Above Suspicion

Above Suspicion

Lynda La Plante

SIMON &
SCHUSTER

LONDON · NEW YORK · SYDNEY · TORONTO

First published in Great Britain by Simon & Schuster UK Ltd, 2004
A Viacom company

1 3 5 7 9 10 8 6 4 2

Simon & Schuster UK Ltd
Africa House
64–78 Kingsway
London WC2B 6AH

www.simonsays.co.uk

Simon & Schuster Australia
Sydney

A CIP catalogue record for this book is available from the British Library

Hardback ISBN 0 7432 5253 5
Trade Paperback ISBN 0 7432 5254 3

Typeset by SX Composing DTP, Rayleigh, Essex
Printed and bound in Great Britain by
Mackays of Chatham Plc, Chatham, Kent

Acknowledgements

I would like to thank all those who gave their time to help with my research on *Above Suspicion*, in particular Sue Akers, Raffaele D'Orsi, Lucy D'Orsi, Dr Ian Hill and Dr Liz Wilson, Dr Helen McGrath, Hazel Edwards and Dr Adam Johannsen for their valuable input on police and forensic procedures.

Thank you to my committed team at Plante Productions: Liz Thorburn, George Ryan, Pamela Wilson, Richard Dobbs, Hannah Rothman and George Robertson, and a very special thanks to Jason McCreight. Thanks also to Alison Summers, Kara Manley, Stephen Ross and Andrew Bennet-Smith.

As always, thank you to my wonderful agent Gill Coleridge and all at Rogers, Coleridge and White. Very special thanks to Suzanne Baboneau, Ian Chapman and all at Simon & Schuster who I am very happy to be working with.

I dedicate this book to my son Lorcan William Henry La Plante

Chapter One

Detective Chief Inspector Langton stared at the women's dead faces. All six of them appeared to have the same joyless, haunted expression. They were all of similar ages and worked in the same profession. The first victim on the file had been strangled twelve years ago.

It was six months ago that the last victim was found; she had been dead for at least eighteen months. Langton had been brought in to Queen's Park to oversee the case. Without a suspect or a witness, he had begun to cross-reference the way the victim had been murdered, and subsequently discovered five identical unsolved cases.

He was certain that they had all been killed by the same person, but to date he had no clues as to who that person might be. It was turning into the most frustrating, dead-end case he had ever worked on. The only thing he was sure about, and that he and the profilers agreed on, was that there would be another victim.

Due to the length of time between each gruesome discovery, there had been little media coverage. Langton wanted to keep it that way; hype and panic would do his investigation more harm than good, and police warnings usually had little effect on the prostitutes. Despite the Yorkshire Ripper being headline news for years, he was finally caught with a tart about to do the business in his car. Police warnings didn't mean much to the street girls when they needed money for drugs or rent, or their kids or their pimps.

Langton leafed through the latest batch of missing persons' files. A photograph caught his eye. 'Melissa Stephens', he read. According to the report sheet, she was seventeen. The photo showed a stunningly pretty girl with shoulder-length blonde hair and the sweetest of smiles. Compared to the other women on file, this girl looked like an innocent angel. How had the photo ended up in this folder?

Langton put the girl's details to one side and went back to the files of missing prostitutes in their late thirties and early forties. He studied the photos of their beat-up looking faces intently. He took note that many of the women in this file were European; some were Russian.

Langton's detective sergeant, Mike Lewis, interrupted his concentration. 'She doesn't fit the profile.' He leaned across the desk and picked up Melissa's photograph.

'Yeah, I know. That's why I put her to one side.'

At first, the team had concentrated their search on the local area, but now the net had spread to include Manchester, Liverpool and Glasgow. They were monitoring missing persons for women with similar profiles to the victims. It was sick, but it was all Langton could do; a fresh victim might provide the vital clue that would lead them to the serial killer.

'Did you hear about Hudson?' asked Lewis.

'No. What about him?'

'He called in sick. He was taken to hospital. May be serious.'

'Shit! The Boss is already checking us out. We'll lose half the team if we don't get a result soon.'

'He might be out for a while.'

Langton lit a cigarette. 'Get someone in to cover him, and fast.'

'OK.'

An hour later Lewis placed half a dozen folders on Langton's desk.

'Christ! Is this all you could come up with?' Langton complained.

'It's all they've got.'

'Leave them with me. I'll get back to you.'

Lewis shut the door and went back to his desk. Langton started to glance through possible replacements for Hudson. The first file belonged to an officer he had worked with before, and didn't get along with. He opened the next one.

Detective Sergeant Anna Travis's file was certainly impressive. After graduating from Oxford University in economics she had done the usual eighteen weeks' training at Hendon, then taken a uniform posting with a response team. Towards the end of her probationary period she had been attached to the local borough CID Robbery and Burglary Squad before switching to the Crime Squad. A memo from her superintendent under-lined in red that Travis was a very 'proactive' officer.

Langton flicked through the rest of her CV with less interest. Travis had moved quickly up to the Home Office's High Potential Scheme. The list of attachments she had covered made him smile: robbery, burglary, CID, Community Safety Unit. About the only thing she hadn't worked on yet was a murder team, though he noticed she had applied three times without success.

He was beginning to feel his age. Slightly depressed, he read on. The glowing recommendations from her superiors he took with a pinch of salt; he needed someone with street knowledge and initiative, not just an impressive CV. It was the last paragraph that seized his attention. He straightened up as he read the words: 'Anna Travis is the daughter of the late Detective Chief Superintendent Jack Travis'. Langton started tapping the file thoughtfully with his pen: Jack Travis had been his mentor.

In the outside office, Mike Lewis answered the phone promptly. Then put his head through the open door of Langton's room.

'Gov?'

Langton looked up from his desk, distracted. 'Who is it?'

'Wouldn't say. You want to take it or not?'

'Yeah, yeah,' said Langton, reaching for the phone. 'Stay.'

Mike leafed through some paperwork while Langton spoke tersely: 'How old? Who's on it? OK, thanks. Get back to me. I appreciate it.'

Langton put the phone down. 'Body just found on Clapham Common.

I don't think it fits with any of ours – she's young, apparently – but they're only just on the callout.' He rocked back in his chair thoughtfully.

'Mike, do you know DCI Hedges? Crew-cut, square head, and full of himself?'

'Yeah. A right arsehole.'

'It's his case, his area. I want you to stand by. If we get any more details I might want to crash in on it.'

Lewis looked at the photos spread out on the desk: 'Are you thinking maybe it's the missing angel?'

'Maybe.' He held out a file, and stood up. 'Get this Anna Travis on the team.'

'What, the rookie?'

'Yep.'

'She's never been on a murder team.'

Langton shrugged himself into his coat. 'Her father was Jack Travis. Maybe taking on his penpusher of a daughter will be good karma.'

He stopped at the door. 'Anyway, rate we're going, we might not even have a case. If the chief puts them all on file, we'll be stuck with a skeleton team until they've all been shelved and sent over to the dead file warehouse. G'night.'

'Night.'

Lewis returned to his desk in the incident room and dialled Anna Travis's number.

By quarter to eight the next morning Anna Travis was sitting in a patrol car speeding to the murder site. Although all she had been told was that she was replacing an officer on sick leave, Anna was excited to be finally working in the field for which she had trained so hard.

With Anna in the patrol car were Lewis and another seasoned detective, DC Barolli. Mike Lewis had square shoulders, and a body running to fat. His round face and red cheeks gave him a look of perpetual good humour. Barolli was smaller, with dark, Italian looks but an East London accent.

As they drew up to the Clapham Common parking area, she noticed the presence of the forensic van, and numerous unmarked cars. Although police cordons allowed no one but officers entry, an exception was made for the catering van which was already in place and serving pies and sandwiches to the teams setting up the base.

What surprised her was the lack of a sense of urgency. Lewis and Barolli went straight from the car to 'Teapot One' to get some coffee. Unsure of the procedure, Anna just hovered nearby. When she looked further across the common towards the yellow ribbons cordoning off the car park, she could see white-suited forensic officers moving around.

'Is this the murder site?' she asked Lewis.

'Pretty obvious. Yeah.'

'Shouldn't we go and sort of make our presence known to DCI Langton?' she said hesitantly.

'You had your breakfast, then?' Lewis asked.

'Yes, before I got the callout.' Actually, she'd had just a cup of black coffee; she had been too nervous to eat. Anna waited while Lewis and Barolli queued up for their bacon sandwiches. They made short work of them, after which the three began to make their way to the murder site. Anna let them lead, deliberately falling behind. After eight hundred yards, they slithered down a sloping bank. She noticed both officers tense up. Lewis removed a handkerchief from his pocket and shook it out; Barolli unwrapped chewing gum.

They approached a group which stood by a clump of trees in a small hollow. There the forensic officers were kneeling or moving deliberately around the area. Anna stepped onto the duckboards placed strategically along the muddy incline. Though the two detectives nodded towards various people, no one spoke. The quiet was unsettling. Then it hit her. The smell was like dead flowers left too long to rot in water, when their stems become soggy and discoloured. Soon it was overpowering.

'You took your time,' DCI Langton barked at the two detectives. He turned to light a cigarette and she saw a tall rangy man in a forensic–issue white paper suit, five o'clock shadow already breaking the surface of his angular chin. Langton had a hawk nose and hard piercing eyes which made it difficult to meet his gaze. Neither detective answered him now, both turning to look instead towards the white tent which had just been erected. Langton inhaled deeply, then the smoke streamed from his nostrils.

'Is it a possible?' she overheard Lewis ask his superior quietly.

'Yeah. But you watch. The dickhead in charge is going to hang onto the case if we can't prove it — and fast.'

Now Langton's gaze fell on Anna. He stared unapologetically at her.

'You the new DS?'

'Yes, sir.'

'I knew your father. Good man.'

'Thank you,' she said softly.

Detective Chief Superintendent Jack Travis had retired two years ago, only to die from cancer six months later. Anna still missed him terribly. She had adored her generous, loving and supportive father, and it was a source of grief for her that he was gone before she made it in plain clothes. She felt that grief even more keenly now that she was on the Murder Squad which had become such a prominent part of his adult life. His nickname had been 'Jack the Knife', for his ability to cut through the dross. More than anything, Anna wanted to be as successful as Jack Travis.

The smoke trailed from Langton's cigarette as he pointed to the tent. 'I think it might be our angel, the missing girl.' He headed towards the open tent flap. 'Want to take a look?' he asked Anna over his shoulder.

Lewis and Barolli were given white paper suits and overshoes so as not to contaminate the area. 'They're short of masks,' Langton explained as he delved into a cardboard box and handed Anna her suit packet. 'Gown up, then keep to the duckboards.' He squeezed the butt of his cigarette, placing it in his pocket.

Anna hastily opened the packet and removed her paper suit. She hauled it up over her skirt and jacket, then closed the Velcro, which stuck to her tweed jacket. As she balanced on one foot and then the other to fit the overshoes over her low-heeled court shoes, she kept taking deep breaths to ward off the strong stench, breathing through her mouth in short sharp intakes, then hissing out the air.

Behind her, she was aware of one officer grumbling to another.

'What's he doing here; this isn't his turf, is it?'

'No, but he wanted to take a look. He's handling that dead-end case over at Queen's Park. Cheeky sod; I'd like to know how he got here so fucking fast. Plus he's got those two goons with him. Don't know who he thinks he is. DCI Hedges is going apeshit.'

When Anna stepped into the tent, she remembered what she'd been told: no training ever prepares you. They can show you mortuary shots, you can discuss post mortems (she'd even been present at one), but not until you confront your first real corpse does the impact hit you. They always say it's the first one that stays with you for the rest of your career.

'You think it's her?' she heard Lewis whisper.

'Maybe,' Langton said. 'Right age, right colouring.'

'She's been here for a while.' Barolli was sniffing with disgust. 'In pretty good shape, though. No decomposition. It's the bad weather. She's been covered in snow, but yesterday was a freak day, almost seventy degrees.'

While Langton chatted with his two detectives, Anna edged across the duckboards to move closer.

'We think she's maybe a student, reported missing six weeks ago,' Langton broke off mid-conversation to explain to Anna, 'but we won't know for sure until they've done the post mortem.' He turned back to address his detectives. Langton became a blur; she could see his lips moving, hear him faintly, but as those in front parted ranks to give her a clear view of the corpse, Anna wanted to vomit. Now she was close up, the stench was thick and heavy, worsened by the confines of the tent.

The victim lay on her back, her long, blonde hair splayed around her head. Her face was swollen, her eyes sunken and crawling with maggots, which explored her nostrils and fed in her mouth, squirming and wriggling: a sickening, seething mass. Around the girl's neck was what looked like a black scarf. It had been knotted so tightly her neck was ballooning. The victim's skin tone was bluish and puffy. Her arms were

7

behind her back, her body slightly arched. Her T-shirt had been drawn up over her breasts, her skirt pushed up around her belly. Both legs were spread-eagled, one shoe on, the other close to her side. The knees were scraped and the bloody scratches were covered in flies and maggots, which clustered all around the body. Rising above it was the buzzing sound of bluebottles. Bloated by their feeding frenzy, they clung to the detectives' white suits.

'This weather's got them out early,' Langton said, swatting a fly off his suit.

Anna could feel her legs start to buckle. She breathed deeply, trying hard not to faint.

'Let's go.'

Langton watched Anna stumble ahead of him, desperate to get out of the tent. He knew exactly what was going to happen next. She made it as far as a tree and stood there retching. Her stomach heaved while her eyes streamed tears.

The other two detectives were stripping off their white suits and dumping them in a waste disposal bin provided.

'See you back at the car park,' Langton called out, but Anna couldn't lift her head.

When she finally joined them, they were sitting on a picnic bench. Langton was eating a sandwich and the others were drinking coffee. Anna's face was almost as blue as the dead girl's as she perched on the edge of the bench.

Langton passed her a paper napkin.

'Sorry,' she murmured, wiping her face.

'We'll get over to the station. Nothing much we can do here; right now, she doesn't belong to us.'

'Sorry?' she said.

Langton gave a sigh. 'The little girl isn't ours. The local police called in the murder team for this area, so by rights it's their case, not mine. We're not allowed to take it unless we prove a connection. Fucking red tape! The arsehole in charge is a right little prick.'

'You still think it's the same bloke?' Lewis asked.

'Looks like it, but let's not jump to conclusions,' Langton said. She noticed Langton could smoke and eat at the same time. He was chewing his sandwich while smoke drifted from his nose.

Lewis persisted. 'Looks like the same bloke to me, way he tied her hands.'

Barolli chipped in. 'I agree.' Anna noticed he was still chewing gum. 'They only found her last night. How did you call us here so fast? You get a tip-off?'

'Heard the callout over the radio. Got here almost the same time as the SOCO lads.'

Lewis knew his gov wasn't telling the truth, because he'd been with him at the station when he had received the tip-off. It was obvious he was protecting his source.

'I've already had a run-in with DCI Hedges.'

Both detectives followed his gaze to the blond man getting coffee at Teapot One. Feeling their scrutiny, the man glanced their way before returning to his mug of coffee.

Anna wanted to say something, but felt too wretched even to attempt to string a sentence together. They drove towards the station. Queen's Park was a good distance from Clapham Common. The police station local to the murder site would automatically be setting up their own incident room.

Anna had never been to the Queen's Park station, so she had no idea where she was going when she followed Mike Lewis up one flight of stairs towards the incident room. The station itself was old and rundown; the walls of the stone corridors were painted in lavatorial green, as were the stone stairwells. The second floor had worn lino on the floors and paint peeling from the ceiling and walls. Numerous offices led off to glass-panelled doors, interview rooms, filing sections. There was a sense that things were up in the air, with filing cabinets left at various intervals down the corridor. It was all confusing and bore no resemblance to the training manual, nor to workshops she'd been in at the college.

Barolli had disappeared to the toilet; she had no idea where Langton had gone.

'You're replacing Danny, aren't you?' Lewis panted as he reached the top of the flight of stairs.

'I think so,' she answered.

'He got some kind of stomach bug. One minute he was fine, next buckled up in agony. I thought it was appendicitis, but it's some intestinal bug. Did you know him?' Now Lewis was barging down the narrow corridor.

'No,' she said, trying to keep up.

Lewis reached double doors at the end and banged them open. The doors swung back and Anna would have been clipped if he had not grabbed a door in time.

'Sorry,' he said absent-mindedly.

Anna had not anticipated the number of people she found working on a case where the body had only just been discovered. Eight desks were lined up, four to four on either side of the room. The desks were manned by male and female uniformed officers and two clerical workers. There were stacks of filing cabinets, overflowing files and masses of paperwork. Running along the length of one wall was a whiteboard covered in dates and names scribbled with felt-tip pen by various hands. Besides this was the unnerving display of numerous mortuary and life shots of the different women.

On one desk was a missing persons file. Anna opened it and found herself staring at a photograph of a stunning-looking young woman, Melissa Stephens — age seventeen, last seen in early February. There was a list including her eye colour, clothes she was last seen wearing and other details.

'Has the victim from this morning been identified?' she asked Mike Lewis. He was sitting on the edge of a desk, talking to one of the female officers.

'Not yet,' he replied over his shoulder, then went back to his conversation.

Anna moved along to the board to look at the other photographs. Side by side were six photographs of victims. Beneath them were descriptions, locations and ongoing enquiries. These women's faces were hard and old compared to Melissa Stephens, with tough-eyed stares.

'Are these all ongoing cases?' she asked Lewis.

He did not hear her as he was talking to Barolli, who had just arrived.

Anna continued reading. Each of the victims had been raped and strangled and their bodies dumped in various local beauty spots: Richmond Park, Epping Forest, Hampstead Heath. All of them had their hands tied behind their backs and they had all been strangled with their own tights.

'The victim this morning and all these victims – are these ongoing cases? I mean, are they connected?'

Barolli came over to join her. 'Hasn't anyone filled you in on why the governor got us out of bed so early this morning?'

'No. I was just called at seven to say I'd be joining Langton's team. Nobody's told me anything about the enquiry.'

'You're replacing Danny, aren't you?'

'Mike mentioned he was in hospital.'

Barolli indicated the victims' photos. 'This investigation has been going on for months; six months to be precise. Five of the cases are years old. Their cases were left on file, until the gov dug them up.'

'Six months?' she said, shocked.

'Yeah.' He jabbed the board. 'This was our most recent victim and by the time she was found, she'd been dead over a year. We started grouping them together a few months back: they've got the same MO, as you can see.'

'You mean it's the same killer?'

'We think so, though so far we've come up with fuck all. But if the stiff found this morning is connected, we might get some leads. There again, we might not and we won't get the case. The gov is really wanting it as we'll be bound to get more evidence with it being fresh.'

Then the swing doors banged open and all eyes turned towards Langton.

'It's Melissa. The dental records match.' Langton moved further into the room, which fell silent. He looked haggard, his eyes sunken and his five o'clock shadow was now even darker. 'They moved fast for us, but we'll have to wait for any further results. I'm going over to the lab now. Until we get those details, I won't know if I need to set up a strategy meeting with ACPO. Mike, you want to come with me?'

Feeling a bit like a schoolgirl, Anna raised her hand. 'Could I come too, sir?'

Langton gave her a slow, studied stare. 'You been to a post mortem before?'

'Yes.'

'You keel over on me and I'll send you packing, understand?' He pointed at Barolli. 'You handle things for me here. Anything they get in, we need to know immediately. Start up a board.'

Barolli's black stencil pen was in his hand as he looked at Melissa's photograph. He made a note of the dental records on the board as identification, then he wrote *Melissa Stephens* in large letters, *Victim 7*, with a question mark.

Langton sat in the front seat of the car, head leaning on the headrest, his eyes closed. Anna wondered if he was asleep. She leaned back, intent on keeping her mouth shut. Finally, he spoke. 'This will be a big media show. She's young and she was beautiful. I've got to convince the commander in charge of Pan London Homicide to award me the case. What we've been working on isn't exactly high profile – six old tarts, or old drippers as your dad used to call them, don't warrant *Crime Night* specials or reconstructions – but if they give it to me, I'll get the team I need and with the Holmes database to help, I'll get a result.'

Anna nodded, still a little confused. 'Thank you.'

Anna and Langton walked across the car park to the hospital. He knew exactly where he was going and walked fast, pushing doors vigorously without looking behind him, expecting her to make it through after him. Finally, they reached the mortuary, where Langton pointed to a door marked 'Ladies'.

'Gown up in there and then come straight through,' he said.

Anna tied a mask around her head, slipped her feet into overshoes and then tied the green ribbons of her protective gown. She entered the morgue, shivering. It was freezing cold.

Though recently modernized, the morgue had retained its Victorian tiles, though the swill area and the steel tables and equipment were up to date. At one table a group of assistants cut away the filthy, torn clothes from the corpse of a junkie found that morning. The floor was white tiled and slippery. A second table was empty, being swilled down with a high-powered water jet. On the third table, or 'slab', lay their victim, covered by a green plastic sheet.

While his assistant listed the victim's clothes, the pathologist, Dr Vernon Henson, spoke quietly to Langton. Anna watched as a black T-shirt and pink skirt were placed in an evidence bag for the forensic lab.

'No underwear?' Langton said quietly.

'No panties,' said Henson. 'But there's a bra. You probably want to have a look at the way it was tied.'

Langton gestured for Anna to move beside him as Henson was removing the plastic sheet from the body. It was at this moment that a gowned-up DCI Hedges walked in, snapping on rubber gloves. He glared at Langton. 'You still breathing down my neck, Jimmy? Or are you just here for the thrill?'

'I'm here, Brian, because if this girl is mine, you'll have to give her up.'

Hedges shrugged. 'You'll have to prove it first. Right now, this is my case. So, if you don't mind, butt out of my way.'

Langton stepped to one side. Hedges moved closer to the table as the two pathologist's assistants turned the body over gently to face down. The hands were held together with a white cotton sports bra. The bra had been wrapped tightly around the wrists, then tied with some considerable force. Henson stepped aside to allow photographs to be taken from every possible angle before attempting to undo the knot. It resisted his efforts.

'I'm going to have to cut it free,' he said, almost apologetically.

'Go ahead,' Hedges instructed.

Trying to cause as little damage as possible, the pathologist snipped the material from the corpse's wrists. The hands stayed in tight fists. The weals around the wrists were a dark plum red. When the girl was carefully laid face upwards again, her arms were drawn out to her sides, but her fists remained clenched.

'We have what I think are her tights; again, they've been pulled exceptionally tight round her throat, cutting into the skin, so I doubt I'll be able to undo them by hand.'

More photographs were taken of the way the tights had been knotted. Langton and Hedges virtually nudged against each other to get a clearer view.

The tights were pulled so taut that it was almost impossible to remove them. Eventually Henson clipped the knot away from her neck. The swelling had made the girl's neck almost twice its normal size. The marks around it were deep, breaking through the skin; the tights had been pulled so roughly around her throat that the bruises were black, vermilion red and a deep purple shade. It was hard to recognize the girl on the slab as the same one in the photograph.

'We've sent a lot of the larvae from her eyes and mouth over to the lab; they will give us an indication of how long her body has been in the woods. The insect infestation is more like we would experience in summer, due to the extraordinary weather conditions. I've got roses blooming in my garden and a few days ago, they were snowbound.' Henson had a low, deep voice. His tone seemed more conversational than deferential to the work at hand.

'Can you clean her up? Just so her family don't see her like this,' Hedges suggested.

Langton's eyes widened. Henson, offended by the suggestion that, as chief pathologist, he would allow any relative to see their loved one's corpse without 'cleaning it up', changed the subject quickly. 'Stand back, please. Once I cut her up, the swelling will be released. We'll be drawing her eyelids down, so the relatives won't see her empty eye-sockets. You'll see the little buggers have invaded her gums and the tip of her tongue is missing; could have been bitten by a fox.'

He turned to Langton and took a spatula to indicate the chewed tongue. 'Unless she bit it off herself. If she did we'll find it in her stomach.'

'Took quite a blow here to her right temple, just above the ear.'

The camera continued to flash, taking the close-ups as required: face, neck, eyes, mouth and nose.

Henson waited till it was done, then drew back the long blonde hair to reveal a dark circular bruise congealed with dry blood.

'I'd say it was a blunt, round-edged object, size of a ten pence piece. Once again, we have maggot infestation around the perimeter and there are eggs, so they'll give us more to go on as to the time she's been dead.' Henson pulled at his mask.

Langton nodded. 'Off the cuff, how long would you say?'

'Bloody hard to tell. Decomposition is not that bad, but if she was left during the past month, well, we've had freezing weather, snow and ice, etc., etc. She has very dark areas over the entire underside of her body, which indicate she's been in this position for a considerable time. Could be a few months, or a few weeks, definitely not days.'

Henson began to prise open her fingers.

'Nails are in good condition. Looks like I won't get much from underneath, but we'll check, obviously.'

Henson stood back to observe the length of the body in more detail from the pink-painted toenails to the top of the head.

'There are no scratches, or other signs she tried to fight back. Hopefully, the crack on her temple rendered her unconscious. I'd say by looking there was vaginal and anal penetration.'

Henson indicated the girl's vagina, his fingers brushing her skin softly. 'You see these bruises? That indicates it was pretty brutal. We'll take swabs, obviously, but the anus is split on two sides. Basically that's it until we cut her open and find out more, so let's get started, shall we? She's been weighed: just seven stone ten, little thing. The X-rays will be coming back to us shortly. I didn't find anything broken, but we will get them to you

15

anyway. There's a small birthmark on her right shoulder, but apart from that, she is blemishless. A very pretty creature at one time.'

Langton nodded. He had not glanced in Anna's direction once and she was thankful, as she knew her face above the white mask was about the same colour. But so was DCI Hedges's face and she was surprised when he turned to Henson.

'Keep me updated, I want to see if forensics get anything from her clothes.'

Hedges walked out and Anna heard Langton give a soft, derisive laugh. Henson caught it and his eyes crinkled above his mask.

'She's already been washed down, so we'll get started. I just need the stabilizing block under her head.'

Henson picked up the scalpel. Leaning in closely to make the Y-incision, he cut shoulder to shoulder, meeting at the sternum and then slicing down to the abdomen and into the pelvis. When the internal organs were exposed, the stench of rotting flower stalks was overpowering. As the hiss of body fluids and gasses permeated the room, Anna took fast intakes of breath, fighting to stay upright. Her head felt fuzzy. No wonder Hedges had made his exit quickly.

Next, Henson cut through the ribs and collarbone before lifting the ribcage up and away from the girl's internal organs. Henson removed the organs individually to weigh them. After he had taken samples of fluids in the organs, he opened the stomach and intestines to begin an examination of the contents.

Despite her fuzzy head, Anna observed that Henson's assistants worked as a tight unit. He never had to give an order and while they were doing the weighing and blood tests, he could concentrate on the corpse's head.

As Henson probed Melissa's eyes, Anna's view was obliterated. Without looking back, Henson addressed the room. 'Well, she'd had severe haemorrhaging, which is usual for strangulation and we still have a veritable feeding frenzy in her eye-sockets. Nasty little sods.'

Anna focused her mind on trying to assimilate what he was saying, rather than looking down at the sliced-open body. Though the stomach contents had almost brought her to her knees, somehow she was still standing. Henson began the incision to lift the scalp. He sliced from behind the head, then peeled the scalp forwards over the face to expose the skull. At that point an assistant handed him a high-powered, high-speed, oscillating saw to open the skull. Next he was handed a chisel to prise off the skullcap.

So far Anna had managed to stay upright. It had seemingly become easier; the stench had mingled with antiseptic which helped. The sound of the chisel finished her off. Unable to control her retching, she only just made it to the ladies' toilet in time. Banging past the cubicle door, she gasped for breath. She knelt over the toilet bowl and heaved. After several minutes, when she attempted to stand, her whole body was still shaking.

At the basin she ran cold water and kept splashing and dabbing her face with a paper towel, but every time she stood straight, she felt her stomach heave. The stench seemed to cling to her clothes, her hair and her hands, even though she washed and rewashed them using soap from the dispenser.

Still feeling dizzy, Anna leaned against the corridor wall and waited.

Langton eventually strode out of the morgue. 'Dead approximately four weeks,' he muttered to Anna and pulled off his green tunic. 'She'd been lying there all that time.' His mask hung by its thread. 'It's bloody unbelievable.'

Not waiting for her response, he continued towards the gents and disappeared inside. A moment later he emerged and gestured for her to follow him along the corridor.

'You ever done synchronized swimming?' he asked, still zipping up his trousers.

Anna was unsure if she had heard him correctly. 'Sorry?'

'They have these nose clips so they can stay underwater. They're very useful. You clip one on and it forces you to breathe in and out with your mouth.'

'You can also suck Mint Imperials.' Langton turned round towards Anna once they were in the patrol car. 'Those little round mints.' He rested his arm along the back of the seat. 'You get used to it; when you know what to expect, it's easier.' He returned his gaze to the front again.

'Thank you,' she murmured, embarrassed. She was at a loss what to say next, or whether there were questions she should have been asking.

The smell of the soap dispenser's liquid, an odour like pinewood forests, was making her feel car sick. As if she didn't have enough to contend with already. She closed her eyes, praying that she wouldn't start retching again.

'Sorry,' Langton murmured as she opened a window. She noticed he had a lit cigarette in his hand. 'Can't smoke in the station. Well, not supposed to, anyway. Can't smoke in most places now, so . . .' He shrugged, then, inhaling deeply, leaned back on the headrest. A few moments later, somewhat out of the blue, he asked her, 'Your mother still alive?'

'No, she died two years before my father.'

'Right. I remember, now. What was her name?'

'Isabelle,' she said, bemused.

'Isabelle? Yes. She was very beautiful, I remember.'

She watched him flick the cigarette butt out of the window. The cool air from the open window was making her feel less nauseous. To her surprise, she found herself saying, 'I take after my father.'

He chuckled, 'I guess you do.'

Her father had been a heavy-set man: square-shouldered, with thick red curls. Her mother on the other hand had had olive skin and deep-black hair. She had been a stunning woman, tall and slender and very artistic; a designer. Anna had her dad's hair, which sprouted all over rather than growing in a specific direction. She wore hers cropped short. For a redhead, she was unusually dark-skinned, unlike her pale freckly dad, and had inherited her mother's dark eyes. She was short, also rather square, but she carried no fat; it was all muscle.

Anna had ridden horses since she was a toddler. She had won so many rosettes that she could cover herself from top to toe in red and blue ribbons. Once her dad had pinned them all over her and taken a photograph; she had only been eleven years old.

Anna's thoughts turned towards Melissa. What had her young life been like, before she was reduced to her present state? She thought of herself at that age, then younger. She realized Langton was talking to her and she leaned forwards. 'Sorry, sir, I missed that.'

'The reason I force myself to go through the post mortem, to see that little soul cut to shreds, disembowelled, dehumanized, is because, somehow, it makes it easier. It steadies the anger. That prick Hedges couldn't take it, of course. Wimp!'

He closed his eyes; conversation seemed at an end for now.

Anna followed Langton to the incident room, where he threw off his coat, took a marker and headed towards the board. He began listing the information he'd received from Henson. Without turning, he called out, 'Jean, can you get me a chicken and bacon sandwich, no tomatoes, and a coffee.'

Jean, a thin-faced constable in uniform, was working at one of the computers. She stood up as soon as he called her name: 'You want a Kit-Kat, or anything else?' She didn't look as if she suffered fools gladly.

'No, thank you. Bacon and chicken sandwich, no tomatoes.'

Mike Lewis walked in as Langton continued to mark the board: 'Mike, it looks like our tip-off was right.'

'OK! We got a time of death?'

'Not yet, but she's been dead four weeks at least. Strangled and sexually abused. Get onto the super, tell him we have a critical incident. We'll need a Gold Group set up; we're in danger of losing the public's confidence. Contact the murder review team, let them know that we are now handling the enquiry. Is Barolli back yet?'

'Nope, but he shouldn't be long. He went over to forensics.'

'Gather the team together, we'll have an update at . . .' Langton glanced at his watch, then checked on the wall clock. 'It's already three o'clock. Fuck. Say half four?'

Everyone in the incident room, apart from Anna herself, was getting

19

ready for the meeting. None of her training had prepared her to join an up-and-running team like this one.

'Excuse me, sir. Is there anything you want me to concentrate on?'

Langton sighed. 'Familiarize yourself with the case histories. Find a desk, Travis and get started.'

He pointed to the noticeboards, then waved his hand towards a section of filing cabinets which lined one wall.

'Right, sir.'

She tried her best to look as if she knew what she was doing, but she was at a loss as to where to start and she could not figure out the filing system. Many of the cabinets had stacks of loose files balanced on top of them.

A uniformed PC passed, carrying a tray of teacups.

'Excuse me, which is the first case file?'

'One nearest the wall,' answered the PC, without looking back.

When Anna opened the top drawer, she found it fully stacked with rows of files. Removing an armful, she turned to survey the room. The same PC passed by with the empty tray.

'Erm . . . is there a desk I could use?'

The desk in the rear of the room was cluttered with cartons of takeaway food. The wastepaper bin beside it was overflowing with empty hamburger cartons and cold chips. Anna tidied a space for herself.

Suddenly there was a bellow. Langton was holding up his sandwich, waving it around.

'I said it not once but twice: no fucking tomatoes, Jean!'

'I asked them for no tomatoes.' Jean was red-faced.

'Well, it's full of them! You know I hate tomatoes!'

'Would you like me to take them out?' Jean retorted, but Langton was already chucking them into the bin.

Anna lowered her head; she hadn't eaten since breakfast. No one here had offered her so much as a cup of tea or coffee. Her presence seemed to go unnoticed. She located her briefcase and had just taken out new pencils and a notebook when she realized it was almost four o'clock.

★

Teresa Booth was forty-four when her body was found on waste-ground near the Kingston bypass. She had been a prostitute, though not from that area. Teresa worked the red-light district of Leeds for many years.

With the busy road so close, not many pedestrians used the area and the victim had been found by a boy whose scooter had broken down. Wheeling it off the busy road onto the narrow pavement, he had glimpsed a foot through the undergrowth. After scrambling up the ridge, the boy found the body. The corpse's hands had been tied behind her back with a bra; she had been strangled with a pair of black tights. The body had remained undetected behind bushes for three to four weeks. It had taken longer – four months – to identify her. This discovery was in 1992.

The mortuary photographs were attached, with pictures of the murder site. Teresa's face in death had a terrible, haunting ugliness. Her skin was pockmarked and she had a deep scar on one cheek. Her bleached blonde hair had black roots showing. The initials 'TB' on her arm appeared to have been scratched or cut and she had a faded pink heart tattooed on her right thigh. She had severe bruises to her genital area.

'TB' had been traced to Terence Booth, her first husband. Teresa had subsequently been married three times. Though she had three children, none of them appeared to be by any of her husbands. Two were sent to foster care at a very early age, while the youngest, a boy, had been living with her mother.

Teresa looked a lot older than her forty-four years. Hers was a sad, murky history. She was an alcoholic who had spent time in prison for persistent prostitution offences and for 'kiting', which meant she was caught with using stolen credit cards and passing dud cheques. She was identified by her fingerprints and from her photographs.

'Travis!' Anna looked up. Mike Lewis was gesturing at the door for her to get a move on. She had been so engrossed, she hadn't noticed the gradual emptying of the incident room. 'Briefing room,' Lewis explained before disappearing.

Anna was hurrying after him when Jean called out: 'Don't leave the files out, please; return them to the cabinet.'

Anna zigzagged back to the desk, where she collected the half-read file and replaced it. When she asked where the briefing room was, Jean said sharply, 'Second door on the left, one flight down.' As Anna exited rapidly, she could hear Jean moaning to another woman. 'I'm sick to death of him having a go at me. It's not my job, anyway, to go schlepping out for his lunch. They're all bloody foreign in there, don't understand a word you say to them; "no tomatoes" and he gets layers of them!'

Anna flew down the narrow stone steps and along a murky corridor. The hubbub of noise drew her easily to the briefing room. Rows of chairs had been placed in haphazard lines and a desk and two chairs faced them. The large dingy room smelled of stale tobacco, even though there were stained yellow notices demanding 'No Smoking'.

Anna skirted her way along to a vacant chair at the back, where she sat clutching her notebook. Up front, Lewis and Barolli were joined by eight detectives and six uniformed officers. The two female detectives were a large blonde woman who looked to be of retirement age and a tall thin-faced woman in her mid-thirties with badly capped teeth.

The superintendent who had overall charge of the enquiry, DCS Eric Thompson, entered, closely followed by Langton. Thompson had an athletic look about him: his face fresh, his shoulders upright; he stood as if poised on the balls of his feet. His thinning hair was combed back from a high forehead. Langton by comparison looked tired and crumpled and in need of a shave. Barolli was loosening his tie in a seat nearby.

'Quieten down!' Langton barked. He perched on the edge of a desk and leaned forward to address the room.

'The victim was formally identified today by her father. She is, or was, Melissa Stephens, aged seventeen. We suspect she is a "possible". Her boyfriend's statement on the night she went missing is all we have to go on so far, but it is my belief that Melissa strayed into our killer's target area.

To date all his victims have been hardened prostitutes, all in their late thirties or early forties. Melissa may be our biggest breakthrough yet. It's imperative we move like the clappers.'

Anna made copious notes, but not being privy to any of the previous case files, she had no idea what Langton was talking about most of the time. What she picked up was the following: on the night Melissa disappeared, she had an argument with her boyfriend. This had occurred at a late-night café close to Covent Garden. She was last seen walking in the direction of Soho. The boyfriend assumed she was heading towards Oxford Circus tube station. He finished his drink and headed after her. But Melissa, it seemed, had found a shortcut, perhaps down Greek Street. Inadvertently, she went through the red-light district.

Though Melissa's boyfriend, Mark Rawlins, called her mobile phone incessantly from the tube station, it was useless. The phone had been turned off. Frightened for her, he retraced his footsteps, hoping he'd bump into her. After returning to The Bistro, around 2.30 a.m., he went back to Oxford Circus tube station, then on to Melissa's flat, but she had not arrived home. Neither Mark nor her three flatmates ever saw Melissa again.

The following day, after calling her parents in Guildford and everyone else he could think of, Mark finally contacted the police. Forty-eight hours later, a missing person's file was lodged and circulated, along with photographs and requests for information.

No one came forward, even after a television reconstruction shown four weeks after her disappearance. They had not one eyewitness who could give a clue to her disappearance, with the possible exception of a waiter who had been smoking a cigarette outside a renowned gay club and who saw a blonde girl talking to the driver of a pale-coloured, or maybe white, car. At the time, he assumed she was a prostitute, he said. Though he didn't get a good look at her face, he did notice her black T-shirt, which had diamanté studs that sparkled in the neon lights outside the massage parlour opposite.

Langton suggested that their killer, who haunted red-light districts, could have mistaken Melissa for a call-girl: outside a strip joint very late at night, a blonde in a sexy outfit, short skirt and strappy sandals – could their killer have been the one to pick her up?

Though the briefing continued for another hour, the super finally insisted they did not yet have enough information for him to take to the commander and request this murder enquiry be handed over to Langton's team. Hearing this, Langton jumped to his feet, holding the photos of the six dead women like a pack of cards.

'Their hands tied with their bra, strangled with their own tights. If forensic can verify that the knots around the neck and wrists were tied in a similar way, then Melissa Stephens becomes the latest victim of a serial killing. If we get this case then we've some hope of catching the bastard, but we've got to move! Any time lost in farting around begging for the enquiry is a fucking *waste* of time!'

With that, the team broke up; they would simply have to wait until the following morning.

After the team had left the briefing room, Langton sat moodily in a hard-backed chair. He looked up when he heard Anna crossing the floor towards him. He held in his hand the photos of the dead women.

'They were all alive, once. Albeit in one wretched condition or another, but nevertheless they were alive, with families, husbands, sometimes kids. Now they're dead and whether or not they were junkies, whores, drunks, or just fucked-up human beings, they have a right to have us hunt down who killed them with as much press as Melissa Stephens.'

He sighed, pinching his nose. ''Course, on the other hand, I could be wrong. We won't know one hundred per cent until we get the forensic evidence back.'

'But you really do think it's the same man.' Anna felt more at ease with him now.

'Thinking isn't good enough, Travis. It's evidence that counts. If they tell me that Melissa's bra or the tights that throttled the life out of her weren't tied in the same way as these poor bitches then no, it's not the same killer.'

'Was there any DNA?'

Now he turned that laser stare on her. 'Read the case files; don't waste my time.'

'Would it be possible to take a couple home to read? Or I can stay late and do it here, so I'm up to speed with everyone else?'

'Sign for anything you take out.' Langton banged through the doors.

Anna shook her head; these guys certainly liked to make an exit. She collected her notebook and pencils. As she walked towards the open door she gave a backward glance to the still-smoky room. The chairs were now even more jumbled, the cups and saucers used as ashtrays overflowed and screwed-up paper and old newspapers littered the floor.

She closed the door behind her quietly. She felt a strange sense of elation to be part of her father's world.

Chapter Two

It was past midnight when Anna finished compiling her shorthand notes on the Teresa Booth case, and by the time she had finished the file on the next victim, it was after two o'clock in the morning.

Sandra Donaldson, aged forty-one, had a similar background to the first victim: a life of abuse, drugs, alcohol, four children all fostered out and a junkie boyfriend. She was first arrested for prostitution when she was twenty and then numerous times after that for theft and handling stolen property as well as further arrests for prostitution.

According to postmortem reports, she had been more severely beaten than the first victim. Her bruises looked horrific: some old and yellowing, some fresh. Her black bra had been used to tie her hands behind her back and she had been strangled with her tights. When Anna matched the two large blown-up photographs depicting the way the items had been knotted, she was hardly surprised to find they were identical.

Sandra had been raped brutally, with damage to her vagina and anus. Like Teresa's, her body was dumped and left rotting like rubbish. Anna reflected on this sad end to a sad life. It had taken weeks before anyone claimed her body for burial. The only reason she had been identified in the first place was because her fingerprints had been on file. Anna wrote a memo, reminding herself to check if all the other victims had police records too. It was the last thing she did before she collapsed exhausted into bed.

However, none of this weariness was evident in her face or demeanour the next morning when, just before nine o'clock, she arrived at work in her brand new Mini Cooper. A uniformed officer directed her to a car park round the back of the station, which was completely full with patrol cars. Obviously there had been no space allocated for her, so it took a few tours around the car park before she wedged her car in beside a battered old Volvo. As she locked her car, she prayed that whoever drove the Volvo wouldn't scratch her baby on their way out.

The incident room was quiet that morning and, with some relief, she noted that the used food cartons had been removed from the desks.

'Good morning, Jean,' she said, brightly. 'Nobody here yet?'

Jean, the only other occupant, returned her greeting with a lukewarm smile.

'You must be joking. They've been in the briefing room for an hour. There's a big strategy meeting.'

'Nobody mentioned it last night,' Anna protested, taking off her coat. She quickly returned the files to the filing cabinet before heading to the door.

'Did you get permission to take those away? They are supposed to stay here, you know.'

'I am aware of that, Jean,' Anna replied, trying to curb her irritation, 'but I asked DCI Langton if I could take them, to catch up. I signed them out in the logbook and desk diary. Who's down there at the meeting?'

'The commander. If DCI Langton can prove our murders are linked to the Melissa Stephens case and we have in-depth knowledge of all the linked offences, we'll have all the help we need.'

Anna waited for her to explain.

Jean did so carefully, as if dealing with a half-wit: 'The Department of Public Affairs will liaise with the D/SIO and the SIO and will provide press statements and organize briefings. It's all political now. Drives me nuts. There's more and more paperwork required on every investigation.'

'Has any conclusive evidence come up since last night that links Melissa Stephens to this enquiry?'

'I don't know, but the gov was in before the cleaners this morning, so I'd say he's found something.'

Jean looked smug as she resumed typing on her computer. Anna walked out of the room.

There wasn't a soul in the corridor or on the stairs; in fact, it seemed almost ominously quiet as Anna made her way to the briefing room on the lower floor. Since this was the headquarters of the day-to-day operations of the station, on a typical morning phones could be expected to be ringing constantly, with the sound of voices wafting up the stone steps to the next level.

Not today, however. The double doors to the briefing room were closed and, unlike the interview rooms, there were no glass panels in them. Anna leaned against the doors, hoping she could hear something, anything. Apart from a low murmur of voices, she heard nothing. She couldn't bear to barge into the room, so she turned round, planning to head back to the incident room, and almost collided with DC Barolli as he came out of the gents, wiping his hands on a paper towel.

'How's it going?' she said, in a low voice.

'I couldn't tell you. The commander's not one to give anything away.' He lobbed the paper at a bin, missing it.

'Did we get anything from forensic?'

'You must be joking. They take their time.'

'So, no other details came in?'

'Not that I know. Those pricks over at Clapham wouldn't give you a pot to piss in.'

He continued down the corridor, so Anna returned to the incident room, where she read the third case history. This victim's name was Kathleen Keegan. She was aged fifty, of below average intelligence and illiterate. She had been beaten down by depression and ill health. There had been numerous arrests for drunk and disorderly conduct and, as with the others, arrests for prostitution and streetwalking. She had once been a redhead, but the hair in the photographs was badly dyed blonde and in texture resembled frizzy door matting. The mortuary pictures of her sagging, overweight body and her flattened breasts were depressing. Six babies had gone to care homes, or been fostered, due to her inability to care for them.

When her decomposing corpse was found, it was lying in a public park, hidden under stinging nettles. Her body was tied in exactly the same way as the other victims', but these pictures were particularly gruesome. The victim's false teeth were protruding from her mouth, almost as if she was laughing: a hideous horror clown with red lipstick smudged over her face.

It was a repellent, tragic pattern, thought Anna and even though Kathleen had already been brutalized by life, her death was still a wretched and undeserved end.

It was after twelve when the meeting broke up and Langton and his team returned. Anna noticed he was smiling. While everyone in the incident room grouped around him to hear what had happened, she remained at her desk.

'Right. We have the case of Melissa Stephens. The commander will instigate bringing in fifteen detectives. We're still short of legs, but we can't argue with that. We will also get another office manager, two more admin staff and Holmes Two. The Home Office will back us up and place us now on a major-enquiry system. This will give us greater input to the enquiry.'

Langton hushed the ensuing applause. 'I want someone over to Clapham to get all the details they have on the Melissa case. While we wait for anything to come in from the lab, we start work.'

He pinned up Melissa Stephens's photograph. Then he picked up a black marker-pen and ringed the number '7' twice.

'We know she left her boyfriend at half past eleven and headed towards Oxford Circus tube station.'

Langton instructed his team to cover every route from Covent Garden to Oxford Circus. They were to hound the strip-club joints; often they were kitted out with hidden cameras for their own security.

'Check out any CCTV footage used in clubs, pubs, car parks, in all the various routes. Get what you can. After four weeks, I suspect most of it will have been destroyed. I want to know the exact route Melissa Stephens walked that night. A witness has come forward, a waiter. He was sure he saw Melissa talking to someone in a car, the make he can't remember, or the colour – in fact he can't even be sure it was her – but I want that tape of the reconstruction, I want that driver, I want that car. Because –' Langton gestured to his wall of death – 'we have a serial killer. I am hoping to Christ that Melissa's death was his first and last big mistake. Let's get moving.'

While the officers grouped to divide up the orders, Anna remained sitting at her desk, feeling like a spare part. No one had acknowledged her, or spoken to her yet. As the room thinned out, she stood up and approached Langton.

'Am I still attached to the case, sir?'

For a moment Langton looked as if he couldn't recall who she was, then he tapped his desk with his finger. 'Go out with DS Lewis, he's picking up the TV reconstruction.'

'I think he's already gone,' she said, looking around nervously.

'Then stay with me. I've asked for Melissa's boyfriend to be brought in. You can come to the interview. You had lunch?'

'No.'

'Go and get some in the canteen. Be back at quarter past one.'

'Thank you.' She headed back to her desk, then turned. 'I didn't think forensic had brought in a report yet. Did we get evidence in last night that tied Melissa to our case?'

Langton gave her a strange, cold stare. 'No.'

Anna couldn't hold his piercing gaze; she went to her desk, where she didn't look up, afraid she might find he was still glaring. She walked over to the filing cabinets to replace the Kathleen Keegan file. She was certain he was watching her, which turned her cheeks vermilion red. It made her angry, to feel so inadequate. She couldn't wait to get out of the incident room.

The canteen on the top floor was small in comparison to the Met stations she'd worked in before. Almost every table in the room had been taken.

Balancing a tray in one hand and her briefcase in the other, she headed towards the far side of the canteen, where some uniformed officers were leaving a table. She pushed the dirty plates aside and opened her yogurt, turning her back unintentionally on the next table where DCI Hedges and two of his team were sitting.

'All I am saying is, who the fuck does he think he is?' DCI Hedges continued loudly. 'That was my case. You tell me how he gets away with saying his six victims, his six ancient hookers, have the same MO? It's bullshit and he's the biggest fucking bullshitter I've ever come across!'

Anna half turned, in time to see DCI Hedges jabbing his fish and chips with his fork. 'No fucking way. So her hands were tied? So fucking what? He didn't have any forensic evidence, no postmortem report, and he gets the full fucking Monty and we are left out of it, like pricks. No way are his old tarts connected to the murder of that little girl. It's bullshit. Unless he is getting it across with the commander. She was on his side before we even started!'

There was the clatter of their cutlery during a pause while they ate their lunch, but soon Hedges was at it again. 'He's going to get all the press, all the media coverage. It's fucking disgusting!'

'What if it's true?' asked a sullen, pockmarked officer.

'What's true?'

'That he has some serial killer.'

'Bullshit. No way is that little girl part of his enquiry. Six months he's been on it, collecting old slags from all over England. I'm telling you, DCI Fuckface Langton is desperate. He won out because he's brown-nosed the commander, or fucked her, because there's no other way he could have got this case, no fucking way.'

While Anna finished her lunch, the three men continued to slag off Langton, paying her no attention. She was making her way back to the incident room just after one o'clock when it occurred to her to check whether her new Mini was still intact. It was. She was at the rear entrance of the station when she saw Langton with Commander Jane Leigh, one hand at her right elbow, as if steering her to her waiting car.

Anna watched Langton laughing with the commander as they approached her car. He opened the rear door. There was an obvious familiarity between them. When she got in the back seat, he leaned in to finish the conversation.

Anna got back to her desk just ahead of Langton, who banged into the incident room.

'Have a good lunch?'

'Erm yes, thank you. And you?'

'Not had time. I'll get a sandwich.' He nodded to Jean, who gave him a wry look.

He checked his wristwatch and looked over at Anna. 'Interview room two. I'm going for a slash.'

'Yes, sir,' she said, getting ready with her notebook and pencils as the doors swung closed after him.

It was almost a quarter to two when Langton walked into the interview room where Anna was waiting. He held a beaker of coffee in his hand, wrapped with a paper napkin.

'He's just arrived,' he said, sitting beside her. 'His name is Mark Rawlins, student. London University. Business affairs.'

He sipped from his takeaway coffee. 'You were at Oxford, right?'

'Yes.'

'Jack must have loved that.'

'Yes. My father was very proud, you know, that I made it to Oxford.'

'What do you think he'd feel now?'

'I'm sorry?'

'Well, here you are in a rundown station with the Murder Squad, on a case full of tarts and—'

Before she could think of an answer the door opened and Jean, holding a chicken sandwich, peeked in.

'Your order, sir, minus tomatoes – and there is a Mark Rawlins in reception.'

'Is he on his own, or with someone?'

'He's with his father.'

'Well, tell his father that I just want to see Mark. No, forget it. Let him bring in who he wants.'

Jean closed the door.

'Is he a suspect?' Anna asked.

'Not yet,' Langton said, biting into his sandwich. He chewed rapidly; as if he had a train to catch, thought Anna. 'You look at me as if you know something I don't. Or you disapprove of me. Which one is it?'

She flushed. 'Sorry. Just over-eager, I guess.'

'Really? Is that what it is?'

There was a pause: he took another bite of his sandwich.

'I overheard DCI Hedges talking in the canteen.'

'Yeah, and . . .?' he said, with his mouth bulging.

'He doesn't like you.'

'Tell me something I don't know.'

'He said he didn't know how you'd got this case, unless you were having a scene with the commander. He said there was no connection between the murders,' Anna continued. 'That what you said about there being a connection was all bullshit.'

Langton finished his sandwich and wiped the table in front of him with his hands, picking up a few crumbs.

'What do you think?'

'I don't know,' she said, hesitating. 'Melissa was young and beautiful. From what I have read so far, your killer goes after a specific type: bruised, old, beaten – so unloved they wouldn't even make it on to the missing persons list because nobody cared enough about them to report them missing.'

'I agree, but the way her tights were wrapped round her neck three times was what swung it for me.'

'But at the postmortem . . . I can't recall Henson saying that—'

'You were throwing up in the toilets,' snapped Langton.

'No, I was there when he cut the tights away from her throat.'

Langton rubbed his eyes. 'Last night I went to the forensic lab, checked the fucking tights: three times, three times wrapped around her little white throat. It's the same killer.'

'And the bra? Was that tied in the same way?' Anna felt that Langton had just lied to her, but before he had a chance to answer, there was a tap on the door and Jean ushered in Mark Rawlins and his father. Langton transformed himself before Anna's eyes. Genial and relaxed, he stood to shake the visitors' hands, then gestured for them to sit.

'Thank you for agreeing to come in. I hope we can get through this as fast as possible and with as little pain.' He gave an avuncular glance at Mark, a fresh-faced youth who looked closer to sixteen than nineteen. 'This must be torment for you; it's a terrible thing.'

Mark's father, white-haired, well-dressed, was far more nervous.

'Is my son a suspect?' He addressed Langton brusquely.

'Not at all. But he was the last person we know who saw Melissa alive. Anything he might recall could be vital.'

The interview was an eye-opener for Anna. Langton spent time putting the emotional boy at his ease, before he scrutinized his original statement, section by section. When Langton pressed him as to what the young couple had been fighting about, the boy became nervous. The room was tense as Langton started to put the pressure on.

'You were Melissa's boyfriend for eighteen months,' he said impatiently, 'and you have said over and over again how much you loved her, so you might understand why I am confused as to how you could just let her walk away. It was half past eleven at night, Mark.'

Mark had been constantly glancing at the upright figure of his father, but Mr Rawlins had said hardly a word throughout the interview.

'I was only going to wait a few minutes, then go after her and that's what I did. I paid the bill and walked off in the same direction.'

'Which was?' Langton waited.

'She went across Covent Garden, I presumed she was heading for the tube station, but when I got there it was closed. I wasn't sure if she would go towards Leicester Square or Oxford Circus, so I then walked back to the Square down Floral Street.'

Langton passed across a street map for Mark to highlight the route he had taken. His hand was shaking and beads of sweat stood out on his forehead.

'Did you and Melissa have a sexual relationship?'

When Langton repeated the question, Mark started to cry.

'Is this really necessary?' said his father quietly.

'I need to know, Mark, if you and Melissa had a full sexual relationship.'

Mark shook his head.

'There is a possible witness who said he might have seen Melissa talking to someone in a car.'

Mark raised his head.

'Was Melissa the type of girl who would ask for a lift?'

'No. She wouldn't do that.'

'Was she promiscuous?'

The boy's eyes widened in shock.

'No, no. No!'

'What did you argue about, the night she walked away from you?'

Mark's fingers gripped the pen so tightly it looked as if he was going to snap it.

'I'm trying to ascertain the mood she was in; that's all I'm trying to do, Mark.'

'I told you. She was angry.' Mark threw the pen across the table, then he started to sob, his whole body shaking. After a few moments, his father moved over to comfort him, gripping his arm tightly.

'She wouldn't let me do it.' Mark muttered something else, his face red with torment.

'What?'

'I said, she wouldn't let me have SEX WITH HER,' he shouted. 'That's why she walked away: because I wanted her to come home with me. I wanted to have sex with her but she wouldn't, she refused . . .' He broke down.

'Are you telling me that Melissa was a virgin?'

Mark struggled for self-control. 'Yes, and she would not have got into

35

a stranger's car; she wouldn't have done that. What you're trying to make her out to be is disgusting! *You* are disgusting!'

It was a while longer before Langton released father and son. As they left the interview room, Mr Rawlins glanced at him over his shoulder with disdain.

'My son is bereft. To imply that Melissa was anything but an innocent in all this is most cruel. I hope to God you treat her parents with more respect.'

The door closed quietly behind him. Anna shut her notebook. She was of the same opinion, not that she could say anything. She was, therefore, surprised by the quiet fury in Langton's voice.

'A virgin and she gets sodomized, raped and murdered! Life stinks.'

'Yes.' She suddenly had an almost overpowering impulse to reach out and comfort him.

He sighed, rubbing his head. 'Right, let's get over to forensics. See if they've come up with anything.'

He strode out of the room. She just made it to the door before it closed in her face.

In the forensic department, Melissa's clothes had been laid out on the bench tables. Langton and Anna stood before a black T-shirt with a pink sequinned logo that spelled out the word 'strip'. To one side there was a small square of pink velvet and on that, a single diamanté stud.

Langton shook his head. 'Strip?'

'It's actually a very expensive T-shirt,' Anna hastened to explain. 'See the way the "t" is picked out? That's the logo for Theo Fennel.'

'Who?' he snapped.

'Theo Fennel. He's a high-society jeweller, has a shop on the Fulham Road.'

Langton turned to the forensic assistant. 'Did you get any fibres from it? The sequins have sharp edges.'

Coral James, the forensic scientist, took off her glasses.

'No; we had hopes, but the T-shirt was drawn up, covering the sequins. As you can see, one is missing.'

Langton and Anna looked closer. On the 's', picked out in sequins, one stone had gone, leaving the four small claws empty.

They turned their attention to a pink cotton mini skirt with an elasticated belt. The fabric was expensive and shiny and offered little hope of anything clinging to it. Melissa's shoes, low-heeled and expensive, were scuffed, but with little trace of mud. Langton turned to Coral James.

'No mud? It was like a mud bath when we were there. We are hoping for confirmation soon that she was killed at the site.'

'Well, it was cold. Then we had that odd snowstorm. It's hard to tell; the ground might not have been muddy when she was taken there.'

'Or carried.'

Next, they scrutinized Melissa's white sports bra, which the pathologist had cut and pinned to a sheet. Next to it were drawings of the fabric knot itself and then photographs of how the knotted bra had been found on the body.

'We finished the tests you requested. Over at the far side, you'll see other tests we've been working on.'

Across the lab, on the table by the wall, the bras from the other victims had been laid out. There were more photographs, arrows or markers to show similarities. The dirty discoloured underwear was an unpleasant sight.

Coral led them to a table where a life-size dummy was lying face down.

'The way each of the victims' bras were tied we think is virtually identical. Let me show you.'

Coral expertly crossed the dummy's wrists with a black bra, demonstrating how Melissa's bra had been wrapped twice around and the section with the hooks and eyes used to secure the knot.

'They were all drawn very tight, cutting the wrist and almost wrenching the arms out of their sockets. You can see the bonds are very secure. But the sports bra was more difficult; it's not got as much give as the other ones; they were elastic and nylon. The silk bra was torn in the process of tying it.'

Coral now moved on to the tights. It had been necessary to cut them away from the neck. In each case, she indicated that the tights had been wound three times around the victim's throat and drawn in a knot. Anna found it hard to believe the smallness of the garrotte, no more than two inches in diameter.

She made copious notes, following Langton from bench to bench. Sealed in plastic bags were some of the previous victims' clothes that had been retained. Langton had declined to view them again. He kept looking at his watch impatiently. He asked the vital question when they returned to Melissa's clothes.

'So, is it good or bad news?' he said quietly.

'I wouldn't say it was good, whatever way you look at it.' Coral removed her rubber gloves. 'But I know what you're asking me and the answer is yes. We believe your little girl was killed by the same person: the knots, the method of tying them, are identical.'

'Thank you,' he said, tight-lipped.

'We are still working on her clothes, so you might get something new there; but, as yet, we have nothing.'

Outside in the car park, Langton lit a cigarette. 'Unbelievable, isn't it? Not so much as a carpet fibre.' He sucked in the smoke and half turned towards Anna. 'The fucker must know exactly what he's doing.'

'You think there's a place he takes them to?' Anna asked. 'Maybe he kills them and dumps the bodies elsewhere.'

'Nope. Killed at the site, or near it. In all the cases, they had to agree to go with him.'

'That's true with the prostitutes. But Melissa wouldn't have agreed to go with him unless she knew him and she was found a long distance from her flat.'

Anna would have continued speculating, but Langton had flicked his cigarette aside and was walking towards the waiting patrol car. 'We're going to see Henson next, at the pathology lab,' he shouted to Anna behind him. 'Maybe he'll have something for us.'

He slammed the passenger door shut. She just managed to scramble in the back seat before the car drew away.

In the pathology lab, Henson sat before a large slice of cream cake and a cup of coffee. He smiled when they entered his lab. 'Just having my elevenses, albeit at four o'clock, but that's my life whenever you lot start screaming for results. And I have no intention of hurrying. It's my career on the line if I make a mistake, so I'm not quite ready for you.'

Langton pulled a face.

'All right. I give you one thing: I do know her last meal was a hamburger, fries and Coca-Cola. No alcohol, no drugs. A very fit young woman. Beautiful muscle tone and fresh, unblemished skin. She was a natural blonde with well-cut hair; no dye, but a few highlights. She was wearing very little make-up.'

Henson polished off his cream cake and wiped his mouth with a tissue. 'Give me another twenty-four hours, I'll have all the results. Then the coroner should be able to release her body for burial. We have taken slides, etc.'

He gave a sidelong glance at Anna. 'Let's have a look. You shouldn't pass out this time. Easier to digest, slides.' Henson smiled sympathetically as Anna flushed. Then, crossing the room to the area where all the pathology slides were blown up onto light frames, he addressed Langton with a new seriousness.

'See this mark on her neck? Not having much joy in giving you possibilities: odd shape, size of the old shilling, but with a bulbous area at the top.' He pressed his own neck with his forefinger. 'Went in quite deeply: half an inch. Didn't kill her, though; I would say she was already unconscious. We're testing her brain matter, so I will have a result on that.'

'Thank you,' Langton said. 'Fast as you can, yes?'

'Yes,' Henson said with a sigh. He walked into the lab next door.

Langton looked at Anna. 'Right, let's go back to the station. See if the lads have anything for us.'

'Yes, sir.' She was tired out, even if he wasn't. Next time she would need more than a yogurt for lunch.

The incident room was crowded. Someone was sitting at her desk but before she could say anything Langton was clapping his hands for attention. Then they were joined by the newly added detectives, office manager and clerical staff, so Langton took the next few moments to meet everyone before he provided the update. First he confirmed that the person who had tied the bonds on Melissa was the same person who did it to their other six victims. 'Number seven' was now legitimate.

A large TV set was wheeled in. Langton held up a videocassette. 'OK, everyone. This is for those of you who didn't catch the reconstruction that was made when Melissa was just a "missing persons". After we watch, we'll throw out to anyone who's got a result today. Best news we've had yet is the verification we're hunting the same bastard for—' He never finished. The theme music for *Crime Night* started and the room fell silent, except for the underlying ringing of phones.

A photograph filled the screen and a voice-over began: 'Melissa Stephens, last seen here at The Bistro in Covent Garden. She was wearing a distinctive black T-shirt with pink diamanté logo and a pink skirt. We wish to hear from anyone who saw her that night after eleven thirty.'

The film continued for five more minutes, with a running commentary, as 'Melissa' was shown walking away from The Bistro, headed towards the tube station. A short interview with her parents ensued; they begged anyone who might have information about where their daughter was to come forward. They said repeatedly that Melissa would never have taken off without calling them and they feared the worst. The tape was then fast-forwarded to the next section, which ran at a spot two hours later the same night. There were details of call-ins. Finally, the announcer said they had received a call from a witness who was sure he had seen Melissa that night. Another full-screen picture of Melissa followed and under it, the phone number to call.

The TV set was turned off. It was a while before talk broke out again. The general atmosphere was one of depression caused by the realization that when the show had aired, the Stephenses' young daughter was already dead.

Together the detectives went over their orders for the following day. Langton returned to the board.

'OK, coffee's on its way; in the meantime let's crack on. Any new assignments from the update will be given out.' He pointed to Mike Lewis, who moved to stand beside him. 'For now, just sit and listen. Mike?'

Mike opened his notebook.

'I interviewed the call-in witness from the show. The guys handling the missing person case had already traced him, so we got to him fast. His name is Eduardo Moreno; he's Cuban and speaks very little English. He works at the Minx Club, on the corner of Old Compton Street in Soho. The club is a transvestite hang-out; members only, know what I mean? Across the street is a massage parlour, real cheap dive; bright pink neon sign outside, that sort of thing. The neon is quite important because not only is it pink, it flashes. So Mr Moreno, who works as a waiter-stroke-dishwasher, is standing outside the club having a cigarette at about midnight. He is certain the girl he saw is Melissa, though it gets a bit screwed up, because he thought she came *out* of the massage parlour-stroke-knocking shop.'

Lewis described how Moreno had seen Melissa bending down to talk to someone in a car. He could not say the colour and make, just that it was a big car and pale. He was also unable to say if Melissa got in the car; just that he'd turned away to talk to someone passing and when he looked back both the car and Melissa had gone. He was also unable to describe the driver, but he thought it was a man.

Langton gave instructions to bring Moreno in and show him every make of car. He was sceptical about his claim that his English was poor since he had managed the phone-call. Lewis explained that another waiter made the call for him as they both thought there could be a reward. The good news was that the Minx Club had CCTV security cameras, as did the massage joint and after a lot of persuasion both establishments had agreed to allow their tapes to be viewed. There was plenty of footage and only one camera was time-coded. Any film of Melissa could then be enhanced by the lab and returned quickly. Mike planned to view the tapes first himself.

Alan Barolli was up next. He told them he had spent the day exploring the streets around the possible routes Melissa had taken. The film crew had only forty-eight hours to compile their footage and so had gone for the most direct route. Barolli had spent time checking out every other path Melissa might have taken. The result was that he had more than six additional CCTV tapes and they were being reviewed in the hope they would provide details of the exact journey she had taken from Covent Garden that night. However, as Langton had suspected, due to the passage of time, a number of places using CCTV had already recycled the tapes.

Langton threw the discussion open to the room for questions. Anna put up her hand, then found herself flushing when the entire room turned to look at her.

'Two things, really. It must have been cold that night. Melissa, we know, was wearing a T-shirt and short skirt. Do we know if she had an outer garment, say a jacket or coat?'

Observing a few looks and shrugs in response, Langton gave instructions to check with her boyfriend. He was about to move on when he saw Anna's hand was still raised; he nodded.

'Also, the T-shirt has that sequinned logo. It's possible that our killer, who has only picked up prostitutes to date, thought Melissa came out of the massage parlour. The T-shirt saying "strip" across the chest might have given him that idea.'

Langton nodded and checked his watch. 'OK, it's eight o'clock; let's call it quits tonight. Tomorrow, full steam ahead. Get the Cuban in, the CCTV footage sorted out, and we'll see if the postmortem reports can help.'

There was a mass exodus to the doors; some of them, like Anna, had been on duty since nine or earlier. She collected her coat and briefcase and headed towards the filing cabinet.

'Gov, can I take the file on victim four?'

Langton gave her a perfunctory nod and continued to confer with the office manager about the duty roster. In preparation for all the new officers, copies of the files had already been made, so Anna just removed one, signed the report logbook and left, feeling very tired.

Reaching the car park, she was more than a little pissed off to find her beloved Mini with a scrape down one side. It was impossible to tell if the beat-up Volvo next to it was to blame. Anna chucked her briefcase onto the back seat and sat for a moment, wondering if she should return to the station to complain or perhaps request an allocated parking space, but in the end her tiredness prevailed and she just drove home.

Chapter Three

Anna had only been in this job for two days, but already it had taken a toll on her domestic life. There was dirty washing in the bathroom and she badly needed groceries. She jotted several items down on a shopping list and decided to pick them up on her way into the station the next morning.

That finished, she poured herself a glass of wine and set about making supper. It was after eleven by the time she had eaten and she realized as she opened the file on the fourth victim that she was too tired to take anything in. She set her alarm for half past five the next morning and crashed out.

In the morning, she had a shower, got dressed and made some coffee. By six o'clock she was feeling much brighter as she opened the file.

Barbara Whittle, another well-known prostitute, had been forty-four at the time of her death. Her body had been found in a state of advanced decomposition. There were the usual on-site photographs, plus close-up shots of her tied hands and her neck, where her tights had been wrapped and drawn taut to strangle her in the same way as the others. This case was put on file in 1998.

Barbara was almost five feet eight and her body was ravaged by alcohol. The corpse showed severe bruising, numerous abrasions and lacerations. The ligature mark, which ran in a horizontal groove around her neck, was embedded deeply. Due to the lengthy period of time before discovery, the victim's bound hands were white and swollen and a wedding ring cut deep in the bloated skin.

Barbara was quite dark skinned, with frizzy permed hair. Anna thought she must at one time have been very pretty. Like the others, she had numerous children, of unknown whereabouts. Though murdered in London, Barbara Whittle had resided in Manchester. Her body waited six months to be identified.

Anna felt a chill running down her spine. They should not hold off a press release: these women, whatever their lives had become, had deserved a warning of the horror that awaited them. If the killer planned to continue murdering these working girls, they should know of the danger they were in. Anna glanced up at the clock at that moment and panicked: she was going to be late for the office.

By the time she arrived, Langton had already left the incident room for the pathology lab. She drove there, aware that by this time it was half past ten and she was very late. After hurrying into the building, she found Langton with Henson, staring at an illuminated X-ray unit. They turned as she came into the room and apologized for her lateness. Langton returned to his scrutiny.

Enlarged on the screen, the strange circular wound to Melissa's neck was deep, just breaking the surface of the skin. Langton peered closer. 'Maybe a ring with a rounded stone?'

'Possibly,' murmured Henson. 'But if it was punched in her neck, it would have left more bruising. I've no idea. By the way, at the back of her head, there's a small bald patch. Looks like a clump of hair was torn out.'

Henson switched on the next light box. 'Right, next. This is an X-ray of the brain tissue – see where we've got the blue and green areas? The blue is enlarged. This means your girl was unconscious for some time prior to death.'

Henson clicked on the next photograph, which showed the ligature wound to her neck. 'It's so tight that it's almost cut through to the jugular, pressing onto it. The skin abrasions from the garrotting are really appalling. Poor little soul didn't stand a chance.'

He lit up another X-ray; this one focused on Melissa's belly. 'This is interesting. You can see there are marks on her stomach. I would say these came from being carried, possibly over someone's shoulder. See the indentation here and just beneath her belly button?'

Henson cocked his head, still looking at the picture. 'I'd say he was right-handed.' He mimed lifting something heavy and placing it over his shoulder. 'Yes, could be right-handed.'

'Could they be punches?' Anna ventured.

Henson narrowed his eyes. 'Punches?'

'Yes, the one on her stomach looks like part of a fist to me.'

Henson pursed his lips. 'I doubt that is a punch. As I said, more like a bruise from being carried.'

Langton was growing visibly impatient, but Henson hadn't finished his deliberations.

'She died where you found her. The time of death we've got down to approx five weeks ago. We're expecting more details of the insect infestation, but it's difficult to get all that much as the weather plays such a part. It went from very cold to nearly seventy degrees in a matter of a day.'

Langton stated that he did not want the coroner to release the body until they were certain it would not be required for further examination.

'Have it your way. The parents have been calling constantly. They want to arrange a funeral service. But if you need her, fine; we'll keep her on ice.'

Depressed about the limited information he had gained, Langton walked silently with Anna through the car park. As she stopped by her car, she said, 'Sorry I was late, sir.'

'That yours?' he asked, still glowering.

'No, I stole it to get here. Joke.'

She was fumbling for her keys and when she looked up to smile, seemingly oblivious to her, Langton was walking away towards a patrol car and uniformed driver.

She got into the Mini only to find a notice plastered across her windscreen: 'Private car park. For medical employees only. Your car will be towed away'.

Her attempts to rip the notice off left strips of partly glued paper across the windscreen. She swore softly and repeatedly, for a very long time.

Mike Lewis glanced up from his desk as Anna put the Barbara Whittle file back and signed out her fifth victim for more late-night reading.

'Get anything helpful from that old fart Henson?'

'No. Murdered where she was found,' replied Anna. 'Possibly carried over the killer's shoulder. You?'

'Yards of fucking CCTV footage, plus two hours with that Cuban fruit and nut. His BO is the worst I've ever come across and I've had my fair share of smellies.'

They were interrupted by a sudden burst of laughter from a group of detectives round DC Barolli's desk. He was holding up an article from the internal Met newspaper.

'Says here, they're lowering the physical entrance requirements for women; they just can't keep up. You read this, Jean?'

Jean gave them a sour-faced glance, but Moira, a big blonde with heavy breasts, grinned with derision. 'Wankers. It's brains, not brawn, that cracks a case.' Though Moira waited for a response, they avoided her scrutiny and returned, mumbling, to their desks.

'Any of you beefcakes traced the girl's handbag yet? You should try getting off your arses—' Moira broke off as Langton appeared in the doorway. She returned to marking up the board.

'What was that?' he asked as he joined her.

Anna listened curiously. She had also been struck by the fact Melissa had no handbag and that none of the other victims' handbags had been recovered.

Moira answered Langton earnestly. 'I know they never mentioned it in the reconstruction, but surely she'd have had one? Why would she walk off from her boyfriend without a purse when she was supposedly heading for the tube?'

'Boyfriend couldn't recall if she had one or not.'

'Yeah, but they don't notice. He said the same thing about her coat.'

Moira flipped through her notebook. 'All she had on was a T-shirt and mini skirt? When it was cold out? But the no-bag thing really worries me. Doesn't make sense.'

'Yeah, I know.' Langton turned to Barolli at his desk. 'Have you been back to The Bistro?'

'Yep. We questioned waiters, the owner and managed to trace a couple of customers. No one remembers much. The place was jammed, so even though it was cold, some of them were eating outside. Melissa and Rawlins sat at the table ringed on the right of this photo.'

Langton frowned over the photographs of the restaurant.

'CCTV footage ready yet, Mike?'

'Any minute, gov. There's a hell of a lot of tapes to be checked over. If our sighting of her from the Cuban is correct, we've got her at Old Compton Street, corner of Greek Street, so we've had to cover a lot of possible routes.'

'Put some pressure on them. We need to see what they've got. Or haven't got. Did The Bistro have a security camera?'

'No. And during video reconstruction, they never mentioned a handbag.'

'She had no pockets in her clothes,' Moira reminded them.

'Maybe she expected the boyfriend to catch up with her,' Langton said, flatly.

Two hours later, when the tapes from all the security video cameras had been gathered, DS Mike Lewis stood by the TV screen, the remote control in one hand and addressed the team.

'We got some good news and some bad,' he said as the blurred black and white film began.

Lewis did a running commentary. They had identified Melissa in frame, as she passed by Paul Smith's boutique in Floral Street. He froze the film at that point.

'Look: no handbag. No coat. She's really hurrying. Now you see her, now you don't.'

Lewis replayed the moment Melissa passed the security camera. She was in quite a hurry, almost running. The next sighting was Melissa going down Exeter Street near Joe Allen's restaurant, walking at a slower pace, but looking confused. She turned back, giving the camera two hits.

'Now we presume she's heading past the Opera House towards Bow Street mags court.'

'Or she could have been going back to the boyfriend,' Moira said.

'No, wait now, we've got something good coming up. There's a time code on this section: it's eleven fifteen and here she comes.'

All heads craned forward to watch, as Melissa came in shot, passing the Donmar Theatre. The footage had been taken from across the road. 'Two black kids, with grey anorak hoods pulled over their faces, try to get Melissa to stop and talk to them. As one puts out his arm towards her, she backs away. She will have nothing to do with them. They follow for a few feet, then she starts to run. The two boys look after her, as she disappears out of frame. They walk away.'

Lewis pressed fast forward, then stopped the frame again.

'The theatre was already closed; so was the Pineapple Dance Centre. Now, just on the edge of frame, is that her boyfriend? I can't be one hundred per cent, but it looks like Rawlins to me.'

They rewound and replayed, all the time peering at the fuzzy frame. All they could agree on was that it could have been Mark Rawlins, but it was impossible to be sure as he was hardly in shot.

'Get that blown up,' Langton said.

'Already in the pipeline.' Lewis picked up the remote. 'On to the next section.'

'Why didn't she get the tube at Covent Garden?' Moira asked.

'They shut the gates at half ten; congestion on the platform. OK, this is the best we've got and it tallies with our Cuban friend. It's footage from the Club Minx and buttressed onto it is the footage from the massage parlour opposite. So we're getting two hits of the same sequence, from different perspectives.

'There's our Cuban pacing around, lighting a cigarette. He is directly opposite the massage parlour. Passing him are a number of cars, one is a

Range Rover and the other is a Jaguar. You can see the flash of the neon sign outside the massage parlour; it's giving us that strange light. Now, there's a vehicle on the inside of the Range Rover, but hidden; it's some kind of low car and it's turning right. You can see his indicator flashing, along with the neon light. But there's no way we can tell the make of the vehicle. We've got the reg of three of the passing vehicles but no luck with the other two.'

There was a brief pause as the footage jumped to the next segment.

'OK, now we're seeing footage from the massage parlour security camera and again the Cuban's statement bears out. Here she comes, just entering right of frame, maybe intending to walk down Greek Street, to Soho Square. If we believe the boyfriend, she was heading towards Oxford Street, either to get on the tube at Tottenham Court Road or to continue onto Oxford Circus tube. That would make more sense since she lived in Maida Vale, which is on the Bakerloo line. There's a clear shot of Melissa for only a second, passing the massage parlour and again she looks as if she were unsure of her direction. She stands a moment. She turns back to walk past the massage parlour again. She walks virtually out of shot, then she can be seen looking towards something or someone, before disappearing out of frame.'

Lewis held up his hand. 'Now, on the freeze frame, you can just see a small section of a pale coloured vehicle. It could be white or grey, but all we've got is that fraction of the side and a minuscule section of the back bumper. See it?'

Lewis had to rewind the tape twice before it was clear to them what he was pointing at on the edge of frame: there was a fraction of the side of a car and a small section of the vehicle's bumper.

'It could be the same car that was on the inside of the Range Rover; either that, or he's driving down Old Compton Street from Tottenham Court Road and parking up on the corner. We'll get that section blown up and see if we can tell the make of the car, but I think it could be a Mercedes, an old one, maybe thirty years old.'

The video ended and Lewis rewound the tape.

★

Viewing the video had left the team with a strange, almost surreal feeling. Melissa had come to life in front of them and yet they seemed as far away as ever from trapping her killer. Langton closed his office door with unusual quietness. Everyone went to work on their various assignments.

Anna studied the file of the fifth victim. Beryl Villiers was thirty-four. Younger and fitter, she had put up more resistance than the others. Nevertheless, both her eyes were blackened and swollen and her nose had been broken; two front teeth had been knocked out and were found near the body.

She, too, was a known prostitute and had a history of addiction, but her autopsy showed no signs of her still using, nor any alcohol. Her home address was in Bradford. When all else had failed to produce anything, Beryl had finally been identified by the number on her breast implants. Once she was identified, the police leading her enquiry had questioned all the working girls around King's Cross station. None could recall who Beryl had picked up earlier that night, after a couple of punters she'd taken to the old station arches. She was last seen patrolling her beat, around ten fifteen, but no one could recall seeing her after that. Four weeks after she disappeared, in March 1999, Beryl's body was found on Wimbledon Common.

Beryl was younger than the previous victims. She had no children. She was a 'weekender', travelling from Bradford every Friday night and returning home on the following Monday. She originally hailed from Leicester, where they located her mother; she seemed more distraught to learn her daughter was a prostitute than to learn that she was dead.

Anna made copious notes and returned to the filing cabinet for the last case history.

'What are you doing?' Moira asked.

In reality she was making herself busy. 'Just familiarizing myself with the case files,' she said.

'You're Jack Travis's daughter, aren't you?'

Anna's eyes lit up. 'Did you know him?'

'Everybody knew Jack. He was something else. I was sorry he died.'

'It was cancer.'

'Yes, I know. We sent flowers. How's your mother handling it?' Moira asked.

'She died two years ago.'

'Oh, I'm so sorry. She was very beautiful. I remember meeting her once. None of us could believe that old codger had kept her secret for so long.'

'He worshipped her.' Anna smiled.

'We all pretty much worshipped your dad. If he'd been handling this case, he'd have got a result by now. I think Langton's out of his depth. And I tell you something: that girl had to have a handbag. Why aren't we concentrating on that?'

Anna felt an urge to defend Langton. 'We are, though.'

'Bloody haphazard way of going about it. And that reconstruction? They didn't have her with a handbag in the video. They're bloody amateurs. Why didn't they ask her mother if one of Melissa's handbags was missing from home?'

'Have we checked Melissa's flat?' Anna asked.

'Of course we have. She had a wardrobe full of handbags.' Moira stared at the photographs on the wall. 'Better life than any of these poor bitches. Seeing them up there, it's as if their eyes follow you around, like wounded dogs. All got the same expression, haven't they?'

'Have you noticed how many come from up north?'

Moira nodded. 'Leeds, Liverpool, Blackpool, Manchester, Bradford . . .'

'I was just wondering if there was a possible connection; whether they knew each other.'

Moira shrugged. 'You ask around the big stations: Euston, King's Cross, Paddington – a big percentage come down on the train from the north and scrabble for punters. They're like hornets. Usually junkies, who get hooked up with a pimp, or drugs, or booze. I know, I was on Vice for six years.'

Moira was walking away as if the conversation was over. Anna took the last file to her desk. Langton opened his office door and called, abruptly: 'Travis! Come in here a minute.'

Anna picked up her notebook and headed for his office. Moira smirked at Jean.

'Keen, isn't she?'

Jean pursed her lips and returned to her computer. 'Maybe she's after a spot on *Crime Night*!'

Anna stood in front of Langton's desk. He rolled a pencil, flicking it back and forth. 'You were late this morning. You threw up at the murder site yesterday and then again at the post mortem. I was beginning to think you were a waste of space, Travis.'

She bristled.

'But Henson's just called. It seems you're right. The marks to Melissa's stomach are part of a fist. The punch wasn't directly to the skin but through her T-shirt; there are fine fibres embedded in the skin that match the material. It makes it hopeless for us to get a clear print but Henson believes that they'll have every indication of the size of fist, so there's a possibility that if we find the killer, they might be able to make a match with his fist!'

'That's good,' she said quietly.

He gave her a beady look. 'What is it?'

She hesitated. 'Erm, I was just thinking we should issue a press release to warn the girls.'

'Won't mean anything. Nothing stops them.'

'I've been reading up on the fifth victim and—'

'Beryl Villiers,' he said to himself.

'Well, she wasn't as washed up as the others, no alcohol or drug problems and—'

'You are not telling me anything I don't know, Travis,' he interrupted impatiently. 'And we are giving a press conference. Soon.'

But Anna held her ground. 'Did you ever find if there was a connection between the victims? I noticed they're all from the north of England.'

'You noticed that?' He leaned back in his chair. 'Well, continue to read the case reports; after that, read up on the enquiry details and the thousands of statements taken and you'll find we didn't come up with any connection. They didn't know each other!'

Mike Lewis popped his head round the door. 'Did you want Rawlins brought in? We've had another look and still think it might be him, edge of frame.'

'Yeah, wheel him back in. Soon as you have something, call me.'

'Right.'

Lewis shut the door behind him and there was a pause.

Langton's eyes were closed; he was resting on his folded elbows. Anna was just wondering if she should leave when he spoke. 'Something's wrong. The way she's running in the footage. Something isn't right.'

'Well, she'd had a fight with her boyfriend,' Anna said tentatively.

'It's the way she's running. Doesn't look like a kid pissed off with her boyfriend. Looks more like she's scared.'

Anna was trying to recall the order of the footage. 'The two boys that approached her?'

'Yeah – I think she might have been mugged and we're missing that section. All we do know is we have a witness and a time coder that makes her still alive at half past eleven.'

He lifted his head and looked at her.

'You worked with that profiler, Michael Parks, didn't you?'

'Erm, yes.'

'I never give those profilers much kudos. It's all about stating the obvious.'

'I think he's very good,' she said, nervously.

'Do you indeed? Well, if DS Travis rates him, I should do as the Gold Group request and get him in then, shouldn't I?'

'He did some very good work when we were on a kidnap situation.'

'Really? Well, let's hope he can do some good work for us.'

Anna waited to be dismissed. Langton picked up a file and started reading. Glancing up a moment later, he seemed surprised that she was still standing there and said she could leave.

Anna returned to her desk, irritated with him. At the far side of the room Moira was engaged in conversation with Mike Lewis.

'If she got mugged and they took her handbag, makes more sense that she maybe could have accepted a ride.'

Eavesdropping on their conversation, Anna pretended to give all her attention to the file. Soon, however, she was absorbed in what was written. Langton did seem to cover everything in his own way. She knew that after reading the next victim's report, she had better give herself enough time to check out the actual police enquiries. She didn't want to give Langton any opportunity to get in another snide dig.

Jean appeared with a tray of coffee. 'Not a doughnut left and the vultures have already started cleaning out the canteen. Press conference starts in the briefing room, fifteen minutes.'

As the coffee was passed round, Jean looked over to Anna. 'Sorry. You weren't here when I took the orders.'

'That's OK,' Anna said, tired and still busy.

'Who does he want to go in with him?' Moira called out. 'Barolli and Lewis?'

'Yes, that's right. Tweedle Dum and Tweedle Dee,' Jean said. She turned to Anna. 'He wants you too, Travis.'

In the briefing room, the press had arrived in force. Seated on the rows of chairs, they read the press release that had just been handed out. The office manager had consulted Langton about what else should be included in the press package: selected photographs and some details of the crimes. A long desk with a microphone had been placed in front of the chairs. Two video cameras were recording.

Anna waited outside the double doors. The noise from inside was a low buzz as the journalists talked quietly amongst themselves. She saw Langton coming towards her down the corridor, flanked by Lewis and Barolli. She noticed all three had shaved and put clean shirts on. Langton was wearing a grey suit and a navy blue tie. He seemed ill at ease as he turned to his sidekicks. 'Right, let's go. Travis, sit next to me.'

'Yes, sir,' she said, following them through the double doors.

The room fell silent as they took their seats at the long table. On the wall behind them there were large blown-up photographs of Melissa Stephens. Anna, next to Langton, was surprised at how nervous he was. He removed his notes from the file and placed them down in front of him. He coughed a couple of times, then tested that the microphone was on.

'Firstly, thank you for coming,' he began. 'I am eager for your assistance. We have always maintained a good relationship with members of the press and with this specific case I must ask you, once more, to stick to the guidelines issued. You are all aware, I believe, that Melissa Stephens's body has been recovered, after she was declared missing six weeks ago. What we did not know until today, erm . . . In examining the evidence, we have decided that Melissa's murder is, we believe, connected to others already under investigation.' Langton then opened the meeting to questions from the floor.

By the time the press briefing was concluded, it was after half past seven. Langton had given reporters enough, but not all, of the information his team possessed and sidestepped the more probing questions. He was patient and informative, but also guarded. Anna had been impressed by his handling of the situation. Langton disliked using the term 'serial killer' and mentioned it only once, but during the questioning the journalists were quick to bring up the Ripper murder case.

After the press had gone, Langton addressed the team, loosening his tie. 'Right. Tomorrow will come the blast. We're probably all going to have to work the phones. This will create a lot of extra work, separating the nutters from anyone that has legitimate information. It will take days, maybe weeks. So be prepared. I want everyone in the briefing room at two o'clock. We have a profiler, Professor Michael Parks, coming in. The Gold Group has briefed him and he has had access to all our files for three days now, so let's hope he can give us something to go on. OK, that's it for tonight. Get some sleep. It'll be mayhem tomorrow.'

After packing her briefcase, Anna left the room with Jean. On the stairs, she asked the older woman about Langton's private life.

'What do you mean?' scoffed Jean. 'He doesn't have one. He's a workaholic. First in, last to leave. He hasn't gone home tonight, you know. He's gone over to the edit suite to look at the CCTV footage. Poor Mike is pissed off: it's his wife's birthday. She's cooking up a storm and she's pregnant. He won't get home now until past eleven.'

'Does Langton have a wife?' Anna asked.

Jean stared at her. 'Oh, that kind of private. Well, he's had a couple of them; lived with a few women. But who or what he's doing now, none of us know. That he does keep private.'

'I see,' Anna said. She stopped, before heading down the stairs to the back exit and car park.

'Can I give you a lift, Jean?'

'No, thanks. My old man is waiting for me.'

'Goodnight, then.'

Anna couldn't believe it. Her back bumper was dented. The mini now had a scratch down one side, sticky paper on the windscreen and a crumpled back bumper. Her shiny new car, her pride and joy, saved and scrimped for.

Early next morning, Anna pored over the details of victim six, aged thirty-four. A bleached blonde, with a sexy curvaceous figure and a known cocaine habit, Mary Murphy was a prostitute with no police record. Her body, discovered in July 2003, had made her the most recent victim until Melissa Stephens. Mary was found only three days after her murder on Hampstead Heath. She was originally from Preston in Lancashire. No handbag. Her corpse remained unidentified for two weeks.

Mary Murphy was the first case that Langton had headed up. She had a profile different from the others, being middle-class and well-educated. After her divorce five years before, Mary's twin daughters had gone to live with their father.

Mary probably started to sell herself when her cocaine habit took hold. She worked for an escort agency, though her last known client had been questioned and was no longer a suspect. She had left his suite at the

Dorchester Hotel at one o'clock in the morning and had died between one and three hours later. The last sighting of Mary was by the doorman at the Dorchester, who recognized her as she was leaving the hotel. It was presumed Mary went looking for another client. After that last sighting, she had been picked up by the killer.

The file contained the same wretched photographs. The shirt was drawn up to the victim's neck, her tights wrapped around in the same way. Her hands were tied behind her back with her red lace bra. Though she had been raped and buggered, no DNA was found; as with the other victims, the killer had used protection.

After she had finished reading the file, Anna opened her front door to pick up her newspaper. The case had made the front page: 'Suspected Serial Killer on the Loose'.

Though DCI Langton had not wanted mass panic, that's what he'd got. The case was headlined in every newspaper. There were constant references to both Jack the Ripper and 'his Yorkshire namesake'. One tabloid had two-inch letters screaming 'Jack is Back'.

On arrival, Anna made her way down the station corridor towards the incident room. As she approached, all she could hear was the non-stop ringing of telephones and the babble of voices growing louder and louder. The incident room now had an extra four phones installed in one long section. The phones on all the desks were ringing and every detective was hard at it. All calls were logged: names, addresses and relevant details were then transferred from the officer to the office manager. When Anna reached her desk, the phone was already ringing. Jean gave her a rueful look.

'Welcome to Bell City. It's a quarter to nine and we've had a hundred and fifty calls in. So get started.'

Anna took out her notebook and reached for the phone. 'Queen's Park incident room. This is DS Travis speaking.'

It was a long and ear-splitting day. Amidst it all, staring at the mayhem with their dark helpless eyes, were the seven victims: Teresa Booth, Sandra Donaldson, Kathleen Keegan, Barbara Whittle, Beryl Villiers, Mary Murphy, and now, Melissa Stephens.

Chapter Four

Thousands of phone calls had poured in, yet little information had resulted. However, forensics had come up with what could prove to be a significant piece of evidence. The tests performed on the DNA swabs, while yielding neither blood nor semen, had identified the type of condom worn by the killer as 'Lux-Oriente' which was made in America and easy to pinpoint because of the unique lubricant used by that company. While the indication that their killer had made his purchase in the United States was heartening, the discovery that Lux-Oriente sold millions of condoms every year made the purchaser virtually impossible to trace.

Another breakthrough occurred in the investigation when Rawlins, the murdered girl's boyfriend, broke down and confessed that their final argument had turned physical. He had followed Melissa and continued to row with her as they walked away from The Bistro. Rawlins remembered that Melissa had carried a small envelope bag, which he had thrown at her. While he couldn't recall the colour, he remembered it was made of soft dark leather. Between the empty stalls of Covent Garden Market, there was a scuffle which ended when he punched her.

While the imprint on Melissa's belly could no longer be considered evidence which might lead them to the murderer, some compensation was forthcoming. Rawlins had recalled that Melissa was carrying a black woollen cardigan on the last night he saw her alive. He remembered that they had tugged it between them during the argument, which had occurred when he caught up with her near Floral Street.

After the punch Melissa had angrily declared that she never wanted to see Rawlins again and, furious, he had walked away. When he changed his mind and tried to catch up with her, she had disappeared – for ever.

Rawlins had become deeply distressed at this point in the interview. He blamed himself for her death. If he had only apologized for his action and taken her home, Melissa would be alive today. Shame had made him keep the quarrel a secret. That was the reason he had not told the full story to the television reconstruction team.

Langton ordered that Rawlins be released. Not only had they lost valuable time, but also the chance that someone might find and recognize either the black cardigan or the bag. However he saw no reason to charge the boy with perverting the course of justice; Mark Rawlins had received his sentence. He would have to live for ever with the knowledge of his culpability in Melissa's death.

A press release was issued, calling for anyone with information about the girl's missing purse to come forward. Though discretion had been assured, along with the reassurance that the police were only interested in the location where the purse was found, or snatched, not one caller could help them. The police had to presume that somewhere on Melissa's journey her bag had been stolen, since on the CCTV footage she carried neither cardigan nor bag.

There was some cold comfort in the fact that Langton had been correct regarding Melissa's scared run: that somewhere between leaving her boyfriend and her appearance on another security camera, something had happened to frighten her.

The Cuban was brought back three times, but he became more confused on every occasion. Even an interpreter was unable to extract any further information. The section of the car was determined to be a Mercedes, possibly circa 1970, though they were unable to ascertain if it was white or merely pale since the film was in black and white.

★

The mood of the murder team changed when the profiler arrived. Professor Michael Parks was in his mid-forties, balding and wore horn-rimmed glasses. He stood in front of the team over the course of two hours, displaying a calmness that seemed at variance with what he was saying to them. He advised them to look for a male, mid-thirties, affluent, possibly attractive. Despite these attributes he would be unmarried and in a profession that enabled him to travel.

Parks regarded the irregular time gap between each murder as worrying. The first kill was in 1992, next came one in 1994, then 1995. Then, after a lengthy gap, another in 1998, then 1999 and following a gap of almost three years, Mary Murphy, killed in 2002 and then the last victim, Melissa, in February of this year.

The team listened carefully as Parks explained that a serial killer can become dormant, 'killed out', as he described it, his desires satiated. In some cases, he might never kill again. However, Parks believed that their killer would not stop. He was almost certain that between those lengthy gaps, other murders must have been committed.

Parks indicated the victims' photographs; the faces now as familiar to the team as their own families'. He continued: 'One obvious common denominator is that the women are known prostitutes. Another thing I have noticed and this is very common with serial killers, is the physical similarity of the victims. All the women, including the last victim, had brown eyes. They all had bleached, dyed or natural blonde hair. I believe this man started out by killing a woman who hurt him, maybe left him, possibly a mother figure, a prostitute herself. He would therefore, to begin with, be killing his mother. However, towards the end of the line-up of victims, he is killing younger women, seemingly indiscriminately. This means he has not satisfied his urge. The way he leaves their bodies exposed and humiliated is a sign of his hatred. This man detests whores and seeks to defile them in any way possible.'

The room was silent. Many of them, including Anna, wrote copious notes. But Langton sat impassive, staring at the floor.

'Most serial killers,' Parks continued, 'usually take some kind of token. It is possible our man took their handbags. This would provide him with the pleasure of later sifting through their belongings. While he may keep a number of small items, the bags themselves would be too large an item to keep, too dangerous; they would eventually be dumped or burned.'

Parks removed his glasses. 'He's very intelligent. He leaves no DNA, no clues. To the outside world, he probably seems the personification of respectability.

'The first four victims were used to getting in strange men's cars. There is little sign of struggle because they would have consented to being tied by their wrists. None of these women were gagged, which proves they must have complied with his desire to tie their hands behind their backs. I would say the ones that struggled, like Beryl Villiers, may not have consented. Melissa, we know, was unconscious at an early stage.'

Parks folded his glasses, placing them in his top pocket. 'That is all I have for you today. All I can say in leaving, is this.' He paused theatrically. 'He isn't yet satiated. I would say quite the opposite. The murder of Melissa and its subsequent press coverage will have heightened his drive to kill again, if he has not done so already.'

The team continued over the next four days to interview and cross-question callers they felt to be legitimate. In the end, the most informative and legitimate-sounding call came from a woman with a very deep voice, who insisted on anonymity but said she was certain she had seen Melissa on the night she disappeared.

It had been almost midnight when she had noticed a girl fitting Melissa's description on Old Compton Street, bending down to talk to the driver of a pale blue sports car. She could not identify the make, only that it was an 'old type'. She never saw the driver's face clearly, though she said he was clean-shaven and 'blond-ish' and, although it was evening, he was wearing dark glasses. She was about to cross the road and confront the girl about poaching on her patch when Melissa got in the car and was driven off.

They put a trace on the call. It was from a mobile phone but they couldn't get a fix on the caller's location. Langton ordered Lewis to try harder to track the caller down.

'Track her down?' Lewis shook his head, disbelievingly. 'How? We don't know what she looks like; we don't have a name. We've got nothing.'

'The voice!' Langton snapped. 'Mike, for God's sake, play the call and listen! You know she works Old Compton Street. She's probably a transvestite: right area, Club Minx. Go and talk to as many of them as you can find. Match the voice! He or she's all we've got so far.'

'Right, gov. Will do.'

'Now, everyone else pay attention. We need to go back to square one. Open up Teresa Booth's case. Go through every one of the victims again. See if we've missed anything.'

Three weeks had passed. No new witness had been traced, there were no further clues as to their killer's identity and the Murder Review Group had started sniffing around, wanting results. The commander heading up the Gold Group also wanted results, which they didn't have. Without any new evidence, Melissa's case could be taken over by a new team, or the present team could be halved. The case was heading slowly for the dead files and Langton, frustrated beyond belief, knew it. He still maintained a gruelling schedule, though they were coming up empty-handed every day.

It was a quarter past three in the afternoon when the call came in. Jean took it and handed it over to the office manager, who forwarded it to Langton.

'What's this?'

'Call yesterday afternoon. From Spain.'

'Spain?'

'Caller said he was Barry Southwood, ex-detective. Said he had information about the serial murders. Left his contact number.'

'Southwood?' Langton said, frowning.

'Said he was an ex-police officer.'

'Yeah, right, I heard you. Anyone checked him out yet?'

'Yep – Barolli. Turns out he's a dirty cop. Fifteen years with Vice. "Enforced retirement".'

'OK. Get everything you can on him. Then we'll call the old sod back.' Langton paused by Anna's empty desk.

'Where's Travis?'

Barolli looked up. 'With Lewis. They've had no luck finding our gravel-voiced tart yet; they're still trawling around Soho. You want me to call them back in?'

'No,' he growled, retiring to his own office.

It was almost six o'clock; Anna and DS Lewis were standing outside a small, dingy café near King's Cross station. It was a known haunt for pimps and hookers, especially on a rainy night. The two detectives had spent hours stopping known street girls on every corner of Soho. They had also walked through the main train stations, but again their questions met with no luck. With the only description being 'a gravelly voice, male or female', there was not a lot to go on. It was worse than looking for a needle in a haystack. Lewis called it quits. They would both fill in their report the following morning at the station. Lewis went for the bus, but Anna decided that she would take the tube home.

She spotted the tube station and headed down the escalator. Her feet ached like hell and she was exhausted. Coming up the escalator was a tall, rangy woman with thick, black, curly hair. She wore a tight red leather skirt, a leather jacket with studs and a low-cut vest. She was carrying a big bulging shoulder bag and talking animatedly to a short, plump, blonde woman.

'I said, "For a tenner, I wouldn't light your cigarette!" The cheeky sod! So then he says—'

Anna turned. She was certain it was 'the voice'. She stepped off the down escalator and jumped onto the one going upwards. At the top, she glimpsed the red leather skirt disappearing; the woman was walking away on strappy, red high-heels.

Outside the station Red Leather was nowhere to be seen. Frustrated,

Anna checked the taxi rank, then returned to the station, but she'd lost her. She sighed, then noticed a sign for the ladies' toilets. Red Leather's dressing room?

Inside, the plump blonde was at the mirror, outlining her lips with gloss. A toilet flushed. Anna checked her make-up.

The blonde called out to her friend, 'My mum said she wanted me to pay her the going rate. I said to her, that's a bit much!'

Red Leather exited a cubicle and tottered over to the washbasin.

'Mmm,' she said.

'I mean, these bleedin' childminders are getting twenty quid an hour, you know?'

'Mmm.'

Anna washed her hands. Her back was to the two women, but she could see them both in the wall of mirrors above the sinks. They finished their make-up, frizzed up their hair. The blonde never stopped talking, while the woman in red leather, whom Anna was desperate to hear, still didn't say a word.

'Tarra, then. See you Monday.' The blonde walked out. Anna crossed to the hand-dryer wafting her hands, playing for time. Her heart quickened as Red Leather washed her hands, shook the water from them and turned to Anna.

'Those things take a hell of a time, don't they? I mean, they should just provide paper towels.'

Anna was certain it was the same voice. Red Leather clicked over to an empty cubicle and withdrew reams of toilet paper. The prostitute returned to the mirror, drying her hands.

Trying to sound casual, Anna walked over and said, 'Tell me something. You called Queen's Park police station, didn't you, and said you had information about Melissa Stephens.'

Red Leather looked up sharply. 'So what? I said all I knew.' She sidestepped Anna. 'There's nothing more. Excuse me.'

'I would like to talk to you,' said Anna, astonished she was right.

Red Leather stood licking her lips at the mirror. 'Well hard luck,

65

sweetheart. I've done my good-citizen shit. How in Christ's name did you find me?'

'You have a very unusual voice.'

'Yeah. Comes from a punter stepping on it, squashed me larynx. Tarra.'

As Red Leather walked to the door, Anna hurried after her. 'Could I just have ten minutes, please?'

Red Leather's hand was on the door. 'I felt sorry for the little girl, right? I told them all I saw. I'm not gonna walk out with you. In that suit, those shoes, you got Vice Squad virtually stamped on your forehead. It'd bring me a lot of grief.'

'I'm not with Vice.'

'Sweetheart, I don't give a shit if you're with the Royal Ballet.'

Red Leather walked out, Anna hot on her heels. 'I'm with the murder team. Look, don't make me arrest you.'

Red Leather stopped and snarled, 'On what fucking charge?'

'Couldn't we just have a coffee?'

'Jesus Christ!'

'I'll pay you for your time,' Anna said.

'Fifty quid. Go back inside the toilets. I'm not being seen out here with you.'

'You go in first,' said Anna, sure that otherwise she would walk away the moment her back was turned.

Red Leather sighed noisily and returned to the ladies. Anna followed her.

When Langton finally put in the call to Spain, Southwood's answering machine was on.

Moira had her coat on ready to leave. 'All I know, gov, is he was a bent cop. Real piece of work. I was still in uniform; it was that long ago. We called him the Groper.'

'You think this information he's got could be for real?'

'I dunno. It's not like he called straight away; it's been weeks. And he kept on about a reward.'

66

Langton smiled ruefully and told Moira she could go home. He knew he would have to take the call seriously, but his budget was tight. A trip to Spain was the last thing he needed in the report book, especially if it was a waste of time. When he tried the number again, the machine was still on. Depressed, he hung up.

It was almost nine o'clock: the skeleton night shift was on duty. Langton stood in the centre of the room. They hadn't had a break for weeks. It seemed the case was drying up. Anna burst into the room, her face flushed.

'Oh, good, you're still here.'

Langton smiled. 'I'm thinking of moving in.'

She took off her coat. 'I found the witness.'

'What?'

'At King's Cross station. One reason we had no luck is that she's a weekender; gets the train in from Leeds every Friday, leaves on the Monday. She's not a transsexual, by the way, she's female, but one of her punters—' She had to gasp to catch her breath; she was so excited.

'Take a deep breath, Travis, then give me the details.'

Anna got out her notebook and began flicking through the pages. Langton perched on the edge of her desk. 'Her name is Yvonne Barber. She's a prostitute; she shares a room with two other girls above a bondage shop in Old Compton Street. Yvonne was certain the car Melissa got in was a Mercedes, an old one.'

Anna had shown her a clutch of vehicle pictures and she had picked it out, unhesitatingly.

'It was this one, drophead Mercedes SL; the colour was pale blue.'

Langton clapped his hands. Anna beamed.

'Her description of the driver is still vague: mid to late thirties, clothes well cut, short, pale brownish or blond hair, wearing dark glasses. But here's the most interesting thing: she said it looked as if Melissa knew him.'

'What?'

'She said Melissa didn't look afraid; she was smiling and talking to him as she moved round to get in the passenger seat. She said it really looked like she knew the driver.'

'Knew him?' Langton was still frowning.

'Yes,' Anna said. 'That was why Yvonne walked away. She had been going to have a go at her because that stretch of Old Compton Street is her patch, right?'

'Well, that opens a big can of worms.' Langton reached out and touched her shoulder. 'Totally unexpected. Good work.'

'Thank you.'

It was after half past ten by the time Anna had written up her report. As she left, she saw that Langton's light was still on in his office. She didn't get home until half past eleven. As she got into bed, she touched the photograph of her father and whispered, 'I found her, Dad!'

When Anna went in the following morning, Lewis held up her report.

'You got lucky.'

'Yes, I guess I did.' It wasn't exactly the reaction she had hoped for. She sat at her desk and asked Moira, 'Where's the gov?'

'At the lab. You know this trip to Spain: do you want to put your name down for it? The gov will choose who goes, but there could be a bit of Euro shopping up for grabs.'

'Spain? Why Spain?'

'Call in from an ex-policeman; says he has information on the killer. We think it's bullshit. He was as bent as a hairpin. So you want to go on the list or not?'

'Yes, sure.' There were sly glances around the incident room. No one else wanted it. It meant an EasyJet budget flight, there and back in a day, not to mention the schlep out to Luton airport.

Meanwhile, Langton was impatiently pacing up and down outside the lab. Eventually a gowned-up Henson came out, removing his mask. 'You can get me at the end of a telephone, you know.'

'I wanted to see for myself.'

'See what?'

'Melissa Stephens's body.'

In the cold storage area, Henson slowly pulled out the drawer containing her body.

'We are still waiting for the insect infestation details.'

Langton shook his head. 'It's not that. At the post mortem, you said the tip of her tongue had been bitten, possibly by foxes. Correct?'

'Yes. We have examined her stomach contents; she didn't swallow it.'

'What size is the bite?'

'See for yourself.'

Henson withdrew the sheet covering her head. He used a spatula to open the mouth and then, with an object resembling flat-edged tweezers, he gently prised forward Melissa's tongue. 'As you can see, it's the tip and a fraction more that's missing.'

Langton cocked his head to one side, then looked at Henson.

'You sure it was a fox or a dog?'

'To be honest: no, I am not. I understand where you're going with this, but I am very doubtful.'

'Can you run a test?'

'I'll get the odontologist to test it for you. We might need to cut her tongue out, so you will need her parents' permission. They continue to call around the clock; they very much want to bury her. It's been weeks.'

Langton stared at Henson. 'I'll get the permission; maybe say they can have their daughter back if they allow us to do these tests.'

Henson re-covered Melissa's head with the cloth and slid the drawer back.

'I want this done today,' Langton said.

Henson nodded. He didn't like to admit fault, but he knew he should have explored the possibility that it was a human bite even if, as he still believed, it turned out to have been the work of an animal.

Langton was smiling when he banged into the incident room. As he bellowed for attention, Anna anticipated that he was going to tell everyone she had traced Yvonne. She sat back nervously in her chair and heard Langton's words: 'We have a big development this morning.'

There were murmurs; everyone gave him their full attention.

Expressions of shock showed on their faces when he announced that Henson was doing tests on Melissa's tongue.

'If our killer bit off the tip, we might have dental impressions. The family has given permission to remove the tongue. So, we wait. In the meantime, we go back to Melissa's family: did anyone they know own a blue Mercedes-Benz? We go back to Rawlins, the boyfriend and we tap into all her friends and see if they know of anyone.'

Langton looked over to Anna. 'We had a good break last night. Travis tracked down the gravel-voiced caller. Her name is Yvonne Barber; she has a record for soliciting as long as my arm. She was certain that Melissa knew her killer. So, let's get moving. At long last, we're getting a few breaks.'

After Langton had slammed his office door shut, the office manager asked who had volunteered for Spain. There were a lot of sidelong glances as Anna put up her hand.

'You won the ticket, Travis. Come and see me; we'll make arrangements.'

Anna quietly smiled. She wondered if Langton had pulled a few strings on her behalf.

Later that morning she took him the updates on calls to his office.

'Tomorrow you'll come to the lab with me, they'll be testing the tongue and—'

'I can't. I'm going to Spain. Majorca, actually,' she said, surprised.

'What?'

'To interview Barry Southwood in Palma. I got lucky.'

Langton grinned. 'You got suckered in by the rest of the team.'

'I'm sorry?' she said, stunned.

'Never mind, you're the best person for it. I can't afford to lose any of the others.'

Perplexed, she returned to her desk to find her itinerary for the following day already marked up, with a note that the ticket was to be collected at the EasyJet desk.

As she read the instructions, she caught her breath. She had to be at the airport two hours before takeoff? This meant she would have to leave home at four o'clock in the morning. Reading further, she had to take a deeper breath. The return flight was the same afternoon! The plane would land at Luton at nine o'clock at night. When Anna looked up, bewildered, she caught a lot of naughty-boy grins. She laughed involuntarily.

'You bastards really got me. There and back in a single day?'

'It's Professor Henson.'

Langton snatched at his desk phone and snapped, 'Put him through.'

'DCI Langton?'

'Speaking.'

'I had the "tooth fairy" in to look over the details.'

'What?'

'Just a joke name we use for the odontologist. You were right and I was wrong. He agreed with you, it was a human bite. Although we have only the top row of teeth, we should be able to make a good impression and get a set made up.'

'Human?' repeated Langton.

'Yes,' Henson admitted rather sheepishly. 'So, all you need to do now is find him.'

'Well, I'm working on it. Thanks for getting back to me so fast.'

Langton replaced the phone. This was a step forward, though deeply worrying.

Though they still had no suspect, they now had confirmation that their killer was becoming more sadistic. He was not dormant, far from it. The monster who murdered Melissa Stephens was active and would kill again, unless they stopped him in time.

Chapter Five

Anna stood in the long line of passengers at Luton airport, waiting to board from Gate 4. The plane was half-empty and it was no wonder, she reflected, given the ungodly hour of the check-in. She sighed; it was going to be a very long day.

In London, Langton was watching as Henson carefully splayed a section of tongue cut from Melissa's mouth in order to record and photograph every detail. He placed one ruler along the side of it and another lengthwise. The angle of the camera had to be precise, exactly perpendicular to the bite mark. These photographs would later be enhanced by computer technology using an infrared camera. The painstaking procedure would take a long time.

Henson was using a sterile cotton swab, moistened with distilled water and gently taking swabs from the tongue. The hope was to find traces of the killer's saliva and therefore his DNA.

'It's got clear indentations,' remarked Henson. 'The odontologist was able to get a good impression.'

The airport at Palma was so stiflingly hot that Anna was thankful she had travelled light. Exiting the terminal, she found the taxi rank and gave her driver Southwood's address: Villa Marianna, Alcona Way. The taxi driver wore a baseball cap, a T-shirt and dirty jeans. He seemed to be sweating, an indication the taxi had no air conditioning, though it was a registered cab, with a radio.

'Do you know the area?' Anna asked the driver. He turned, grinning, and with a broad Liverpudlian accent, said he knew the whole place like the back of his hand. He informed her that Southwood's address was on the outskirts of Palma. Anna leaned back and opened her window for some air as the driver, whose name was Ron, gave her his life story. He had met his wife in Palma on a package holiday. Now he had turned his hand part time to carpentry and also helped in real estate deals.

Without drawing a breath, he focused on Anna now. 'So, what you over here for? Lookin' fer property, are you? See ya got no luggage, like. How long you stayin'? I can show you some nice places, dependin' on the price range. There's some good bargains still to be had, but yer gotta know where to look, like.'

'I'm a police officer,' she said.

'Gerraway. A cop! Christ, they're gettin' younger! What you over 'ere for, then?'

'Just an enquiry. Is it much further?'

Unfortunately, it was. The midday sun beat down relentlessly. Even with the window down, Anna was sweating.

'What's the enquiry about, then?' Ron asked. Not for the first time, Anna caught him watching her in the rearview mirror rather than the road ahead.

'Can't discuss it, I'm afraid,' she said, hoping it would shut him up. It didn't.

'Drugs, is it? We get a lorra junkies over 'ere, 'specially in the high season. Is it drugs?'

'No, it's not drugs.' To distract him from this line of questioning, she asked the driver to give a rundown of the area. For the next half hour Ron gave an informed commentary on the best restaurants, hotels, clubs and pottery factories.

'Me brother-in-law works in the biggest pottery factory, in the centre of Palma. Got some lovely plates. You should make a trip of it. I can give you a guided tour; just call anytime. Call me direct and not through the company. I'll give you a good rate!'

His hands left the wheel. The taxi veered across the road as Ron produced various cards for his other careers.

'Please concentrate on the road,' Anna instructed.

'What I'll have to do is pull over. Check me map.'

The taxi lurched to a stop. 'Right. What was the name of the area?'

'Alcona Way.'

He turned the pages, frowning, flicking from one page to another. It was obvious Ron didn't have a clue where the villa was. Anna was gritting her teeth as he got out of the car. He crossed the road to a traffic policeman. Sighing, Anna watched them confer, look at the map dubiously, up and down. Then followed lots of arm gestures and hand flapping before Ron eventually returned to the taxi. Anna looked at her watch. It was almost two o'clock.

'Right, I just gotta turn round. Head back towards the marina, then go left, up behind the old town.'

'That's the opposite direction,' Anna snapped, on the verge of losing her temper.

'It's quite hidden. Part of a new development . . . that's not quite developed,' he laughed. 'If you know what I mean.'

Fifteen minutes later, they left the old town behind them. Some distance further on, they came to well-cut hedgerows and good roads. The villas were now very exclusive, walled properties with glorious coloured bushes in full bloom. For a moment, Anna wondered how a retired ex-Vice cop could afford to live in this area; then the roads became uneven. Suddenly, she saw a lot of half-built properties and then Ron turned up a dirt track.

'Should be up at the top here. Look for the road sign. It's gotta be up here somewhere.'

Stones flew as the taxi bumped along the road, swaying and dropping into the occasional pothole. The sign 'Alcona Way' was lying on its side. Ron backed up a few yards and turned in to what was little more than a cart track. At the end of the track there was a large, electronically controlled gate. 'Villa Marianna' was picked out in scrolled wrought iron with a Spanish dancer beside it.

Anna climbed out of the back seat of the car and pressed the security button. Before she could say a word the gates opened, revealing a paved driveway curving to the right. The taxi passed a large swimming pool with various sun loungers nearby, all in a bad state of repair. A ripped canopy hung limply, providing limited shade to the pool area. And there, behind the flowering bougainvillaea, was a sprawling villa: two storeys high, with white shutters, many of them hanging loose.

Ron had been silent until they drove to the front porch, where a number of very expensive cars were parked: a Porsche, a Saab convertible and a yellow Corniche, its white roof pulled back to reveal creamy white leather seats.

'Bloody hell! Very nice. Very nice,' Ron muttered, pulling on the handbrake.

'Can you wait to take me back to the airport?' Anna asked.

'I'll have to charge fer waitin' time.'

'Charge me. But don't leave, I have a plane to catch.'

Anna got out of the car and pressed the intercom. She waited a good few minutes before she pressed it again and then had to jump backwards quickly as a man swung open the door. He was tanned, with dark, silky, shoulder-length hair. His washed-out denim shirt was open to his navel.

'Yes?' he said, bored.

'I'm here to see Barry Southwood.'

He hardly glanced at her again as he led the way into a large tiled reception area.

'Barry! Barry!' he shouted up a sweeping wide marble staircase. 'BARRY!' Without another word, he ran up the stairs two at a time, disappearing past a landing.

Anna stayed in the hallway, only turning as she heard the sound of an electric wheelchair behind her.

Ex-detective Barry Southwood wheezed as he brought the chair to a standstill. He was grossly overweight, his belly almost resting on his knees.

'Barry Southwood?' she asked.

He stared at her, red-faced with thinning, greased-back hair.

'I am Detective Sergeant Anna Travis.' She was about to open her bag and show her identification.

'Jesus Christ! How old are you, for God's sake?'

'I'm twenty-six.'

'Twenty-six and a DS? Fucking ridiculous! My day, you'd have to have been in the force a good ten years. You come out of university a pen-pusher and they bump you straight up through the ranks!'

'Could we go somewhere to talk?' Her jaw felt tight.

Southwood shook his head, sweat drops flicking like the spray from a shower. 'They took their fucking time, then they send me a fucking kid! Disrespectful load of shites. Well, you can fuck off, tell them to send me a real copper.'

'Mr Southwood, I've come a long way to talk to you. I am on the murder enquiry and you said you had some information that might help us.'

'Well, you can just go back and tell them to fuck themselves.'

Stepping closer, Anna could smell the alcohol.

'Moira Sedley sends you her regards. She spoke very highly of you,' she lied.

'Who?'

'Moira Sedley. She was with the Vice team you used to be on. Blonde.'

'Oh yeah, big tits. Slag.'

From above came the sound of moaning, then a high-pitched howl, followed by further moaning. Southwood started to turn his chair round, wheezing as he did so.

'Don't pay any attention. Come on through.' His chair disappeared through two open double doors at the end of the hall.

Anna could identify the sound of a girl's moans and groans and then, as she entered the massive open drawing room, the sound behind her changed to shrieks of laughter.

Southwood was pouring himself a drink. 'Used to have a view of the marina before the cunts built up that block of flats.' He indicated the bottle of Scotch.

'No, thank you. But I wouldn't mind a glass of water.'

'Help yourself.' He opened a bottle of soda and poured some into a tumbler half full of Scotch. 'What did you say your name was?'

'Anna. Anna Travis.'

'Cheers.' He gulped at his whisky and then burped loudly. The chair buzzed over to the open window.

'I have a return flight,' she said, following him. The floor-to-ceiling windows opened on to a terrace. 'I have to be at the airport by three.' She was grateful for the slight breeze from the window.

Southwood gazed out to his empty pool.

'Is there a reward?'

'I'm afraid not, no,' she said matter-of-factly, sipping some water.

Opening a flap on the side of his chair, Southwood took out a pack of cigarettes. Heaving for breath, he lit up. Anna watched his face getting redder as he sucked in the smoke.

'You said that you had information,' she repeated.

'Maybe. Sit down.'

Anna sunk into a large sofa with pale pink floral cushions and gilt fringes hanging loose. She positioned herself away from the overflowing ashtray on the coffee table in front of her. Southwood had aimed his ash towards it, but missed.

'Who's heading up the enquiry?' he gasped.

'DCI James Langton and the chief superintendent is Eric Thompson, Commander Jane—'

He waved his hand, impatiently. 'All right, all right . . . never heard of them. Bloody female commanders now. I know they gotta put the friggin' women up the ranks, 'cos it's all discrimination nowadays, but they're bloody useless. Never met one that knew what she was doing.'

'How did you hear about the case?'

He sipped his drink, clutching the glass with puffy fingers stained with nicotine.

'I was at the dentist. Someone had left some English newspapers. I don't usually bother with them: out of sight, out of mind. Said you got another Ripper on the loose.'

'Yes, the media have inferred—'

'"The media have inferred",' he mimicked.

'If you do have information, I would be most grateful if we could discuss it.' She sat upright as he leaned forward to address her.

'You telling me there isn't a reward? With seven victims? I dare say there isn't one for the old drippers, but this last little girl was lovely.'

'There is no reward.'

'Haven't her family put one up?'

Anna put her glass down carefully. 'No. As I said, I need to be back at the airport by three, so there really isn't much time. Please, if you have information . . .'

From outside the window there came a screech of laughter and the sound of voices and loud music. Southwood manoeuvred his chair round quickly and headed back to the window.

Sighing with frustration, Anna rose and followed him. She looked outside and was so shocked that she froze, her mouth open.

A cameraman was filming a blonde girl, stripped naked, lying across a sun lounger, her legs spread open. A naked man's head was buried in her crotch, another naked man masturbated by her face and a third kissed and sucked her breasts. The hunk stood to one side, yelling directions.

As Southwood protested, Anna slammed shut the window and dragged the curtain across. 'I have not come here to waste my time. If you have any information, then you'd better tell me what it is.'

Southwood whizzed his chair away.

'I can tell by looking at you, you've never had a decent fuck. Tight-arsed little bitch.'

'And I can tell by looking at you that you're not long for this world.'

Southwood's mouth dropped open. 'What?'

Anna was red-faced with anger. She approached and leaned both hands on the sides of his wheelchair. 'Take a look at yourself,' she said

78

scornfully. 'You were a bent officer. And now? You go one better. Ex-Vice cop renting out his crumbling wreck for porno flicks. I'll wager that girl is under age. I could have you picked up by Spain's Vice Squad, you sick bastard.'

Southwood pushed her away from him. 'You don't even know the law, pen-pusher. Spanish Vice Squad? That's a fucking joke! You want to lay anything on me, you'd better go back to training school.'

The sweat was dripping down his face as he buzzed his chair to the front door.

'Get the fuck out of my house,' he yelled with fury.

Moments later, Anna stood outside his villa. She knew she had blown it. Explaining why to Langton would be difficult and if Southwood did have vital information, they were unlikely to get it now.

'That was quick,' Ron said, grinning at her. 'Where next?'

'Back to the airport,' she snapped.

She was sweating as much as Southwood. Moira had suggested she wear something buttoned to the neck and she had foolishly chosen a cream sweater. It was damp now and clinging to her like a limpet.

At the airport she had plenty of time on her hands. She sat in the departure lounge, figuring out what she would say to Langton. Maybe she shouldn't admit to losing her temper; perhaps just say that the cop was a drunkard and had no information.

At half past six, an announcement came over the tannoy. Due to an electrical fault, the last plane to Luton would be delayed. Twenty minutes later, passengers were informed that the flight was cancelled; the next available plane to Luton would leave first thing next morning.

Langton was in a foul mood when Moira tapped and entered his office.

'Travis won't be back until the morning.'

'What?'

'Just had a text from her. The flight was cancelled. Says she's got nothing from Southwood.'

Langton shook his head. 'Bloody knew it'd be a waste of time. Does this mean we'll have to pay for an overnight stay? The ticket cost over a hundred pounds.'

'They'll sort that out. It's the airline's responsibility.' Moira was eager to get home.

'Tell Lewis I want to see him,' Langton muttered before she closed the door.

The commander had called asking for an update. They had no DNA from the swabs and although they had the teeth impressions from the lab, even these were of no use without a suspect. Time was against them. Over four weeks had passed since Melissa's body had been discovered. Her case was getting colder by the day and the longer the enquiry limped on, the less information they could expect to come in.

Mike Lewis entered, looking glum. 'No more phone calls. We've still got the lads out. We've finished questioning Melissa's friends and family and none of them have a Merc. It's drying up, isn't it?'

'Yeah,' Langton said, equally depressed. He passed over the lab photographs of the dental impression. 'This is all we've got. Bastard bit the end of her tongue off.'

Lewis glanced at the photographs with distaste.

Langton tapped one of them. 'Henson said the sicko was probably biting down on her tongue when he raped her to stop her from crying out.'

'Bastard,' Lewis said. 'Did Anna get any information?'

'Travis? She's drinking sangria in a seafront bar, for all I know. Her plane's delayed. She's staying overnight.'

'Shit,' Lewis said. 'Wish I'd volunteered.'

Anna decided that she would return to Southwood's villa. She couldn't walk away without at least trying one more time to see what he might have. She went outside the terminal to be confronted by Ron.

'I just heard yer flight was delayed. Thought you might come out. I can take you to a nice B and B. Very cheap; pal of mine runs it.'

'No. Take me back to the villa, please.' She sat back in his smelly taxi.

She hadn't a hope in hell of getting another cab, as all the delayed passengers were lined up waiting.

'Yer know that bloke you went to see? Does he own that place?'

'Yes.'

'He's an ex-cop.'

'Yes, I know.'

'I spoke to a pal of mine.'

'Did you?'

'They make porno flicks at his place. That Corniche belongs to a right ponce of a bloke. He directs them. You with the Vice Squad, are you?'

She closed her eyes, leaning back. 'No.'

'What you doin' here, then?'

She sighed. Ron looked at her via his driving mirror.

'I am part of a murder team,' she said flatly.

'No kiddin'? You look too young.'

'Well, that's as maybe.' She was trying to fathom out what she was going to do when she returned to Southwood's villa. She wondered what her father would have done in her position.

Ron persisted. 'What you want to see him for, then?'

Anna opened her eyes, her jaw tight. 'We are hunting down a serial killer. He says he has information, but he won't give me anything unless there's a reward.'

'Well, you was in and out of there like a blue-arsed fly,' Ron said.

'He threw me out!'

'And now you're going back?'

'Yes, that's right, Ron. I am going back.'

'What you gonna do?'

'I don't know.'

Ron did his 'hands off the steering wheel act' and turned to face her. 'You know what I'd do?'

'If you don't look where we're going, we'll both end up in the morgue,' Anna snapped.

'Sorry. Got me all excited.'

81

They drove for a while in silence. Then Ron turned towards her once more. 'Threaten him,' he said.

'I'm sorry?'

'Fear makes people talk, love. You gotta make him scared: if you're shittin' in yer pants, you talk. I know about these things. That's why I got out of the Pool. Bizzies there are right bastards: knee in the groin, head-butt and they put it down to trippin' up the stairs.'

'Will you please watch the road?' She leaned forward.

'Sorry. But yer should put the pressure on him, love, if he knows about this series killer. You have a go at him!'

'Thank you, Ron, but I doubt I'd go as far as a knee in his groin.'

Anna was certain that asking Southwood for his help 'nicely' would not produce anything. And she was not about to head-butt him either.

The main gates to the villa were open, much to Anna's relief. She instructed Ron to park the taxi outside the gates, not wanting Southwood tipped off that she had returned. Ron got out, eager to accompany her, but she told him to remain by the taxi and wait.

'I gorra cosh in me glove compartment. For me own safety. You know, if I get a dodgy customer. You want it?'

'No, thank you. Just wait.'

In the darkness she seemed small and vulnerable. He watched her straighten her jacket and head up the drive to the house.

She rang the intercom and before she could speak, Southwood's gasp rang out.

'You're fucking late! Just leave it inside the door.'

When the front door was buzzed open, Anna stepped inside the house. At first the hall was dark and then it was flooded by a hideous, yellowish light. She heard Southwood's chair buzzing towards her. Then, a dis-embodied voice: 'You gonna stay an' have a quick snifter with me, Mario?'

As the chair wheeled around the corner, Southwood's face appeared, shocked. 'What the fuck is this? I thought you were deliverin' my booze.'

Anna shook her head.

'No such luck, Barry. It's me again. I am not leaving until you've told me what you know. I'm not alone, either. I've got a patrol car waiting at the gates.'

'What?'

'I can have you arrested, tonight,' she warned.

'Oh yeah? On what charges? Wetting me pants?'

'On allowing your premises to be used in the making of pornographic material.'

Southwood chuckled mirthlessly. 'Bullshit. They're consenting adults and there's no law against making adult movies. I know, sweetheart, I was on Vice for long enough.'

'So you admit to allowing your premises to be used for pornographic films?'

'YES. I gotta earn a living. So if you want to pay for what I know, then we got a deal. If you've come to sweet talk me, then you can piss off. There's the door, use it.'

Southwood turned his chair and headed back towards the lounge. Anna stood watching him and, after a moment, followed. The lights, obviously on some kind of timer device, went out.

Southwood was sitting at the open french windows, lighting a cigarette. In the compartment of his chair was a half-filled bottle of Scotch. She watched him steer his chair out of the room on to the patio, as if to make sure she had left the house. She walked silently to the windows and could hear his chesty cough.

She stood partly hidden by the curtains as he moved the chair towards a makeshift ramp down the stone steps of the veranda. She edged further forward, just making out the dark shape of Ron's taxi waiting at the gates.

As he crossed the patio near the pool, Southwood fumbled for the bottle at the side of his chair. He was so busy trying to open the bottle while at the same time looking towards the gates that his chair veered dangerously close to the side of the swimming pool. When it bumped over a ridge, the worn parapet lifted. She watched silently as he tried to move the chair backwards, the bottle smashing to the stone and then breaking.

'Shit,' he growled, still fumbling with the controls.

'Need some assistance, Barry?' she asked softly.

Southwood craned his neck to see her, squinting in the darkness. The chair whirred and buzzed, each motion moving it closer to the edge of the pool.

'Pull me back, will ya? Me batteries need recharging,' he snarled.

Anna moved closer, but remained directly behind him.

Again he swivelled round to try and see her more clearly, but every motion he made now inched the chair closer to the pool.

'Jesus fucking Christ, what're you doing?' His voice rose in panic.

Anna remained silent as he sweated and tried again to get the chair out of the rut.

'All right. All right. I have information. You get it, if you pull the bloody chair back. Did you hear what I said? PULL THE CHAIR BACK!'

'I will. But you'd better start talking.'

'What?'

'I think you heard me.'

'I'm gonna fall into the fucking pool,' he shouted.

'I'll tell you what I'll do. I'll hold on to the back of the chair, just to make sure you don't fall. So the sooner you tell me what you know, the better.'

Southwood gripped the arms of his chair. 'It's maybe worth shit. For Chrissakes help me out here. I can't fucking swim, never mind bloody walk.'

Anna now positioned herself directly behind the chair, as the big man sweated in fear.

'OK, OK, this is what I've got. Just hold on to the chair. Don't let me get any closer to the edge.'

Southwood began, sotto voce, alternating between rasping coughs and puffs on his cigarette. Twenty years ago, before he moved to London, he was a DC attached to Vice with Greater Manchester Police. A well-known prostitute called Lilian Duffy had been found dead, strangled with her own stocking. Her hands had been tied behind her back with her bra. Duffy had been raped. She was forty-five.

Anna listened. She didn't respond when Southwood asked if it was ringing any bells.

Southwood continued with his account. Duffy had been arrested numerous times before by the Vice Squad. She had served a short prison sentence for prostitution. Southwood described her as a real hardened whore: a 'dripper', he said. On their files there was an assault charge filed by Duffy a year or so previously. She claimed to have been raped by a man who had picked her up and then tried to strangle her.

The Vice Squad responded only half-heartedly. Duffy, after all, was a known alcoholic and drug abuser. But she had provided a very good description of her assailant and they began to run it through records. Suddenly, she withdrew the charges, which had pissed everyone off because of the time already invested. When she was arrested for prostitution again, a female Vice Squad officer had tried to find out why she had withdrawn her charges. Duffy had stunned everyone by claiming 'personal reasons': the assailant attacker was her own son.

Anthony Duffy, seventeen years of age, was subsequently arrested. He denied attacking his mother. A year later, Lilian Duffy's body was found in a wooded area, strangled, with her hands tied behind her back. The murder team, now provided with the Vice Squad's reports, brought in Anthony Duffy for questioning. There were no DNA specialists twenty years ago and with no witness and the body in a badly decomposed condition, they had not pressed charges. Anthony Duffy had been released from custody, though the feeling in the office was that he was guilty.

Southwood waited for Anna to respond. As he turned, she could see the sweat dripping down his forehead.

'That's it. That's bloody it!' he gasped.

'Why?' she asked.

'Why what, for Chrissakes?'

'Why did you feel that Anthony Duffy was the killer?'

Southwood wiped his face with the cuff of his shirt.

'Just a gut feeling. He was a real odd kid, very calm. He had been brought up in foster homes, but around fifteen he traced his mother. She was living with this Jamaican pimp. Had a whole string of girls living in a shit hole in Swinton, on the outskirts of Manchester.'

'So, was he well brought up? Had he been abused?'

Southwood was shaking. 'Nah. Good education . . . very intelligent. Come on, now, wheel me back inside. I gotta have a drink.'

Anna had to really jerk the chair hard to free it from the rut. Southwood yelped with fear, sure she was going to tip him into the pool, but she managed to ease the chair round. He fumbled with the controls, but the battery was now very low. She had to push him back up the ramp. He weighed at least twenty stone, but at last she got him back into his drawing room.

Anna went behind the bar and poured him a glass of water. He almost snatched the glass from her and gulped it down.

'Gimme some of that vodka. I'm out of Scotch. That's why I let you in. I thought you was Mario, the guy that delivers for me. And can you plug in the battery recharger? It's by the coffee table.'

Anna switched on a lamp and found the recharger. She then fixed him a drink as he watched her with angry, watery eyes. She calmly took out her notebook and, leaning against the bar, made notes of everything he had told her. Southwood remained silent, drinking thirstily, before holding up his glass for a refill.

'I'll check all this out,' she said, pouring more vodka. 'Is there anything else?'

'Nah, that's it. Like I said: it might mean fuck-all. There was just something about him.' He hesitated. 'Made you feel uneasy. I think it was his eyes. He'd got these big, wide-apart eyes.'

'Anthony Duffy,' Anna said, softly.

'Yeah, he was a really handsome boy. Christ knows where he is now. That was twenty years ago.' Southwood looked pitiful: hunched in his chair, clutching his glass. 'It's all I have, swear on my dead mother's grave. That's it.'

Anna put her notebook away. 'We'll check it out. Thank you.' She started to walk to the door.

'Why don't you stay and have a drink with me?'

She glanced at him and shook her head. The big, foul-mouthed man looked vulnerable. Though he was obviously lonely, she couldn't stand to be in his presence a moment longer.

'No. Thank you.'

By the time Anna left the villa a crate of Scotch had been deposited on the doorstep by the front door. Southwood called after her from his chair. 'Good night,' she said, and walking outside, closed the door behind her. They had a possible suspect. Anthony Duffy. She'd finally got what she came for.

Ron jumped out of the waiting taxi and opened the passenger door.

'You all right?' he said. 'I was getting worried.'

'I'm fine. Just find me somewhere quiet where the food is good and cheap, and has some decent sangria to go with it. And then I need to find a hotel.'

'On our way,' he said as the taxi swerved down the hill, away from the decaying villa and its equally decaying, drunken occupant.

'Did you get the information you wanted?' Ron asked.

'Yes,' she said, repeating the name 'Anthony Duffy' to herself. It might prove to be unconnected. But if it didn't, they had, at long last, a suspect.

Chapter Six

L angton kept staring at the memo.

'Anthony Duffy?' He looked at Lewis. 'What's this about?'

'Travis sent a text message to Moira. Here's the printout.'

'This is it?'

'Yeah, that's all she said. And that she should be back this morning.'

'So what's with this Anthony Duffy?'

Lewis scratched his head. 'We don't have any record of him; he's not on any files. I guess we have to wait until we get the details from Travis.'

Langton pursed his lips in anger; he returned to his office.

Moira looked over. 'I told you to wait until she got here.'

Lewis whipped round on Moira. 'This is a fucking murder enquiry, Moira! She needs to get herself organized: sending bloody text messages! She never even contacted the Spanish policeman we arranged to help her.'

It was a nightmare journey home for Anna. Ron's friend with the B and B, was in fact the proprietor of a seedy, rundown hostel. The room was cramped and damp and she had to share the dubious bathroom. That, with the after-effects of the awful sangria, greasy hamburger and french fries from Ron's favourite café, had kept her up most of the night before she re-boarded the plane. She staggered back and forth to the toilets throughout the trip. She wasn't exactly sick, but she did feel like someone with a cement mixer in her stomach.

When she arrived at the station just after two o'clock, she wasn't feeling any better. The cement mixer kept on churning, but now she was feeling light-headed, too. Moira came to her desk.

'Gov is very spiky about your text message,' she whispered. 'You wanted me to pass it on, right?'

'Yes, of course.'

'Well, he's ready to have a go at you.'

'Go at me? My God, I've had no sleep, I have worked my butt off and Southwood is even worse than you described. He's got no idea what I had to go through to get the information out of him!'

'Travis!' There was a bellow from inside Langton's office.

Anna made her way there.

'Sit down,' he snapped. 'What the hell were you doing? You did not contact the authorities. You did not use the patrol car provided.'

'Nobody told me to contact anyone,' she spluttered.

'It's fucking procedure, Travis! You think we'd just let you loose without any backup? Then I get handed this text message! Lost your voice, did you? Couldn't call in?'

'It was very late when I got the information.' The cement mixer was churning faster, making her break out in a sweat. 'I think I've got a bit of food poisoning,' she added.

'Take some Bisodol! You going to be sick, is that it?'

'No. I just don't feel very well.'

'Neither do I. So, let's have it! Who is this Anthony Duffy? This suspect? Jesus Christ, who the fuck is he?'

It took Anna over fifteen minutes to explain how she had eventually been able to gain the information from Southwood. Langton listened without interruption; though he made a few notes, his anger was palpable.

'So, if the profiler is right about our killer taking his revenge against his mother, then Southwood's suspect could be the man we are looking for.' Anna swallowed audibly.

Staring at her, Langton now held up his hand.

'You think this cab driver saw what you did by the swimming pool?'

'No, sir. I am sorry if it was unethical, or against usual procedure, but I did get a result.'

'True. Well, I hope to Christ it doesn't have any repercussions for us. Go and fix your stomach and we'll get onto this.'

'Thank you.'

Langton's expression softened a fraction. 'I'm sorry I sounded off at you, Travis. You look terrible, by the way.'

'I feel terrible.'

Lewis was standing by the computer. Having run the name Anthony Duffy through the 'known felons' database, the team still had no result. Social Services also came up blank; Passport and Immigration likewise. Anthony Duffy didn't appear to exist. They had requested information from the Greater Manchester murder team and Vice Squad, but many files had been lost in a fire at the station fifteen years ago,

If alive, Anthony Duffy would now be in his late thirties. They contacted Housing, Benefits and Inland Revenue; no one had a record of Anthony Duffy. They had numerous Duffys, of course and even eighteen Anthony Duffys, but none of the correct age. There was not a parking ticket in his name, no police record and he had never been called for jury duty. It seemed that he had disappeared off the face of the earth.

Then their luck seemed to turn. The address for the mother, Lilian Duffy, had been found on an old electoral register. The house she had lived in was owned by Jamail Jackson, a small-time con artist and pimp in the Swinton area. But then, no sooner did they glimpse a light at the end of the tunnel than it flickered out. The house had been demolished fifteen years ago and Jamail murdered in a pub fight four years later.

Langton ordered the search to spread to foster homes and adoption agencies. But by six o'clock that evening, they still could find no trace of Anthony Duffy. He could be living abroad; he could be lying in the cemetery.

Anna had stayed the course all afternoon but by that time she was feeling even worse. She had not dared eat anything all day, only spooning in her mouth half a bottle of Bisodol. Lying in bed later that evening with a hot water bottle across her stomach, she went over and over everything Southwood had said.

Duffy was well educated. The profiler Michael Parks had described the killer as having above average intelligence. There was also the connection with his mother being a prostitute. He had to be a very viable suspect.

Could there be a link between the older victims? They were all from the north of England and had moved down to London for one reason or another. Or they had become weekenders. Could one of the victim's relatives have a clue to Duffy's whereabouts? Sleep didn't come easily to Anna that night.

By the time she got to work the next day, Langton had divided up the team and sent them to interview relatives and other contacts of the victims. So it continued for the next three days, as the team worked on tracing and interviewing people. On the fourth day everybody was called together for a briefing.

Langton asked for an update. One by one, the officers detailed their interviews with the victims' relatives. Many had moved on, or were dead, so tracing them had taken time. The children of the victims were spread far and wide, many of them on the same downward spiral towards drug and alcohol abuse as their mothers. No one appeared to have ever heard the name Anthony Duffy and there was as yet no photograph of him to show.

Langton suggested they return to Southwood and get an e-fit picture made of their suspect. Anna had written in her report that he had a very good recall of Duffy's face. The picture could be aged, then released to the press.

Then the breakthrough they had been waiting for came. Mike Lewis up in Manchester found a possible link in the files of an adoption agency there. The woman running the agency had no papers going back further than twenty years, but acting on her own initiative she visited Ellen Morgan, who had been the administrator at one time. Since then, laws and restrictions regarding the foster programme had been tightened, but twenty years ago Mrs Morgan not only arranged foster care for numerous children, she was also a foster mother.

It was Moira who took Lewis's call. Mrs Morgan had at one time cared for a boy called Anthony Duffy. Her address was a nursing home, Green Acres, in Bramhall, near Manchester.

Langton chose to do this interview himself and ordered Travis to accompany him. It was to be another day trip. They boarded the eight o'clock train at Euston the next morning. Langton wore a smart suit and held an armful of newspapers.

'Mike's also managed to track down an ex-Vice cop who might be able to help,' he told her as they made their way along the narrow aisle to their seats.

'I thought we'd interviewed them all,' she said.

'This one was invalided out, eight years ago. Shot in the leg. He lives at Edge Hill. I've got a car waiting for us, so we can zap about, see what we can get.'

Langton settled in his seat, opposite Anna. He took out one paper, proffered another, but she shook her head, indicating her own *Guardian*. She was ill at ease sitting opposite him. She couldn't help wondering how it would be, being in such close proximity to him for the three and a half hour journey there and the three and a half hours back. She sat back to read. Occasionally she would steal a glance at Langton, but he appeared oblivious to her presence. The entire journey passed mostly in silence.

She just managed to avoid the train door slamming into her as he charged off down the platform once they reached the station.

Outside, a Greater Manchester Police patrol car was waiting for them. Langton sat in the front seat with the driver, a friendly, chatty officer. They did not discuss the case. Instead, the two men engaged in a lively conversation about the rise in property prices.

'You married?' the officer asked.

'Nope. Been there twice though, so I've got the T-shirt.' Langton grinned. He turned suddenly to Anna in the back seat.

'What about you?' he asked.

'Am I married?'

'Yes?'

'No, I'm not.'

The driver offered the information that, not only was he married, he had five children.

'Five?' Langton said, shaking his head in astonishment.

'You got any?' the driver asked.

'Yes, one daughter. She lives with her mother. Lovely girl, very bright. I have her some weekends, when I'm free.'

As Langton chatted, Anna was amazed to hear so much about his personal life. By the time they reached their destination, Langton in turn knew virtually the driver's entire life history.

The nursing home looked pleasant, set in the middle of a well laid-out garden. The reception area seemed light and friendly. There were flowers on the desk and cards pinned up on the bulletin boards. Mrs Steadly, the cheerful administrator, was a woman in a pink suit.

'You can see Mrs Morgan in her room, unless you prefer to have coffee and biscuits in the sun lounge. You won't be disturbed there. It's not that warm today and with all the glass it can get a bit chilly. We really need to put central heating in, but we have to raise the money first!' she said as they crossed the reception area with her.

'I think we'd prefer to see Mrs Morgan in her room,' Langton responded, smiling.

The room was fairly large, with numerous pot plants on the windowsill. Mrs Steadly introduced a frail, tiny woman with a halo of snow-white hair. Crippled by painful arthritis, Ellen Morgan moved with the aid of a walking frame.

Mrs Steadly backed out of the room and closed the door. Laid out on the bed were two large photo albums. Anna took a seat by the window, Langton sat on the bed and Mrs Morgan leaned on her frame.

'I knew you wanted a photograph. So I got everything out and went through them. It brought back memories, I can tell you.'

Langton smiled. 'You had a very full life. How many children have you cared for?'

'Too many. But I keep in touch with most of them and they come and see me,' she said, moving across to the bed.

Langton gently helped her to sit beside him and placed the album she was pointing to in her lap.

'Tell me about Anthony Duffy,' he prompted.

'Anthony was four when I first met him. He was only supposed to come for a few weeks, but he stayed with me eight months. He was very shy, exceptionally nervous. He looked like a skeleton when he arrived,' she chuckled.

Langton watched the bulbous, distorted fingers turning the pages. Then she pointed. 'Here's one from that time. It was taken at one of the boy's birthday parties. There's Anthony, at the corner of the photograph.'

Langton gazed at the face, then removed the photo, which he passed to Anna. Anna was struck by the image of this tiny boy, with his paper hat, wearing a striped, knitted pullover. His pixie-like face was unsmiling; he had large, extraordinary, beautiful blue eyes.

'He was very much a loner. Not that he was trouble; well, he was young, but he didn't mix with the other children. His mother was in police custody and went to prison for six months. When she came to collect him, he clung to the banister rail, screaming. It was very sad. There was nothing I could do in those days. She was his mother.'

Mrs Morgan removed another photograph from the album. 'He came back to me four years later. This is him. He'd grown quite tall for his age. He wasn't as shy, but he still wouldn't mix with the other children. He was very bright, but he had become more difficult to control. When he didn't get what he wanted, he would throw the most terrible tantrums; you've never seen the like.'

Langton passed the snapshot to Anna. Anthony, at eight, was tall and skinny. He wore shorts, a shirt and tie and his hair stuck up in odd tufts, looking as if it had been cut with garden clippers.

Mrs Morgan stared at the empty space in the album. 'I said I would have him for the eleven months his mother had left to serve in prison, but I couldn't handle him. The house was cramped with two girls of my own and the four other children living with me. But that wasn't the real reason. I just didn't want him disrupting everyone the way he did. He'd get angry—' Mrs Morgan stopped for a while, as if remembering something.

'He had the most extraordinary eyes, "Elizabeth Taylor eyes", I used to call them. He could be very foul-mouthed. That I could deal with. But we had a big, fluffy old cat, Milly. She gave him asthma. I explained that he should not stroke her or go near her, really, because if his asthma got worse, he wouldn't be able to stay. Then his asthma cleared up. I will never forget finding Milly. He'd wrapped her body in a tea towel. I confronted him and he didn't lie, didn't try to make an excuse. He had taken the cat down to the garden shed and strangled her. He said he loved me and didn't want to be taken away again.'

The tears started to flow. She dabbed at her eyes with a folded tissue.

'There was a couple, they had fostered before. They were very nice, elderly, quite well off. They agreed to take him. I packed up his few things and they came round in a very expensive car. He was so excited about the car that he never even looked at me when they took him away. Anthony was fostered by a couple called Jack and Mary Ellis in 1975. They are both dead now.'

'Did you ever see him again?' Langton asked.

'I saw him once; it would have been about six or seven years later. I was drawing the living-room curtains and I saw this boy standing outside the gate. Just looking at the house, staring really. He was in a school uniform: blazer, a yellow and black school scarf, long grey trousers. I knew it was Anthony because of those eyes. But by the time I got to the front door, he'd gone. He never came back. I never saw him again.'

Back in the car, Langton's mood was subdued. The driver started up the engine, asking if they wanted to go to lunch or should he drive them to Edge Hill to see ex-Detective Richard Green.

'Straight to him, please,' Langton said without hesitation. 'What did you make of that, Travis?'

'Very sad,' she said. Her stomach was growling.

'Yeah, shoved from pillar to post. If we don't get any joy from this chap Green, when we go back we might try to do a composite picture ourselves and age it up.'

'How did you track me down, then?' Green said when they met at his house.

'It wasn't that easy,' Langton said, smiling. 'You certainly move around.'

'Yeah, well, with the pension I get, money is tight, so we buy houses, do 'em up and sell 'em on. The wife made all the curtains and covered the sofas. She's also a dab hand with the paintbrush, decorating. I do a spot of carpentry.'

'I've been thinking about what you want,' he continued. 'It was a long time ago. Must be twenty years. I was with Vice.'

Langton nodded. 'Yes, I know.'

'Hated it. That's why I moved over to the Robbery Squad and what happens? I'm only there two years and this bloody little junkie fires off a round in my leg.'

'Bad luck.'

'I'd call it more than that; thirteen years old, the little shit! If I'd got my hands on him, I'd have been put away for murder.'

'Anthony Duffy,' Langton reminded him quietly.

'Oh, right. We had him in for questioning. You know Barry Southwood?' Green laughed. 'He had to get out of Manchester. He was a devil with the hookers. He was warned over and over again. Sex mad, he was.'

Langton repeated, 'Anthony Duffy.'

'Right. I've been racking my brains, to get the events as clear as possible.'

'And?' Langton prodded.

'We had him in for questioning, that'd be 1983. His mother, Lilian, had been brought in, beaten up badly. She was screaming the place down.

Anyways, once she was calmed and cleaned up, said she wanted to make a charge of rape and assault.'

'Did you take any swabs?'

'We weren't all that up to speed on the DNA, like we are now.'

'She pressed charges?'

'Yeah. She said this guy had tried to strangle her and she had fought him off and escaped.'

'When did she say it was her son?'

'I'm not sure. To be honest, none of us was that interested in her; she was a real pack of trouble. She would have been seen by a female officer on the rape team. She came back, saying how she wasn't going to press charges. She wants to change her statement and when we have a go at her, she starts howling, saying it was all a mistake, it wasn't a punter. It was her son and she didn't want to get him in trouble.'

Langton held up his hand. 'Do you think when she was attacked she didn't know it was her son? Maybe she found that out later?'

'I don't know. Could be. She lived in a house full of old slags, all as bad as each other. Shallcotte Street, it was; number 12. Place was a hellhole. There were so many fights and beatings, the ambulance could practically find its own way to the house without a driver.'

Langton leaned forward to change the subject. 'When was the next time Anthony Duffy's name came up?'

Green pursed his lips. He took out a small notebook with jottings in it and flicked the pages backwards and forwards.

'You got to remember, I was on Vice, not the Murder Squad. Oh, here we are. I don't have the exact date, but it was maybe fifteen, twenty years ago. It was on some wasteground. There were a lot of old junked cars, fridges that had been dumped and the council ordered the place to be cleared. That's where they found Lilian's body. She hadn't even been reported missing. Murder team is called out. Been dead at least six months. I saw the morgue shots when they called me in. It was a mess: dogs and foxes had been at it. She had been strangled with a stocking, her hands tied behind her back with her bra. They called in the Vice Squad and there were the notes about the assault charge. I think Barry Southwood gave them some details. Next thing I heard was they arrested her son, Anthony Duffy.'

'Did you see him?'

'No, I didn't. One of the girls said they couldn't believe that a tart like Lilian could have such a good-looking boy. Seems he was well dressed, quietly spoken. He was at some college or other. Anyway, after questioning him, they released him without charges.'

'And? Anything else?'

Green shrugged his shoulders.

'That's about it. I had a few pints after, with his arresting officer. He said the consensus was Duffy might have done it.'

'What do you mean, "might"?'

'Because of the way he was. It was weird, they said. He was so quiet, so unemotional.'

'Why did they release him if they had suspicions? Did he have an alibi?'

'I don't know. Maybe. Listen, she'd been dead a long time. There was no witness, no weapon. The girls who had seen her last were all screwed up. They couldn't remember where she had been, or who she had been with. She hadn't even been reported as missing.'

Langton looked across to Anna.

'You want to ask anything?'

She hesitated.

'Do you recall any of the names of the other girls that lived at the house?' She opened her notebook.

'You're asking the impossible,' said Green, scratching his head.

'If I was to read out a few names, can you tell me if any are familiar?'

'Sure. But this was a long time ago. Most of them are probably in the cemetery.'

Langton gave her a brief nod.

'Teresa Booth?'

He shook his head. She continued at random through the list of victims and got the same response to Mary Murphy; he shook his head for Beryl

Villiers, again for Sandra Donaldson, but when she said the name 'Kathleen Keegan', he hesitated.

'I think she was at the house. Name sounds familiar.'

'And Barbara Whittle?'

'Yeah. That sounds familiar too.' Green could not elaborate on whether or not the two women were residents, claiming he just recognized their names. 'There were all sorts, different ages, living at that place. Lot of kids too, just running wild. Social services wore out the path to the front door.'

The house had been demolished. This would mean another extensive search of past records. And the Keegan and Whittle families would have to be questioned again to see if they recalled either victim living at 12 Shallcotte Street.

Langton weaved his way down the aisle of the carriage, carrying two cups. He set the coffees down on the table between them. He lit a cigarette.

'How much do I owe you?' she said.

'On me. Really.'

Langton took out his mobile phone and began to scroll through his calls. He went to stand by the door and Anna watched him through the glass partition, talking. He made call after call, his face concentrated and unsmiling. He did have, she thought, quite a handsome face. His nose was too thin and hooked slightly, but his eyes were nice, expressive, as were his hands. The dark shadow round his chin gave it a bluish hue, both attractive and not. For a police officer, he also didn't dress that badly, she decided. His suit was quite stylish; so were his shoes. She turned quickly to stare out of the window as he returned.

Langton drained his cold coffee and slid back in his seat.

'Good work, Travis, listing the victims. Good thinking.'

'Thank you.'

He leaned back, loosening his tie. 'It's been one step forward, two steps back. But today, I think, we paced a bit ahead. What do you think?'

She took a deep breath. 'I think if he is our killer, something happened to him at that house in Shallcotte Street. The picture of him screaming at being forced to leave Mrs Morgan's care is tragic. The cat incident shows how scared he must have been. From four to eight years. That's a long time for a child to be in a hellish place. That would have shaped his character, if he is our killer.'

Langton said something so quietly that she missed it.

'Excuse me?'

'I'd put money on it. It's him.'

They remained silent for a while. When she stared at her reflection in the window, she saw her hair was standing up on end, like a kid's.

'How's your stomach?' he said, yawning.

'It's fine. Thank you for asking.' She was trying to think what she could talk about. 'How old is your daughter?'

'Kitty? She's eleven; lives with my ex-wife.' He patted his pocket and took out his wallet. He sifted through receipts and crumpled banknotes before withdrawing a small photograph.

'This was taken a few years ago. She'd just lost her front teeth.'

Anna looked at the photograph. Kitty had dark curly hair, big bright eyes and was giving a wide grin to the camera.

'She's cute.'

'She's a right little tomboy.'

She watched as he replaced the photograph in his wallet. Then he stared at his reflection in the window.

'You're divorced?' she asked tentatively.

He slowly turned to face her. 'Yes, I'm divorced.' He smiled and regarded her almost with amusement. 'Got a boyfriend?'

'Oh . . . few people around, nothing serious. Well, I wouldn't have the time right now, you know, to have a relationship. I suppose it must be even more difficult for someone like you.'

'Why?'

'Well, you know, it's a full-time occupation, isn't it?'

'Is that why my marriage broke up?' he asked.

Anna was unsure how to respond. 'Sorry?'

He gave a soft laugh. 'Travis, you are obviously pumping me for information. Truth is, I am a workaholic, but work had nothing to do with my divorce. I would put my marriage failure down to extra-marital liaisons.' He was silent for a moment. Then he looked up and laughed. 'Especially blondes. I'm a sucker for blondes.'

There was a glint in his eye. She couldn't tell if he was telling her the truth or sending her up.

He leaned back. 'What are you a sucker for, Travis?'

'Toasted cheese and bacon sandwiches.'

He grinned, then closed his eyes. 'Your old man would be proud of you.' She felt a compulsion to cry. When she looked at him again, he seemed fast asleep. She watched his head slowly slide to one side. After a while, she too leaned back and closed her eyes.

Anna jolted awake; Langton was lightly touching her cheek.

'Just coming into the station.' He sat up and started straightening his tie.

'Oh, I must have dropped off.'

'You certainly did. I've been trying to wake you for five minutes.' They were in the last carriage. When he slid the door open, a large gap was revealed between the platform and the train. Langton jumped. Then to Anna's astonishment, he turned back, grabbed her by the waist and swung her down to the platform. She was so close to him, she could smell the nicotine and coffee on his breath.

'My God, you're heavier than you look,' he joked. After making sure she was on terra firma, he strode off at his usual pace. Anna scurried behind him. She might look like a mere slip of a thing, she reflected ruefully, but she was muscular. One of her father's favourite jokes was to take her on his knee, feel her little legs and say they were all muscle. Then he'd moan, 'HEAVY muscle. She weighs a ton.'

Her mother, Isabelle, had long, slender limbs. Her dad would tease Anna that she should have been a boy, because the next baby would take after her mother. She never did have a sibling, though. It was not a source of pain or conflict in the family. It had simply never happened.

Outside the station, they parted ways. Langton had decided to take the tube home and Anna told him she would be catching a bus. In fact, she didn't. Once he was out of sight, she hailed a taxi. She always did this when it was late. Jack Travis had made his daughter extremely aware of the risks for young women of walking home on their own from a bus stop or tube station late at night.

His love and care for her had been like a protective cloud. As she flopped down on her pillow that night, Anna could hear her father's voice. Sometimes, though rarely, she heard her mother's voice. Once, at the dinner table, she had teased her husband about his 'scaremongering'. 'You shouldn't scare Anna,' she said. In answer, he came over to where his wife was sitting and wrapped his arms tightly around her.

'Izzy, if you saw what I do, day in and day out, you'd understand. I have the most precious two women in the world. God forbid anything should harm them.'

Anna was missing her parents now. At such times she felt herself very much an orphan.

Unable to sleep, she started to mull over the day's work. Finally she sat up and picked up her notebook. Mrs Morgan had described a school scarf; perhaps they should focus on tracking the suspect from that quarter.

Yet again, Langton was one step ahead of Anna. He already had a member of the team tracking the college their suspect may have attended. Langton hoped to find a later photo of Anthony Duffy to put out to the public, to see if anyone had information. It didn't come in until late afternoon the next day.

Anthony Duffy had not attended school in Manchester, but rather in Great Crosby, on Mersyside. The Merchant Taylors School confirmed that a pupil named Anthony Duffy of the same age and description as their suspect had attended their school. They had a number of photographs of him. He had been an exceptional student. Anthony had gained an A in every subject at A level. The headmaster himself did not really recall Duffy, as twenty years ago he had been a junior teacher and taught much younger pupils.

An elderly maths teacher remembered him. He had been puzzled that Duffy had never returned to collect his certificates. The boy was by then eighteen years old and could have been accepted at any number of universities. No one had seen or heard of him after the end of that term.

By six o'clock, the special courier had arrived with a list of pupils from Anthony Duffy's class and their last known addresses, but the most important evidence lay underneath the list: a packet of photographs.

There were two pictures of Anthony Duffy with his rugby team. His face had been ringed by the helpful headmaster. His head was turned away slightly but part of his profile was visible. There was another picture of him with the swimming team: eight boys lined up in swimming trunks. Once again, Duffy seemed to shrink back behind a boy in front, who held the large cup for the winning team. This time the other side of his face appeared. The school dramatic society provided three photos. They, too, were group shots, but they showed far clearer images of Anthony Duffy, albeit in wigs and hats.

In one photograph he was playing King Henry from Shakespeare's *Henry V*. He stood in his armour, holding a helmet with a red plume which blocked part of his face. His legs were apart and his chin up; those mesmeric eyes drew you to the young boy's face. In another he wore a long wig and a black moustache. His costume suggested King Charles I. He was surrounded by boys dressed as women.

In the last photo, which was of the amateur dramatic society itself, he stood next to a boy wearing a fool's costume. Duffy was holding a skull, suggesting he was playing Hamlet; luckily, in this photograph, his face was in focus and without the embellishment of a wig or make-up.

The photographs were enhanced in the lab. Everyone around Duffy was deleted and the two pictures showing partial profile were dismissed.

They had also been able to contact two ex-school friends, but neither had seen him since he left school twenty years before. One couldn't, at first, even remember him. A third school friend, now living in Australia, was being tracked down for questioning. The other names given by the present headmaster from the school register were either deceased or uncontactable from their last known addresses.

The following morning the photos were ready; their 'Hamlet' was pinned onto the noticeboard. His boyish body was muscular and fit. He had blond hair, high cheekbones and a tight-lipped mouth. His unusual eyes gave his face a prettiness that was almost feminine.

An expert was coming in to 'age' the picture, since Anthony Duffy would now be nearly forty. The room was humming cheerfully when Jean approached Anna at her desk.

'Can I tell you something?' she said quietly.

Anna smiled up at her. 'Of course.'

'I just don't want anyone yelling me down and I could be wrong. You know what I mean?'

'Go on. What is it?'

'Anthony Duffy.'

'Go on.'

'Well, like I said, I could be barking way up the wrong tree. It's just those eyes of his. I mean, they're unusual, aren't they?'

'Yes.' Anna waited.

'I think I recognize him. But as nobody else has, either I'm wrong or they don't watch as much TV as I do. Anyway, there was this show on quite a while ago. I was a real fan. It used to be on every Saturday and he played a detective. It was called *Sin City*, on at half ten in the evening. He looks like the actor. Since then he's been in films rather than anything else on the telly, but I'm pretty sure.'

'Let's have his name.' Anna picked up her notebook.

'Alan Daniels. They're also the same initials.'

'Thanks, Jean.' She stood up from her chair. 'Let me run this by the gov and see what we get.'

Moments later, Langton was leaning back in his office chair.

'Alan Daniels? Never heard of him. Have you?'

'No. But Jean is a big fan. He starred in some detective series called *Sin City*.'

'And what is he up to now?'

'Apparently he's sort of well known; he's in films these days.'

'Is she serious?'

'Yes. She thought hard about mentioning it. She was pretty nervous about it.'

'*Sin City*? I bet she fucking was. Well, Travis, we leave no stone unturned. Get onto that actors' thingy, Equity. They'll have photos of everyone in the profession. Later, you can have a go at Jean. I suspect she's heading for hot flushes.'

The following morning, Anna visited the offices of Equity and sat thumbing through the pages of their copy of *Spotlight*, a directory of every actor registered with them. Alan Daniels had a half-page spread. There was no age given, but in the photograph he appeared to be in his mid to late thirties. His agency was called AI, Artists International and was the UK's biggest management company. Anna took down the particulars. Daniels was described as 'six feet one, blue eyes'. As soon as she left the building Anna rang the station, hardly able to contain her nervous excitement.

'It's Travis. I need to talk to the gov.' She waited a few moments.

'Langton.' His voice was terse.

'It's him,' she said quietly.

'What? Are you certain?'

'It's his eyes. Yes, I'm certain. What do you want me to do?'

'Don't say anything to anyone. Just get back here fast and we'll decide how to proceed.'

'OK'.

'Anna, listen to me. If he's a fucking TV star, we have to tread very carefully. The last thing we need right now is a media cock-up.'

Anna shut off her phone and took a deep breath to calm herself.

Back in the incident room, Jean almost had heart failure. Langton cupped her face in his hands and kissed her soundly on the lips.

'I was right?'

Langton crossed her lips with his finger. 'Shh. Don't say a word to anyone. Do you hear me, Jean?'

Jean nodded solemnly. After Langton returned to his office, Jean glanced to the victims' photographs, then stared at the boyish, smiling face of Anthony Duffy.

Chapter Seven

Anna stood shoulder to shoulder with Detectives Lewis and Barolli in the small office. Langton stood behind his desk, facing them. He looked quite sharp in his grey suit, crisp white shirt and blue tie. He had shaved closer, Anna mused, noting the absence of his usual five o'clock shadow.

She started to attention when Langton began abruptly: 'We're bringing him in this afternoon. The consensus is we take this softly softly. The commander wants Daniels questioned without it becoming public knowledge. Only if further evidence is corroborated do we go for an arrest. Remember, first off, he's just helping our enquiry.'

He smiled. 'I don't want you telling your wives, or girlfriends – um, boyfriend, in your case, Travis – understand? When the media acts like vultures in these high-profile cases, it just makes our job harder, sometimes impossible. Now, we've only got circumstantial evidence in the first six cases, but it's a bit better for Melissa. And if Alan Daniels did the lot of them, that's what we want to get him for: all seven murders.'

Anna felt the tension rising in the room. Stacked high on Langton's desk were fifteen or more videos, all films or television series featuring Alan Daniels. Anna noted a number of film and TV magazines nearby.

Langton indicated the pile of videos. 'I've been through most of these and I expect all of you to do the same. Use the video set up in the briefing room. No need to wade through the entire thing, just fast forward to

Duffy. Be aware of who we are dealing with. Keep foremost in your mind that he's an actor. Over there are some back issues of film magazines and *Hello!* and *OK* that I want you to check. Guess what? He's in all of them.

'He lives alone in a substantial property on Queen's Gate, Kensington. The only access is the front door; there is no rear exit. The basement is occupied by four students from the Royal College of Art. Two women from the Victoria and Albert Museum rent the top floor from Duffy. Right now, though, he's the only occupant in the building.'

Langton continued to bring them up to date. Their suspect did not drive a Mercedes, but a Lexus saloon. He was wealthy, with over two million pounds in the bank. He paid his taxes on time, seemed law-abiding; so far had not even had an outstanding parking ticket.

His theatrical agent had been helpful, according to Langton. Seemingly unaware of the serious implications of the situation, the agent gave Langton details of his client's availability and schedule. He was currently filming at Pinewood Studios but had a four-day break coming up when he would be available for interviews. Langton promised to get back to him.

He wrapped up the briefing with one final piece of information: two officers had been outside the Queen's Gate address for twenty-four hours. They had orders to report back to base, if Duffy, as he continued to call him, left home. Langton was due to arrive at Duffy's residence at two o'clock, to escort him in.

There was a strange air of unease back in the incident room. Langton was under heavy pressure to make a fast decision regarding Duffy's involvement in this case, so they would know later in the day if they had captured a suspect at last.

When Travis, Lewis and Barolli went to the briefing room to watch the tapes, Lewis was surprised to discover how many of the films he had seen. Not great blockbusters, he explained, but some of them were good genre films.

Anna found it eerie to watch Daniels age onscreen. In the films he made as a young man, his voice had not matured, but by the early 1990s the older Daniels had acquired a deep, resonant voice with an upper-class, aristocratic tone. He seemed best suited to costume dramas.

Lewis had control of the remote in his hand and was constantly fast-forwarding or rewinding without consulting the others. He stopped the tape suddenly and said earnestly, 'I saw this film. Funny I'd never heard of his name till now. Parts are getting bigger; see, he's in this one in almost every scene.' Lewis fast-forwarded again.

'Could we just actually watch a couple of sections?' Anna said impatiently.

'Turning you on, is he?' Lewis sniggered.

'I would just like to get a good look at him.'

'It's odd how he can be making a fortune, when people like me have never heard of him,' Barolli contributed.

An hour later they sat watching *Falcon Bay*, an American mini-series. The men's constant banter was starting to irritate Anna. She was relieved when Lewis and Barolli decided they had seen enough for one day and left her to watch alone. She took the remote. Now she could pay closer attention to Alan Daniels, whose talent was obvious. His onscreen presence grew more commanding with every scene. It was his stillness, she thought, that was most compelling.

She fast-forwarded to a scene set in a vast bedroom swathed in silks and billowing curtains. Daniels was sitting on the bed, a shotgun held loosely in his hands. His costume – riding boots, tight britches, shirt open to the waist and a silk scarf loosely draped around the neck – showed his lithe, muscular body to perfection. When he turned slowly, Anna noticed the woman who lay behind him, her dark hair spread across the pillow. She wore a lace nightgown, with the frill loose around her shoulders.

'How long have you known?' he asked softly.

'Since Christmas,' she said, eyes closed.

'And you haven't told me until now?'

'I didn't know how to tell you. I didn't want to lose you. Please, come to bed. Lie beside me, just once more.'

Anna drew closer, fascinated by Daniels's performance. His sexuality exuded mystery. Slowly, he drew the scarf away from his neck and discarded it. He knelt at the end of the bed, as if to pray.

'Come to me, darling,' she pleaded.

As she held out her arms he raised the shotgun. Her eyes opened wide with fright as he fired, her blood spattering his face and white shirt. Slowly, he reloaded the gun; then suddenly, unexpectedly, he turned it towards himself.

As the camera moved in closer, Anna's attention was glued to the screen. His eyes at that moment were like a wounded animal's, full of pain. He was about to pull the trigger when he paused and threw the gun aside. He crawled over the bed, to get closer to the woman's body. Then he lay down beside her and gently drew her nightgown down to reveal her breasts. He rested his head against her heart.

'One last time, my darling,' he murmured, then he turned to kiss her breasts.

Anna almost shot out of her seat. The door had banged open and now Lewis leered at her from the doorway.

'Aha! You're still watching! Can't get enough, eh?'

She picked up the remote, red-faced and turned off the set.

'Gov wants you!'

'Me?'

'Needs a woman's touch. In his office.'

She ejected the video and placed it in its box where, on the cover, Alan Daniels, shotgun in his hand, stood like a character out of *Gone With The Wind*.

Lewis was still hovering at the door. 'Looks like you and Langton are getting to be quite an item.'

'For God's sake, Mike, leave off.'

'I wouldn't let it go much further, Travis.' He smirked. 'He's got a bad reputation.'

'Why are you doing this? Is it because you're pissed off he didn't ask you to go to Queen's Gate?'

'God, no. Just being a friend,' Lewis muttered as he left.

Langton was on the phone when she entered his office. He gestured for her to wait for him to finish his conversation, then continued in the mouthpiece: 'Right. Yes, yes, we'll do that. Yes, yes. Travis and I are going to pick him up now.'

He threw Anna a pained expression.

'Fine. Thank you. Talk later.' He replaced the phone. 'They're certainly getting hot under the collar. They don't want Daniels questioned without legal representation. So when we pick him up, he gets to make his call.'

'Did you tell Lewis you wanted me to go with you?'

'Yeah. Way I want to work it is "slowly, slowly catchee monkey". If he isn't the one, we'll know fast. Since so many of these fucking solicitors run the show now, I just want one crack at him before he starts the "no comment" game.'

He looked at her steadily for a moment.

'Does your hair grow like that, or is it some kind of style?' He cocked his head to one side.

She ran her fingers awkwardly through her hair.

'It just has a bad habit of doing this.'

'Well, go and tidy yourself up. We leave at a quarter past one. Get some lunch too, if you haven't had any.'

She was headed for the door.

'Travis?' he said quietly.

'Yes?'

'What did you think of the film retrospective?'

Anna hesitated. 'He's talented and the parts are getting bigger. If he is our man, he's going to lose all that. It's a lot to risk. And if he's not?'

'Yes. That's why we have to be careful. There's quite a few embassy top dogs living along Queen's Gate so they're used to seeing cops around. It's not going to put the wind up anyone.'

'Do you think he's the killer?'

'No point in thinking, unless I have the evidence to prove it. What's your gut feeling, though?'

'I honestly don't know.' She looked at her shoes. 'With his looks, he could get any woman he wanted. And he's linked in those magazines with all the starlets and socialites. It doesn't make sense in one way that he'd gamble a future like that, but if he is a psycho, maybe he'd get off having a secret life and being able to disguise it.'

'He certainly found the right profession for disguise.'

'Those celebrity magazines keep pumping out who he's seen around town with, but there doesn't appear to be any one woman. Maybe he's gay; thirty-eight, never married? Makes sense.'

Langton flipped open one of the magazines. 'Better do some reading. I hate this stuff.'

Since he seemed finished with her, Anna walked out of his office.

By one forty-five they were in the patrol car outside Daniels's house, which was on the left-hand side of Queen's Gate at the Kensington Gardens end. According to the two officers outside who had seen him that morning at a first-floor window, Alan Daniels had not left home.

Langton turned and gave Anna a small half smile before he preceded her up the stone steps of the large, pillared entrance of the elegant house. The bells for the other floors had the residents' nameplates, but the section occupied by Daniels showed no identification.

Langton rang the bell. After a few minutes a disembodied voice said, 'Yes?'

'Mr Daniels?'

'Yes,' the voice said carefully.

'It's the police.' Pause. 'Could you open the door, please?'

The door opened with a click. Langton and Travis stepped into a beautiful, high-ceilinged hallway which smelled of polish. The floor was covered in mosaic tiles, which encircled the statue of a Greek goddess at the centre of the hall. There was a gleaming mahogany hall table, on which a few letters were neatly piled. The door, presumably leading to Daniels's apartment, was at the right of a wide, crimson-carpeted staircase. Oil paintings lined the walls, as the staircase soared upwards to the floors above.

It gave Anna a momentary shock when the door swung open to reveal Daniels to see the celluloid image she had been staring at all morning become flesh and blood. He appeared taller and slimmer and his hair was different: blond, silky, cut in what seemed to her a Victorian style. His features were more delicate and the high cheekbones rendered his face more gaunt than on the screen. But his eyes in real life remained the most extraordinary violet colour, enhanced by his dark eyelashes. He wore a black polo-neck sweater, faded jeans and a pair of old velvet slippers with an embroidered gold monogram.

'Is this about the residents' parking?'

'No.' Langton took out his ID badge. 'I am Detective Chief Inspector James Langton and this is Detective Sergeant Anna Travis. We need to talk to you, Mr Daniels. Could we come inside?'

'I suppose so.' Daniels hesitated, then stepped back in the lighted hallway. 'Come in.'

Nothing about him gave any indication of his background, thought Anna; certainly not his aristocratic tone of voice and haughty manner. They followed him into a vast dining room, where light entered from a wall of glorious stained glass. Anna gazed in wonder. Over the dining table hung a crystal chandelier, and impressive crystal lamps had been placed at either side of the fireplace. The table must have been twenty feet long and the accompanying chairs had red velvet seats.

'Every time there's a concert at the Albert Hall, they insist on removing the residents' parking bays,' Daniels was complaining earnestly to Langton. 'It's disgusting that we all have to pay to park here.'

Langton nodded, showing little interest. Anna was studying the pattern on the oriental rug beneath her feet when Daniels interrupted her reverie.

'This way, Detective,' he said with a faint smile. Embarrassed, she followed the two men into the drawing room at the front of the house, overlooking Queen's Gate. Two tiger skins were splayed impressively across the polished wood floor and several distinguished oil paintings hung from the walls.

Daniels gestured for them to be seated. Anna sat down awkwardly on one of the huge white sofas with brilliantly coloured silk cushions. She had never seen such wealth in all her life. Langton remained standing, unaware of his image caught behind him in a fifteen-foot mirror. Daniels sat down on the edge of the sofa opposite, paying Anna little attention. Between the two sofas there was a carved coffee table, piled with expensive magazines and art books.

'This all feels very serious.' Daniels's head was tilted towards Langton.

'I'm afraid it is,' Langton said quietly. 'We are investigating a series of murders. We would like you to answer some questions.'

In this big room, Langton's voice made a slight echo.

'It's more serious than parking, then,' Daniel responded with a self-deprecating smile. 'May I offer you anything? Coffee? Tea?'

'No, thank you, sir.'

'Were the murders in this area?'

'Yes. We would like you to accompany us to Queen's Park police station.'

Daniels's eyes widened in surprise.

'Why is that?'

'It is preferable we question you at the station rather than in your home. Would you agree to accompany us?'

'Of course, but I'd like some more information. I mean, is it anyone I know that has been murdered? Were they neighbours of mine?'

'You can, if you wish, have representation,' Langton added.

Daniels's face showed a slight annoyance as he checked his watch. Then he looked up at Langton: 'Are you arresting me?' It seemed to Anna that he had become completely oblivious to the fact there was a third person in the room.

'We simply want to see if you can help us in our enquiry.'

'Are you saying I might know the murderer?' Alan Daniels remained casually perched on the arm of his sofa.

When Langton said nothing, Daniels continued quickly, 'At the very least I should be told what it is you wish to question me about. Anything less is unacceptable. Surely you see that?'

'I am investigating a series of murders; that is all I can tell you.'

Daniels ruffled his hair.

'Do you agree to accompany myself and DS Travis?' Langton persisted.

'This is all a bit weird, but obviously, if I can help you in any way possible, I will endeavour to do so. First, I think perhaps I should talk to my lawyer.'

Daniels crossed to a white marble side table and picked up the phone. As he dialled, he gave Langton a small smile.

'Is this what they call "helping police enquiries"?'

'Absolutely, sir,' Langton replied smoothly.

Daniels spoke to someone he called Edward. Anna and Langton exchanged glances. What was interesting was that he did not appear nervous. In fact, contrary to their expectations, their only suspect had started treating the situation as a bit of a joke.

'Yes, Edward, I'm fine. Look, I need your advice. I've got a detective here and he wants me to accompany him to – what station is it?'

'Queen's Park,' Anna responded sharply. Langton raised his eyebrows, amused.

'It's connected to some murders,' the actor continued. 'He thinks I might know the killer, or the victims.' He went on to explain that, since they had declined to give him any details, he had no idea what they wanted from him but, he joked, a visit to the police station might be useful material one day.

'He'll join us there.' Daniels replaced the phone. 'So, I'll just put on some socks and shoes, then we can go.'

Anna sat next to Daniels in the patrol car. He made numerous calls on his mobile phone, one to someone he was meeting at the opera later. He was generally so casual, so relaxed, it was unnerving. Something had come up, he said chattily and he might be late but they weren't to worry. Next, he called his cleaner about groceries he required and informed her that he needed some dry cleaning collected. All the time, he leaned into his phone and as far away from Anna as possible, only speaking to apologize to her when his foot accidentally touched hers.

On their arrival at the station, they went in through the back way, avoiding the day's action. Langton left Anna in charge in the interview room while he went outside to await the arrival of Daniels's solicitor.

Since making his phone calls, Daniels had hardly spoken. Now, inside the room, he looked bemused. There was a table with four chairs, two on either side. Stacked on the table were numerous files, some containing photographs.

Anna directed him to sit with his back to the door and took up her seat opposite him. She opened her notebook. Langton was not yet with them and it seemed an interminable time to be alone with Daniels.

Edward turned out to be Edward Radcliff, one of the most notorious heavy hitters in the legal system. His chambers were almost as famous as his reputation.

Langton asked if he could speak with him alone, before they saw his client.

'By all means. I'd like to know what this is all about. Sounds very unethical to me.'

'I am simply protecting your client. Alan Daniels is a known name. Rather than make a spectacle of bringing him in for questioning—'

'Questioning about what?'

'I am leading the enquiry in a series of murders. The last known victim was Melissa Stephens—'

'Jesus Christ.' He stopped walking.

Langton continued, 'But we have six other victims we believe were killed by the same perpetrator.'

'This is unbelievable. I mean, it is inconceivable Alan could have any connection to these tragic women.'

'I need to ask him some questions; if he is able to give me the answers, then he will be free to leave. I will be taping and filming the interview.'

'You haven't charged him, I take it? You've not arrested him?'

'That is correct, but I will still need to follow procedure.'

Radcliff took a deep breath; then, after a moment, suggested they get on with it.

There had been no words spoken between Daniels and Anna as they waited, apart from his polite refusal of her offer of tea or coffee and his request for water instead. A tape recorder and a video camera had been brought in and set up. When Langton ushered Edward Radcliff in the room, Daniels stood to shake hands with his solicitor, who then sat beside him. Langton took his seat beside Anna and rested his hands on the table. The tape and video camera were turned on.

Langton stated the date and time and that those present in the interview room attached to Queen's Park Metropolitan Police station were himself, Detective Sergeant Travis, Alan Daniels and his solicitor, Edward Radcliff.

Daniels glanced at Radcliff, seeming slightly perplexed at the formality. The lawyer reassured his client that it was all just procedural and that he had to be given his rights for his own protection.

Langton continued, 'Mr Alan Daniels has agreed to help our enquiries. He is not under arrest, but has come to the station of his own volition. Mr Daniels, you do not have to say anything—'

'Now wait a minute—' Radcliff began to protest.

'Sorry,' said Langton. 'I mean, were you under arrest, you would not have to say anything but it would harm your defence if you did not mention here something you were later to rely on in court. Anything you do say could be used in evidence against you.' He looked at Radcliff. 'If it were to come to that, of course.'

Daniels shook his head, nonplussed. The tape in the machine was turning and he stared at it, frowning.

Langton waited a few moments before asking the first question.

'Mr Daniels, is your real name Anthony Duffy?'

Daniels blinked. He waited a moment before he answered.

'Yes; yes, it was.'

Radcliff glanced at him, then made a note.

'Did you change your name by deed poll? Or by some other method?'

Daniels leaned back in his chair, looking uncertain.

'We were unable to trace you for some considerable time. Did you apply to Births, Deaths and Marriages for the name change to be legally registered?'

There was another lengthy pause; Daniels stared at his hands, then he looked up and answered quietly.

'It was more than fifteen years ago. There was another actor by that name, so I changed it. I was in Ireland. They would have a record of it, but yes, I was originally Anthony Duffy. It was all legal.'

'Was your mother Lilian Duffy?'

His face fell. He became stressed, starting to twist his hands.

'Yes, yes, she was. Whether or not I'd describe her as a mother is another matter. I was brought up in foster care.'

'And is it true that your mother was murdered?'

Daniels leaned forward. 'What on earth has this got to do with anything?'

'Could you please just answer the question, Mr Daniels.'

'Yes, I was informed that she had been.'

'And were you questioned by the Greater Manchester Police at the time of her murder?'

'Christ! I was seventeen years old. I was brought in. They brought me in to tell me she was dead. For God's sake!'

Radcliff was making notes. If he was surprised by what he was hearing, he didn't show it.

'We both know it was a bit more than that,' said Langton. 'You were arrested and questioned.'

'I was released. Why on earth are you bringing this up, twenty years later?'

'Were you also questioned about a previous assault on your mother?'

'What?'

'Your mother alleged you had attacked her.'

'No. No, that is not correct.' His eyes flashed with anger, then he turned to Radcliff. 'There were never any charges. What the hell is this about, Edward? I have come here in good faith.'

Radcliff stared coldly at Langton. 'Do these questions have some bearing on the reason Mr Daniels is here?'

'I believe so.' Langton opened the file in front of him.

'Could you please look at these photographs, Mr Daniels and tell me if you knew any of these women?'

He withdrew the first photograph and glanced at the video camera.

'For the benefit of the video and the tape, I am showing Mr Daniels a photograph of Teresa Booth.'

Daniels glanced at the black and white mortuary picture, then shook his head.

'No, I don't know her,' he said firmly.

Out they came, one by one: Sandra Donaldson, Kathleen Keegan, Barbara Whittle, Beryl Villiers, Mary Murphy. To each 'Did you know this woman?' Daniels shook his head and said that he did not. He was sitting very upright, gripping the edge of his chair.

'Did you reside at number twelve Shallcotte Street, Swinton?'

Daniels gave his solicitor a helpless look.

'Just say yes or no, Alan,' he said.

'I believe I did. Until I was four or five years of age, and again after a period of foster care.'

'Do you recall Kathleen Keegan as also living at that address?'

'I was just a child. Of course I don't,' he snapped angrily.

'Do you recall Teresa Booth living at that address?'

'No, I don't.'

'Do you recall any of these women living at that address?'

'No, I don't remember any of them. I have just said: I was only a small child.'

'Thank you. Could you tell me where you were on the night of seventh February this year?'

Daniels closed his eyes, sighing.

'When?'

'Saturday, seventh February; between the hours of eleven o'clock that evening and two o'clock the next morning.'

'Probably in bed. I was filming all of February; in fact, I was on location in Cornwall. I can check this for you, but I am certain that's where I was.'

'In Cornwall?'

'Yes. There's a new version of *Jamaica Inn* being filmed.'

'I'd appreciate it if you could verify if you were in Cornwall on that date.'

Daniels told them that his agent would supply the exact schedule. He was shaking his head in bewilderment as he turned to Radcliff, saying, 'I don't believe this, Edward; it's inconceivable.'

The lawyer patted his arm reassuringly.

Lastly, Langton laid the photograph of Melissa Stephens on top of the others.

'Do you know this girl?'

Daniels chewed his lip.

'No. No, I don't think so. What's her name?'

'Melissa Stephens.'

Daniels looked closely at the photograph.

'No, I don't. Is she an actress or something?'

'She was a student.'

Langton packed up the photographs and carefully replaced them.

'Would you be prepared to have an odontologist make a cast of your teeth?'

'What?' Daniels leaned back in his chair, incredulous.

'This is getting to be rather silly now,' Radcliff said, tapping the table with his fountain pen. 'You have brought my client in. You have not arrested him. He has answered all your questions. I suggest we call this a day. Unless there is something else?'

Langton explained firmly that if they were to eliminate him completely from their enquiries, they would need to take an impression of Daniels's teeth. When Radcliff demanded a further explanation, Daniels touched his arm, demurring. 'No, wait, Edward. If they want me to do a test, I'll do it. I am sure they must have a good reason for bringing me in, so I might as well give them every assistance possible. If I do whatever they want now, my time will not be wasted again.'

'Very well.' Radcliff looked at Langton. 'Do you need anything else?'

Fifteen minutes later Daniels was allowed to leave with his solicitor. He stopped in the open doorway and looked back to Langton sadly.

'Lilian Duffy was a sick woman. I have tried my hardest to forget my early childhood. If I hadn't been fostered by an exceptionally kind couple—'

'Mr and Mrs Ellis?' Langton volunteered.

'Yes!' He gave a mocking glance. 'You have done your homework on me!'

'Previously to that, you were cared for by Ellen Morgan.' As Daniels showed a flicker of emotion at her name, Langton continued: 'We talked to her.'

The suspect lowered his voice. 'Well then, you know how much my life improved after I was taken from Lilian Duffy. I have endeavoured to put my wretched past behind me. I didn't think I would be so affected by what has been brought back to me this afternoon. However, the most important thing to me now is that my past continues to be kept out of the press.'

'There is no reason why it shouldn't,' Langton replied.

'Thank you; I would appreciate it. I am due to start a film in the United States and any bad press, especially of the type this awful case would encourage, could damage the granting of my visa at a time when my career is really taking off over there.'

Edward Radcliff murmured it was time to leave and with a brief glance at Anna, their so-called prime suspect walked out.

Langton removed his jacket and loosened his tie. Anna stood at the door, watching him for clues about how he thought it went.

'They agreed to visit the dental department at the lab, first thing in the morning,' she offered.

'It will be a waste of time.' His tone was sullen.

'Why?'

'His teeth are capped.' He took out a cigarette. 'They're very good ones. I noticed the difference as soon as I saw him.' He tapped his own teeth.

'Maybe we should find out when he had them done?' she ventured.

'Maybe.' There was a pause. 'Meanwhile, check out his alibi. Filming in Cornwall?'

'Will do,' she said, approaching the desk. 'Did you notice how he refers to Lilian either by her full name, or just as "she"? He's unable to say the word "mother".'

'Yeah,' Langton said wearily, in the process of lighting one cigarette from the butt of the last one.

'I thought the speech at the end was contrived as well.'

'He's a fucking actor,' he muttered. 'Probably got it off one of his films.'

'Should we let Michael Parks have access to the video tape? See what he can come up with?'

'Yeah,' he muttered again.

'Are you coming? Everyone's waiting in the incident room for an update—'

'Anna, get the fuck out of here, will you?' he fumed. 'Just leave me alone for a few minutes.' She stared at him. 'Go on, get out! For Christ's sake!'

Anna left, slamming the door behind her. This was getting to be an infectious habit, she thought grimly.

Half an hour later, the entire team had been assembled. Langton appeared, looking tired and unshaven. His mood seemed dark.

'Right. We had him in. He was questioned and released. The dental match won't do us much good; he's had his teeth capped recently.'

Anna put up her hand.

'YES!' He glared at her.

'Dentists have to make sets of the old teeth before doing implants and capping them. We could get in touch with his—'

'Yes, good. Do that. Thank you, Travis.'

Langton took a deep breath. 'We need more evidence. The truth is, we have nothing on him. So tomorrow, we start from scratch.' He indicated the photos of the dead victims. 'We turn over every single one of these cases until we find something. If we don't, we're well and truly fucked. The Gold Group is coming in to hear about the Daniels interview.'

He looked around at his team's waiting, expectant faces.

'The reality of the situation is, we didn't get enough. That said –' Langton paused to shove his hands into his pockets – 'even if the team gets cut by half, which is on the cards, I am not prepared to let this go back on the case files. I am going to fight like hell to maintain this incident room. Because I truly believe that Anthony Duffy, aka Alan Daniels, is our killer.'

There was a low murmur round the incident room.

He gave a rueful, boyish smile. 'All we need is the evidence to prove it, so let's get cracking in the morning. For now, we all need a bloody drink. Let's adjourn to the pub. First round is on me.'

The tension of the day was finally taking its toll on Anna. She felt exhausted and was packing up in preparation for home rather than the pub when she looked up to find Jean standing beside her.

'What was he like?' Jean whispered conspiratorially.

Anna smiled. 'Well, he certainly is good-looking. Lives in a fantastic house, beautiful furniture. He's charming and he's in great shape.' She frowned, trying to put her finger on what was wrong.

'Go on,' Jean encouraged her.

'I can't quite fathom it out. He has a kind of mysterious manner about him. It's like he knows something that you don't; a big secret.'

'If the boss is right and he killed all seven of them, that is one hell of a secret.' Jean leaned closer. 'Did you find him sexy?'

'I'm not sure. Those eyes are amazing. When he turns them on you, it's like he's looking right at you, or through you.'

'Every Saturday I'd sit glued to the TV. You have no idea what a fan I was. *Sin City*. You don't remember it?'

'I was still in school uniform, Jean.'

'I wasn't long out of my gym slip either. I was hoping I'd get a glimpse of him. Didn't you find him attractive at all?'

When Anna saw Jean's eager expression, she realized what it would be like if Alan Daniels's involvement in the case became public knowledge. There was something avaricious about Jean's curiosity and there were no doubt hundreds of Jeans out there who would be snatching up the morning's papers to read the latest about Daniels. The background details alone would create a tabloid frenzy. Perhaps what he had said on his departure was really heartfelt. To have succeeded in recreating himself and putting his troubled past behind him, was admirable. If the information was leaked that they had questioned him, it could destroy an innocent life.

'Is it him, do you think?' Jean was watching her face with interest.

Anna shook her head. 'I don't know.'

'Langton seems to think it is,' Jean persisted.

'Thinking isn't good enough,' Anna protested. 'He also said that.'

'No need to get shirty with me,' Jean retorted. 'I was just curious what you felt.'

'If you must know, I felt sorry for him.'

'Ah, he got to you, did he?'

Anna grabbed her briefcase. 'No, he did not get to me, as you put it. Anyway, whatever I felt is immaterial. Goodnight.'

''Night,' Jean said. Moira was packing up. She nodded to Anna's retreating form.

'What was that about?'

Jean whispered across their desks. 'I'd say she fancied Mr Alan Daniels.'

Moira chuckled, though she didn't take Jean's comment seriously.

'She doesn't have a chance,' Moira whispered back. 'Have you seen the way she dresses? He's got his pick of every woman in London.'

'I doubt he gave her a second glance,' Jean concurred. 'She really needs to do something with her hair.'

Anna, mortified, stood outside the doorway to the incident room. She could hear their laughter as she made her way to the stairs, holding back tears.

★

Anna had bought some groceries at the small supermarket round the corner from her home: fresh coffee, lots of canned soups. Now she stacked them in her cupboards. Then it was time to do a load of washing, after which she selected garments for dry cleaning, all the while trying to push Jean and Moira's disparaging comments from her mind. However, as she checked over her outfits for work, she saw their point: charcoal grey pleated skirt with matching jacket; dark grey straight skirt with matching jacket; two pairs of dark brown trousers and one pair of black trousers.

'Boring! Fucking boring!' she muttered. She was a plain-clothes detective, who had 'designed' herself a uniform. Nothing in her wardrobe had a glimmer of personality and that included the plain, court shoes. She dressed like a frumpy school-teacher, circa 1960, she thought mournfully.

Even in the shower Anna couldn't get the women's comments out of her memory. Her mind zigzagged between the contents of her wardrobe and her next available shopping opportunity. It had hurt her to hear what they really thought of her appearance, because she knew they were right. It wasn't just that Alan Daniels would not be giving her any second glances, but she reckoned it could be true of any male. After all, she had not had a steady relationship since Richard Hunter, a detective inspector with the Met Drug Squad, and he had seemed more interested in her partnering him in the squash tournament than in his life.

Hunter was a pleasant guy and they did play squash well together. His prowess in the bedroom, though, had not been as good as his game. They had called it quits pretty amicably.

Anna sat up and punched the pillow a couple of times before flopping back down in her bed, but it was no use. Sleep would not come. She got up and sat on a stool in her neat, tiny kitchen, sipping a cup of tea and asked herself honestly what was the matter.

She took out a mirror and regarded herself with a critical eye. Her hair. She really did need to have something done. It was about five inches long and, as Langton had pointed out, it did sprout up in odd places. She wondered whether she should have it cut really short. It was so thick, just another inch and she would have curls, like the child in the old Pears soap advert.

She resolved to cut it as soon as she got time off. She would also have to buy a more stylish wardrobe. She was not going to be a frump. When she went back to bed, she touched the photograph of her father and said softly, 'G'night, Dad.'

Chapter Eight

As Langton suspected, Alan Daniels's teeth impressions were of no use. His new dental work had not only been extensive, it had also been done in the United States, where his dentist was not helpful. Apparently, Daniels had suffered considerable pain after teeth implants and developed an infection. He requested his original X-rays and impressions in order to take them to another dentist. Once his teeth settled down, he had destroyed the X-rays and impressions, but refused to pay the dentist the full amount, an astonishing fifty-two thousand dollars.

His appointment had been made before the murder of Melissa and the work was completed after her murder. A coincidence? Or yet another false lead?

The most vital piece of evidence in possibly linking Daniels to the murder of Melissa Stephens was gone. Daniels's solicitor had provided the details of his dental history, along with a written explanation as to why the dental work had been necessary: a film stunt had gone wrong, a fall which caused damage to his upper front teeth, requiring the emergency dental work.

The only evidence now was circumstantial. They knew that as a child, Daniels had resided at 12 Shallcotte Street along with his mother, Lilian Duffy and two other victims, Teresa Booth and Kathleen Keegan. They still lacked verification that any of the other victims, either Mary Murphy, Sandra Donaldson, Barbara Whittle or Beryl Villiers, also lived there.

The splintered team decided to concentrate on one victim each and continue enquiries. Anna had been allocated Beryl Villiers, the woman identified by her breast implants. She had called Beryl's mother. She was friendly on the phone and agreed to see Anna. She had remarried and was now Alison Kenworth. Her new husband, Alec, was a long-distance lorry driver. Mrs Kenworth worked as a manageress, six days a week, at a boutique, she said and could either talk to Anna there, or at her home after she had left the shop.

Confirmation came from his agent that Daniels had indeed been in Cornwall, shooting the remake of *Jamaica Inn* during the week of 7 February. They seemed to be going downhill fast. Langton obsessively maintained they had the right man, but was aware that if they did not gain fresh evidence soon the team, already halved, would be disbanded. His office door was almost off its hinges, it had been slammed so often.

Anna was sitting on the train to Leicester, musing over the first stage of her 'makeover'. She had been to the hairdresser, who had given her a new, cropped hairstyle. It did not seem to have made very much of an impression in the office, though Langton had remarked that it made her look like a boy. There had been no time, as yet, to assemble a new wardrobe, though she had done a bit of surveillance. A sharp suit in Emporio Armani was earmarked along with some of their silk shirts, but the prices were out of her range so she was waiting for the sales.

Arriving at Leicester station, Anna was collected by a local patrol car and a driver. The driver would be on call and available to drive her when required. Langton had informed her in a barbed, throwaway manner that since the car was at her disposal, this time she should consider using it and not rely on local taxis.

She was dropped off at the small boutique at three o'clock. Mrs Kenworth – a well-dressed woman in her fifties – led Anna to a small back room.

'Will this be all right?' Mrs Kenworth asked nervously.

'It's fine,' Anna said, putting down her briefcase.

Mrs Kenworth held out her arms for Anna's jacket, which she placed neatly on a hanger behind the door. In a prominent position on a small desk there was a headshot of Beryl Villiers. Until then, Anna had only seen mug shots and mortuary pictures.

'This is your daughter?' she asked, rather unnecessarily. Anna was unprepared for how beautiful Beryl Villiers once was.

'She used to do some modelling. I have more pictures.'

Mrs Kenworth opened a drawer in the desk and removed a large brown envelope containing eight colour photographs. Anna glanced through them. The photographs had been taken in a studio. Beryl seemed to be between eighteen and twenty years of age.

'She's lovely.'

'From the time she was a little girl, she was always so confident and pretty.'

'She took after you.'

'Thank you.' Anna noticed Mrs Kenworth's eyes rapidly filling with tears and added quickly: 'Did Beryl ever live at an address in Shallcotte Street, Swinton?'

'I don't know. Shallcotte Street?'

'Yes. It was demolished fifteen years ago, so this would have been before then.'

'Oh no, I don't think so. Though, to be honest, I couldn't really tell you. From when she was seventeen, she moved around so much.'

'When she left Leicester, did she give you an address?'

'No.'

'Do you know if Beryl ever knew someone called Anthony Duffy?'

'I don't recall that name.'

The doorbell pinged and Mrs Kenworth looked into the shop. She excused herself and went to serve the customer.

Anna sifted through the photographs. It didn't yet make sense to her that such a lovely girl could become a prostitute.

'Sorry about that,' Mrs Kenworth said on her return. 'Regular. She's taken a couple of outfits to see which her daughter likes. She's getting married.'

Mrs Kenworth reached for the coffee pot. The tray, with cups and biscuits, was already prepared.

'You said she left home at seventeen. Why? Did you and your daughter have a falling out?'

'She got in with a really bad bunch of girls. She was just sixteen. She had been getting good results at school. She was also really talented, said she wanted to be an actress.'

Mrs Kenworth continued talking as she poured the coffee. She had done everything possible to persuade her daughter to stay on in school, but she had refused; she had started work at a local health spa and began to train as a masseuse. 'At first I got her a flat with two of her friends, not far from where we lived, so I could keep an eye on her. I paid the rent.' Next thing, Beryl had left, without telling her mother her whereabouts. It turned out she had gone to Southport to be with someone she had met at the spa.

'She turned up one Sunday, driving a new MG. She said she was living with this man, but she wouldn't even tell me his name.'

Suddenly, Mrs Kenworth broke down.

'I don't honestly know why she wouldn't let me into her life,' she wept. 'She insisted she just wanted to live her own way and without any interference from me. But I wasn't interfering, I was concerned; she was only seventeen.'

'What about Beryl's father?'

Mrs Kenworth dried her eyes. She said that George Villiers, her first husband, had divorced her when Beryl was ten years old. The little girl had worshipped him. At first, Beryl had gone on weekend visits to see him, but after a few years he and his new girlfriend went to live in Canada and they had never heard from him again.

'I met Alec six or seven years ago. He's a wonderful, kind man. I don't know what I would have done without him.' Tears came splashing down her face again. She blew her nose, apologizing all the time for crying. 'Sometimes I would get a phone call, always saying the same thing: life was wonderful, she was happy. She used to come home periodically, always in another flashy car, a different one. One time I said to her, why couldn't I meet this man she was living with?'

Mrs Kenworth took a deep breath. Beryl had told her that she had left the man from Southport and was now with someone else, someone even better and much wealthier.

'Did you find out the name of the new boyfriend?'

'No. As ever, she was very secretive, but she was wearing expensive clothes and a big diamond ring; diamond earrings as well. She always wanted the best things, ever since she was a child. I was too weak with her. I'd give her whatever she wanted, just to keep the peace. She had a wild streak in her, a terrible temper.'

Anna checked her watch. She didn't seem to be getting anywhere; certainly she was not getting the connection she hoped for.

'It was drugs,' Mrs Kenworth offered quietly. She poured more coffee and went on speaking in the same quiet voice.

Two or more years later, Beryl had turned up on the doorstep late one night. Her mother hadn't heard from her, or seen her, in all that time. She was alarmed to see that Beryl had got very thin. 'I put her to bed. She looked terrible, kept on saying, "I'm sorry, Mum. I'm so sorry." She was covered in bruises. She wouldn't talk about it. All she'd say was that she had got herself into a bit of trouble. There were a lot of telephone calls, late at night. Then, once she was better, she started not coming home until morning.'

Mrs Kenworth swallowed. She just sat there for a moment, her eyes full of pain.

'We had another terrible row. She was gone the following morning. Under her bed, I found hypodermic needles, drug things. It broke my heart. She was destroying herself.'

'Did you know where she had gone? Did she leave an address, or contact number?'

'No, she never did.' An expression crossed the mother's face, as if remembering something.

'Manchester. That's where she went, that time. Manchester. I found a phone number on a bit of torn paper. I called it. The woman that answered sounded drunk, or maybe she was drugged. I called a few times and the same woman always answered. Told me Beryl wasn't there. She told me to stop calling.' She pursed her lips. 'I thought she was lying.'

'Why?'

'Call it mother's intuition. I contacted the phone company. I thought they might give me the address. I was really worried about Beryl using drugs. They wouldn't help. I went to the police, told them about Beryl, what I was worried about. I gave them the number.'

Anna spoke up. 'I don't suppose you still have the number?'

'No. She came back. She was hysterical, shouting at me. She kicked at the front door. Said I was causing her a lot of trouble, that her friend had been visited by the police and it was all my fault. I said that I was worried about her, that I knew about the drugs.'

Tears started streaming down Mrs Kenworth's face as she told Anna that Beryl had become like a stranger. She was abusive and violent. She warned her mother that she was not to call her friend, Kathleen, again. That if she did call, she would be getting her daughter into a lot of trouble.

'From Kathleen?'

'Yes. I said that she wasn't much of a friend since she'd lied about not seeing her. Then she sort of collapsed crying and did the old "sorry" routine. I put her to bed and that's when I saw her breasts. She'd had implants. She'd always had beautiful breasts. She was perfect. She could have done anything, been anything.'

Mrs Kenworth closed her eyes. 'I know I was naive, but until then I'd never really considered that my daughter might be selling herself; that she might be a prostitute. If anyone had told me, I wouldn't have believed it.'

The shop bell rang. While Mrs Kenworth went to serve the customer, Anna took down some notes. Could the Kathleen be their victim, Kathleen Keegan? If so, they would have three out of the six that knew each other. If the Leicester Police had kept records that far back, it would be another link in the chain.

Mrs Kenworth entered with a blue two-piece suit on a hanger. She put it onto a rail at the back of the office. 'I can lock up now.'

'That's nice,' Anna said, coming closer to inspect. 'Really nice. I like the colour.'

'I was just about to mark it down for sale. It was in the window; there's a slight sun mark on the shoulder. What size are you?'

'Twelve, I think.'

'Would you like to try it on?'

Anna smiled hesitatingly.

'Yes, thank you. Do you have any shirts that might go with it?'

It was a quarter past five when Mrs Kenworth drove Anna to her home. Upon their arrival, Anna placed a call to the local police. It was a far-reaching hope that they might still have a record of Mrs Kenworth's visit but if so, they might possibly have the Manchester address.

Mrs Kenworth's flat was in a well-kept council estate. The flat was immaculate, though stiflingly warm. Mrs Kenworth opened the door to her daughter's old room. 'I've kept this the way it was when she first ran away. All her pictures are in here.' She touched a photograph of an incredibly pretty, dark-eyed young girl on a pony; then one photograph after the other, showing a pretty little girl growing into a stunning-looking teenager. 'I still come in here to sit, sometimes, just to talk to her.'

The room was a shrine, permeated by a sickly perfume. There was a frilly pink nylon bedspread, with matching pink pillows and cushions. A collection of dolls had been lined up, all dressed in pink. The white and gold wardrobe still contained the dead girl's clothes, yet she had not lived in the flat for most of her adult life.

'I never saw her again after that. She sent me a Christmas card from London. Said she had a job in a fashion house, that she'd gone back to modelling. She had such beautiful brown eyes,' Mrs Kenworth whispered, heartbroken, holding out another picture.

'Yes, she was lovely,' Anna said, taking it.

She looked at the professional headshot. It seemed impossible that this lovely girl had been found dead on wasteground and the only way she could be identified was by her breast implants. Mrs Kenworth's daughter could have had the world at her feet, but she had been murdered at thirty-four, her beauty completely laid waste by years of prostitution, violence and drug abuse.

Mrs Kenworth raised her eyes to Anna. 'I wouldn't believe it when the police told me she was a prostitute.'

When Anna's mobile phone rang, it startled them both. Anna excused herself and murmured instructions for her driver to collect her from the flat. It was with relief that she finally climbed into the patrol car a few minutes later. The interior heat and the mother's anguish had sapped her energy.

On saying goodbye, Anna had glimpsed another side to Mrs Kenworth. Anna had just mentioned Beryl's father again: did he know of her death? In response, Mrs Kenworth's face became tight and vicious and her lips pulled tightly together.

'I didn't know where he was to tell him his daughter was dead. He never had to deal with the local press banging on the door, asking me about the prostitute murdered and left unidentified for six months. You saw all those lovely pictures of her; they could have picked any of them, but no, they had to print that terrible picture from the murder. She looked like a mean-faced whore. Not like my daughter at all. He never sent a penny for her. He never even sent Beryl a birthday card, a Christmas card – nothing! He left me for a bitch that I trusted as my friend. And he broke his daughter's heart. And then she broke mine.'

Anna touched Mrs Kenworth's hand as the older woman blinked the tears back.

'I really have to go. The car's waiting. But thank you so much for your time and for helping me with the suit.'

'Any time, dear.' Mrs Kenworth managed a half smile. 'You know where I am. I'll always give you a good price.'

Reclining against the back seat of the patrol car, Anna closed her eyes and gave a silent prayer of thanks for a happy childhood and two loving and understanding parents.

At the police station she headed straight to reception, where the desk sergeant lifted the flap in his counter and said, 'Come on in. We've roped in a retired officer. Some kind of friend to the Villiers family.'

The small interview room smelled of paint. A white-haired, rotund ex-detective stood up to shake Anna's hand as she was led into the room. Anna was amused to find he didn't waste any time on a preamble, but went straight to the subject.

'You wanted to know about Beryl Villiers? How long have you got?'

'Not long, actually,' Anna said. 'I'm on the seven o'clock train back to London.'

Ex-DS Colin Mold leaned back, clasping his hands over his belly. 'Right, me duck.' He gave a different version of the Villiers family as troubled, with numerous domestic callouts. Villiers and his wife were always scrapping. 'The fact is, the man couldn't keep his dick in his pants. He knocked her around, but his wife always dropped charges before they went to court.' Then, Mold continued, Villiers had run off with his wife's best friend, a hairdresser. In the divorce proceedings, he failed in his fight to get custody of Beryl, but he did get access to her. Not long after, he had dumped the hairdresser and skipped, with another girlfriend and a lot of rent owing, to Canada. Nobody had heard from him since. The real victim was Beryl, who had loved him.

He chuckled about how the two women, older and younger, were at loggerheads. Even at the tender age of eight, Beryl was fighting with her mother. A couple of times she had run off and her mother would drag her back home from the hairdresser's. Then he went quiet; just saying not much had happened until Beryl had left home at sixteen and her mother had found a little flat for her with two friends.

Anna opened her notebook. 'This was when she went to work at the health spa?'

He snorted. 'There was another name for it: bloody knocking shop. Open until late at night; a lot of hanky-panky went on.'

'The most important period I need to know about is the time she went to Manchester.'

'Right. So they said.' Mrs Villiers had found hypodermic needles in

Beryl's bedroom and she turned up at the station in a terrible state. She also had a phone number. She believed that Beryl was in Manchester. 'She even had this idea she was being held against her will by some woman. So I pulled in a couple of favours. You have to understand: I'd known this girl since she was a toddler.'

'Who was the woman?'

'Her name was Kathleen Keegan: a real hard tart. She was running a brothel and using drugs and booze and Christ knows what else. Pal from Vice Squad went in, put a bit of a threat about. Beryl, they said, had been there, but had left before the visit.'

'Can you give me the address?'

He nodded, adding that it wouldn't be much use, as the house had been torn down.

'Was it Shallcotte Street?'

'Not that shit-hole, excuse my language. That was also demolished when this new housing development went up all around that area. But you know, they're like rats. You drive them out of one place and they just turn up in another.'

Anna passed over a list of the six victims.

'Do you recognize any of those names as being connected to Kathleen Keegan?'

He rubbed his nose, as he looked down the list. Then, shaking his head, he passed it back.

'No, duck, just Beryl and the Kathleen Keegan woman.'

His watery blue eyes assumed a sad expression.

'I wish I had found her. Might be alive today.'

Anna put out her hand to shake his. He gripped it tightly.

'I appreciate your help.'

'No trouble. She was very beautiful, lovely face. Pity the dirt bags got to her when she was young. They never let her go and to die like that: unidentified, left to rot? She didn't deserve that.'

'No, she didn't,' Anna said.

'You got a suspect?' he asked hopefully.

'Not yet.'

'I always think if you've not got him in the first few weeks, you never will. When it's white hot, you stand a chance. Body left to rot for weeks, hard to find witnesses, harder to get evidence.'

'Yes, yes, it is.'

'If I can be of any further help, you just have to call.'

Anna had turned to walk out, when he called after her.

'You've forgotten your bags.' He was holding up the three shopping bags from Mrs Kenworth's boutique.

Embarrassed, Anna took them from him.

'Got a bit of shopping in as well, did you?' he teased her.

She had only just made it to the train station in time. When she got home, she hung her new suit and the two new blouses on hangers on the wardrobe door, then stepped back, her head to one side. The sun damage, which made the right shoulder a slightly lighter shade than the left, was hardly noticeable. She closed the wardrobe door, pleased with her purchases and was just getting ready for bed when her phone rang.

'Hello. It's Richard.'

'Richard?' It had been over six months since they had last been together and that was such a disappointment she had doubted she would bother seeing him again.

'Richard, hello,' she said cheerfully. 'I was only thinking about you the other night. I haven't heard from you for weeks! How are you?'

'Terrific. You don't fancy an early morning game of tennis, do you? Only Phil Butler's partner's got flu and I've booked the court: the Met's Athletic Club.'

'Oh, I don't know, Richard. I'm on this really big case and you know me, I'm better at squash than tennis.'

'Aren't we all? Come on, sweep the cobwebs out. Half six? I can collect you.'

'No, no. I'll make my own way there.'

'Terrific. Let's meet up at quarter to seven, do a catch-up and then we can all have breakfast after the game.'

Anna replaced the phone. It would do her good to get some exercise. Unlike the bad-tempered Langton of late, who never took any and smoked like a chimney. The more she thought about it, the more she looked forward to it. She set her alarm for half past five.

Next morning, Anna got into her car wearing her tracksuit with her squash shorts and T-shirt on underneath; she put her new suit on the back seat. She would shower and change at the club after the game.

The garage was below the block of flats in which she lived in Maida Vale. It was a new building, quite small, with only six apartments. One of the attractions had been that it was very secure, with a locked garage for the residents' cars and an access door to the ground floor. There was a well-lit staircase and a small lift to the top floor, but as her flat was only three floors up Anna rarely used it.

Richard, who was always early for everything, greeted her warmly. He looked different.

'Have you lost weight?' she asked.

'I certainly have. Down by ten pounds and I've got another five to go.'

He seemed more attractive than she remembered. Perhaps it was the different haircut. There wasn't long to catch up before Phil Butler arrived. He was a bald, thin-faced DI attached to the Robbery Squad. He crushed Anna's fingers as he shook her hand. 'Glad you could make it. This is a double or quits match. Rich and I have been going at it hell for leather for months. It's the final today. I need to win and my partner gets flu. I tried to cry off, but there's a hundred quid on it and you know him.'

'Yes.' Anna smiled, thinking she didn't really, but she wouldn't mind seeing more of him again. Was it only the haircut? And she reminded herself, on the last night they had been together, he had been on duty after all for the last twenty-four hours.

Richard went off to find his partner, also a police officer. Her name was Pamela Anderson which was a bit unfortunate as she was not blonde, had no visible breasts and looked like more like a rake than a babe.

But Ms Anderson was a whizz on the court. She served so hard that

Anna took four games before she could make a return. Her partner kept on saying, 'It's OK,' then whenever there was a ball close to the net, he would yell 'MINE!' which really irritated her.

They were pretty much evens: one set and four games each. Richard had, time and time again, lobbed some really great shots and Anna kept thinking perhaps she had underestimated him. He'd never played so well. It got to five–four, with Richard and Pamela leading, when Anna got into her stride. Her serve picked up and she started slamming back the spin serve from Ms Anderson. Suddenly it was six–five and time was running out on their court. She dodged Phil twice to make a slam from the nets. Then on a vital shot, the one they needed to win the next set, she had bellowed, 'Mine, MINE!' just before missing it.

It should have gone to a tie-break, but there were people waiting for their court. They shook hands. 'Another time,' Phil said. A towel around his neck, he opened his wallet and begrudgingly handed over a fifty-pound note to Richard. Though he did not say it, she knew Phil blamed her for the outcome. She was astonished when Richard laughed and refused to take the money. 'We'll play again when Tara's fit.'

She noticed how fast the fifty-pound note went back into Phil's pocket.

Ms Anderson was nowhere to be seen in the women's changing room. Anna applied her make-up, wondering if another date with Richard might improve his performance. His tennis had certainly improved. She made her way to the canteen. It was almost eight o'clock, just time for a quick breakfast before she had to leave for work.

The boys had ordered bacon sandwiches and coffee for the table. Richard got up to draw Anna's chair out for her and she sat down, impressed. He was improving every minute. She noticed he did the same for Pamela, who had now changed into her uniform.

Phil said between mouthfuls, 'I hear you're working with Langton.'

'Yes, I'm with the murder team now.'

'I worked alongside him once. That was enough.' He pulled a rasher of bacon from his sandwich and took a bite. 'Mind you, that was a good few years ago.'

'Didn't get along?' Anna asked innocently, disliking Phil even more.

'He could be a nasty sod at times. You ever played tennis with him?'

Anna gave him a surprised look. She could not have imagined Langton playing anything, except perhaps the odd hand of poker.

'Got a sliced serve,' Phil slurped his coffee, 'that's a bitch to get back.'

Then he stood up, announcing that breakfast was on him. He gave a brief smile to Anna and mentioned to Richard that he would book another court.

There was an uneasy silence after he'd left. Pamela nibbled at her sandwich, while Richard said confidentially to Anna, 'So, how is it working out? Word is, not too good.'

'We just got some big leads,' Anna protested.

Pamela laughed. 'I know your commander's DCI. And she's not a happy bunny.'

'Oh, really? Well, perhaps she hasn't had the update. When you're dealing with seven murders, some as far back as—'

'I know James Langton too.' Pamela dabbed her lips. 'He used to be part of the Met's athletic team, bicycle racing. I often saw him at the athletic track in Maida Vale.'

'Langton on a bicycle?' Anna asked, surprised.

'That was a while back, of course, when he was married to Debra Hayden. Did you know her?'

'No.'

'She was amazing. She used to race with him – "the Demon Duo", they were called. It was all very sad.'

'You mean the divorce?' Anna was fascinated.

'No, Debra was his first wife. She died of a brain tumour. Tragic, really; she had a great career ahead of her. And she was very beautiful.'

Anna noticed that Richard had gone quiet, but she couldn't resist.

'I know he has a thing about blondes.' She was trying to sound casual.

Pamela looked up sharply.

'I couldn't say. Debra was Persian, though, so I doubt it.'

'Oh,' Anna said and would have liked to continue, but Pamela was checking her watch. She collected her bag and leaned over to kiss Richard.

'See you later, darling,' she said. She smiled at Anna. 'Nice meeting you. Richard's told me a lot about you.'

Richard fiddled with his teaspoon, embarrassed. Pamela waved as she left the canteen.

'What do you think of her?' he asked nervously.

'She seems very nice,' Anna replied, with some confusion.

'Congratulate me. We're engaged.'

'Oh! Congratulations! I'm, uh, speechless. How long have you been together?'

'Six months, on and off.'

'Six months? Really!'

'I didn't mention her before, because when I last saw you, I wasn't so sure.'

'And now you are.'

'Yes. We're living together.'

'Oh. Wonderful.'

'Yes. Pammy put me on the Atkins. And I'm working out. I've never been fitter. I've got ten times the energy I used to have!'

'I can see that. Look at the time. I can't be late.'

As she stood up, Richard kissed her cheek. She couldn't believe it; he was wearing aftershave.

'Thanks for stepping in this morning. Phil's a really nice guy, recently divorced. You two seemed to get along well. Maybe we could do it again sometime?'

'Sorry,' she said, gathering her things. 'Work's really busy right now.'

She couldn't wait to get away from him. She could have kicked herself. Why the hell hadn't she put him on the Atkins diet? All that potential and she hadn't spotted it? Some detective!

She returned briefly to the ladies to comb her hair. She adjusted her new suit in the mirror. Her white shirt was open at the neck, revealing the gold chain and small diamond that had once belonged to her mother. She looked great.

At the station, Anna was disappointed that no one remarked on her makeover. They had all gathered in the incident room for the latest briefing. Langton sat on the edge of the desk and, on the board behind him, the dead women's faces looked out at the assembled team.

'Mike, what you got?' Langton asked Lewis.

Lewis had been allocated the second victim, Sandra Donaldson. He reported that he had traced one of her kids to Brighton. The boy was working in a seaside fish and chip shop. According to Lewis, he was one sandwich short of a picnic and all his questions only produced monosyllabic grunts. The boy had been brought up in various foster homes. He claimed he didn't know any of the women, he didn't know anyone from Manchester, he hadn't really known his mother. He described his sister as a slag and his brother as a criminal, presently a guest of Her Majesty in Brixton prison.

Barolli had had no luck either. He, too, had begun tracing relatives of the victims. The ex-husband of Mary Murphy had left England to live in Germany, taking her twin daughters with him. She had no other contact-able family. Barolli had then turned to Kathleen Keegan's children in the hope that they could help. Since they were scattered all over the place, he had gone for the eldest: a married daughter, living in Hackney with five kids.

'She was unable to recall anyone called Anthony Duffy, or if her mother was acquainted with any of the other women. She did remember that Kathleen had lived in Manchester and supported Manchester United; she said her mother had probably screwed the entire football team, given that she screwed everything else. She hated her.'

As Barolli sat down, Moira stood up to address the room. She told them about her visit to Emily Booth. Teresa Booth's mother was still alive, residing in a care home for the elderly. The old lady was feisty and still had all her faculties. Moira had them laughing with her mimicry of the woman's Newcastle accent.

It had been a lengthy interview. Though the old lady did not recognize any of the victims' names, she handed Moira photographs of her daughter, including a group shot of three women sitting on the railings at a sea front. Moira held up the photograph.

'I thought it was Brighton to begin with, but the old lady said that it was Southport, Lancashire. Not far from Manchester, right?'

The photograph was circulating round the room and had reached Langton.

'Now I may be wrong, but take a look at the woman to the right, wearing a black skirt and sun top. I think she's Beryl Villiers.'

While Anna waited for her turn, she opened her briefcase and removed a selection of the photographs Beryl's mother had provided. After Moira's photograph was passed to her and she had examined it, Anna stood up, heart pounding, to address the room.

'It's either her, or a doppelganger. I brought this picture from Leicester.' The second photograph began to circulate.

Langton was the last to compare both pictures. After considering them, he approached the wall and pinned up both pictures.

'What else have you got for us, Travis?'

'Kathleen Keegan,' she said. The room erupted.

Anna described the interview with the ex-detective, then the one with Mrs Kenworth. Jean was writing the updates on the board, marking the connection between those women in red felt-tip pen. Now that four of them had been connected to each other, possibly all of them would be connected to the house in Shallcotte Street. The only two unlinked as yet to the others were Sandra Donaldson and Mary Murphy.

'Good work, Travis. Barolli, I want you to contact Manchester Vice Squad. We need to know about any working girl – well, she'd be an old woman now – who was had up for prostitution before Shallcotte Street came down.'

Lewis put up his hand. Langton nodded.

'Gov, even if we get each woman knowing each other – maybe even knowing Lilian Duffy – what does it prove?'

Langton exhaled a sigh. 'That the killer also knew them; perhaps all of them. That's what these links are providing.'

'Yeah, well, I know that part,' Lewis said.

'So what's your problem?'

'I just can't get my head round the fact that Duffy would kill them one by one. There's years in between the murders, in some cases. I think we should be looking elsewhere, one of their pimps, or a client. Duffy, or Alan Daniels, was only eight years old when he finally left Shallcotte Street. We know where he went, what school, etc. What does tracing the slags who knew each other give us? I mean, Lilian Duffy? It was bloody twenty years back when he's down for possibly killing his mother! And the latest murder is Melissa Stephens? She's not a hooker, she's not a slag: she's a seventeen-year-old student.'

'You're saying you don't think we have a serial killer?'

'We *know* there is a serial killer. Everyone's agreed they've got the same MO.'

The tension in the incident room was uncomfortable, as Lewis went head to head with Langton.

'So?'

'I'm saying we should back off these old cases. Only concentrate on Melissa Stephens. We're wasting valuable time on the case and as time goes on, we'll lose any leads we might get.'

'We haven't got any leads, Mike!'

'I know that,' snapped Lewis. 'But we've all been schlepping around the fucking country when we should have been here. What I'm saying is, if you think Duffy is the killer, get the Cuban in.'

Langton's jaw was working overtime. 'He never saw his face.'

'OK, get the gravel-voiced tart in. She said he was blond. She saw part of him.'

'She said she only saw him from the side and he was wearing shades.' Lewis sat down, sighing.

Langton looked around the room, his eyes shifting from one to the other. 'You all have the same feelings?'

Everyone looked uncomfortable under his individual scrutiny, until he got to Anna. He raised his eyebrows. She hesitated; Langton was just about to pass over her, when Anna raised her hand. 'I think we should stay on trying to discover if the women all knew each other.'

'Thank you,' Langton said and shoved his hands into his pockets. 'I don't know if Daniels is our man either, but I do not believe we are looking for a random client of these girls as Mike suggested, or one of their pimps. These murders do have a link: the girls knew each other. That should lead us to anyone they had in common.'

He paused. 'If that person was Alan Daniels, that makes him a suspect. If the same man killed Melissa Stephens, it could mean that the killing cycle that had him murdering prostitutes may be complete, but he can't stop. What may have started out as a series of revenge killings could have gone into override. He could be enjoying the act of murder too much to stop. In which case, I do not think he will stop.'

Everyone in the room was hanging on his words. You could have heard a pin drop.

'Whilst you have been schlepping around the country, I have been working on the dates.'

Langton gestured for Jean to draw up the big diagram board. 'These are the time gaps that have been blocked out.'

Jean turned over the first sheet of thick white paper.

'I have not included the murder of Lilian Duffy, only the other women, because of their time frame. There are big gaps between the murders, as Mike was saying. Nearly three years in the longest case.'

Marked up were the names of the victims and beside them the dates. Langton then took the marker from Jean. Beside the time gaps, he wrote in big letters: USA; USA; USA. 'These dates are when Alan Daniels was filming in the United States.'

He turned to the room. 'I don't know in which US cities, or locations, his filming took place and at this stage I don't want to go back to Daniels, or his shark of a brief. We'll go to his theatrical agent. But once I know the cities he was filming in, I will be enquiring Stateside to find out if they had any victims found with our MO.'

Anna sat back in her chair. Langton never ceased to amaze her. She had watched him quietly wipe the floor with all of them and by the end, there wasn't a man or woman in the room who didn't feel the same awed respect that she did.

'Travis!' Langton gestured towards his office. When Anna grabbed her notebook, she suddenly noticed the doodles covering one page. Before closing the book, she quickly ripped out the page with the rows of hearts. She was irritated to find herself acting like a schoolgirl with a crush on her teacher.

She closed the office door. He had his back to her. 'What do you think, Travis?'

'You may be right.'

'I could also be wrong.'

'Yes, of course.'

He turned, gesturing to the chair in front of his desk.

'Thank you for backing me up in there.'

'I think everyone has come round,' she said.

'I appreciate it.' He looked at his watch: 'I'm seeing the agent at half past eight. He said by then he will have the information I asked for. I'll pick you up at your place.'

'Fine,' she said, surprised.

'Good work in Leicester and—' He cocked his head to one side, studying her. 'What's going on?'

She lowered her eyes, self-consciously.

'Is there something odd about the right shoulder of your jacket?' She made a swiping movement with her hand. 'It looks like a stain, or something.'

'Oh, it's just, erm, it was in the sun in the shop window. Oh, God, is it that noticeable?'

'Only from a certain angle,' he smiled. 'Where you were sitting, you had the light from the window behind you. With your red hair, you

146

looked like a friendly little beacon.'

She was silent, nonplussed.

'OK, that's it for now. I'll pick you up at eight.'

'See you in the morning, sir.'

'No, Travis.' He gave an impatient sigh. 'Tonight!'

After Anna had left his office, she paused in the corridor outside. Well, she decided, better to be noticed as a friendly little beacon than not be noticed at all.

Chapter Nine

Being a neat and methodical person, Anna took the rubbish out every Monday, did her laundry every Tuesday and until now had required no cleaner for the rest, as the flat was so compact. Nevertheless, times had changed. At ten to eight when her doorbell rang, she was eating an impromptu dinner of cornflakes, having arrived home from the station half an hour before, with just enough time to change her shirt and freshen her make-up.

As she hurried to open the door, she spilled the last dregs of milk and cornflakes down her skirt. She swore and with a tea towel wiped herself furiously. There was another sharp ring of the bell. Noticing the small fluffy bits left behind on her skirt, she chucked the tea towel aside, grabbed her bag and opened the door.

'I'm sorry to keep you waiting,' she said breathlessly.

She followed the uniformed driver towards the patrol car. Langton sat in the front seat, reading the *Evening Standard*. He addressed her without looking up.

'We're going to see a Mr Duncan Warner. He couldn't give us an earlier appointment. He's been making calls to the States to double check a few things, so with the time difference . . .'

'Oh, right,' she said, surreptitiously picking off bits of fluff from her skirt. She noticed he had shaved and changed his shirt and wondered if he kept a wardrobe in the office.

'Did you get home?' she asked. She had no idea where he actually lived.
'No, I didn't.'

'Is it too far away?'

He looked up from his newspaper and faced the road ahead.

'As a matter of fact, it's not far from you. Kilburn.'

'Oh.' She smiled; bit by bit she was discovering more about his private life. She wanted to ask exactly where, but restrained herself.

They drove into the West End and entered Wardour Street. They parked outside a four-storey office building, with *AI Management* printed in tasteful lettering on the glass door.

Down the staircase inside came a tall, slim girl with a short, tight black skirt and white silk blouse. She looked exactly the way Anna would like to look if she was five inches taller.

'Do you want to come this way?' she said, smiling as she let them in. 'It's only two floors up.'

Anna couldn't help noticing her incredibly white teeth. Her blonde hair was cut with a low fringe and the rest of it was caught in a slide at the back. That was how Anna would have liked her hair to look if it wasn't short and curly and red.

'I'm Mr Warner's secretary.' She shook Langton's hand. 'Jessica.'

'This is Detective Sergeant Travis,' he gestured towards Anna.

'Can I offer you a drink?' Jessica asked once they were in the AI office.

'No, we're fine, thank you,' Langton said reassuringly.

There was an undercurrent of something in the atmosphere. Anna just wasn't sure what it was.

'I'll tell Mr Warner you are here.'

Langton surveyed the reception area, its walls lined with film posters and client photographs. He seemed taken with a poster of a haunted house; the windows had enlarged, frightened eyes peering from behind them. The title of the film, *Come Home, Emma*, was slashed across the poster. He moved closer to read the small print and then turned to Anna. 'He's in this. Looks like a load of old tosh.'

Anna walked over. During the day, she thought, this area would probably be a hive of activity, but at night there was something eerie about the quietness. The door to Warner's office opened. Jessica, backing out, said: 'I'll see you in the morning. G'night.' She turned, opening the door wider. 'Would you like to go in?'

'Thank you,' Langton said. As they passed, Jessica flashed her teeth again, then she was gone.

The office was large, dominated by a massive desk. There were scripts crammed into bookcases and piled on the floor. Lining every available space on the walls were actors' photographs, most with messages scrawled across: 'To darling Duncan—; 'To the best—', 'To my beloved Duncan—'

The 'Duncan' referred to was balding, fifty-ish and wore a pair of steel-rimmed glasses perched on his nose. His attire included a silk shirt, cord trousers and old, worn carpet slippers. A pair of his shoes was placed by the side of his desk.

'Come in, sit down.' He seemed very affable. 'Now: tea, coffee or a glass of wine?'

'Nothing, thanks.' Langton sat down, but Anna responded, smiling: 'I'd love a glass of water, please.'

'Right, water it is.' He crossed to a fridge and opened it. 'I am obviously very concerned.' He took out a bottle of water, unscrewed the cap and passed it to Anna. 'And, to be honest, not quite sure what this all means.'

'Thank you,' she said. They sat down on a low, black leather sofa. She positioned herself as far from Langton as possible to give him space. Warner sat in a high-backed swivel chair. Behind the desk was a black pug dog on a cushion. Its huge, watery eyes had blinked at Anna when she entered the room, but otherwise it had been so still, it could have been a stuffed animal. When Warner returned to his chair, the dog, as if offering proof it was a living creature, half turned its head before flopping down on its cushion and going to sleep.

Feeling uncomfortable in such a low position, Langton tried leaning forward. 'We want to protect your client as much as possible, which is why I asked to see you here. At the moment I can't really give you details. I just wanted to let you know that in order to avoid publicity, we need to get certain information, information that will hopefully eliminate your client from our enquiries.'

'Is it fraud?'

'We would prefer not to disclose the reasons. As I said, we might be able to very quickly eliminate Mr Daniels from the enquiry.'

'Does he know you have come to see me?'

'Not unless you have told him.'

'Me? Oh no, I haven't said a word. It's just – well, you can understand why I am concerned. Alan has just finished filming. Next week there's a number of things we're negotiating. How serious is this?'

'It is very serious. But as I have said, it could be a misunderstanding and rather than make this public, I felt this was the best route we could take.'

'Yes, yes, I am sure it is. But you do understand why I am nervous about any police enquiry? I mean, is it a sexual thing?'

'Partly. Yes, it is.'

'Christ, it's not little kids, is it?'

'No.'

'Good. If it was that, then, you know, I wouldn't give a shit what happened to him. I can take just about anything, but not that.' Warner started rubbing his head agitatedly. 'If you knew what scrapes I've had to get some of the stupid buggers out of and it's not just the men.' He opened a cigar box, proffered it to Langton. 'Unbelievable.'

'No, thank you.'

'So Alan doesn't know?'

Langton balanced himself on the end of the sofa. 'We have had one interview with him.'

'He's been in to see you?'

'Yes, accompanied by his solicitor.'

'So, this is serious. And you say it's not fraud?'

'No, it is not fraud.'

'And it's nothing to do with kids. Is it porno, that kind of thing?'

Anna could feel Langton's impatience. It was obvious that Warner would continue his fishing trip, until he was satisfied.

'It's a murder enquiry. Now could we please get to why I am here?'

'Murder?'

'You said you would be able to supply me with a list of dates.'

Warner's face had drained of colour. 'Is he a witness? A suspect? Or what?'

'At the moment he is just helping our enquiries. You can understand now why we have not made this public.'

'Oh yes; right.'

'If it was out in the open, it could create very unpleasant publicity.'

'I understand, I understand. Then there's the whole immigration problem.' Warner was sweating. 'I've got one star they won't let into the States, because when he was a student he was arrested for smoking a joint.'

Langton stood up. 'Do you have the information for me?'

Warner nodded. 'I was on to LA when you arrived. I was able to check the other dates from my own records. One film was shot in San Francisco and another in Chicago. These weren't leading roles. Alan is yet to break it big over there –' he was opening his desk drawer – 'but it's beginning to happen. I didn't get this typed up, though I can if you want.'

Warner handed Langton a handwritten page of foolscap paper.

'No, that'll be fine. Thank you.'

When they returned to their car and driver, Anna looked up at the lit window on the second floor. She tapped Langton's arm. 'He's on the phone. I bet any money he's repeating it all to someone else.'

'Probably his boyfriend,' Langton said lightly, getting into the car. Langton gave the driver instructions to drop Anna home first. Then, as they drove off, he silently checked the dates against a list in his own notebook. After a while, he snapped the notebook closed triumphantly.

'The gaps between the murders all coincide with periods of time Alan Daniels was filming in the States.'

'How long was he there for, each time?'

'It varies. Sometimes five weeks, other times just two and there was one long stretch of six months.'

Langton passed Anna his notebook and the sheet of paper from Warner. She started looking over them.

'I'll get onto the US tonight and start the ball rolling,' he said, staring out the window. Then, almost as an afterthought, 'Might have to take a trip myself.'

'To the States?'

'No, Travis, the moon!'

She handed him the notebook, which he replaced in his pocket. When his mobile phone rang, he checked the caller ID before he answered it. 'Hi. Should be with you in about three-quarters of an hour.' He listened, then said quietly, 'That sounds good. Or we can go and get something to eat at the Italian.'

Anna had wondered if she should offer to cook him something. Now, she pressed back into her seat, looking out of the window, as he continued what was obviously an intimate conversation. He laughed softly before switching off the phone.

'You want the newspaper?' he asked without looking back at her.

'Thank you.'

He extended the paper backwards over his shoulder.

They didn't speak again for the rest of the journey. Langton went to sleep. When the car stopped to drop her off at her home, he briefly woke to grunt goodnight. It was almost a quarter to ten. She wondered who was waiting to have dinner with him. Whoever it was, she did a good job ironing his shirts.

Anna's flat had only one bedroom with an en-suite bathroom, a large living room and a small kitchen. The carpets throughout were a soft oatmeal colour. There was plenty of cupboard space, which made her happy. It was a very orderly apartment, reflecting little of who Anna was, perhaps because she was still unsure of that herself.

This was the first time she had bought her own place instead of renting.

After her father died, she could not bear to live in the old garden flat in Warrington Crescent, Maida Vale. But Anna had not moved too far from her old home and that had a comfort value. She knew the local newsagent, the post office and the small community knew her. She liked that.

In the shower, Anna chided herself for trying to find out more about Langton's private life, especially since he had demonstrated no interest in hers. Why should he? She was just his DS, with a crap haircut and an irregular suit. She had just stepped out of the shower and was towelling herself dry when her phone rang. She jumped and quickly checked the time. She wondered who would be calling her at this hour.

'Travis?' his familiar voice drawled.

'Yes, sir.'

'We got a hit: body found in San Francisco with the same MO. They'll be sending in details tomorrow. Thought you'd like to know.'

'Thank you, that's—'

But he had already hung up. She looked down at the receiver still in her hand. Well, she thought, at least he wasn't having a candlelit dinner with his girlfriend in some groovy Italian restaurant. She flopped onto her bed happily. She gave her goodnight glance to her father's photograph. 'Sorry, Dad. I just fancy him rotten!'

When she closed her eyes to sleep, her father's words came back to her. 'If you ever become a copper, sweetheart, best not to get married. You'll never find a man as understanding as your mother.' He was standing with his arms wrapped around her mother. He had been working on a case and they had not seen him for days. Her mother never seemed upset by his lengthy disappearing acts, or jealous of his work. She would simply use the time to write her journal, or to paint.

Isabelle had just laughed at him, saying she hoped he wasn't advising their daughter to turn gay, since that was the only way she'd get a partner with a skirt.

Her parents' banter had fascinated her as a child. Theirs was a strong relationship, built on a foundation of trust that now, as an adult, she wondered whether she would ever find. They were obviously in love, yet neither seemed dependent on the other. Her mother was very self-sufficient and took Jack's absences in her stride, certainly more than young Anna did.

Anna wondered if she would ever acquire that same independence in a relationship. So far she had hardly been able to maintain a relationship at all. She was her father's daughter, married to the job. Until DCI Langton had slammed the door open and walked into her life.

The next morning the incident room was abuzz with the news from San Francisco that a body killed using the same MO had been found in a very decomposed state, strangled with her own tights and with her hands knotted behind her back by her underwear. Her name was Thelma Delray and she was a prostitute, aged twenty-four.

The approximate time period of the American murder fitted within the lengthy gap between two of the English victims. There had been no witness, or DNA and without a suspect the case had been left open on file.

The fact that they knew their suspect was in San Francisco at the same time was not enough to warrant his arrest. However, Langton ordered one of the enquiry team to obtain a magistrate's warrant to search Alan Daniels's premises. The following evening they received an email from Chicago.

There was another victim, this one slotted in the time gap between the murders of Barbara Whittle and Beryl Villiers, when Alan Daniels was in the same area. The buzz was getting stronger; this was too much to be coincidence. The woman was found on wasteground. Same MO. She was a well-known prostitute, Sadie Zadine. Her body had not been discovered for six months. The pattern of the murder, the type of victim, was virtually identical.

Still there was the commander to keep in the loop. She had taken a very keen interest in the enquiry and wished to be kept up to date on any new developments. The evidence they had, however, was still only circumstantial, that Alan Daniels happened to be in both areas at the time of the murders. With no DNA and no witnesses, it would never make it to trial.

On the third day, they received news from Los Angeles; their third hit. Their victim was younger: Marla Courtney, a heroin addict, aged twenty-nine. Same MO: strangled and trussed with her own underwear. The LA PD emailed photographs of the victim in situ, including close-ups of the method of strangulation. All three US victims had been raped and showed signs of anal penetration. None of them displayed bite marks, or appeared to have been gagged. Still, there was not one witness, not one shred of evidence that could lead them straight to the perpetrator. None of the American victims had been linked, until now. Marla Courtney's time of death fitted in between victims six and seven, Mary Murphy and Melissa Stephens.

The Gold Group had decided that, given the high profile of their suspect, the enquiry team must seek approval at every stage of the investigation. Langton was almost apoplectic with rage and frustration when he was refused permission to arrest Alan Daniels. His superiors agreed it was highly 'coincidental', but there was not one shred of evidence that physically linked Daniels to the murders, nor did the fact that Daniels had been in the vicinity prove his guilt. Neither did the possibility he may have known all the UK victims. The commander was very apprehensive about criticism from the media, should it transpire that they were wrong about Daniels. The word 'circumstantial' was bounced around harder than a cricket ball.

The profiler, Michael Parks, was brought back in. He looked over the chart, nodding occasionally. 'It's as I expected: the killer never stopped and the victims are getting younger. Since Melissa, whose tongue was bitten, it is quite likely the murders will become more violent. He's worked this down to a fine art. He is not going to stop, that is for sure.'

Parks's inability to provide further insight made Langton even more obsessive. His office door was banging continuously through the next days as the team gathered details from the US, requesting as much information as possible to be sent over. Langton's new concern was that if Alan Daniels returned to the States for his next job, he might disappear. Even with his high profile, they might never find him again.

'It isn't fucking England. He could just keep moving from state to state over there.'

Being constantly told they did not have any proof was frustrating the entire team now. 'Let me fucking search his flat. I'll get the proof,' Barolli muttered.

It wasn't until four thirty, Thursday, that they were given the go ahead: a search warrant had been issued.

This was the chance Langton had been waiting for. He called in the POLSA 'specialist' search teams to assist, though it seemed unlikely they would uncover any forensic evidence since none of the murders had been committed at Daniels's flat.

At the briefing, Langton told them they were looking for anything whatsoever that could tie into the murders. They had to be diligent.

Langton ordered them to arrive in visible patrol cars. Barolli and Langton went ahead. Travis and Lewis followed. Lewis was constantly on his mobile to his pregnant wife who was over nine months gone. Lewis had been in a state about it for days.

They convened outside the Queen's Gate house. They knew from the two officers on round-the-clock surveillance that Daniels was at home and that he had seen them arrive: one of them had seen him look out from the bay window. The foursome, plus two more from POLSA, moved up the steps to the front door and rang the bell. Without any exchange on the intercom, the front door buzzed open.

As Langton and his detectives entered the hall, Daniels appeared at his front door, his face drawn and angry. 'Well, you couldn't make yourselves more obvious if you tried. I was expecting you to use a sledge hammer to open the door!'

Langton presented him with a copy of the search warrant which he read carefully before allowing them into his apartment.

'Well, come in, I suppose,' he said flatly. 'Be advised, if any damage occurs, I will sue. There are some very valuable items, so I'd advise you to be as careful as possible.'

Daniels gestured for the police to file past him. Once they were inside the flat, he closed the front door and asked abruptly, 'Where do you want to start?'

'Wherever is convenient to you,' Langton said coolly.

'Nowhere is convenient,' Daniels drawled sarcastically. 'But I suppose you can start in the bedrooms,' he nodded towards the bank of stained-glassed windows, 'and I'll continue my work in the drawing room.'

He turned on his heel and disappeared through the door to the drawing room.

'Some place.' Barolli looked around in awe.

Lewis was peering at an oil painting. Over his shoulder he said, 'You could fit my flat into this room.'

Langton exited the dining room. He turned left into a small corridor. The others were virtually at his heels as they entered a small, well-equipped kitchen. Expensive cutlery, crockery and cooking utensils were stored in shiny white cupboards, with the lighting hidden in strips behind cornicing.

'Check this out,' he ordered Anna, crisply. She went to work.

Lewis had opened another door and was looking in. 'Bloody check this bathroom out: marble, sunken bath, like a palace.'

Barolli and Langton caught up with him and looked into the exquisite, tasteful bathroom. It was wood-panelled with elegant bowls of soap and perfumes lined up alongside rows of candles in squat silver bowls.

Lewis left them to examine the bathroom and stopped in front of a door with stained-glass panels. After he disappeared inside, Langton heard him gasp, 'You better come in here and look at this.'

Langton and Barolli quickly joined him. The room was sumptuous: there was a grand piano, two velvet sofas and a glass-topped coffee table with art books piled upon it. But the highlight was the vaulted, stained-glass ceiling, from which different coloured lights shimmered over the white-panelled, vastly proportioned room.

'There was nothing in the kitchen. It didn't look as if it was used; well, the cooker didn't,' Anna said, joining them. The three men were silent, standing in awe as she continued: 'The fridge is stocked with fresh fruit and vegetables and – my God, this is so beautiful!'

Langton murmured, 'Go upstairs – start up there.'

'Right.'

Anna moved cautiously up the narrow, winding staircase leading to the upper floor, where there were two bedrooms: a master suite and bathroom and a guest suite. The master bedroom was almost as large as the entertaining area below. The four-poster bed was made of heavy oak, with draped panels of the palest green. The walls were also washed green and there were banks and banks of floor-to-ceiling wardrobes. Built inside one was a mirrored dressing table, perfumes and oils neatly lined up. The room was immaculate and smelt of a light perfume.

Anna searched the clothes, their pockets, the turn-ups in the trousers, the racks of hand-made shoes. All the shoes had fitted heavy wood inserts to retain their perfect shape. Only the velvet, monogrammed slippers looked worn. There were three pairs: pale green, royal blue and black. She held a slipper in her hand. It was hard to believe its owner was once Anthony Duffy, the child of a beat-up prostitute called Lilian.

She patted and checked the rows of cashmere sweaters and silk shirts. The bedside tables held books, mostly historical, no paperbacks. She lifted the green silk bedspread, to find it was lined with dark green cashmere. Alan Daniels certainly knew how to live. She noted the absence of knick-knacks and memorabilia.

When she stripped the bed, the sheets looked fresh and laundered. She found nothing in the bedroom. POLSA searched the carpet; there were no bloodstains, or stains of any kind.

'Found anything?' Langton at the doorway had made her jump.

'No, nothing. I was just thinking how strange it was to have no personal items around. You know, photographs . . .'

'Same downstairs.'

Langton walked to the four-poster bed. 'Be nice to have a session in this,' he said softly. 'Did you look under the bed, the mattress?'

'Yes,' she said, flushing.

'How about on top of the thing?'

'Not yet; I was just about to do that,' she lied.

Langton stepped up onto the bed. 'Nothing.' He jumped down and opened a wardrobe. 'So start up on the next floor.' He felt one of the silk shirts and murmured: 'These are nice. Certainly has enough of them.'

Anna went into the narrow corridor outside the bedroom and climbed another small, winding staircase to the top floor. This area was very different, although still sizeable. It seemed to be his library and office. The desk was stacked with scripts, documents and banks of photographs, mostly of women, with loving messages scrawled underneath. There were also numerous photographs on the walls: the suspect with other actors, on location. There was a laptop computer on the desk and drawers underneath containing files with neat headings: Tax, VAT, etc. There was an entire drawer for fan mail. She began to pore through the documents and letters. She heard footsteps on the stairs and Lewis appeared.

'Knows everyone, doesn't he?' He had turned a full circle in the room and now walked from one picture to the next.

'You should read some of these fan letters; he'd never be short of female companions.'

'This is gonna take hours, wading through all this lot.'

Langton appeared at the top of the stairs. 'Travis, we'll take over in here. Start on the front room, where he is.'

'Right.'

After she left, Langton surveyed the photographs. He paused at a picture of Daniels lying on a yacht with two blondes in skimpy bikinis.

'Some great-looking women,' he said.

'That's why it doesn't make sense to me,' Lewis protested. 'Why would a man who can get his hands on women like these want to shag stinking old prostitutes?'

Langton turned on the laptop.

'That's why I think we've got the wrong bloke.' Lewis, who was searching through files looked up. 'Hang on – he said he'd lost his dental records, didn't he?'

'What about it?'

'Well, look what's in here: X-ray, plus payments, etc.'

'We'll take that. Let me see.'

Langton examined the X-ray, holding it up to the light. 'Keep going; things are getting warmer.'

Anna tapped on the closed door to the drawing room and Daniels opened it.

'Could I come in here, please?' she said.

'Yes, help yourself.'

He returned ahead of her to sit on the sofa, curling his legs beneath him, picking up a script.

'You have a beautiful house,' she said awkwardly.

'Thank you.'

Embarrassed, she began to sort through the magazines.

'Was it necessary to visit my agent?'

'Sorry?' She could feel him looking at her.

'I said, was it necessary to visit my agent? I came to the station. Why didn't you simply ask me what you needed to know while I was there?'

'I don't think we had the—' She stopped herself, the colour rising in her cheeks. 'You should ask DCI Langton.'

She continued flicking through to the next magazine, checking for any loose note, or scrap of paper.

He cocked his head to one side, amused by her. 'What on earth are you looking for? Incriminating evidence in *Architect's Monthly*?'

'You never know,' she said, looking up with a half smile before turning back to flip through the pages of *Vogue*. 'Have you ever been married?'

'Been close. I am not the easiest person to live with,' he said, stretching out his legs to lie on the sofa. 'I am obsessively neat. But I suppose you've noticed.'

'Yes.' She walked round to start searching the books. 'I'm a bit that way myself.'

'It probably comes from never having anything as a child that belonged to me. My clothes were always second hand, or hand-me-downs. When you are fostered out, they often have numerous other kids that they care for and so you get their stained clothes with the holes. I grew to hate the smell of other people's bodies: their vomit, or their piss.'

'I don't have that excuse. It must be in the genes or something.'

As she continued searching, he swung his legs down and watched her.

'I don't think I've quite got that obsessive compulsive disorder, but I must be close. I spend a fortune at the dry cleaner's. And I've had the same woman cleaning for me for years: Mrs Foster,' he said, chuckling. 'She's remarkable. She even cleans under the rim of the taps, which is a particular phobia of mine. I should give you her number, if you ever need a cleaner.'

'What phobia is that?'

'The one where you go into a sparkling, clean bathroom but, if you get a quick glimpse under the tap, it's – horrifying; it's gunge.'

He was making a joke, trying to charm her. She smiled back and moved on to examine the mantelpiece.

She watched him in the large wood-framed mirror as he kept talking to her.

'As a child, I could go months without a bath; sometimes the grime around my neck was as thick as the gunge under the taps. I didn't know for years that your hair should be washed. Can you credit that?'

She moved on to the table beside the sofa. 'There were a lot of women living at Shallcotte Street. Didn't any of them help to look after you?'

He rested his chin on his hand and looked at her. 'Are your parents alive?'

'No. Sadly they've both passed away.'

'Did they love you?'

'Fortunately.'

He was giving her his full attention and she found it hard to look back at him. He was an exceptionally handsome man; his eyes were incredible, she thought.

'What did they do?'

'My father was a police officer. And my mother was an artist.'

His gaze never faltered. 'I never knew my father. In fact, I don't believe she knew him.'

'Have you ever tried to trace him?'

'Why would I want to do that?'

'Well, if you ever have children, it is always useful to know.'

'Whoever he was, he'd only come after me now for my money.'

'I suppose so.' Anna moved closer to the side table nearest to him. He rolled languidly onto his stomach and continued watching her.

'Life is strange, isn't it?'

She was forced to kneel down quite close to him. His head leaned over hers.

'Do you know what it would do to me if the press found out that a murder team were searching my place?'

'I can imagine.'

'Can you?'

'Of course. There has been enough, over the past few years, of celebrities being arrested.'

'And released,' he said, pulling back.

'Yes, with damaged careers. We are trying to be very diplomatic in your case.'

'It wasn't diplomatic to go to my agent. He has a big mouth. He called me straight away, in a state of panic. It was very unpleasant. I could feel his gossip-mongering adrenalin hit the roof. Did you notice he and that disgusting pug dog of his have very similar eyes?' he asked.

She laughed uncomfortably.

'It's awful going out to dinner with him. Takes it everywhere; slides it into restaurants and it sits there, under the table, letting out small, puffy farts. Ghastly creature.'

He was very amusing company, she thought. Anna tried to distance herself from him, walking away to search the far side of the room.

'Are you married?' he called out, flirtatiously. 'Sorry, what is your name again?'

'Anna Travis. No, I'm not.'

'Anna,' he said appreciatively. 'Anna is a lovely name.'

'Thank you.'

He stretched his arms above his head. 'Do you want to feel under me?'

She stifled a smile and he responded in mock surprise.

'I mean under the cushions, obviously.'

'Yes, obviously.' She played along, amused. 'Thank you, yes. I'd better check.'

He stood up. 'Here, I'll help you.' He started lifting the cushions for her to inspect underneath.

Together they replaced the cushions; then followed the same procedure on the opposite sofa. 'Look how neat we are. We should be married,' he joked, trying to catch her eye. He suddenly reached out and held her hand. 'Anna, as you can see, I am trying to be helpful, but it is so very upsetting.'

'I am sure it is.' She nodded sympathetically. He was closer than she felt comfortable with. She could smell his cologne. But he was holding her hand too tightly for her to move away without causing offence.

'I did not do these terrible murders.' His eyes momentarily shone with tears. 'You know that, don't you?'

She was at a loss as how to respond.

He suddenly dropped her hand and opened his arms expansively. 'Would I risk losing all of this? Especially now I finally have the chance of making it big time. If this new film comes off, it'll mean I've got a chance to work in Hollywood. Mainstream success has eluded me, until now.'

She looked to the door, hopefully.

He chewed his lower lip. 'All I am guilty of is hiding my past. I buried it and if it was to surface, it would—'

'We have every intention of keeping this private,' she said firmly.

Daniels gave a soft laugh. 'It must appear very shallow, my life, compared to yours.'

'No.'

'You probably think it all rather sad, to be so dependent on material things?'

'I do understand,' she said helplessly. Part of her couldn't believe that a famous movie star was being so familiar with her. The other part – the professional part – disapproved strongly.

To her alarm, he threw his arm around her shoulders. 'Anna, I want to show you something.'

When she shifted position, he looked at her, surprised.

'I just want to show you something.'

He kept one arm around her shoulder and produced from his back pocket a slim kid-leather wallet.

Langton arrived soundlessly in the doorway and watched them. Their heads were bent close to each other.

'I have never shown this to anyone before,' Daniels was saying softly.

He indicated a small black and white picture of a little boy with frightened eyes. His hair was plastered down and he was wearing baggy grey shorts with a knitted jumper. 'It is the only photograph I have from my childhood.'

Opposite, was a scaled-down version of his headshot. He was tanned, handsome and looked ahead with confidence. Alan tapped the photograph. 'See? They face each other. One lives inside the other. One comforts the other. Both of them are the reason I am so ambitious.'

There was a loud cough. Anna broke away, embarrassed.

'We've finished, Mr Daniels,' Langton said coolly. He looked strangely at Anna.

'Have you?' said Daniels lightly. He replaced his wallet into his back pocket.

'Yes, sir. I am taking a few items that I will need you to sign for.' Langton walked further into the room. As he passed Anna, he gave a curt nod. 'If you wish to accompany me around your apartment, to see there has been no damage? You can return to the car, Travis.'

'Yes, sir.'

As she passed, Daniels took her hand. She stopped, confused and watched him lift it to his lips.

'Goodbye, Anna,' he said, quietly playful.

Flushed to the roots of her hair, Anna left swiftly.

Outside the house, she found Lewis and Barolli had already gone.

She climbed in the back of the patrol car, waiting for Langton with some trepidation. As Langton exited from the house, she saw Daniels appear at the ground-floor window for a moment, then disappear. Langton opened the front passenger door, got in and then slammed it so hard, the car rocked.

'What the fuck was that about?' He spun around to confront Anna.

'What, exactly?' she stammered.

As the car moved off, Langton's face remained taut with anger. 'You were supposed to be searching his fucking room, Travis. I walk in there: you are standing with his arm around you. I felt like I was intruding. And allowing him to kiss your hand? What the fuck do you think you were doing?'

She swallowed.

'What the fuck was going on? I have never seen anything so fucking unprofessional.'

'If you would just calm down and stop swearing at me, I can tell you.'

He glared at her. 'Asking you out on a date, was he?'

'No! He was talking about his childhood. He'd opened up. And then, just before you came into the room, he wanted to show me a picture.'

'What kind of picture, Travis?'

'Similar to the ones his foster mother showed us: a black and white snapshot. And opposite it, a recent one.'

'Really? And what do you deduce from that?' he snapped.

'He said that one lived inside the other. He also talked about his fear of losing all he had gained. I suspect he fears becoming that wretched child again.'

Langton groaned. 'Well, that's fucking brilliant psychology, Travis. I'm glad you compromised your dignity for that nugget of wisdom. He didn't identify the wretched child as the real serial killer by any chance, did he?'

Sullen, she did not reply.

Several minutes later, Langton turned back to her, more calmly. 'We found his dental X-rays. So he lied about them being lost.'

She stared out of the window wordlessly. She decided not to say what she thought, which was that Daniels's compulsive neatness would, in her opinion, mean he knew exactly where everything was. If they were in any way defamatory, he would have destroyed them.

Langton unbent a little more. 'So, after your tête-à-tête with Anthony Duffy – what do you think?'

She took a big intake of breath. 'He has too much to lose. I don't think he would jeopardize the life he has now.'

There was a pause.

'So, in your humble opinion, is he our man or not?'

'No, I don't think he is.' She leaned slightly forwards. 'What about you?'

'I'd like his wardrobe.' He smiled ruefully.

'That's not a proper answer.' She managed a half grin.

'It's all you're going to get,' he said. Langton knew they might have come up empty-handed and it hurt.

Peace had been restored between them.

Chapter Ten

Anna was at her desk by nine o'clock the next morning, when Lewis and Barolli strolled out of Langton's office. Lewis gave her a lewd wink and whispered, 'Heard he almost got into your pants!'

'What?' she hissed.

'Just a joke, all right?' Lewis grinned. Suddenly his mobile phone rang and he went into a flap, trying to get it out of his pocket. He listened, then he grabbed his coat, yelling, 'It's coming! The baby's coming!' and legged it fast out of the incident room, followed by hooting and cheering.

When the noise had died down, Moira looked at Anna. 'Come on. You can tell me. What happened between you and Alan Daniels?'

'Christ!' Anna pushed back her chair in a temper and stomped off to the filing cabinet where Barolli was sifting through the photographs from Daniels's flat.

Jean called out to him: 'Hear he's got a great place.'

Barolli nodded. 'It was a palace. Course, I didn't get to see the master bedroom. Travis checked that herself. Right, Travis?'

Anna slammed the filing cabinet drawer closed. 'What is it with you lot?'

Moira told Anna to ignore them, they were just trying to lighten things up. Barolli grinned in response.

Langton walked in, his raincoat drenched and his umbrella dripping. 'It's pissing down,' he said, unbuttoning his raincoat. Taking some pages from inside his breast pocket, he passed them to the nearest officer. 'Report says the X-rays are no good; bite won't match the impressions. It wasn't Daniels's teeth that bit Melissa.'

'We get anything from his laptop?' Barolli asked.

Langton shook his head. He looked crumpled and badly in need of a shave. Anna noticed he was still wearing the same shirt from the night before.

'Where's Lewis?' he asked.

'His baby is on the way,' Jean said, smiling.

'That's good.'

Langton walked into his office, the dripping umbrella leaving a trail of water after him and closed the door.

'Eh, Travis. Come and have a look at this, will you?'

Barolli was holding a magnifying glass. She crossed to Barolli's desk and bent down to look at the photograph.

'Is that Julia Roberts he's got with him?'

Anna turned away. 'I wouldn't know.'

Jean replaced the phone and announced the commander and the chief superintendent were on their way in. She hurried to Barolli's desk and took the magnifying glass.

'No! That's nobody. It doesn't even look like Julia Roberts. He's got a great body, though, hasn't he? Is he coming in again, Anna?'

Anna switched on her computer and said tersely, 'I wouldn't know, Jean.'

'But do you know, is he or isn't he a suspect now?'

Anna started typing furiously as Langton put his head around the door. 'Jean, can you check out the cost of a flight to San Francisco? And internal flights to Chicago and Los Angeles.'

'Yes, gov. Hotels, as well?'

Langton gave a brief nod before retreating.

Jean started to log onto the internet. As she checked for the airlines, she glanced across to Moira.

'Be a nice little trip for someone. He won't go alone.'

'Not me, I hate flying,' Barolli said, replacing the photographs into their envelope.

'Could I see those?' Anna put her hand out. Barolli, at his desk, tossed the packet across to her.

Suddenly everyone froze. The big brass had just entered the incident room. The commander, two members of the Gold Group and their chief gave frosty nods and muttered a few good mornings on their way towards Langton's office. Jean grabbed her phone, then replaced it.

'Shit. I forgot to tell him they were coming in. I'll get a bollocking.'

The team went quiet as the blinds that covered the window looking into the incident room were drawn down.

'I think that's his American trip out the window,' Moira said quietly.

Barolli took a deep breath. 'Tenner on it; they're scaling us down.'

'But they can't do that,' Anna said, shocked.

'Yes, they can. We were brought in for Mary Murphy. That was over eight, nine months ago. It's been two months since Melissa Stephens was found and we've no bloody result on that, either. It's too costly to keep us all on the case.'

They all gave an involuntary glance at the shuttered window and began working at their desks.

At one o'clock, Jean took coffee and sandwiches into Langton's office. Back in the incident room, she reported a very tense atmosphere. 'The gov looked as if he was being hauled over the coals.'

Inside his cramped office, Langton sat in mute fury. He had not, as yet, even broached the subject of a trip to the States.

The commander put her sandwich aside. 'I mean it, James. We are seriously going to have to consider scaling down the team. As far as I can gather, your suspect, Alan Daniels, has co-operated on every level. The search warrant and subsequent search of his flat resulted in nothing whatsoever that implicated him. With no new evidence forthcoming, it's a very costly operation to keep so many officers on.'

'I am aware of that,' Langton said coldly.

'I do understand the reasons for focusing on Alan Daniels, but the evidence is totally circumstantial. There is nothing corroborating it and even though intuition is something we can't dismiss, we nevertheless have to seriously contemplate how you intend to take this further. Now is the time to give me – everyone here – details.'

'Results, so far, are these: we have a serial killer on the loose and, as you've read the reports, you know as well as we do that he could also have been committing the same crimes in the United States.'

Langton opened the file on the American victims.

'I read it, James,' Commander Leigh said curtly. 'But that brings up the possibility that the perpetrator could be American.'

Exasperated, Langton threw up his hands. 'That isn't feasible. Daniels was in the States: filming in Chicago, in Los Angeles and San Francisco. That is too bloody coincidental. We also know there were two periods when he was in New York. I am getting them checked and—'

She interrupted him. 'I am aware of the latest report. But being in the same place does not automatically mean he was involved. That said, it could let us off the hook if the killer turns out to be an American. We could feed that information to the press.'

He knew what she meant.

'If you can take it, Ma'am. I wouldn't want the responsibility of closing us down and then another victim being discovered,' he said. 'Because I am damned sure he's not stopped.'

'It's not a question of me taking it,' she snapped. 'The costs to date outweigh the results. I have to present my report to the assistant commissioner. That means making a decision about bringing in a new team, which I am loath to do, as it will spiral the cost even further.'

'Give me more time, then. Let me take a trip to the States; check out their records of the victims. They've sent over only case reports and the fact they have the same MO, but if I could get more details, I would, at least for my own satisfaction, eliminate Alan Daniels.'

She sighed, impatiently. 'Eliminate him? You don't have one scrap of evidence to implicate him, for Christ's sake, and definitely nothing to link him to the Melissa Stephens murder. All you have is a group of women who may or may not have known him and who may or may not have known each other! I have read the reports.' She was fighting to retain her temper. 'You have had every possible opportunity. You have not, I am sorry to say, given me anything today that warrants keeping an entire murder team here in Queen's Park.'

'You've already halved the team. I won't let this go,' he said firmly.

'It is not a question of what you want,' she said angrily. 'Look, let's not get into a shouting match over this. I will consider giving you two more weeks.'

'Give me three days. That's all I need to go over there and check out these cases.'

The commander looked at Chief Superintendent Thompson, who, till then, had not said more than a few words. 'I trust James.' He carefully placed his coffee cup on the desk. 'If he feels there is a possibility of gaining a result, I'd send him to Alaska, if necessary.'

Langton gave him a grateful look. The commander collected her briefcase and walked to the door.

'Three days and keep me informed. Because we are going to have to prepare a press release.'

The team watched curiously as the procession of brass walked out, but could find nothing in their manner to indicate what had happened inside. A call from Lewis lifted the gloominess in the atmosphere. Barolli yelled out the news: Lewis had a son, weighing in at seven pounds, six ounces. After a moment of quiet conversation, he replaced the receiver.

'He's going to put in for maternity leave,' he said, surprised.

'I think you mean "paternity" leave,' Jean commented wryly.

'What did you tell him?' Moira asked.

'I just said that from what has been going down here, I didn't see why not.'

Langton appeared. He called out to Jean, who was printing material from the internet. 'You get the information I wanted?'

Jean gathered up all the pages. 'Mike Lewis has just had a baby boy,' she informed him.

He looked puzzled for a moment; then gave a half smile.

'Moira, send him a bottle of champagne and some flowers for his wife. From all of us.'

He returned to his office, Jean following on his heels.

'Christ, Jean, is this the cheapest deal you can get?'

'Yes. I checked with all the airlines and the Virgin Atlantic flight is the cheapest, direct to San Francisco.'

She passed him another sheet. 'I would suggest you hire a car from San Francisco and drive to Los Angeles, then get an internal flight from there to Chicago.'

'Thanks,' he said curtly. Then he reached for the phone.

When Jean returned to the incident room, she grinned at Anna conspiratorially. 'He's having kittens about the price, but it's not that bad: round trip for under six hundred quid.'

Moira had taken a call from the NYPD in New York. 'No joy in New York; they've not got anything on the dates Daniels was over there.' She buzzed the message through to Langton's office.

She took a couple of notes and looked over to Jean. 'Jean, can you get onto CAP in San Francisco. That's the division that handles the murders of prostitutes: Crime Against Prostitutes, it's part of the Vice Division in the San Francisco Police Department. You need to ask for Captain Tom Delaware.'

Moira leaned on Jean's desk, watching her write it all down. 'He wants a hotel. Somewhere in a place called Tenderloin.'

'Tenderloin?' Jean asked. 'You sure you got that right? Tenderloin?'

'That's what he said. Tenderloin.'

Having just walked in, Langton overheard the conversation: 'It's called that because during the Depression era, only police officers earned a good steady wage and could get a decent steak.' The two women turned to him, astonished and he shrugged. 'Now you know!'

Jean and Moira seemed to return to their work in hand, though when they noticed Langton lean on Anna's desk, neither of them was averse to watching from a corner of her eye.

'We're on the eleven o'clock flight tomorrow. Heathrow direct to San Francisco. Can you drive an automatic?'

'Yes,' said Anna. 'San Francisco!'

Langton straightened up. 'Jean, check out the visa situation ASAP, for Travis and myself.' He returned to his office.

Moira and Jean threw a glance at each other. Barolli pushed back his chair, irritated. It wasn't that he wanted to go to San Francisco; it was just that it would have been ethical to ask him, since he'd been there longer. He also wanted to know what the hell was going to happen in London when his gov jetted off to the States.

Langton looked round the corner of his door at the sight of an uptight Barolli and added, 'With Mike out being a daddy, I need you to run the incident room.'

'So, we still have one,' Barolli said moodily.

'We are hanging onto it by our fingernails. We only have two weeks. I'll be giving a briefing in fifteen minutes.'

'Right,' Barolli said, still not mollified.

'And I know you bloody hate flying. I've got a long drive from San Francisco to LA, then an internal flight to Chicago. And only three days to do it, there and back.'

'Bloody hell,' Barolli whistled.

'It's make-or-break time.' Langton rubbed his chin, which was really in need of a shave. 'So whilst I am gone, you need to dig harder; find anything that'll get that woman off my back.'

'Right. Will do.'

Anna was so excited she could hardly contain herself. She had never even been to America, let alone to three of its major cities. Secretly, she also liked the fact that she would be travelling with Langton alone: just the two of them.

In the flat, Anna spent most of the evening selecting what to pack. She had arranged to meet Langton at the airport at half past nine the next morning. She took out her passport and made sure she had some money to change into dollars at the airport. All done, she put her wheelie suitcase by the front door, ready for the morning's departure. It was just after ten when her phone rang. She ran to pick it up, thinking it might be Langton.

'Anna,' a man said softly.

'Yes. Who is this?'

'Come on. Don't you recognize my voice?'

She felt the hairs on the back of her neck prickling. 'No, I'm sorry, I don't,' she lied. 'Who is this?'

'OK, play hard to get. I don't mind,' he laughed. 'It's Alan Daniels.'

She tried to collect her thoughts. 'How did you get my number?'

'You're in the book, of course.'

'Oh, yes.'

'Do you want to know why I am calling?'

'Yes, it's late.' She wished she could tape the call.

'Do you like ballet?'

'Yes. I do. Very much.'

'I have been given two tickets. I would love it if you could join me; perhaps we could have a little supper afterwards, at the Ivy?'

'Oh, well, er, yes. I love ballet.' She swallowed hard. 'When are the tickets for?'

'Tomorrow night. Very short notice I know, but—'

'I'm so sorry, Mr Daniels—'

'No, no, no – Alan,' he interrupted.

'Unfortunately, I will be away.' She almost said she was going to America, but stopped herself. 'Thank you very much for thinking of me, Alan.'

'Where are you going?'

'To Manchester,' she lied.

'What are you going to Manchester for?' he asked.

'Erm, on business.'

'We might still be able to get together. What time do you get back?'

'The thing is, I might have to stay over. My chief said it was possible.'

'Ah, well, perhaps another time, then. Would you like me to call you again?'

'Yes, yes, I would. Thank you for thinking of me.'

'Of course. Goodnight, Anna.' He replaced the receiver.

Her phone number was not in the book. How had he got it? In the shower, she went over every word of their conversation. No way had Alan Daniels simply speculated that she might like ballet. She adored ballet. How did he know that?

She made herself a sandwich and a cup of tea. The call had really taken the edge off her excitement at leaving for the States. Eventually, she got into bed. Reaching for the bedside lamp, she stopped and withdrew her hand. The photograph of her father had been turned out to face the room. She touched it every night before she went to sleep. It was always facing towards her, towards the bed, not away from it.

She squeezed her eyes tight shut. She was scared. Had she moved the frame when she was tidying up that morning? She tried to recall exactly what she had done, but inside she knew she hadn't moved it. She had left her front door open when she went down to the bins, but only for a few minutes. Had he been in her home?

Anna got up and walked round her small flat. After making sure that nothing else had been moved, she double-locked her front door, throwing the bolt across it, which was something she rarely ever did. She returned to bed, pulling the duvet up to her chin. In the darkness, what had felt safe before now felt frightening: the way the dressing-table mirror reflected the street-light through the curtains and the sight of the wardrobe door left slightly ajar all of a sudden made her heart pound. Could someone be hiding in there? She told herself not to be such a wimp, but she turned on her bedside lamp all the same. She looked at her father's strong face in the photograph and whispered: 'Was someone here, Daddy?'

At the airport next morning, Anna spotted Langton immediately. He carried a lightweight, folding suit bag and no other luggage. She joined him at the Virgin desk with her suitcase.

'Can you carry that on the plane?' he said sceptically.

'I can put the handle down,' she insisted.

'Good. The less time we waste hanging around for luggage, the better.'

After they were checked in, they headed through to Departures. Langton did his usual fast-paced walk; Anna, wheeling her case after him, had to trot to keep up.

'I want to buy a camera,' he said, hastily heading towards duty free. She waited in the background as he trailed from counter to counter, musing and picking up one camera after another. He eventually decided on a small zoom-lens job and after he had paid for it, set off at his usual fast pace, this time to buy cigarettes and a bottle of malt whisky. Next, he was inspecting perfumes and asking her which one she preferred, since he was at a loss.

'It depends on who you are buying it for,' Anna replied, itching to know.

'Just give yourself a spray of that and let me smell it.'

She sprayed her wrist with a tester bottle. When he held her hand and sniffed, it was like an electric shock.

'Right, that'll do.' As he sniffed her wrist again, she started to redden.

'She'll like that,' he said, meeting her eyes. Then, as an afterthought, he added, 'It's for Kitty,' before he was off to the counter to pay for the bottle of perfume.

She watched him go. He was wearing a grey suit she had never seen before and a pale blue shirt with white cuffs and collar. All that and a close shave; he was looking very attractive.

Eventually they were on board. She sat herself into the window seat and fixed her safety belt while he removed his jacket, folding it neatly to place above him in the locker. When he sat beside her and drew his belt closed, they were so close her shoulder touched his.

'Did you know Barolli hates flying?' he said, reaching to take the in-flight magazine from the seat pocket in front.

'Daniels called me last night,' she said quietly.

'What?' He put his magazine down and turned to face her.

'He called me at home, after ten. He said my number was in the book, but it isn't.'

He stared at her, uncomprehending. 'Why didn't you tell me before? What did he say?'

She repeated the conversation, almost word for word.

'That it?' he said, when she had finished.

She hesitated. When she woke up that morning, she was less sure that she had not moved her father's picture herself. 'Yes.'

'Tell me something, Travis. Do you fancy him?'

'No, I do not!' she said sharply. 'Speaking of which, I don't know what you told Barolli went on at Queen's Gate, but I don't find his jokes very funny.'

'Don't be so uptight. Listen, if Daniels asks you out again, I want you to accept. We'll monitor your calls. And if you go out with him, we'll keep tabs on you.'

He was looking so elated by her information that Anna felt a little resentful.

'Oh, thank you very much. Don't ask how I feel about it!'

'It's the classic syndrome, don't you see? He wants information.'

'I don't suppose there's an option then, is there?'

'He will be getting a kick out of being close to the investigation, close to someone involved in trying to capture him. It couldn't be better, Travis.'

'So, you still think it's him?'

He ignored the question and delved into the arm of his seat, bringing up the video screen,

'But if you're wrong?' she persisted. 'What if he's innocent?'

'You mean what if he just fancies you?'

'I didn't mean that.'

'Really? This movie star who could have any woman he wants falls for DS Anna Travis. Somehow he gets hold of her number and calls, hoping for a date? That sounds plausible? Come on, grow up!'

'All I said was: what if you're wrong?'

He stubbornly fixed his earphones onto his head.

'Conversation over!'

'I have had men ask me out in the past,' she said with pursed lips.

He half lifted his earphones. 'Don't get your knickers in a twist. I believe you. But how many of them were under suspicion for murder? Date any serial killers lately? Get real, Anna. The guy is dangerous. He's coming on to you because it's a game he gets a kick out of playing.'

'What about the fact his dental X-rays don't match the bite mark from Melissa's tongue?'

In response, he sat back and closed his eyes to listen to the in-flight music programme.

She stared out of the window. What if he was right? At the same time, what if he was wrong? Why couldn't the truth simply be that Daniels liked her? After a while, she too eased her seat back and tried to sleep, but she kept thinking about Daniels: remembering the picture he had shown her of himself as a child. Was it true that he had never shown it to anyone before?

She needed to use the toilet. Unfastening her seat belt, Anna climbed over the reclining Langton. He did not sit up when she left, nor as she clambered back to her seat, though he did turn over in his sleep. She watched, alarmed, as his head lolled closer to hers, then came to rest on her shoulder. It was a strange feeling: to have him so close. What a pity she didn't like him any more. And it was quite obvious he didn't think very much of her.

Somewhere on the flight, she too closed her eyes. Their positions changed. Anna woke up to find her head was now on his shoulder and he was gently stroking her cheek. She sat bolt upright.

'Sorry,' she said, embarrassed.

'That's OK. I was trying to wake you. We're landing in fifteen minutes.'

'Right.' She felt disorientated, even more so when he leaned closer.

'You were catching flies and snoring,' he said, amused.

She looked at him, perplexed. 'So were you! But I was too polite to tell you.'

He laughed. 'Well, fingers crossed we get a result today.' He eased his seat forwards into the upright position. Then he smiled at her. 'You sleep like a little girl. I was just teasing.'

She said nothing, but she decided she liked him again.

It was much warmer in San Francisco than either had anticipated. The temperature had reached the mid-seventies by two o'clock. Langton ordered the taxi driver to take them to the Super 8 Motel on O'Farrell Street, which was only a fifteen-minute drive from the airport. The motel was situated in the Tenderloin district close to the police station. This area was the red–light district, probably the worst neighbourhood, with a flood of drug dealers and drug addicts and prostitutes patrolling the streets. The driver explained: 'It's a great place, but you gotta be careful: the streets ain't the cleanest and you gotta watch out for oddballs coming up to you. So stay alert and don't let 'em get to you, but the 'Loin is a great place, an' you got the greatest diners and restaurants.'

When they arrived at the motel, Langton said he would meet Anna in the lobby in twenty minutes. There was hardly time to unpack, so she had a shower and quickly changed her shirt. In the lobby, she found him talking to the concierge. He had maps and was already on first-name terms with the man, who handed him the car-hire documents and keys.

They went into the car park. When Langton located their rental car, he was taken aback by the size of it. It was a bright blue Chevrolet Metro; inside, it smelt like a rose garden.

'Right. You drive, I'll direct,' he said, getting into the passenger seat and opening the map. Anna took a deep breath. 'You take a right out of the gates and remember, you are on the other side of the road. Keep driving and then it's left, right, right and another left and we should be there.'

He told Anna they would be meeting the deputy chief first, at the Bureau of Investigations; then on to Captain Tom Delaware, who headed up the CAP division, attached to the Vice Squad.

Anna managed to get them to the Police Department without a major accident. Whenever Langton rapped out his instructions en route, she just gritted her teeth. Finally, as they were driving round the large car park in front of the San Francisco Police Department, Langton snapped at her to 'just park the car'. She pulled on the brake and fumed at him.

'Do you want to drive? Or will you let me do it?'

She finally parked the car in a space marked 'visitors'. She and Langton walked in silence towards the main entrance of the San Francisco PD.

It was freezing inside the air-conditioned building. Their meeting with the deputy chief, thankfully, was short and to the point. When he checked their credentials and passports he seemed almost apologetic, reassuring them it was just a necessary procedure, since they were being given access to files and case reports.

A young female officer led them to Captain Delaware's office. She tapped and ushered them inside.

Tom Delaware was a rotund, beefy man, with a gut hanging over his pants and a big personality to go with it. He greeted them warmly and offered coffee. They refused. Langton passed over the duty-free malt whisky. Delaware grinned. 'You touch my heart.' He examined the bottle then put it into his desk drawer.

'I know you're on a tight schedule, so let's get started.'

From a thick file on his desk he withdrew a photograph of the victim: Thelma Delray, aged twenty-four. Langton thought she looked older, but he said nothing. Her sad story mirrored the British victims' pasts. 'Trixie', as Delaware referred to her, was a well-known hooker, having worked the red-light district since she was a teenager. Every time they placed her into a foster home, she ran back to her pimp and was subsequently out on the streets. She was a drug addict and Anna also thought she looked older than her age.

The mortuary shots were very reminiscent of their own victims. The close-up photos showed her murder had the same MO. The way her bra was tied looked the same. The tights were wrapped around her neck, three times.

'What about suspects?' Langton asked.

Tom said her pimp had no apparent motive: Trixie was earning good money for him. Why kill his golden goose? He also had a strong alibi. He was in their apartment in Bay View, with two witnesses, on the night she was last seen alive. Three weeks later she had been found face down in John Macaulay Park, very decomposed. It had been a hot summer.

'One of the park keepers discovered the body here. Son of a bitch dumped her that close. Any one of the little kids could have found her.'

On the last night Trixie was seen alive, a number of girls recalled her talking to someone in a car. It was midnight; she never came back to her patch.

'Who identified her body?' Langton asked.

'Her mother.'

Langton put Alan Daniels's photo on the desk.

'You ever seen this guy?'

Delaware frowned. 'Nope. No, can't say I have.'

The captain drove them to the park, to show where Trixie's body was discovered.

'We believe the killer brought her here, took her out of the car and into the bushes over there. Killed her on site. A witness saw a car parked there, but he couldn't recall what make it was. No registration and he said the lights were out.'

It was half past six and in the red-light district the girls were on the streets. Anna stared out of the back window of the patrol car. She was so tired she could feel her eyelids drooping. Of course, it would be after midnight, London time. Langton seemed not to flag at all. He suggested dropping Anna back at the motel, while he took Tom to a few bars for an evening out.

Anna felt irritated, because she knew she was being dismissed. But back at the motel, she felt relieved. She went to the hotel restaurant for a hamburger and then straight to her room. She checked the route on the LA freeway map before bed. The following day was going to include a long drive.

Langton, meanwhile, was barhopping with Tom Delaware. Or, as Tom described it, 'girl shopping'. At first he wondered if Langton was looking for himself, but he soon realized he wasn't. By the time they reached Joe's Restaurant in a really rough area, Taylor Street at Turk Street, Tom's feet ached and he was hungry. As they leaned back in their comfortable black–burgundy leatherette booths, Langton asked Tom if he recalled there being a film unit in the area at the time Trixie was murdered.

Tom didn't, but he put in a call to an ex–cop pal who supplemented his pension by working as a location manager for film units. They talked more over supper as they waited for him. At midnight, he arrived and over coffees, the photograph of Alan Daniels was again produced.

Anna woke with a start. There had been a loud crash from the room next door. She looked at her watch: it was half past three. Another crash. She suspected this one was the fall of the ironing board. So he not only slammed his office door, he knocked over everything no matter where he was. Next, the toilet flushed. That was followed by more bangs and thuds. She heard Langton swear a few times, then there was the clicking of lights being switched off. Then on, then off; she couldn't keep track.

Then, finally, silence. She found it difficult to go back to sleep. Perhaps because now, in London, it would be eight o'clock in the morning.

She got up reluctantly and had another shower to wake up properly. At five o'clock, she lay down and closed her eyes, thinking what she would order for breakfast. She woke with a start. She thought she had heard a fire alarm. But the noise was coming from next door. Langton was obviously up and taking a shower. She decided she might as well dress and join him for breakfast.

She knocked on his door. He yanked it open.

'I was wondering if you wanted breakfast,' she said, avoiding looking at him. He was wearing just a towel slung round his hips and holding a muffin in his hand. She could see he was fit, his stomach was tight and he had a hairy chest; not too much, but it was as dark as his head hair, which was standing up on end. She remembered Pamela Anderson saying he used to be very athletic. Nevertheless, it surprised her that he was so lean and in such good shape.

'What?' he barked.

'I'm going to breakfast,' she said lamely.

He indicated his muffin. 'See you at the desk at nine.'

'I'll see you down there,' she said, turning back to her room.

He slammed the door shut. She didn't see him wince; he had a hell of a hangover and felt terrible.

Anna was at the wheel of the car, studying a highway map, when he walked across the hotel car park. He opened the boot and put his suit bag in it. He then got into the passenger seat.

'Do you know where we are going?'

'Los Angeles,' she said.

'Correct. Do you need me to direct you?'

'No, I've checked out the map. It's mostly straight on the freeway, all the way there.'

'Good.'

'Well, all set then?' she asked.

He nodded wearily.

'Have a good time last night?'

He closed his eyes. 'I was working, Travis. What did you think I was doing, partying with Delaware?'

'Did you eat?'

He sighed. 'Yes, Mother. Now, can we get started? I'm going to lie down for a bit.'

As she drove out of the car park, he pulled the seat lever so he could lie almost prone beside her. Anna took a while to find the right turn onto the freeway and ended up doing a few circles around the city, but found she quite enjoyed driving up and down the hills. At least she was finally seeing some of the sights of San Francisco.

They stopped to fill up the car with petrol and then continued on the freeway. It was an experience she was enjoying, when he woke with a start.

'We nearly there?'

'Not yet,' she said. He eased his seat into an upright position and was suddenly alert.

'I talked to a lot of the street hookers last night, Travis, not to mention a few pimps. I showed them all his photo. Didn't get any result.'

'Should you do that? I mean, what if someone recognizes him?'

'That was the point, Travis. Tom Delaware called in a friend who works for a company that finds locations for film units.'

He was staring ahead, in concentration: 'The film Alan Daniels was on mostly used the marina. The cast lived in big trailers, didn't use hotels. But he recognized the face.'

'And?'

'He was there around the time she was last seen alive. They had been shooting for four days, then stayed on another two. By the time her body was found they'd gone to another location.'

She was still listening intently as they drove on.

'He said the crew were known to have been to the red-light district and a lot of the hookers went to where they were filming, touting for business. They had drivers and limos for the actors, but a number of hire cars to go sightseeing when they weren't wanted on the set.'

Anna recalled that the only witness had seen a car but was unable to give any detail of the make or registration.

'So all we know for sure is that Daniels was there and he would have had the opportunity,' she said. 'He may have even seen Trixie around the film set, then picked her up on the night she disappeared.'

'Yeah, that's it,' he sighed. Tom Delaware was going to check whether Alan Daniels had hired a car. None of the film crew or artists were ever questioned by the SFPD; however, it was so long ago, he doubted that they would even remember.

He fell silent. 'Long way to come, for what we basically already knew.' He sighed deeply and rested his arm along the back of her seat. 'You drive well, Travis,' he observed after a moment.

'Thank you. Wasn't that the reason you wanted me along?'

He didn't reply. She could feel the heat of his arm behind her shoulders.

'I know it's him and his victims are getting younger. Trixie was only twenty-four; Melissa just seventeen.'

'I thought you'd taken Melissa out of the equation,' she said. He withdrew his arm.

'No, I haven't. He's a really clever son of a bitch. First he says he destroyed his dental records, or lost them. Next we find them; it looks suspicious and he simply says he forgot where they were.'

'But he didn't know we would get a search warrant, did he?'

He snorted. 'Come on, he's brought in for questioning about seven murders. If he's our man, he's going to be bloody sure we'll want to search his place. I think he just planted them to get us off the scent.'

'It's possible,' she said, not really believing it.

'There's something else.' Langton leaned forward, fiddling with the air conditioning. 'The ex-cop – you know, location guy – he said he'd check out as much as he could that'd help; he also said a lot of the actors came and went although they were down to shoot for all the days. There was a bad rainstorm, so they had a day when they couldn't film.'

'What does that give us?'

'Possibly a new way of looking at Cornwall. We'd checked out the dates and, yes, he was on the schedule for that entire week, but we didn't check if they had a weather problem. What if Alan Daniels was not in Cornwall when Melissa Stephens was murdered?'

Anna was silent. He nudged her.

'What do you think?'

'It's possible,' she said dubiously. 'But what if he was in Cornwall for that entire time? What if he had simply forgotten where he had put his dental X-rays? What if Alan Daniels is not our killer?'

'He is.'

'But supposition and maybes could be wasting valuable time. If you take Alan Daniels out of the equation, what are you left with?'

'Thank you for that vote of confidence, Travis.'

'I'm serious. What are you left with?'

He glared. 'Seven dead women, eight with Trixie, maybe ten, after we leave the States. Left to rot in cold storage, because they were part of society's garbage.'

'That's not quite true!'

'It fucking is true. Except Melissa, of course.'

'All of their cases were investigated.'

'Bullshit. If I hadn't gone back into the dead files, that's where the poor bitches would still be rotting. Look at the Yorkshire Ripper. Eleven women dead before they got him.'

Anna was trying not to argue. At the same time, she wasn't just going to accept everything he said verbatim. 'They had the Ripper in five times. And still they couldn't catch him. He was a dead ringer for the Identikit pictures the witnesses provided. But they released him, because they were concentrating on a tape recording that had been sent in.' She gripped the steering wheel tighter. 'And the man on the tape didn't have a Yorkshire accent. In other words, all that wasted time on a piece of evidence sent in by some sicko, who had nothing to do with the killer.'

'So you think I am wasting my time?' he snapped.

'Maybe you are wasting time with Daniels. That's all I am saying.'

Signs to Los Angeles started appearing overhead. Anna asked Langton to check the map to find out which slip road they should take off the freeway. He looked over the map for a while then, sheepishly, turned it the right way round.

'Just take the next one. We'll find our way from there.'

She took a deep breath.

He leaned back and said quietly, 'Oh shit, shit. Maybe I have lost my way.'

'No, we'll be OK,' she said through clenched teeth. It says "Sunset".'

'I didn't mean that way, Travis. What if you're right and I am chasing up my own arse?' He gave her a sidelong smile. 'Christ, you're like your old man. Do you know that, Travis?'

He could not have given her a better compliment.

187

When he added, 'And just as objectionable,' she started to laugh and so did he, defusing their previous tension. Then he concentrated on the map and started to direct her towards their hotel.

Chapter Eleven

It was even hotter in LA: up in the eighties. Though the Beverly Terrace Hotel was smaller than the one in San Francisco, it had the advantage of an outdoor pool. Their meeting was scheduled with the LA Police Department for two thirty, so there was time to unpack, shower, or just relax. Anna decided on a swim and went down to the pool.

She was on her tenth length, before she caught sight of Langton. She swam to the steps.

'Do you want me?' she asked.

'Finish your swim.'

'No, it's all right.'

She shook the drops of water from her hair.

'It's just, I managed to get an email through to the station,' he said. 'You know, asking for an update.'

She was climbing heavily up the steps from the pool, her swimsuit clinging to her damply. He held on to her elbow as she was clambering out.

'Barolli's getting on to the London company to check out Daniels's schedule. Whether they gave him any time off during the week of seventh February; say, enough time for a return trip between Cornwall and London.'

She turned towards a sun lounger as he handed her a towel.

'Thanks. What about the dentist who did his work over here?'

'I'm getting in touch with him. The dental lab is emailing him the details. We've eventually got to get over to Orange County. That's where the victim from here was found. So we may have to make contact with their department.'

'Right.'

'I think I'll follow your example and have a quick dip,' he said, not moving.

'Did you pack your trunks?' she asked.

'Nope, but I'm OK in my jockey shorts.'

He got up and wandered into a changing cubicle. She collected her belongings and finished drying off; waiting for him to come out, as he'd left his jacket and his wallet.

He appeared with a towel round his shoulders and his clothes in a bundle under his arm.

'You look remarkably fit, considering,' she said, rubbing her hair dry.

'Considering what?'

'Well, you smoke too much, and drink, and – do you exercise at all?'

'Do I exercise?' he said mockingly.

'Yes.'

'Used to, few years back.'

'Oh, really?' she feigned ignorance. When she asked if he'd ever played tennis, he shook his head.

'Used to have a racing bike. You ever use that track, not far from where you live? I'd get there sometimes late at night, haul the bike over the fence and ride round in the darkness. Used to clear my head. Not done that for a while, though.'

'Your head that clear now, is it?' she joked.

He cocked his head to one side. 'Always fishing, aren't you, Travis? Well, my head is clear and it'll be a lot clearer after I've had a swim.'

He tossed his clothes onto her sun lounger.

'When you've finished, could you take my clothes up to your room? I forgot the credit card thingy and my wallet's in the jacket.'

He dumped the towel and after a rather poor dive at the deep end, started to swim a slow crawl. She watched him for a couple of lengths, then picked up his clothes and walked back inside the hotel.

She had just finished drying her hair, when he knocked on her door.

'Any developments from the station?' She handed him his clothes.

'Nope. See you later. Say twenty minutes, down at reception.' With that, he left.

His wardrobe was consistently surprising her. By the time she got to the reception area, he had miraculously appeared in a crisp, white shirt and light suit. He was wearing dark shades.

They drove to the main, massive LAPD building and after fifteen minutes there, got back in the car and drove to Orange County, where they had been informed the police station would be likely to have more details.

The second victim, Marla Courtney, aged twenty-nine, had a long record of prostitution in Los Angeles. She was also a crack addict. Her murder had taken place between the times of their last two victims back home. So, like Trixie's, Marla's case was cold.

Marla had last been seen, by a waitress, coming out of the Blues Club on Sunset, in a very drunken state. No one else had come forward to say that they had seen her after that. Langton was given the waitress's cell-phone number and called her, but her answering service was on, so he hung up.

Her body was found in a known crack area of Orange County. She was, as with their other victims, lying face down, hands tied and strangled by her own tights. Anna and Langton spent the rest of the morning driving to the Orange County Police Department and checking the files and mortuary pictures of the dead woman. At four o'clock they left the department to head back to their hotel. They drove up Sunset past the Blues Club and on to the CBS television studios in Century City.

The black receptionist had to use a pencil to dial the internal phone number. She had the longest false nails Anna had ever seen: they curved over like talons. Her hair was braided in a mass of plaits, with coloured beads that clanked together every time she moved her head.

'I gotta Detective James Langton and I gotta Anna Travis in reception.' She listened, then addressed them. 'You go up to the fourteenth and someone will getchas.'

'Thank you,' Anna said.

They emerged from the lift into a large reception area on the fourteenth floor. A thin young man with round glasses and a face full of pimples approached them. He put his hand out to Anna: 'Detective Langton?'

'No.'

'That's Detective Sergeant Travis,' Langton said tersely. 'I'm Detective Chief Inspector Langton.'

They followed the young man as he weaved along narrow corridors between rows of desks. Finally they reached a line of offices. By now the sound of phones ringing and actors' voices on videotape had created an extraordinary wall of sound.

They paused outside the last office as the pimple-faced youth stammered out their names. The person inside the office kept on talking. As they waited, they couldn't avoid hearing his side of the telephone conversation.

'She wants how much? An hour? You must be joking! No way we could run to that, unless we shoot it in Romania. I am sure she is, but I am going to have to get back to you. Yes, yes, I know she's just adopted a boy. We'll arrange to take a nanny, half her fucking household if that's what she wants, but we cannot agree to that price. Right, right.'

They glimpsed a hand gesturing for them to enter the office. As Anna and Langton stepped in from the corridor, Mike Mullins finished his call.

'Love you too, babe. Get back to me. Fine, thanks.'

He replaced the phone and stood up.

The room was crammed from floor to ceiling with tapes and scripts and on the side of a very large oak desk was an enormous orchid arrangement. Mike Mullins was short, with a suntan, hair plugs and gleaming white teeth. He was wearing a floral shirt which flopped over his stomach and pale blue jeans. 'Right. Now, have you been offered a water, latte, juice or anything?'

'We're fine,' Langton said.

'Sit down, please.'

They sat side by side on a soft, brown leather couch. Mullins passed a script to the hovering assistant.

'I want four copies of each and white page them.'

Mullins then eased back round his desk. 'I am sorry. I can't remember why you are here?'

'You made a TV film last year. It was called *Out of the System*,' Langton answered.

'Oh Christ, yes.'

'It starred an actor called Alan Daniels.'

'Did it?' Mullins said, clasping his hands. 'I can't honestly remember. I must have blanked it from my mind.' His forehead puckered. 'Yes, I think he was in it. British, right?'

'Yes, he is.'

Mullins swivelled to face his computer, where he tapped away at the keyboard, muttering to himself the whole time. He then peered closer at the screen. 'Of course. I know who it is. Yes. Alan Daniels, but he wasn't the lead. Yes, I remember him. I couldn't afford him now.'

'Do you have a record of the locations where you would have used him?'

Mullins pursed his lips and then did some clicking on his keyboard. 'I've got the entire budget here.'

'And the dates Daniels was working?'

Mullins kept clicking his mouse then finally shook his head. 'I know the dates for the entire filming schedule because it's in the budget. Just not artist by artist, but we filmed over six weeks: start date September twentieth, through to the beginning of November. We were LA based, so I don't have the location lists.'

He turned, frowning from his computer screen. 'He's not suing me, is he?'

'No. Could he have been in LA for that entire period of time?'

'Yes, yes, I think so. I'll get the cast and crew list up for you.'

They waited, as he fumbled around. He did a print-off sheet, which he glanced at. 'Alan Daniels stayed at the Château Marmont, just off Sunset; I can't give you the list, as it has private home addresses, etc.'

Langton stood. 'Thank you; appreciate your time.'

'Aren't you going to tell me what this is all about?'

'I'm sorry, but we are just making enquiries.'

'About what?'

Langton shook his hand. 'Just a routine enquiry. Thank you again.'

Disappointed, Mullins followed them to the door. When it swung open, his startled, stammering assistant jumped from the desk outside.

'He played a detective, I remember that. Blond, very good-looking, isn't he?'

Anna thanked him for seeing them. Langton had already disappeared.

The Château Marmont was situated off Sunset, on Marmont Drive. It was almost six o'clock when they drove in and gave the keys to the valet parking attendant. Anna was tongue-tied, overawed by the sprawling hotel and its private bungalows. She wondered if they would see any film stars crossing the lobby.

It was some time before the assistant manager was available to see them. He was very diplomatic and very evasive; he said he was unable to give them any details of any guest staying presently or in the past, as it was against hotel procedure.

Langton flashed his ID. 'I understand you must guard your guests' privacy, but since this is possibly a police matter, it would be diplomatic of you to assist me in every way you can. I don't want to have to return with LAPD and with uniformed officers and patrol cars.'

They left fifteen minutes later with the information that Alan Daniels had been staying at the hotel, in one of the secluded, private bungalows. He had stayed for five weeks, covering the period that Marla was murdered. He had used a hire car during his stay. It was a Mercedes-Benz.

As they drove away, down Sunset, they passed the Blues Club again, a short distance from the Château. Langton raised an eyebrow.

'Very convenient.'

His mobile phone rang and he patted his pockets to look for it.

'It can't be London, it's after midnight there.' He opened his phone. 'Hello? Hello?'

'Who is this?' said a female voice. 'You called my cell phone; didn't leave a message. I just dialled re-call.'

'Ah yes, are you—?' He covered the phone and nudged Anna. 'What was the name of the fucking witness, the Marla case? What did he say her name was?'

'Angie Dutton,' Anna said.

Langton went back to his call. 'Is this Angie?' he asked smoothly.

'Yeah, who are you?'

Anna listened as he gave as little information as possible and said that he would like ten minutes of her time. After a lot of batting to and fro, he said he would meet her at ten. He snapped the phone shut and grinned.

'Well, Angie has a very sexy voice and probably some vital information. She's working at a club: Sequins . . . Takes her break at ten.'

'Can we eat something before then?'

'We can. But you aren't coming with me. This one I do on my own.'

Anna gave him a look, but he didn't catch it.

'You know, I think my luck is changing.'

He decided they should go back to the hotel and freshen up. Anna had just pulled into the appropriate lane of traffic when Langton gave a sudden laugh.

'What?'

'I thought everyone here in LA worked out.' He laid his arm flat along the back of the seat, so his hand almost rested on her neck. 'How about the walking pimple and his hair-weaved gov, Mullins?'

Anna gave a rueful smile. She felt really tired after the long drive from San Francisco and then around Los Angeles. He picked up on her mood fast.

'What's up?'

'Nothing, just flagging a bit.'

'How about we take a trip to Santa Monica, get a bite to eat there? No, on second thoughts, we won't have the time.'

'I'll get something in my room.'

'Hell, no. Why don't we go and eat somewhere famous? You're not in LA every day.'

'I don't really have anything suitable to wear, but—'

'OK, hotel it is then.'

In her room she showered and blow-dried her hair again. With all the showering and the swimming, her curly hair was getting difficult to control. She headed down to the lobby just after eight o'clock. She was surprised to find that this time Langton had pulled out of his ever expanding wardrobe a light sweater and casual jeans.

'Turns out they don't do real food here, just sandwiches, so I booked us into a place the manager said was OK. Don't worry, Travis, I'll drive.'

He was an appalling driver and nearly killed them both just pulling the car out of the residents' car park and onto the wrong side of the road. On two occasions he almost drove over the central line. After that, the car slowly crawled along the road, looking for the right address.

Once inside the restaurant, Langton almost became a gentleman, guiding Anna to the table with his hand on her elbow. He seemed in a really good mood. A phone call from a sexy-voiced woman can do that to a man, Anna reflected.

'This is all right, isn't it?' he grinned, looking around once they had ordered.

'Anything come in from the station?' she asked.

'Let's, for half an hour, not discuss work.'

Surprised, she picked up her wine. 'Cheers!?'

It was so perfectly chilled and delicious that, after a few sips, her mood lifted too.

'Did you and old Jack get along, then?' Langton asked her suddenly.

'Yes. Oh, yes, he was a great dad. Not at home a lot, but when he was we had his complete attention, me and my mother. He was always arranging outings, you know picnics, theatre, that sort of thing. And he always turned up to watch me at gymkhanas. I was obsessed. I wanted my own pony so much, but we could never afford it, of course, with the upkeep, stable fees, horse-boxes, all the stuff that goes with it. But I'd ride every Saturday afternoon.'

'Did you win things?' he asked, draining his glass.

'Yes, I did. Once, Dad pinned my rosettes all over me, covering me from top to toe and took a photograph: firsts, seconds and thirds, all different colours,' she smiled.

'My daughter, Kitty, wants to take riding lessons, but I know what you mean. It costs. Then you've got to get jodhpurs, hard hats and stuff.'

'You can usually get second-hand kit from most stables that teach.' She paused. 'Does your wife ride?'

'No.' He paused. 'Kitty was eighteen months old when we married. I adopted her. Whenever I think I shouldn't really have got married, I remember Kitty. She's an important part of my life.'

She took a bite, thinking him finished and was surprised to find him actually continuing to discuss personal topics.

'When you lose someone you love unexpectedly like that, you get confused by your grief. When it doesn't go away, you start to look for something, anything that'll ease the pain. For a while the second marriage did that for me, especially having Kitty around, but . . .' He sighed. 'I'm sorry, Travis. You're too young – and you don't know any of this. My first wife died of a brain tumour. One night she goes to bed with a bad headache. Next morning, it's still there, but she goes to work. Anyway, she collapsed the next morning. Two hours later, she died.'

'I'm sorry,' Anna said, gently.

He smiled, painfully. 'So am I.'

When the first course arrived, the conversation ended. She'd never seen anyone eat so fast. She'd only had a few mouthfuls by the time his plate was empty.

197

'Do you have a train to catch?' she teased. He looked puzzled and just refilled their glasses.

'My mother used to say that to me, when I ate too fast.'

'Oh, sorry,' he grinned. 'Tell me about your mother.' He tore off some bread and smothered butter over it. 'Isabelle, wasn't it?'

'Yes.'

'Was she a good cook?'

Anna laughed. 'No. She was good at other things, but she was not a good cook.'

He leaned back, allowing the waiter to remove the dishes. 'So who cooked?'

'My father. He was brilliant.'

'Really?' he said, surprised.

'Yes, really good. We had home-baked breads and pies . . .' She paused as her salmon and Langton's monkfish were served.

He actually chewed slowly this time, savouring the taste. Then he went for it at his usual rate of knots. By the time Anna had finished her main course, his hands hadn't stopped flying; he seemed to have eaten the entire bread basket and he had refilled their glasses several times. Then as the dessert trolley was wheeled to their table and Anna was looking on it with interest, he checked his watch. 'No time; we've got to go.'

They arrived back at the hotel at a quarter to ten. If Langton had driven, it would have taken another half hour. As Anna got out of the car, he slid over to the driver's seat.

'Are you all right to drive?' she asked, worried.

'No, Travis, I'm paralytic. Just go to bed. I'll see you in the morning. Eight o'clock, in reception.'

She watched him drive away, hoping she hadn't been too boring. Perhaps the gymkhana conversation had gone on a tad too long. She had enjoyed being with him, though she doubted he felt the same way. As Anna entered her room, the phone started to ring. Alan Daniels's dentist was downstairs. Anna hurried down to meet him.

Arthur Klein was small and tanned. He wore dark glasses and smiled briefly as she shook his hand and thanked him for coming. He carried a large brown envelope and seemed ill at ease. 'I had arranged to meet, erm, Detective Langton here in the morning, but now I can't, I have a seven o'clock.'

'You schedule dental appointments at seven in the morning?' she said, surprised.

'It's an emergency. Lady bit on a nut and cracked a front cap – one, I hasten to add, I didn't fit, but when you work on movie stars' teeth, the hour is immaterial.'

He had an air of wealth about him: neatly pressed trousers, cashmere jacket and a top of the range Rolex which he glanced at constantly. She remembered that the cost of Alan Daniels's new teeth was more than any of them earned in a year.

'Is there somewhere we could talk? I only have ten minutes.'

The small annexe was full of cactus plants and the wicker chairs had seen better days, but it was empty. Klein refused a drink and sat, pinching at his trousers, looking around distastefully at the stained chair cushions. He tapped his thigh with the envelope.

'I have never been to this hotel.'

From his expression, Anna was pretty certain he wouldn't be back if he could help it.

'You're aware, I think, that I am no longer in possession of Daniels's X-rays, nor the sets of teeth I made up for assessment purposes.'

'Yes. My superior explained.'

'The work turned out to be quite extensive: three implants and a bridge, plus every tooth visible on what I call "the smile".' To illustrate, he ran a finger along his own top teeth and the bottom row. 'Now, I have to tell you these X-rays confused me.' He withdrew from the envelope the photocopies of the dental X-ray removed from Daniels's Queen's Gate flat.

'Confused you? Why?'

'Well, if these are indeed Mr Daniels's teeth, then this would have to be an X-ray of work done before I was brought in. I'm speaking from memory, since I no longer possess the X-rays I took of Mr Daniels's teeth. I did bridgework on both sides, you see, which is not shown here. But when I first examined him, Mr Daniels showed extensive work on the back molar teeth, in fact two gold caps. So, if this is his X-ray, it couldn't be recent.'

Anna leaned forward. 'But it could be an X-ray of Daniels's teeth, just from some time ago?'

'I would say this is not and never was, Mr Daniels's X-ray. Whoever these X-rays belong to had quite a distinctive cross bite.'

'Thank you very much.'

Klein nodded, passing her the envelope. 'I'm not surprised he's in trouble with the law. He was exceptionally rude and tried to defraud me. He refused to pay me when I had done the work. It was all very unpleasant.'

'Was your account eventually settled?'

'Only after I threatened a lawsuit. And then only on the condition I sent him everything: records, X-rays and teeth impressions.'

He checked his watch. 'I have to go. I am sorry if I haven't been very helpful.' He stood up. 'Perhaps if Daniels hadn't been in such a hurry—'

'Sorry, what did you say?'

'He was in a hurry. I had to move a whole block of appointments to fit him in. He said the operation was necessary for filming. I only obliged because he was recommended by a very high-powered agent here who sends me a lot of clients.'

In the car park, Anna walked with Klein towards a Bentley convertible, which he bleeped to unlock.

'When exactly was the appointment made by Daniels?'

Klein opened the driver's door. 'Mid-September, initially. It was a long course of treatment. His final appointment was just a couple of months back.'

'Would you say that Daniels really needed the dental work? Or was it purely cosmetic?'

Klein was fastening his seatbelt. Now he settled back into the leather seat. 'Well, the back teeth were not in good shape. He said he used to grind them. But the front teeth were not that bad.'

'So, he didn't really need "the smile"?'

Klein placed his hands into leather driving gloves and held the wheel. 'It was a better look. Truthfully, though, he could probably have gotten away with just bleaching them.'

He flashed his own whiter than white teeth in a farewell smile. Anna watched as he drove out of the car park.

Anna stood in front of the mirror and checked her own smile. Perhaps she should switch to that whitening toothpaste? She lay down on the hotel bed. If Daniels was about to undergo extensive dental surgery, he wouldn't have cared where he left his teeth marks. Could someone be so calculating? So devious?

She recalled finding her father sitting with a glass of brandy and staring in the firelight. She was young at the time and she sat on his knee, trying to draw him back to her from the dark place he occupied sometimes. He gave her a sad smile when she asked what the matter was and gently drew the hair away from her face.

It was inconceivable that something could be wrong with her father. 'Don't you feel well?' she asked worriedly.

He rested his head for a brief second against his child's shoulder.

'I'm fine, sweetheart. It's just sometimes Daddy works with such twisted, devious souls that their sickness clings afterwards, like a bad smell.'

'What does devious mean?'

He sipped his brandy. 'Saying you didn't do something when you know that you did; weaving lies to make everyone believe you didn't do this thing, but you know that you did and you enjoy the fact that your lies have fooled everyone. That's devious.'

'Did someone do something devious to you?' she asked.

'Yes.'

He said there was a man who had sworn he never hurt one little girl and because they had believed him, another little girl got hurt.

Years later, Anna found out from her mother that he was talking about a child killer, a case that had traumatized him deeply. Ever since then, the word 'devious' had a powerful memory association, which she now attached to Alan Daniels.

The door was rapped so hard that Anna almost shot out of her bed. She had been sleeping naked, so she grabbed a large bath towel on her way to the door.

'Who is it?' she asked.

'Me,' Langton said.

Anna unlocked her door. She was still tucking the towel tightly around her chest. He was leaning drunkenly against the frame. He waved the notes she had slipped under his door.

'So, this Klein guy came up trumps? The bastard planted those dental records in his apartment, right?'

She took a step back. 'I'd say it's a possibility.'

'Brilliant! Bloody brilliant!'

'Do want me to order some coffee?'

'Nope, going to crash out. G'night.'

'G'night.'

He tottered off down the corridor. She watched, peeking round her door, as he attempted to slot in the card to open his room door: there were three swipes and some swearing and cursing, before the green light bleeped and he disappeared inside. She shut her door, sighing: even if she had been stark naked when he appeared at her door, he probably wouldn't have noticed.

Anna had ordered coffee, orange juice and a blueberry muffin. What arrived was grapefruit juice, coffee and what appeared to be a banana muffin. There was no time to complain to room service, so she finished it.

She sat in the lobby waiting for Langton to pay their hotel bill. He looked like shit: unshaven and crumpled.

'Sleep well, did you?' she asked sweetly.

He grimaced, obviously hung over. She decided not to ask if he had gained 'vital information'. It did not seem likely.

202

When they arrived at the airport, she traipsed after him resignedly as he strode around, going to the wrong airline first, then swearing as they retraced their steps to the American Airlines desk. By the time their flight was called, Anna reckoned they had covered the entire airport. He really was useless at directions, she realized, and he was constantly checking for his passport, then the tickets.

They at last boarded the plane. As they weren't on the same row, she still could not ask him about his meeting with Angie the previous night.

It was not a long flight: under two hours. Langton had decided not to hire a car on their arrival in Chicago, but to use taxis. Even though the hotel was very inexpensive, it was really not bad. They were to meet up in the hotel lobby at two o'clock.

Langton was pacing up and down impatiently when she arrived. He had shaved and changed his suit and wore a white shirt and his usual dark navy tie.

'Where were you? Let's go. Taxi's waiting,' he snapped.

Tottering after him, she looked at her watch. She was five minutes early.

During the taxi ride to the Chicago Police Department he asked her to repeat her conversation with Klein. He sat with his eyes closed, listening. When she finished, she asked how his meeting with Angie had gone. He shrugged.

'Good. It was good.'

'I'm sure it was. But did you get any information?'

'What's that supposed to mean?' He seemed more tetchy than usual.

'Just that the meeting went on quite late. You do remember waking me up?'

'Course.' He gave her one of his direct stares. 'So, Travis . . . do you always sleep naked?'

Before she could think what to say, they arrived at the Chicago Police Department. He paid the cab fare and walked ahead of her.

'Detective Langton?' A uniformed officer with a crew cut spoke loudly as he approached them across the marble floor of the reception area.

Langton stood and he and the officer shook hands.

He flashed a smile at her. 'Hi, you must be Anna. I'm Captain Jeff O'Reilly.' He shook her hand, squeezing her fingers tightly. Yet another American with really great teeth, she thought.

'Good to meet you. Right, we can go up to Records first. Then, if you want a drive around, I got a patrol car outside.'

Two floors up, Langton and Anna followed O'Reilly through a cavernous room filled with thousands of files until they reached the Z section. O'Reilly removed a file, signed it out and took them into a small room off another corridor with just a table and chairs inside.

He held up a photograph of a blonde woman, with wide-apart brown eyes. 'This is Sadie Zadine. How she was.' Then he took out a second picture of the victim, in situ. She was lying face down, her hands tightly tied behind her back with a red lace bra. Her neck was wrapped in flesh-coloured tights. The identical MO to their victims; no suspect, no witness. Travis had noted one other similarity.

'Sadie's handbag, was that found?'

O'Reilly raised his eyebrows. 'Her what?'

'I think you call them purses. We call them handbags in England.'

'Ah. I'm with you,' O'Reilly said. 'No. No handbag, as you call it.'

Anna and Langton perused copies of the witness statements. Sadie was last seen bending down, talking to a john who was cruising in a car. She slid into the passenger seat and the car drove off. The other prostitutes thought the car was a Lincoln, dark green, but did not notice plates, or anything else that would help identify the driver.

They needed verification that Alan Daniels was filming in Chicago at the same time. O'Reilly took them to his office, where they could go through the lists of film companies. They contacted two location companies. The consensus seemed to be that any major film being shot in Chicago would more than likely employ their own location manager.

O'Reilly asked if they had a suspect and Langton explained they had a possible one. An actor.

O'Reilly suggested that they check with the local television station and offered them his desk. After at least twenty minutes of being redirected to various departments from accounts to costumes to maintenance, their break came. A television director advised them to look in 'Promotional Programs'. This resulted in a further flurry of phone calls until they located a popular show which interviewed book authors on tour as well as film actors promoting movies. Sadie was murdered recently enough to mean they might not only have a record of personalities interviewed that month but also have retained the tape.

O'Reilly was ready to go off duty. He told Langton that if they wanted to stay over an extra night, he would work alongside them the next morning.

'Thank you, but we have to go back to London,' Langton replied.

'So, you gonna tell me who your suspect is?'

Langton hesitated, before telling him. O'Reilly shook his head. 'Alan Daniels? I've never heard of him! I don't go to the movies. I don't have time to watch much TV. Anyway I get sick to death of real-life crime, so I don't need to watch a bunch of ten-year-old-looking women running around with guns. Anna, no offence. I just watch the Sport Channel.'

He shook their hands and wished them luck. 'You know, about finding Sadie's killer, we did give it our best shot. We had a whole team out for two weeks. But these johns, they could be transient, you know what I mean? This city is full of salesmen and business guys flying in, flying out. She was in the wrong place, wrong time. If you track down your guy, I'd like my ten minutes with him.' He gave a rueful smile and left.

As it turned out, the producer of *Good Afternoon, Chicago* was on maternity leave. Eventually they were put in touch with her researcher, who was recording a show for the following morning and said she couldn't check anything until after seven. However, if they gave her the name of the interviewee and the dates they wanted, her runner would start going through the files. Uneasily, Langton gave her Alan Daniels's name.

They returned to the hotel. It was after seven o'clock. They were to catch the first flight out of Chicago to Heathrow the following morning at nine. By now Langton was in a really bad mood: tired, hungry and frustrated. He retired to his room, saying he'd order from the room service menu and wait for the television station to make contact.

Two hours later, Anna's door was rapped so loudly that she panicked. She had been watching Channel 58, *COPS* on Court TV.

Langton was like a kid at Christmas. He was garbling his words, so she had to ask him to repeat them: 'They are sending over a fucking tape. He was here, in fucking Chicago, for the exact dates we want, when the interview took place.'

'My God.' As she stepped back, he dived in, closing the door behind him. He lowered his voice: 'I didn't say why we wanted it. All I said was we were conducting an enquiry.'

'When will it be here?'

'They're biking it over now, by courier. I'll call your room as soon as it arrives.'

She was just closing the door when he dived back in, asking if she had had anything to eat. He was so obviously excited, she found it infectious.

'I had a hamburger,' she smiled.

'How was it?'

'Fine.'

'Right, I'm going to have one.'

She closed the door behind him, her heart beating nineteen to the dozen. Whatever anyone said, this was too much of a coincidence. Alan Daniels had now been in all three US cities at the time of the murders. When the phone rang, she made a grab for it. It was Barolli. She judged it had to be after twelve in London.

'Is he with you?' he said.

'No. What is it?'

'We've got another murder.'

'What?'

'Can't talk. I've got to call him.'

'He's in Room 436.'

''kay. Goodnight.'

Anna put the phone down and sat on the edge of her bed.

'Oh my God,' she whispered.

Chapter Twelve

Anna tapped on Langton's door.
'It's open,' came his voice.

'Ma'am?'

She turned and saw the hotel receptionist walking towards her.

'This just came for Mr Langton.' The receptionist extended a white envelope. 'I need a signature: the courier is waiting downstairs. I've been trying to call Mr Langton's room, but his phone was busy.'

Anna took the bulky envelope. She signed for it and was thanking the receptionist when Langton appeared at the door.

'Is that it?'

She took a video cassette out of the package. 'Yes. Does your TV have a video player? Mine doesn't.'

'Shit, I don't know.'

Inside his room, Langton sat back on his heels and examined the TV set. Frustrated, he called reception and requested a video player urgently.

While Langton paced up and down, waiting for them to call back, Anna cast a look around his room: it was an untidy mess of discarded clothes, half-eaten hamburger and numerous empty cans of beer. There were wet towels trailing from the bathroom and piled up on the dressing-table were the contents of his pockets: coins, banknotes, receipts and his passport.

When the phone rang, Langton grabbed it. 'That's fine. I don't care how much. Just get me one up here.'

He slammed the phone down, swearing.

'Are you going to tell me what's happened in London?' she murmured. She took the wet towels into the bathroom. He must have left the shower running; there were puddles of water everywhere.

'You don't have to do that,' he snapped, when she returned.

'I know. I'm just doing it until you calm down.'

He slumped down on his bed with a sigh. 'Well, they have another victim. They found her early this afternoon. So far, she is unidentified, but it's the same scenario.'

'Where?'

'Just off the A3, not far from Leatherhead. Could be a copycat killing. I've told Barolli to see if we can bring back Mike Lewis. Shouldn't be hard. Barolli says his baby is driving him nuts. We don't have the case yet and he didn't have many details. But it's a fucking nightmare. The discovery is causing a lot of heat around our investigation; the media are rehashing our old press releases.'

He lit a cigarette.

'Commander's shitting herself. She's been on the blower to Barolli all afternoon; said to try and get back tonight. I said it was impossible. As it is, we're getting the first plane out tomorrow.'

He sat down on a stool by the dressing-table and started to flick through the stack of papers.

'O'Reilly gave me the press back issues on Sadie. Apparently, where she was found is pretty notorious.'

'Incongruous name, isn't it: Roseland?'

'Yeah. It's just twelve miles from all the glittering, brand spanking new skyscrapers. All those nice new little houses we saw being built are just a stone's throw away from crack dens and the hookers walk the street in broad daylight. There have been numerous murders in the same area, because of all the derelict houses. For a time, they also had a suspected serial killer on the loose.'

'But only Sadie has the same MO as ours.'

'Correct. But now with this latest murder, my being here is going to look like a waste of public money. Never mind letting that bastard kill again!'

'But you were told you didn't have enough evidence to arrest him.'

'I still don't, but I should be there instead of farting around in Chicago, San Francisco, LA.'

'Hold on – didn't you get anything from Angie?'

He frowned, stubbing out his cigarette. 'I got fuck all from her. Said the victim came in the club alone. Said she was very drunk, so they threw her out. Said the victim then walked towards a car that was kerb crawling. But she couldn't recall what the driver looked like.'

He checked his watch. 'Where's this fucking video? This fucking hotel!' There was a tap on the door. While the man from room service nervously connected the dusty video machine, Anna read the note attached to the tape, dated 12 July 1998. She turned it over.

'It says this was a live interview for *Good Afternoon, Chicago*, "an afternoon women's hour, which promotes the latest movies and authors on book tours". *Good Afternoon, Chicago* is a low-budget, local TV show.'

Langton took the note. 'This could be a waste of bloody time.'

As the man from room service backed out of the room, Anna slipped him five dollars. Before the door had closed behind him, Langton picked up the remote control and pressed 'play'. He patted the bed for Anna to sit beside him and watch.

He fast forwarded through the cooking section, a floral arrangement and a female writer, until at last the presenter was welcoming, 'all the way from England, to promote his latest film in Chicago: Alan Daniels!'

The small, invited audience applauded his arrival as he joined the interviewer on the sofa. Anna and Langton watched intently. He was casual but elegant in a cream jacket, a dark T-shirt and jeans. His hair was much longer than when they had last seen him. The overall impression he gave was of a reserved, rather shy man. He behaved in a modest, self-effacing way and gave a genuine-looking smile as he told the interviewer how pleased he was to be on the show. He created a ripple of laughter in the audience when he added that they were probably wondering who he was. The interviewer laughed and commented that everyone in the city would soon be aware of who he was and that they would now see a clip of his new film, *The Blue Diamond*.

The clip was short: a scene where Daniels was opening a safe vault. The diamond on a velvet cushion sparkled and sent shafts of blue light over his face, making his eyes seem bluer than blue.

At the end of the short interview he was sitting back in his chair, more relaxed, his legs crossed. He gave a slight wave of his hand and a small nod of his head to acknowledge the applause. He had charmed the audience and the interviewer. She reached over to shake his hand and he kissed it, in exactly the same way as he had kissed Anna's.

Langton sat, remote in his hand, rewinding. 'Want to see it again?'

'Yes,' Anna said, slightly stunned.

As they watched a second time, she wondered: could it be that a handsome movie star could be attracted to plain Anna Travis? Or was Langton right? Was he just pretending? In which case, she was in real danger. They watched it a third time, neither speaking, before Langton turned the TV off.

'What do you make of him, honestly?' he asked.

'Honestly, I don't know,' she said quietly. 'He seems charming, he listens attentively . . .'

'Puts on a good act.'

'It's funny. He's easy to look at and those eyes are amazing, but he didn't come over as particularly sexy.' Anna turned towards him. 'Do you think it's him? Is it him?'

He ejected the tape. 'Sometimes I don't fucking know any more.'

Anna straightened the bed cover. 'You've gone cold on him?'

He stuffed his hands in his pockets. 'Let's just say my intuition about him is shakier than it was. Something about him on video did it. It's just that . . . Jesus God, if I have been wrong, we've wasted so much bloody time!'

'What? What on the video?'

He looked up, lost for an answer. 'He was just so likeable, wasn't he?'

'I felt the same way at his flat, when he showed me the photograph. There was also something quite naive about him, but when I spoke to him on the phone, I got scared. Nothing he said, it was just . . . something.'

'Do you want a drink?' He opened the mini-bar with a flourish.

'No thanks. I'd better pack up. We've an early start.'

'OK, see you in the morning.'

'G'night.'

''Night.' He examined a miniature bottle of vodka. She noticed he didn't even look around as she let herself out.

In actual fact, she had already packed. She was just tired of discussing Alan Daniels.

Langton wasn't. He was even more obsessed by him. Alone, he inserted the tape again, fast forwarding to Daniels; he turned down the sound and continued watching, replaying it over and over.

Langton had set his alarm for five o'clock the next morning, so he could contact London for an update. Mike Lewis said that the victim was not a prostitute but a girl of sixteen. He had seen the body and, although her hands were tied behind her back, she had not been strangled with her tights but by someone's bare hands. He was doubtful it was their man. They already had a suspect in custody: the girl's stepfather.

The return flight was uneventful. They talked during their lunch and Langton told her what Lewis had said. He mentioned that he would bring the profiler in to look at the TV interview and see what he made of it. The rest of the time Anna read her book.

As they were told they were about to land, Langton leaned across to her and thanked her. 'You've been easy to travel with, Travis; I'm just sorry we're not going back with more.'

'I think you'll find, when we reassess everything, we've done some good work.'

He laughed softly. 'Thank you for that, Travis. A real boost to my confidence. I can't wait to "reassess", as you say.'

As the plane landed, they both wound on their watches six hours. It was now eleven o'clock in the evening and Langton planned to drop in at Queen's Park. The patrol car took Anna home and Langton said he would see her in the station first thing in the morning.

Mike Lewis was waiting for him at the station. He confided that, in all honesty, he was glad to be hauled back in. His small bundle of screaming joy had kept him awake since the day he'd come home from hospital

Lewis briefed Langton on the latest murder. It was not one of theirs. That was the good news. The bad news was that they still hadn't got a break in their own case.

'So we're hoping you've got something for us,' he said.

Langton was silent.

'Didn't it go well, then?' Lewis asked.

'No. I've come back empty-handed, Mike.'

'Shit. But Daniels was in all three places, right?'

'Yep. But since not one witness puts him in the frame, it's circumstantial. I'm starting to cool off on him.'

'Jesus Christ, that's one hell of an expensive cool.'

'Yep.'

Langton told Lewis to take himself home to the baby. There were only four people working the late shift in the incident room. Since he was too tired to start up a conversation with anyone, Langton went straight to his office, stacking his receipts and ticket stubs in a pile. He put the video down on a desk already piled high with outstanding memos and paperwork, then opened his bottle of Scotch and poured a heavy measure. If they took out Daniels, they were back to square one. No witness. No suspect.

Back home, Anna bundled her dirty clothes into the washing machine. She pottered around for a while; she didn't feel sleepy yet. She checked her answerphone. There were four messages, but when she pressed play, there was nothing there. Whoever had called had hung up.

Though she made sure her father's photograph was in the same position, she was not comforted: in fact, the opposite. The more she thought about it, the more certain she was that someone had moved it, before. She couldn't sleep, from all the tossing and turning. If Daniels had been in her bedroom, how in God's name had he got in? She knew there had been no forced entry. Since no one but she herself had used the flat, she decided that she would take the frame in for fingerprint tests. The plan comforted her and she fell asleep.

Though he had changed his shirt and shaved, Langton looked like he had slept in his chair. By the time Anna arrived the next morning, he was already in his office with Barolli and Lewis. Moira gave her a welcoming smile and asked if she'd had a good trip.

'Yes. But with three cities in three days, I didn't get to see much.'

Jean held up the video. 'This doesn't play on our machine. We're sending it over to the lab to get it converted.'

Anna began work on her American report. She picked up a pile of files from her desk. Beneath them were the photographs taken from Alan Daniels's flat.

'Shit. Did anyone want these?'

'What?'

'The photos from Daniels's flat. They were on my desk.'

Jean wagged her finger at Anna. 'Naughty, naughty. Barolli was looking for those.'

'I'm sorry. I'll give them to him.'

Moira sat on the edge of Anna's desk.

'So, what was it like?'

'You know, mostly hard work.'

She arched her eyebrows. 'I mean being alone with him for three days and nights?'

'Oh, Moira! I was just the chauffeur.'

'No candlelit dinners?'

'Give me a break. No! I've got to get my report done.'

'Your details about driving him around will make very interesting reading.' Moira was teasing her. Anna took a pretend swipe at her.

'I need expenses for both of you and receipts,' Jean called out.

'He has everything,' Anna replied, starting work. Moira wandered back to her desk.

It was after ten o'clock and Langton still had not come out of his office. Lewis was updating the board with the US murder dates, while Barolli stood beside him reading Langton's notes aloud. Arrows joined Daniels to each location.

Anna picked up the envelope containing the photographs. She hesitated and took them out, skimming through one after the other. They were all in social settings: Daniels lounging under a sunshade with a group of people in swimsuits; Daniels toasting someone with champagne at a candlelit table; Daniels leaning against a car. Only part of the car was visible.

Anna turned to the filing cabinets, overflowing with paperwork again. She read the statements from the Cuban waiter, then checked Red Leather's (Yvonne Barber) before returning the statements to the cabinet.

She tapped on Langton's door.

'Yes!' he snapped.

She went in to find him sitting at his desk in front of a mound of receipts, bits of paper and ticket stubs. 'Can you sort this crap out for me? And they have to be in order. Did you keep a record of everything you spent?'

'Yes.'

'Well, attach it to this lot. Jean's got to get it agreed, otherwise it'll be out of my pocket.'

'OK.'

He swept everything into a folder.

'Can I just show you something?' She handed him a magnifying glass and placed the photograph of Daniels leaning against the car in front of him. 'The Cuban couldn't say what make, but he thought it was a pale-coloured car. The other witness said it was a light colour. When we brought the Cuban in, he was shown a number of vehicles. He couldn't pick one of them out, but that tiny bit of the rear bumper we had on the CCTV footage wasn't one of the new Mercedes, but a Mercedes about thirty years old, according to Mike.'

'So?'

'Well, look at this photograph. You can't see much of it, but it's a Mercedes, isn't it? And it's a light, creamy colour.'

Langton looked at the photograph with the magnifying glass.

'Fuck!'

He leaned back, frowning. 'We've got him down as owning a Lexus when Melissa was murdered, haven't we?'

'Yes. Maybe that's not his Mercedes, but we know he hired one in the States. So he must like them.'

Anna continued: while they had confirmed that Daniels had been driving a Lexus for the last nine months, they had not thought to check on other vehicles Daniels owned before that period.

Langton walked to Anna, cupped her face in his hands and kissed her.

'I love you, Travis.'

He bellowed for Lewis and Barolli.

Anna returned to her desk, where she continued typing up her report. Simultaneously, both Lewis and Barolli were checking with the DVLA, the MOT register and Daniels's motor insurance company.

Langton shouted for Travis.

'Yes?'

He seemed in great spirits, flourishing a list in his hand.

'Daniels exchanges his cars like most people change underwear.'

He listed the number of vehicles Daniels had owned. As his wealth increased, he went from one expensive car to another, often changing them within a few months of each other. But the car they were most interested in was a convertible pale blue Mercedes 280SL, circa 1971, the car Daniels still owned up until the time of Melissa's murder. The reason they had slipped up was that Daniels used a company name so it had not been listed under personal ownership.

The news spread like a bushfire and Anna was roundly congratulated. Then came the bad news: there was no record of the Mercedes being sold or under new ownership. Daniels would have to come in again for questioning.

'We've still got insufficient evidence to arrest him,' Langton told Anna. 'We must do this all by the book. It'll be irregular to go and pick him up at his flat, just in case we've got something that incriminates him. We could be accused of failing to give him his rights. We bring him in and caution him, but make it clear he's not being charged with anything and that he has the right to be legally represented. That means another session with Radcliff at his side.'

He gestured for her to come closer, then said quietly, 'When he comes in, I don't want you around.' Then he turned his head to bellow, 'Lewis! Let's get him in!'

Contrary to expectations, Daniels agreed to come to the station straight away. Nor did he insist Radcliff be present.

In fact, their suspect did not appear to be fazed at all. He was even more charming than the time before and seemed to be making an effort to be as helpful as possible. He sat quietly in the interview room with Langton and Lewis while he was read his rights. Then he brought out a small pocket book. He explained that he did buy and sell his cars in quite rapid succession, for, although he had a resident's parking bay, if he went away filming he did not like to leave the cars unattended for lengthy periods. He had been enquiring about renting a garage space in the area for some time, but had not been lucky so far. They were asking astronomical rents.

Langton then asked about the Mercedes-Benz. Daniels smiled, relaxedly. The Mercedes was one of his favourites, he said, but even in the Queen's Gate area a soft-top car was too attractive to thieves.

'The roof was constantly being slashed. It seems any yob passing with a knife—'

'You sold it?' Langton asked, incredulously.

'Worse. I was going to. I had already stopped the insurance. Then I had a prang in it, and so that was that.'

'You sold it?' Langton repeated.

'Well, you could call it that.'

'What do you mean?'

'It went to the crusher. It would have cost a fortune to repair and it had rust, as well. So I paid for it to be destroyed.'

Langton felt the ground moving beneath his feet. Every time they took a step forwards, back they went. He took down the name of the crushing yard and released Daniels. With an equally despondent Lewis, Langton stared from the window, watching Daniels being led out via the rear entrance towards his chauffeur-driven black Mercedes.

Anna was glad she had not had to face him. The breaker's yard was contacted and they confirmed over the phone that Alan Daniels's Mercedes had been crushed into a two-foot square box.

The date was the day after Melissa Stephens was murdered.

Jet lag kicked in for Anna around four o'clock in the afternoon. As for the rest of them, from everyone being so 'up', they had all come crashing down.

Until Barolli pointed out that if Alan Daniels had taken the car to be crushed, it meant that he had lied about not being in London.

When Anna went to see Langton to ask if she could go home, he sighed: 'Yeah. Why not? Fuck all is happening here.'

She rubbed her forehead, which was throbbing. 'But, surely the fact he owned the same type of car Melissa was seen getting in, means—'

'It means nothing,' he interrupted. 'Not without proof it was his car, proof he was driving it and proof that whoever killed her was the driver. It is all circumstantial. It would never even get to trial. If it did and he walked, it would be over. We'd never be able to get him back. That's the bloody law.'

'Is the profiler coming tomorrow?'

'Yeah, he's coming.'

'See you tomorrow, then.'

'Yeah, tomorrow and tomorrow.'

Once she was home, Anna took a couple of aspirin. She felt really awful. Perhaps if they had good news, she would have felt better. All she wanted was to go to bed and sleep it off. She checked her answerphone, remembering to press 'replay' for any calls that had come in when she was away. When the electronic voice informed her that the last caller had withheld their number, she deleted everything.

She went back to the kitchen and picked up a pair of rubber gloves. She took the photo frame from her bedroom and, turning it over, eased back the small clips. She had decided to take the photograph out of the frame, then wrap the materials in a plastic bag for the lab, taking care not to touch the silver surrounds. She carefully placed the glass and frame in the bag and put it in her briefcase.

This particular photograph had been on her mother's bedside table for years, making it the first thing she saw in the morning and the last thing at night. Curious, Anna drew closer: stuck between the photograph and the backing was an envelope. She got into bed before opening it.

She recognized her father's handwriting. On the front of the envelope he had written 'To My Beloved'. Inside, there was a single sheet of writing in his neat and closely written hand.

Bella mia,

I cannot make what happened into something as simple as a bad dream. If I could, I would. I know how it affects you and rules the way you are. I love you with an unconditional love that accepts whatever you can give me. But I am nevertheless concerned. By allowing your fears to rule your existence, you are making the animal a constant presence. To walk outside the fear will make you stronger. I beg you to let me help you. Bella, you are too perfect, too beautiful to make this home a prison, albeit one filled with your sweetness and your darling soul.

I love you.

Papa.

Papa was the name Anna's mother always used for her husband. Anna reread the letter, confused. It seemed like a letter of encouragement to a victim, but she had no idea about what it referred to. There was no date.

219

She folded it and slipped it beneath her pillow, but she kept on seeing the neat, slanted handwriting and the word 'animal'. She tossed and turned, wondering if something terrible had happened to her mother.

The phone rang. It took Anna a few moments to sit up in the dark and find it.

'Anna,' the soft voice breathed.

'Yes.' This time she knew exactly who it was.

'Welcome back.'

'Thank you.'

'Did you have a good trip to Manchester?' he asked.

'Yes, yes I did.'

'But you didn't go to Manchester, did you?'

She felt her body tense.

'I called the station. I was told you were in the States.'

'Yes, yes I was. It was very unexpected.'

'Did you have a nice time?'

'Yes.'

'Whereabouts in the States did you go?'

Her hand felt clammy, from holding the receiver too tightly. 'It's very late, Alan; I'm just going to bed.'

'Late?' he said, teasingly. 'It's only ten o'clock.'

'I know, but I'm very tired. What do you want?'

'I've got tickets for the ballet again. You said you liked the ballet, so when I was given them, I immediately thought of you. It's *Giselle*.'

'Oh. When are the tickets for?'

'This Thursday, at Covent Garden. Are you free?'

'Can I get back to you, Alan? Just in case I'm on night duty. I haven't got my schedule yet.'

'Well, don't leave it too long.'

'I'll call you tomorrow. Goodnight.'

'Goodnight, Anna.'

She took slow, deep breaths and slipped her hand beneath the pillow to touch her father's letter. It had been written to comfort her mother, but it now calmed her. She climbed out of bed and checked the windows, then bolted the front door. As she did so, she had a flashback to her childhood home. There were a number of locks on their front and back door, window locks, security alarms. Had someone frightened her mother? Was that why she had been so cautious all her life?

Anna became certain that something had invaded her family home. The 'animal' her father had described had made her mother a prisoner. As she recalled her day-to-day interactions with her parents, Anna realized that her mother hardly ever left the house; never on her own and only occasionally with her husband. It was Anna's father who came to the gymkhanas. Always him. She turned to look at his picture. For a second, she had forgotten that she had taken it from its frame because she thought it had been touched by strange hands inside her house.

Remembering, she felt no fear; in fact the reverse. She was angry that she had allowed Alan Daniels to unnerve her not once, but twice. If he had some sick plan to frighten and stalk her, then he had chosen the wrong target.

Chapter Thirteen

'I've asked my neighbours,' Anna said. 'No one saw anyone loitering around the block of flats, the garage, or on my floor.'

Langton nodded, lips pursed.

'I could be mistaken, but I thought we should have it dusted for fingerprints just in case.'

He rocked back in his chair. Anna was wearing a new shirt, tight black skirt and new shoes. The plastic bag containing the picture frame was on her knee. She looked good; he knew he didn't. But she also seemed different, more positive.

'So you're agreeing to go out with him?'

'Yes. I think we should grab at anything we can.'

'Well, as long as he doesn't make a grab at you.'

'I can deal with him,' she said. 'Of course, I'd be wired and I could – could I?' – she hesitated – 'Could I have a small hidden camera?'

He laughed. 'Travis, with such a high-profile case, I don't see why the Met wouldn't get you an entire film crew!'

She looked momentarily confused.

Langton's face became serious. 'There can be no camera, no wire. It would be too dangerous for you if he realized he was being monitored. Also, we can't make this look like entrapment. If we filmed him, it couldn't be used in a court; likewise any tapes we made. It sounds good, but it only works in films, not real life. Speaking of which, you have to be very careful, Anna. You must not place yourself in any danger. No going back to his place, do you hear me? Keep it out in the open.'

She passed him the photo frame. 'I'll get his prints when we're at the ballet.'

He shook his head. 'No, you won't. You've been watching too much *Murder, She Wrote.* Just leave that bit to us.' Lewis tapped on the door and came straight in. He said their profiler had watched Alan Daniels's interview three times and was ready to discuss it.

The remainder of the team had gathered in the incident room. The room fell silent, as Michael Parks moved slowly from one victim's photograph to the next, before turning to face his audience.

'I could be wrong. My earliest impression was that we were dealing with a psychopath. If you've got the right suspect, the killer is not a serial psychopath. After watching him on the video, I am convinced that Alan Daniels is a sociopath. It's not much different clinically and it's a no less dangerous breed, but in my experience, sociopaths are by far more cunning, intelligent and personable than psychopaths. They also don't experience fear. They are exceptionally dangerous because their destructiveness is not easily recognized and their talents often bring them admiration, unfortunately.'

Parks stood in front of the flip chart with a thick black felt-tip pen. 'I say unfortunately, because sociopaths are intrinsically evil.' He started to make a long list. 'If a suspect has demonstrated these symptoms, then you can be pretty sure he is a sociopath.'

Parks wrote in large block print:

1 Is he self-centred and egocentric?

'From watching the tape of the Chicago interview, I would say without doubt.'

2 Does he manipulate others by reading very quickly their
   vulnerabilities?

223

He tapped the page with his pen. 'I would say yes. Did you notice that his interviewer was nervous? He put her at her ease by displaying shyness himself, letting her feel she was the one in control. Very quickly, he had her in the palm of his hand.'

3 Does he feel little guilt, shame or remorse? Is he capable of weaving a web of lies and deceit? Above all, does he feel impervious to discovery?

Langton met Anna's eyes. They both knew this was correct. Parks now marked up number four.

4 Does he have a superficial charm: does he relate well with other people at a superficial level?

Parks tapped his pen again. 'Your suspect is an actor. What better profession?' Langton leaned forward, frowning. He could feel the hairs on the back of his neck prickle. 'Watch the videotape again,' Parks went on. 'Look at the way he uses his charm. Watch how he even manages to manipulate the audience.' He turned back to the board.

5 Is he able to love? Or to demonstrate long-term loyalty? Can he feel normal human empathy? Can he possess deep affection for others?

'A sociopath only pretends to have those feelings. I can assure you, they are false.'

Langton thought about how Alan Daniels had refused to use the word 'mother' and how he refused to acknowledge his foster mother. Anna found herself agreeing with everything the profiler said. It all fit Alan Daniels.

6 Does he have an attitude of superiority and an inflated arrogant self-appraisal?

'Did you notice at the end of the interview, how he almost gives a royal wave, with that slight bow of his head?'

'Fuck,' muttered Langton. 'I hadn't picked that up at all.'

7 Does he use others? Is he a cheat? A liar? Does he lie for the pleasure of it, as well as for what he can get out of his lies?

Anna was writing furiously in her notebook.

8 Does he pursue instant gratification? Does he use others for his own self-aggrandizement?

Langton whispered to Anna, 'Buys a new car every six months!'

She nodded and whispered back: 'What about the furniture in his flat?'

9 Has he demonstrated radical mood swings, such as from amicable to angry? Maybe even displaying a trace of violence?

Parks turned over the page to start on a new sheet.

'Now, it seems your suspect is not married and never has been. He appears to have had few long-term relationships. This is another symptom.'

10 Few close friends. Frequently unsettled and agitated. Does not like to be alone. Becomes agitated in his own company.

Mike Lewis shook his head. He brought up the fact they had all seen numerous photographs of Daniels surrounded by friends. Could they all have been just work colleagues?

Parks removed his jacket, which showed sweat stains under his armpits and continued, 'Most sociopaths not only have superior intelligence, they are remorseless egocentrics. To them, people are only objects to be manipulated. If they do have a relationship, it is a very exploitative one.

Do you understand? To them, people exist only to meet their needs. To them, a person is not a separate human being. He or she is just a means to an end.'

Langton put his hand up. 'What about sex?'

Parks stared at him. 'Go on.'

'Well, these murders were sexual: rape and sodomy.'

The profiler sucked in his breath. 'Indeed. OK. While a sociopath can enjoy lustful sex, it's never sex with any real intimacy. They are incapable of falling in love. Nor do they feel commitment: people are like Kleenex to them, easily discarded.'

'Are they as inclined to kill as a psychopath would be?' Barolli asked.

Parks nodded. 'Yes. There are, however, two types of sociopath. One is a passive predator: the type that can con an elderly woman out of her pension and steal from a cripple. They have little remorse and can be just as callous, but the passive sociopath rarely kills. It is the aggressive sociopath that is the most dangerous. They show a complete lack of remorse and have the ability to depersonalize their victims. The victim is just another object.'

Anna lifted her hand. 'The suspect has not shown himself to be very aggressive; quite the opposite, in fact.'

Parks nodded again. 'Good point. However, you must understand that this aggression is very much under control. Though you may not have seen it, it's there; when it surfaces – he kills.'

Parks walked along the gallery of victims, tapping each photograph with his pen. 'There will exist a reason for choosing these sad women, a hatred already in place. But with this young girl, Melissa . . .' He stared at her picture. 'He seems to have made a mistake. She was in the red–light area. She was blonde with brown eyes. Even so, he didn't control himself. Probably he thought: "what the hell? I'll kill her, too." It is as emotionless as that. That is not to say that his method of killing up until then had not been calculated.'

Anna passed her notebook to Langton, indicating something she had written. He handed it back, nodding his agreement. Anna had speculated that the fact that a nice girl like Melissa had climbed into Daniels's car – a fact which had been confusing, not only to the police, but to her own family – was understandable if she recognized him.

When Parks broke up the meeting, many of the team gathered around him to ask more questions. There was an undercurrent of tension in the incident room: Alan Daniels had regained prime-suspect status. There was an adrenalin rush, as if the hunt was closing in on the killer.

Anna waited for Langton in his office. As he shut the door, he whistled: 'I take back what I said about him. This time he pulled out all the stops.'

'He had more to work with, too. That probably helped.' Anna checked her watch. 'I should make that call.'

'Yeah, I know. I've asked Parks if you and he could have a private talk in here. He can guide you through what you should say and how you should say it. But we have to be really careful this doesn't come over as entrapment.'

After what they had just listened to, Anna felt grateful for Langton's idea.

'But I wanted to have a word, before he comes in. I wanted to say that if you've changed your mind, Anna, if you don't want to do this, then it's understandable; all you have to do is say so.'

'Thanks. I'm up for it.'

'I'll get him, then.'

After a moment he returned with Michael Parks, who listened intently as Anna gave details of Daniels's call to her home.

'Right! He must be feeling very threatened to take such a risk, to make personal contact with someone in the investigation. He must also believe he can manipulate you. He must already believe that *you* are no threat. You must play him at his own game. If I am correct, this man has made a career of deceit and charm and he is using you; remember, at all times, never to lower your guard. The meaning of life for him is in the power to take whatever he wants. He is assuming that you trust him and he will continue to try to appear very trustworthy.' He looked up at Anna. 'Would you mind recalling exactly what occurred at your first proper meeting with the suspect?'

Anna described how Alan Daniels had shown her the photographs in his wallet; how he had seemed overly familiar, placing his arm round her shoulder; how he had kissed her hand when she was leaving.

Parks nodded. 'He is a chameleon. He has an ability to read your fragilities – anyone's fragilities – and to become whoever you want him to be. He will behave in whatever manner he is certain will create an almost instant bond between you. From that first meeting, he knew he could be tactile with you, even though you were there as a member of the search team.'

Anna's stomach was churning; she suspected Parks was right.

Parks continued: 'He showed you something very private, the pictures inside his wallet. He drew you in by saying that he had never shown them to anyone else. He displayed his vulnerability: the poor, suffering little boy haunting the successful adult. He is saying, "No matter how successful I am, I can't forget the wretched life I came from."'

Anna nodded. She had felt compassion for him, which he must have recognized. He had been confident enough to call her that same night. And if he had broken into her flat, he knew even more about her vulnerabilities now.

'What does she watch for?' Langton asked.

Parks hesitated.

'Apart from the obvious, I mean. How should she interact with him to gain his confidence and use it for our benefit?'

'It won't be easy. He is an expert at conning and lying about himself. But there may be what I call a "leakage". If you can play him, draw him out, you just might get him to miscalculate, just go that bit too far – maybe by boasting, or telling a story about one of his more anti-social actions. At no time show you are disgusted, horrified, or repelled by what he tells you. Give no indication of what you really think. You might draw out of him something revealing.'

Langton brought up the dental X-ray discovered at the flat. Parks believed it to be, without doubt, planted by Daniels himself. 'If he had anything in the flat that constituted a risk to himself, I guarantee it would have been destroyed.' He would also have been audacious enough to have selected the photos that were later confiscated and now in their possession. 'He probably left them on display.'

Langton nodded. 'They were easily discovered. But one photo shows the vehicle we are certain that Melissa Stephens was last seen getting into.'

Parks shrugged. 'Isn't that the same vehicle which had been sent to the breaker's yard? You see, even if there was a connection, it cannot be traced, or used. His ego is such that he believes he is above suspicion. He knows you have nothing but circumstantial evidence, which will not stand up in court.'

Parks took a deep breath. 'I believe he is very dangerous right now. He might be preparing to kill again and I don't want to scare anyone, but it's possible he's focusing on Detective Sergeant Travis as his next victim. This possibility might excite him because of its danger and audacity. To commit a murder right under your noses would be a great turn-on. I cannot impress on you strongly enough how dangerous this man is.'

'And you have no doubts about it being him?' Langton asked hesitantly.

'None whatsoever. When we first met, I wasn't really up to speed with the enquiry. But since then I have read all the reports and the evidence to date and lack of it. And I believe, as I am sure you do, that Alan Daniels is your killer.'

Langton confessed, unsteadily: 'I have to tell you, I came to the opposite conclusion when I watched his TV interview.'

Parks smiled reassuringly. 'I'm not surprised. Unless you know what to watch for, those tell-tale signs I mentioned, it's difficult to appreciate how clever he is. Only then do you glimpse what is behind the mask.'

As both men turned their attention to Anna, she attempted a brave smile.

'So, when Anna makes the call, exactly how should she handle him?'

'Approach him with a secret,' Parks advised her. 'You'll have to make Daniels believe that you are seeing him without your superior's knowledge. And that you believe him to be innocent. If Daniels has the slightest suspicion you're acting on orders, he will not open up. He must believe you fancy him and for that to happen you'll have to stroke his ego.'

'So he'll trust me.'

'Exactly: gain his trust, but take it very slowly, let him draw it from you rather than blurt it out; you must not make him suspicious.'

They spent another fifteen minutes closeted in Langton's office. Anna virtually had a script to work from and she had agreed to make the call to Daniels at half past six. She returned to her desk; Parks and Langton remained together.

As soon as Anna had left, Langton asked just how dangerous it was to use her. Parks shrugged.

'I would have thought I had made that perfectly clear. She must not at any cost go somewhere alone with him, but stay out in the open. He will at first only want to pump her for information. I hope you get what you need before he wants to take the interaction a step further. I would also say the backup and surveillance must be exceptionally well-orchestrated. Remember, you have had him in for questioning; he will recognize the officers he has seen here. You don't want him to distrust her; if he does, he will try another tactic.'

'Which would be what?'

'Hard to say.'

Langton was uneasy, but having come this far, he decided they would go ahead. After Parks had left, he contacted the Gold Group commander and asked for a meeting. He would need a new backup team unseen by Daniels and unknown to Anna. He would also ask for an extension on the enquiry as he felt they were getting closer to making an arrest.

Next Langton called in Mike Lewis and handed over the photo frame Anna had brought in. When he had told Parks earlier that there was a possibility their suspect had broken into Anna's flat, he got yet another warning. Parks believed without doubt that Alan Daniels was targeting Anna; if they could prove he had illegally broken into her flat, they could arrest him and hold him in custody for breaking and entering. The hope was that because nothing had been stolen, the moving of the photograph might be the 'leakage' Parks mentioned. It would be something to hold him for, but for how long? Langton was doubtful they would get a result, sure that if Daniels had broken into her flat, he would have worn gloves.

Mike Lewis sent the frame over to the forensic lab. As Anna's prints were already on record, as were those of all the officers, they could very quickly get a result. Langton would orchestrate lifting Daniels's prints to make a match.

To give Anna some peace and quiet whilst she made the call, she was given Langton's office. The phone call would be taped and she had by now learned her script off by heart.

She sat at Langton's desk, in his chair. He sat opposite, listening with a set of headphones and gave her the signal to make the call. Daniels's phone rang four times before he picked it up.

'Yes?'

'Alan, is this you?'

'Yes.'

'It's Anna.'

'I know; I'd just about given you up. These tickets are really like gold dust. It's Darcey Bussell dancing a special gala evening.'

'I'm sorry, I just couldn't get a minute alone.' She lowered her voice. 'I'm still at the station.'

'I see. OK, I understand. Well, it's not *Giselle*, but *Swan Lake*.'

'Oh, that's fantastic.'

'Yes, she's brilliant. I don't know if you read about it, but she hurt her ankle and so it's been touch and go as to whether she would be dancing.'

'Gosh! Do you know her?'

'No, but it's been in all the papers. We might be able to go backstage and say hello.'

'Oh, heavens, what should I wear? Is it evening dress?'

'Yes. Now, shall I pick you up?'

'Oh yes, thank you. Should I wear a long dress?'

'Well, they don't dress up as much as they used to do, but it's not casual casual. I'll be wearing an evening suit.'

'What time should I be ready for?'

'Quarter to seven. Sounds early but there's a champagne reception and I've booked a table at the Ivy so it'll be quite a late night. Is that all right?'

'I'll have to ask if I can get off early, but I'm sure it'll be all right.' She dropped her voice to a whisper. 'I won't be able to tell anyone. I don't think they would approve.'

There was a pause; he laughed softly.

'I understand – so what's your address?'

She gave it to him; he confirmed he would be there at a quarter to seven. 'I'm looking forward to seeing you again, Anna.'

'Thank you. Thank you for asking me.'

He cut off the call. Langton removed his headphones as Anna took a deep breath and replaced the receiver.

'Well done,' he said softly.

She showed him her shaking hands and grinned.

'Do you have a decent frock to wear?' he asked meaningfully.

She laughed. 'Frock? What's that?'

'I'm just saying, there's no need for you to overspend your budget. We might be able to hire one for you from somewhere.'

'Of course I have a dress,' she protested. 'It's not like I never go anywhere.'

'The right dress? For a formal occasion?'

'I don't believe this! Yes, I have clothes for every occasion, sir!'

'Don't joke about this, Travis, and don't think for a second that I like it. Now, be ready on time tomorrow. Don't let him into the flat. You will have backup in the theatre and in the restaurant. Scotland Yard are organizing a team. You will be protected.'

'I only hope they'll be able to get tickets. I've heard they're like gold dust!' she joked.

'Get out,' he said gruffly.

When Anna returned to the incident room, there were quiet appraisals of her. Moira looked at her and gave her a wink.

'I've got a great sequinned job if you need it.'

Anna grinned. 'I doubt it'll fit, Moira. I'm not that well-endowed.'

The fact that she was able to joke eased the tension in the room. They started to discuss Michael Parks and how much he had impressed them. Anna was grateful to have his script. She just hoped she would be able to put it into practice. She had never been undercover before, just as she had never been to anything as glamorous as a gala night at the Royal Opera House. Nor had she ever dined at the Ivy. She doubted that she would have to put on much of an act at being overawed. Whatever happened, this was going to be a night she would remember.

By Wednesday morning, the lab had made contact. They had matched Anna's prints easily. They verified that there were three other prints. One was too smudged to ascertain any identification but they were more hopeful of obtaining the other two. It would take more time, since the two prints were lying on top of each other.

There was a new technology for lifting one print away from another, separating them into two clear prints. The method was a major break-through in digital enhancement of crossover prints but at first it had been deemed unacceptable in a court of law. Recently, this had changed as the benefits of the technique had proven significant. Unfortunately, the closest scientist qualified to use it was in Nottingham. She had travelled down on the early morning train.

By the time Langton arrived at the lab, the forensic scientist had treated the fingerprints with DFO. She explained it was a new chemical, similar to Ninhydrin, which becomes fluorescent when exposed to a light source. After this was processed, the DFO would provide and improve ridge detail on the photo. It was, of course, the ridges of fingerprints that enabled identification to take place, as no person had the same ridges as another.

The process was slow and when she removed one set from on top of the other set, the ridge detail appeared blurred, displaying poor general continuity.

Langton sighed, certain they were wasting their time.

However, the scientist wasn't finished yet. She was becoming irritated by Langton's impatient hovering and the way he constantly looked over her shoulder.

'It's going to take some time,' she warned him. 'Now I need to use the photographs to start image enhancing and at each stage, the accuracy of the prints has to be documented.'

'How long is it going to take?'

'About four hours.'

'Four hours?' he snapped.

Her thin lips were being drawn into a thinner line by the minute.

'If this is to be used as evidence, I can't cut corners. Every print has to be documented through a photographic record listing each stage of the enhancement. As it is I've agreed to prioritize this for you, so you'll just have to be patient.'

'Do you think you'll get something?'

'I wouldn't be here if I didn't.'

He looked at his watch. It was almost twelve. He gave her his mobile phone number and asked her to contact him as soon as there was a result. Then he went to Scotland Yard to discuss the surveillance and report to the commander on the new developments.

Steering the commander into orchestrating a round-the-clock team had taken some persuasion, especially with two officers already outside Alan Daniels's home. Langton's request for officers in two locations, the Opera House and the Ivy, resulted in a heated argument which he had won. Alan Daniels's tickets were in the front row of the dress circle, which made them among the best seats in the house. All the seats close to them were sold so it was arranged instead that two female officers should act as ushers.

While the Ivy did not have a table available at short notice, there were always a lot of paparazzi waiting outside the fashionable restaurant to photograph stars coming and going. Two officers were put in place to act as photographers, another two would tail the couple on foot and there was a backup car on standby.

Instead of a depleted team, Langton now had a full deck. There would be undercover officers positioned at every exit of the Opera House and the

Ivy. The cost was astronomical, as the commander took care to point out, but she had given way on everything. The murder that had occurred when Langton and Travis were overseas had unnerved her. Though a different suspect had been apprehended, the fact that there was a serial killer on the loose and the probability of another murder soon, had finally hit home. So had Michael Parks's report; not only had he predicted more murders, but he had also supported the theory that Alan Daniels was their serial killer.

Langton relayed the latest information to the team. He had received a call from the forensic scientist about the photo frame. She had two clear prints which had already been run through the database. The results were nil. The intruder had no police record. Langton listed the details of the surveillance team and where they would be located. This, Anna knew, he was directing at her, to boost her confidence.

After the briefing, he gave her one last opportunity to pull out. To his relief, she refused again, earning his admiration for the way she was handling herself. She was even coming into the station the following morning to work, though she consented to take the afternoon off to get her hair done at departmental expense.

At home that evening, Anna stared at a bed strewn with discarded clothes and thought, ruefully, that her indecision about what to wear to the ballet had at least made the time fly. She finally decided to wear a cream sheath dress and carry a cashmere wrap. Then it was back to the wardrobe to dig around for the matching shoes she was once sure she had. When she couldn't find them she sat back on her heels, crying with frustration.

She took a deep breath to get hold of herself. Her nerves were raw. There would be ample time to buy a new pair of shoes when she went to the hairdresser the next afternoon. She told herself firmly to stop getting into such a state. From her top drawer, she took out a small evening bag, decorated with seed pearls. She opened it carefully: she could smell her mother's perfume.

She took out the letter she had found inside the photo frame and reread it. As she sat with the bag in her lap, tears welled up in her eyes as she remembered how, after her mother died, she had found this very bag, which had contained her mother's make-up. She had sat down at her mother's dressing-table and opened the lipstick. It was a pale coral colour. She had applied the lipstick moulded by her mother's mouth. It felt like a last kiss goodbye.

Thinking about her mother's warm smile made her cry. Afterwards she felt calmer, as she thought about the evening she would spend with Daniels. She selected various items to put into the pearl bag. How good that it had been Isabelle's. She slipped in a pair of her father's cufflinks as well. Now her parents' love would surround her and between the two of them, she felt she would be protected from evil.

Thursday was rainy and time dragged by in the incident room. Anna kept tapping her watch, thinking it must have stopped. Finally, two o'clock came. She knocked, then put her head around Langton's door.

'I'm off now.'

'OK,' he said casually.

'So, see you in the morning?'

'You'll see me before then,' he said, pulling a notepad out of his desk drawer. 'I'll be at your place to see you kitted out.'

'Oh, will you?'

He started writing. 'I'll also be waiting for you to come home.'

'Oh. See you later, then.'

'Yep, see you later.'

He didn't look up when she left. Not until the door closed, did he chuck the pen aside. He'd been watching her through his office blinds. The funny little carrot top was getting to him. He hadn't felt protective about anyone for a long time. He was certain there was no possibility of it developing into anything other than a friendship. Anna was not, in any way, his type. In fact, he didn't even find her attractive. But there were good reasons to feel protective.

Once Anna had left the station, Langton came out of the incident room to have a quiet word with his team. He said that if the fingerprints found in Anna's flat turned out to be Daniels's, he would arrest him straight away. He was not prepared to let her take any unnecessary risks.

Lewis put his head to one side. 'It's not that much of a risk, with her covered on all sides.'

'Well, tonight I'm going to check out her security personally. If it turns out he's been inside her flat then she's a target.'

A few looks were exchanged but no one said anything. Involuntarily, their gazes returned to the noticeboard, where the row of dead women's faces now included the victims from the US. Anna Travis had gone up another notch in their admiration. They were all hoping no harm could possibly come to her.

Chapter Fourteen

Anna wore a plastic shower cap to protect her hair and keep it straight. Her new, rather boyish cut was modern, almost punkish and the highlights made her thick, red hair seem lighter; it suited her.

A new pair of cream high-heeled sandals matched her dress perfectly. It was five o'clock when the doorbell rang. She was sitting at her dressing-table, wrapped in a kimono and applying her make-up. When she opened the door, Langton grinned, indicating her shower cap.

'Very flattering,' he said, walking in.

She only now realized she still had the shower cap on.

'It stops the steam from the bath making my hair curl.'

'You carry on with what you were doing. I'll make myself at home.'

'Help yourself to coffee,' she said, closing her bedroom door. She could hear him clattering around in her kitchen.

'Do you want one?' he yelled through the wall.

'No, thank you.' She had pulled off the shower cap and ran her fingers through her hair as the hairdresser had demonstrated. It fell into place perfectly and it was still straight!

Langton checked the windows in the kitchen, then moved silently round the neat flat. He checked the rest of the windows and the locks on the front door. He had surveyed the exterior of the building on arrival, noting that he was not stopped by anyone. He had in fact seen only one resident, who was walking out of the garage and showed no curiosity about him whatsoever. If Daniels had slipped inside Anna's flat, then he had probably taken the opportunity when she left her front door ajar.

Langton walked upstairs and then down, noting there was a lift. If Anna was walking down the stairs and Daniels had used the lift, they could easily have missed each other. There was no one in the communal reception area when Langton checked; no sign of a porter, for instance. He walked out to the rear entrance where the dustbins were kept and looked over the small fenced yard. A narrow alleyway led from the street for the rubbish to be collected. It had taken him only a few minutes to move down the stairs from her second-floor flat out to the yard and another couple of minutes back up to her flat.

He explored the tenants' garage. It was well lit, with residents' names and their apartment numbers on small plaques. But if the garage doors were open, as they were now, anyone could walk in off the street and enter the building on the ground floor. He noticed that the door from the garage to the reception was unlocked. Anna's Mini was parked in her space; the others were empty.

Langton felt sure that if Daniels had entered Travis's flat, it had been an opportunist entry, not a break-in. He went back in the kitchen and poured himself a cup of tea. He opened a tin of biscuits and sat on a stool by the counter, reading his newspaper. There was a delicious gust of perfume. He looked up. There she stood, in the doorway.

'What do you think?' she asked.

He gave her the once-over. 'Very nice.' Actually he was struck by how almost virginal she looked in her simple dress. Her new shoes, with their high heels, made her look much more slender than usual. He didn't say any of that, though, just commented, 'Won't you get cold in just that?'

'I've got a cashmere stole.'

'Good. You look very good.'

He checked the time: twenty past six. 'Have you had anything to eat? You'll have a long wait until dinner.'

'I'm not feeling very hungry.'

'Well, don't drink on an empty stomach.' He started munching a biscuit.

'You sound just like my dad.' She turned back to the bedroom and smiled at him over her shoulder.

Langton didn't feel like her father, anything but. She had knocked him sideways, she looked so lovely. His mobile phone rang at that moment. He patted his pocket and pulled it out. When he walked into the bedroom to relay the news, Anna was sitting at the dressing-table.

'He's just left Queen's Gate. He's in a chauffeur-driven black Mercedes-Benz with blacked-out windows. It's a hire car from a Knightsbridge company.'

'We didn't expect that,' she said.

'It means he could grope you in the back seat.'

'Oh, please,' she said.

'I'll go and turn off the lights in the kitchen and drawing room. By the way, did you realize the garage doors were open? Are they usually left open?'

'Sometimes, if one of the residents forgets their keys, but usually it's locked at night.'

Langton sat in the darkened drawing room, while Anna stayed in the bedroom. She heard his mobile ring, then Langton was standing at the bedroom door.

'The car's pulling up outside.'

She threw her cashmere wrap around her shoulders and picked up her evening bag. Langton was still on the phone. 'He's sent the chauffeur in to fetch you.'

When the doorbell rang, Anna opened the door. The driver made a very courteous bow and informed her that Mr Daniels was waiting in the car. As she followed him, Langton watched from the kitchen window at the front of the building. It was still daylight.

He saw Daniels step out from the rear of the Mercedes. The chauffeur held the door open for Anna; Daniels got in beside her.

His mobile rang again.

'They're on their way,' said the voice of a surveillance officer from the car tailing the Mercedes.

'Yes, I know.'

He sat in her drawing room facing the back-yard and switched on the television. It was going to be a long wait.

Inside the Mercedes, Daniels's head rested against the window.

'You look charming,' he said softly.

'Thank you,' Anna responded. 'It took me a while to decide what to wear. I'm not used to such glamorous events.'

He gave no reaction and remembering Michael Parks's advice, she flattered him. 'That is a very elegant suit! Where did you get it?'

He had on an immaculate velvet jacket, trimmed with satin, and a white silk polo-necked shirt. The matching trousers were pressed like a knife, with an inch-wide satin border down the outside.

'It was made by Valentino. I wore it in a film and so I got it at a quarter of the price I would have had to pay if I'd bought it in a shop.'

'It really suits you! And that shirt is gorgeous.'

'Thank you. Valentino insisted I have the roll neck, not a black bow tie. It's the purest silk. But look at these.' He held out his cuffs. 'Bit ostentatious, aren't they?' For the first time she noticed the emerald cufflinks.

'But – they're real emeralds!'

'They were from a necklace worn by Empress Josephine. And those are rose diamonds around them.'

'Good heavens.'

'So, did you have any trouble leaving work early?'

'No. I said it was a family matter.'

'You told a fib, then, did you?'

She laughed. 'It's just that I didn't think they would approve of me seeing you socially.'

'But surely, I am not still suspected of having anything to do with the – what was her name?'

'Melissa Stephens?'

'Ah yes, the Melissa Stephens murder.' He scrutinized her. 'Am I?'

'A suspect?'

'Yes.'

She smiled. 'I doubt it, but at the same time, the fact you've been questioned means it's not entirely appropriate for us to be seen together.'

'Then I'm surprised you agreed to accompany me.'

She turned away, feigning embarrassment.

'Why did you?' He moved closer.

'I am a big fan of the ballet, Mr Daniels. I couldn't say no. I have been looking forward to this evening so much.'

'It's Alan, for God's sake,' he teased. He took out his phone. 'Excuse me. It's on silent. If you have your mobile with you, remember to turn it off during the performance.'

'It wouldn't fit in my bag.' She held up her mother's small evening bag, but he was listening on his mobile. She was relieved that Langton had turned down her request for a hidden camera. Daniels would have sussed it out very fast.

He sighed irritatedly into the phone. 'Look, this is all getting out of hand. What I said was I didn't feel like taking an entire day to have a costume-fitting in Paris; it doesn't matter whether it's Eurostar or a private plane.' He covered the phone and whispered to Anna, 'Sorry about this. I wouldn't mind, but it's just a test. I suggested that they bring the wig to London. I could have a fitting here and that would mean I have only one trip to Paris instead of two.'

He returned to the call. 'Yes, I am interested in working with him and yes, tell him I like the script.' He leaned back in irritation. 'Just talk to them again and get back to me. It really isn't convenient right now; I'm on my way to the ballet.'

He replaced the phone in his pocket. 'That was my agent. Ye gods! It's such a simple thing. Why they can't send the wig and hair and make-up over here is beyond me.'

The driver turned around. 'Excuse me, sir. There seems to be a back-up of vehicles for the Opera House. Should I join the queue, or do you want me to drop you off?'

'Drop me off?' Daniels repeated. 'I don't think so! We'll wait in line. This is a very special evening for Miss Travis and myself. Besides, we have time.'

The line of cars crawled towards the Opera House. Crowds of people were standing on the pavement and a red carpet ran downwards from the entrance. Anna turned to him.

'I don't mind walking.'

'I do!' Daniels retorted huffily.

They sat in silence as the Mercedes inched towards the Opera House. When it drew up beside the red carpet, Daniels instructed the driver, 'You'll have to get out and open the door. They won't have flunkies here.'

'Yes, sir.'

The driver hurried to open the passenger door and Daniels stepped out into a battery of flashlights to which he seemed oblivious. He reached for Anna's hand and helped her from the car. He held her elbow reassuringly as she stepped onto the red carpet.

'Mr Daniels, can you look this way? Alan!'

'Right, Anna – full steam ahead,' he said gently.

'Alan, to the right! Alan, just one for us.'

'Do you mind? I'd better give them something,' he murmured.

'No. Of course not.'

He paused to smile briefly, hardly breaking his step.

They reached the end of the red carpet. 'ALAN, ALAN!' the photographers yelled out, in a final burst of frenzied flashlights. Turning round, he put his arm round Anna's waist and murmured to her, 'Last one. Smile for the camera.'

The couple moved into the Opera House lobby, where two girls tentatively approached Daniels with autograph books. He signed graciously, but kept Anna close, his arm encircling her waist.

'The reception's straight up those stairs, one flight.'

He guided her expertly through the throngs of people. Anna was quite overawed by the glamour of the Opera House scene, but Daniels seemed at ease, managing to sign two more autographs, yet all the while making progress through the crowd and into the private reception on the first floor. Though she saw him dig into his inside pocket for the invitation, they were waved through immediately.

The men wore black tie and the women were in elegant gowns. A number of people welcomed Daniels. Whenever he was thanked for coming, he would respond: 'Here's the real reason I'm here. May I introduce you to Miss Travis? Anna adores the ballet.'

A waiter was standing nearby with a tray of glasses of champagne. Daniels handed a glass to Anna with a flourish.

'Thank you.' She was feeling hot in a room with so many people. She had drunk almost half the glass immediately when she noticed he was sipping iced water.

They stood slightly to one side, looking over the throng of people. He whispered: 'The charity event tonight is for Christ only knows what, either AIDS, or breast cancer, or some country overflowing with orphans. They like to wheel in the odd celebrity. There's quite a few here, actually.' He looked over the room appraisingly.

She was very aware of how many glances he attracted. As he put his glass down on a tray carried by a passing waiter, he picked up a fresh glass of champagne for Anna.

'I'm fine, thank you.'

'Nonsense, have another. It's free.'

She took it, smiling her thanks.

'I did ballet as a child.' She offered up this tidbit of information for want of anything more stimulating to say.

'Really? I can't quite see you as a dancer.'

'I switched to ponies. I could never keep time to the music, let alone remember the steps.'

Although Daniels gave a polite smile, he seemed more interested in surveying the guests.

Over the loudspeaker came the sound of a bell. With a flourish, Alan signed a final autograph for the waiter as Anna put her second empty glass on the tray. They strolled towards the Royal Circle. As they approached, an usherette removed a single glossy programme from the stack under her arm and held it aloft in a neatly gloved hand.

'Good evening, Mr Daniels. Welcome to the Royal Opera House. Would you care for a souvenir programme?'

Anna, surprised, watched Alan peel off a fifty-pound note and tell the usher to keep the change.

'Thank you very much, Mr Daniels,' she said.

'My pleasure; it's all for a good cause.'

He guided Anna down the aisle, whispering conspiratorially, 'Whatever it is.'

As soon as their backs were turned, the usherette placed the fifty-pound note in a plastic bag, sealed it and handed the programmes to the head usher, before she quickly left the building. She had done her job for the evening.

Langton received the call to say they had removed a glass with Daniels's prints from the bar at the Opera House, plus a fifty-pound note.

'It's doubtful the note will be any good to us for prints. Christ knows how many people would have handled it before Daniels. How's she doing?' he asked.

'Fine. Apparently the curtain's just about to go up.'

As they waited for the curtain to rise, Anna looked around the sumptuous theatre in total awe. Beside her, Daniels was turning the glossy pages of the programme, occasionally leaning close to show photographs of particular dancers to her, but he did not attempt to touch her. As the first act of *Swan Lake* began, he sat forward in his seat, concentrating on the stage.

Langton was asleep on the sofa when the next call came in.

'Started the last act. So management says that means they should be leaving the theatre in about half an hour.'

'Good. Bloody long show. It's already after ten,' he muttered.

Inside the Opera House Anna was on her feet beside Daniels, applauding with enthusiasm. As the dancers took their bows, there were cheers and bouquets of flowers were presented to the principals before they left the stage followed by the rest of the company.

'Right.' Alan yawned. He checked his watch. 'It's completely up to you. We can push our way backstage and try to say hello to Darcey, or we can go straight to supper. What would you prefer?'

'Mmm, that's an impossible choice,' she said.

'Shall we just go and eat?'

'Yes, please. I'm starving.'

'The Ivy it is, then.' As they left their row of seats and walked up the aisle, he was instructing their driver on his mobile phone to meet them out front.

Their chauffeur was waiting at the wheel. Daniels made sure Anna was seated comfortably in the car before he got in. He leaned back against the headrest, observing her. 'Did you enjoy it as much as you'd expected?'

'Oh yes. The dancing was extraordinary, didn't you think?'

He closed his eyes, which she took as a cue not to speak. The drive to the restaurant took no more than ten minutes. When they got out of the car, a knot of photographers started calling out his name, but this time he ignored the cameras completely, hurrying Anna past the autograph seekers and through the front door.

From their banquette at one of the best tables he pointed out the location of the ladies. He then suggested they order the salmon fishcakes.

'I, er . . . do need to go,' Anna murmured. Daniels rose to his feet and drew the table out for her. 'Would you order for me?' She purposefully left her purse on the table, giving him every opportunity to check the contents.

By the time she returned, a bottle of champagne had been placed on ice and her evening bag seemed to be in the exact same place. Daniels helped her back into the banquette. After the waiter had poured the champagne, he lifted his glass to hers.

'To you.' Their glasses touched and their eyes met. 'After a perfect performance.'

'Do you come here a lot?' she asked.

'I suppose I do, Anna. Well, it's one of the few restaurants that stay open after the theatres close.'

'Have you ever acted in the theatre?'

'I would like to, but they pay so badly. I remain a TV and film actor.'

'Even in the West End?' she asked, but at that moment, he excused himself to visit another table. Anna watched him animatedly talking with a couple. The suspect looked very glamorous in his evening suit, she noted. Of course, he was posing slightly. The three of them were obviously discussing the ballet and Daniels made a number of ballet gestures with his arm, apparently unselfconsciously, though in the crowded restaurant many eyes were on him. He kissed the woman's cheek then returned just as the first course was being served.

'That was an actor I worked with in Ireland. Madman! I don't know how he got up at the crack of dawn every morning, because he never seemed to go to bed. He's just signed to do a big movie in LA and the woman with him is his ex-wife! Bon appetit!' he said, lifting his fork and jabbing a piece of lettuce.

Anna ate her salad in silence, trying to think of something to say which might hold his attention.

He picked up her evening bag. 'This is very pretty.'

'It was my mother's.'

'Really. May I see inside?'

'Yes.'

He unclasped the bag. 'You can tell a lot about a woman by the contents of her handbag.'

Was he flirting with her? One by one, he took out the contents. Anna couldn't help thinking it was like being slowly undressed. He unscrewed her lipstick and opened the powder compact. He held her keys in the palm of his hand, then dangled them on one finger. He took out her handkerchief and wafted it under his nose. 'Old-fashioned, to have a real handkerchief,' he said, adding wistfully, 'it should smell of perfume, but it doesn't.'

'I'll remember to spray some on it next time,' she said.

247

She noticed he had not touched his salad, apart from the initial bite of lettuce.

He carefully replaced the items, one at a time. 'So you think there will be a next time, Anna?'

'I meant the next time I use it,' she said. She hadn't intended to sound curt, but she hadn't liked him handling her mother's bag so intimately.

'Would you like to spend another evening with me?' His blue wide-set eyes were fixed on hers.

'This evening isn't over yet.'

'What do you mean? Are you teasing?'

'Well, I may bore you rigid,' she said uncomfortably.

He gestured to the waiter to pour more champagne. She tried to find her way back to the script as written by Michael Parks. 'No really, I'm fine.' She placed her hand over her glass.

Daniels dismissed the waiter. 'Ah, the gov wouldn't approve. And it might be rather difficult right now, anyway.'

'I'm sorry?'

'What you're saying is that Langton wouldn't approve of you going out with me. Correct?'

'I don't know. I don't care.' Anna was starting to feel uncomfortable.

'You can take it all away,' he said dismissively to a hovering waiter who was ready to clear their plates.

Daniels rested his arm along the back of the booth. She half-expected him to touch her neck, but he didn't.

'Is it uncomfortable for you to be seen with me?' he asked.

'No! Though at first I wondered. You know, someone as famous as you; whether you would really be interested in me, or if you had an ulterior motive.'

'An ulterior motive?'

'Yes.'

'Such as?'

'Perhaps you wanted to find out how the investigation was going.'

Daniels sipped his water then put his glass down carefully. 'That simply isn't true, Anna. Yes, you're different from the people I meet, but that's the attraction. There's a lot of falsity in my world, pretentious people, people attracted to me for the wrong reasons: fame, money, power. I liked you a lot when I first met you. You seemed genuine and caring and upfront. When I showed you the photograph of me as a child, I meant what I said to you. I haven't shown that picture to anyone else. I couldn't help it. I felt drawn to you somehow. I knew you would understand.'

'I was very touched,' Anna said.

'I didn't want you to be "touched",' he remarked sarcastically. Anna felt his withdrawal of interest like a bucket of cold water. 'I don't want your sympathy!'

'Well, I couldn't help it,' she said, striving to get onto Parks's script. She went for flattery. 'You were such a beautiful child. And I had such admiration for the adult in the photo, too. My God, you rose from incredibly difficult circumstances to make a great success of your life. You're world-famous. I can see everybody looking at you here. Of course I was touched.'

Privately Anna reflected that if this was a tap-dancing contest, she deserved first prize.

Daniels's face softened. 'Thank you for understanding. Sometimes it's hard for me to reconcile the two. That's why I keep the child there; he's a constant reminder of my good luck.'

'It's not luck, Alan. You're very talented.'

'Well, talent, yes. I suppose talent did have something to do with it.'

As the waiter brought their main course, they fell silent. When he poured more champagne, Anna did not refuse. She wondered if she was stretching credulity too far, however he seemed to be thriving on it.

'Everything looks delicious,' she breathed.

He gave a casual glance around the restaurant and waved at a group of people at the door. Anna had just started to eat when he asked politely: 'So, how was America?'

She swallowed and looked away from him. 'Hard work; I spent most of my time driving.' This was more like it, she thought. Now he would pump her for information. It had certainly taken a long time to get round to it, considering he already knew she'd been to the States.

'I'm very well-connected. I know everything. I know you went to LA!'

She acted dumbfounded. 'How on earth—'

'Actually, it's simple. My agent uses the same dentist. So the dentist calls my agent and he tells him that this Langton chap is asking a lot of questions about my dental bill. And so he calls me. It's a very small world.'

'Yes, it is.'

'So, are you going to tell me why you created such embarrassment for me? You know rumours do more than gather moss out there. My agent wanted to know why there was such interest in my dental appointments.'

'You know why, don't you?'

'No, I don't. I let Langton take away my dental X-rays, but nobody has told me exactly why they are so important.'

'I don't know if I should be telling you.'

'Why not? It's not as if I am going to broadcast it to the restaurant.'

'Well, the victim, Melissa Stephens . . .'

He waited, fork raised. 'Yes?'

'It's not very pleasant, especially while we are eating.'

'Go on, don't keep me in suspense! What about Melissa Stephens?'

'Her tongue had been bitten.'

'Good God, her tongue?'

'Yes.'

'So what on earth has this got to do with me?'

'We have a set of teeth marks. It really isn't anything to do directly with you. It is to do with us eliminating you from the enquiry.'

'My God, I am stunned.'

'Which we now have done, as your teeth don't match.'

'Well, of course they don't. It's just mind-blowing to me that I was even under suspicion. I am surprised you agreed to come out with me.'

'You are not under suspicion,' she said, sipping her champagne.

'But that is why you went to LA?'

'Yes, one of the reasons. And San Francisco and Chicago. Alan, I really shouldn't be telling you this. You know it's privileged information.'

'Rubbish! You've just said I've been eliminated. Unless you're lying.'

'I'm not.'

He ate for a few moments and then put his fork down. 'So go on, what else did you do in LA?'

'There was a murder victim called Marla Courtney; she had the same MO as our victim here in London.'

'What does MO mean? I can't remember.'

'Modus operandi; means the same pattern.'

'Good heavens! And you think whoever killed the girl here also murdered someone in the States?'

'Yes.'

Anna now began to move her script up another notch. Her instructions were to draw him out, this time flattering not his professional actor's ego, but his other side: the sociopath. She began to describe how clever and cunning their killer was and how they were unable to find any clues anywhere. He listened attentively, sometimes shaking his head as if in awe.

She giggled. 'I must be getting tiddly – I really shouldn't be telling you all this. I'd get in such trouble, you know. We are not supposed to ever discuss the cases we are working on with anyone outside the station.'

'I won't tell anyone,' he said softly, reaching over to take her hand. 'You can trust me, Anna; I would never repeat what you have told me, not to a soul. But it is fascinating. I find it hard to believe that this man has got away with it and even harder to believe you don't have any clues to his identity. That said, it is really terrifying to think you actually had me questioned and for a while even contemplated that I could be involved. This man must be a monster.'

She nodded and leaned closer. 'He is, but he's also incredibly clever. He never leaves any DNA; no fingerprints, nothing. Not that I'm privy to all the details. My chief is a bit of a loner, you know he has a big ego trip going on.'

'But he took you to America.'

'Well, yes, but I was more or less just his driver.'

'So did he get any result from there? You said you'd also been in San Francisco and Chicago.'

She shook her head and then leaned close. 'If we don't get something soon they'll disband the team.'

'No? You're kidding me?'

'It's true.'

His beautiful eyes blinked in astonishment. 'How many women has he killed?'

Anna placed her knife and fork on her plate. 'This is very confidential. We haven't really allowed the press to know just how dangerous this man is.'

Daniels had hardly touched his food. He neatly placed his knife and fork together on the plate and indicated the waiter should remove them. When the table was cleared, he leaned both elbows close to her.

'How many?' he asked in a whisper.

'We think it's ten.'

'Ten?'

'Yes, which is another reason you were questioned.'

'Me?'

'Yes, because you were in the States at the same time as the murders. The gov has been opening up what they call the dead files, here and in the US.'

'Dead files?' He frowned, leaning even closer, but making no reference to the fact that he was actually in the three cities she mentioned.

'Yes, some of the women murdered here knew your mother; they were all prostitutes and may have lived at the same house you were living in when you were a child.'

'No!'

'Yes.'

'Oh my God! Now I understand. It was all so confusing when I was questioned; half the time I couldn't pick up on what they wanted from me.'

Anna looked at him enquiringly. 'What?'

'I understand now why they questioned me about my childhood.'

She leaned close. 'Please, Alan, if they were to bring you in for questioning again, you won't tell them we discussed any of this? Please. I could get in terrible trouble. They might even fire me.'

He took hold of her hand. 'Of course I wouldn't repeat this, not to anyone, but why do you say they may want to question me again? What on earth can they want from me?'

'I don't know.'

'But you must know! I mean, if this was to get in the press it would ruin my life, my career.'

Anna nodded. 'That's why the enquiry is being so diplomatic. As I said, if we don't get a result, it could all be disbanded and put on open files. They may not even question you again.'

Daniels signalled for the waiter. He ordered two coffees, then said quietly: 'You are right, we shouldn't discuss this. I don't want to get you in any trouble, but you can understand why I am so interested; it's pretty obvious and to be honest it really freaks me out.'

'I'm sorry, I didn't mean to—'

'But you have. I am just amazed. How can they even suspect me? And I can't think of anything I could do or say that would help you. I mean, I will really think about it.'

He sat in silence. Anna looked around the restaurant crowd, which was starting to thin out. It was by this time after half past eleven.

She drank her coffee; Daniels swirled the spoon round and round in his cup. He tapped the side. 'You know, it's made me really depressed. I hate to go back to that time in my life – it's like a chasm opens up inside me and it's dark, a terrible place to return to. But there must be some connection if, as you say, these women knew each other and they were all murdered.'

'Yes.'

'But are the women in the States all connected to them as well?'

'No, not that we have discovered.' Anna sipped the dregs of her coffee. 'But whatever made the killer begin his rampage—'

'It's not exactly a rampage,' he said curtly.

'Well no, there are years in between the UK murders, but if you add the American victims, it is a pattern of killing that shows the killer to be moving from perhaps some kind of revenge to being unable to curb his hatred of a certain type of woman.'

'Prostitutes,' said Daniels, staring into his cup.

'Yes, but he may have made a mistake with Melissa.'

He leaned back, his eyes expressionless.

'Mistake?'

Anna nodded and told him they had two witnesses, the Cuban waiter and the husky-voiced call girl.

'They saw him?' he said incredulously.

'Yes.'

'But that's – that's good news, surely?'

It wasn't enough of a response to be useful. If he was their killer, he was playing his cards very close to his chest. Anna was tired and she felt they had reached a dead end. She stood up, saying she needed to go to the ladies. Alan stood, allowing her to pass him.

'I should be going home soon, Alan. I have to work in the morning.'

'I promise, we won't discuss this topic for another second. Now you go and powder your nose and I'll sort out the bill. Unless – would you like a brandy?'

'No, nothing else. Thank you.'

Anna felt totally drained. She had done her best, letting information out that, in actual fact, he could have discovered from press releases. But Daniels had not slipped up or, in Michael Parks's words, given her the 'leakage' she was hoping for. By the time she returned to the table, he stood waiting for her, holding her wrap. He gently placed it around her shoulders.

'You don't think the reason I asked you out was to pump you for information? Please, don't think that. Because it isn't true.'

She said softly, 'No, I don't. I've enjoyed being with you very much.'

He drew her closer. 'You're very special, Anna.'

★

As they drove away from the Ivy, Anna began to wonder about the next stage of the evening, but Daniels was ahead of her. He instructed the driver to take Miss Travis back to her flat, adding, 'As I'm on the way, he can drop me off first, if you don't mind?'

'No, not at all.'

They drove in silence for a few minutes, though he sat some distance from her, his face in the shadows.

His free hand sought hers out in the darkness. 'When I first came to the station you work at, I can't tell you how scared I was. It brought back the time they found her body.'

'Your mother's?'

He sighed. 'I was just a teenager, so they held me in the cells overnight and interrogated me for hours and hours. I had no one to turn to. And now – I feel like it's happening again, but this time, with even more to lose. You saw the press calling out for me. Can you imagine what they would do if it was to be made public that I was even being questioned? You have to help me. Make them understand: I am innocent. How can I still be a suspect? Why are they doing this to me?'

'It's just the connection, Alan.'

'That I was brought up in a stinking brothel, with a bunch of whores? What does that mean?' he said, angrily. 'I wouldn't remember a single one of them. I've tried my hardest to obliterate them from my mind.' She was perplexed to see tears begin to stream down his cheeks. He wiped them away with the back of his hand, sniffing. 'Sorry. I'm sorry, need that handkerchief of yours.'

She went to open her bag, when he shook his head. 'No, no – I'm alright now.'

'Alan, the reality is you are not under arrest and they have no evidence against you but circumstantial. If they had anything, you'd have been arrested by now. You have to believe me that I wouldn't have agreed to see you this evening if I thought for one moment that you were involved.'

He squeezed her hand. 'Do you mean that?'

'Of course I do.'

255

He rested back. 'Thank God. Because I need you, Anna. I'm going to rely on you to get me through this. Come here; rest your head on my shoulder.' He closed his eyes.

Uneasily, she slid towards him. He wrapped his arm round her. She could smell his delicate aftershave, feel the softness of the velvet jacket against her cheek. Her heart was thudding as he tilted her face towards his and kissed her lips: a delicate, sweet kiss. He gently touched her hair. 'You are already very special to me and I am sure, in time, we can mean a lot more to each other.' He was tracing her cheek with his finger.

From the front seat, the driver interrupted. 'Queen's Gate, sir.'

'Goodnight, Anna.' Daniels kissed her hand as the driver opened the rear door to let him out. She watched as he walked to the front steps, turning back to wave.

She was trembling as the car drove away. When it reached her flat, she thanked the driver, insisting there was no need for him to see her to her front door. She was fumbling for her key when Langton opened the door.

'How did it go?' he asked.

Anna slumped onto the sofa, kicking off her shoes. The lounge was strewn with coffee cups and half-eaten cheese sandwiches. Even his newspaper was in pieces, pages left on the floor by the overflowing ashtray.

'Did you get anything?'

'Not much.'

'Fuck. How come? You were out late enough.'

She shook her head, unable to speak. He could tell she was upset, but he had waited all night for some information and the evening had cost a bloody fortune in overtime.

'What is it, Travis? Did he try it on in the car?'

She started to sob. She searched in her bag for her handkerchief and then began tipping everything out as she frantically searched.

'Daddy's cufflinks!' She was distraught. 'They were in the zip-up pocket.'

Langton looked at her, puzzled. With her new hairstyle standing on end and her tear-stained face, she looked about ten years old.

'Shush, it's OK. You're safe now.'

He knew he shouldn't, but he moved to sit beside her and put his arm round her. She started to sob uncontrollably against his chest.

'Shush. Just take deep breaths and try and relax. Then go and mop yourself up and get some sleep.'

She pulled away from him. 'Stop telling me what to do. Just leave me alone.'

Langton took a deep breath. 'Fine, I'll do that. But in the morning, I want a report, Travis.'

She wiped her tears away with the back of her hand.

'Just tell me one thing. Is it him?'

She sniffed.

'*Is it him?*'

'I don't know.'

He stared after her as she headed for the bedroom. 'Well, that's fucking terrific,' he muttered.

Underneath the duvet which she pulled over her head, Anna cried her heart out. She was a failure. Worse, she had allowed her emotions to overrule her logic. She had found herself liking Alan Daniels; the memory of him softly kissing her lips still lingered. She was confused by her feelings for him. How was she going to face everyone in the incident room in a few hours' time?

Chapter Fifteen

Langton listened from the sofa. He had been woken by an odd, scraping sound in the kitchen. He pulled on his trousers and opened the door. There was Anna, clad in her kimono, scribbling away in a notebook, oblivious to the sound that the stool's legs made on the tiled floor.

She shot up from the stool in alarm. 'What the hell are you doing?'

'It's six o'clock in the morning,' he said lamely. 'Sorry if I scared you. I just heard a noise.'

She drew her kimono closer, embarrassed. 'I was just writing notes for my report. I couldn't sleep any longer and I didn't want to forget anything.'

'Do you want a coffee?'

She covered her notes with her hand. 'Yes, please. There's some freshly made.'

'Got a bit of a hangover?'

'No, I have not!' she said angrily.

'Did you find the cufflinks?'

'No. I'll call the restaurant. I was thinking I may have dropped them in the car.'

Langton poured two cups of black coffee and put one down in front of her. He glanced at the notebook.

'You want to talk about it?'

'No. I'll wait for the briefing.'

'OK. By the way, Michael Parks is coming in to see how you dealt with Daniels.'

Anna wrapped her kimono tighter. 'I'll go and have a shower. Do you need one?'

'No, it can wait until I get home.'

She hesitated. 'Wouldn't it be better to just go in together this morning?'

He grinned. 'Travis, are you inviting me to shower with you?'

'Very funny!'

'I meant that I'll shower when I get home tonight.'

'Fine, fine.'

Once he heard the sound of the shower going, he picked up her notebook and started to read page after page of her neat, meticulous writing. His heart started sinking. This was going to give him a lot of flak.

He had finished reading by the time Anna emerged from the bedroom, dressed. He noticed the doleful expression on her face. 'You still upset about your dad's cufflinks?'

'I remember Daniels taking things out of my bag. Maybe they dropped on to the floor then.' Langton perched on the side of an armchair with his mug. 'I kept them in my bag. Silly! Well, you probably think it is, but I took my mother's favourite evening bag and my father's favourite cufflinks.'

'Oh.'

She hesitated. 'My father . . .'

'He was a great guy.'

'Did you know my mother at all?'

'I met her a few times. Long time ago. I wouldn't say that I knew her.'

'I want to show you something. It's a letter. It was in the photo frame, tucked behind my father's picture.'

When Anna was out of the room, he lit a cigarette. She returned with the letter outstretched. 'Will you read it?'

'Of course,' he said, holding out his hand.

'Do you know what Dad's referring to? I don't understand it.'

Langton scanned it quickly, then passed it back.

'He never told you?' he asked.

'Told me what?'

Langton hesitated. 'I'm not sure of the details, but before your dad was on the Murder Squad, he was with Vice.' He inhaled deeply, letting the smoke drift out. 'This was before I even joined up.'

She saw his unease. 'Please, tell me. I need to know.'

'OK. You have to understand that I don't know all the details.'

'Just tell me.' She was almost pleading with him.

'It's not that pleasant. Your mother was a student at art college. She was found brutally raped in her room. It was pretty shocking; she was so traumatized, she lost the use of her voice. Your dad was brought in to oversee the case. He couldn't get your mother out of his mind. She was very beautiful, even when I met her.'

Anna had to sit down; her legs felt like jelly.

'Anyway, he became obsessed. He was determined to catch the rapist. He eventually picked up a student from a nearby college. He questioned him for sixteen hours without legal representation and then released him, which didn't make much sense to anyone, since the kid had broken down and admitted he had raped Isabelle. The kid hanged himself.'

'Did he do it?' Anna persisted.

'Yep. But instead of case closed, get on with your life, your dad kept on seeing your mother. He couldn't get her out of his mind. Her family put her in some kind of therapy and she recovered, gradually. He kept in touch. They were married two years later. Word was she—' he paused.

'Word was she what?' Anna asked, sharply.

'Well, that she remained of a very nervous disposition and she had basically married her protector. Old Jack would have killed for her. I heard that he had duffed the kid up pretty badly.'

'Did he?'

Langton gave her a look. 'You tell me. Anyway, Isabelle never returned to art college. They were married and then you came along. By the time

I met him he was heading up the Murder Squad. Then I don't know how long afterwards, some thug he was after broke into your house. Though he didn't touch your mother, I think it triggered something, because . . .' He sighed, not really comfortable with all this personal stuff.

'Because what?'

Langton shrugged. 'She started remembering things. She got more fearful about leaving the house. Sometimes, when he was pissed, he admitted — well, he did to me — that being married to Isabelle felt like having an exotic bird of paradise in the house that only he ever saw.'

'And me. I saw her too. I never knew.'

'It wasn't easy. Like I said, she was very fragile and I think he knew that if his exotic bird had never been wounded, he would never have stood a chance of marrying her. But from what you've told me, they were happy and you know, Anna, when you get that hurt or frightened, a protector is important, if it means you carrying on living.'

Anna stood up, her father's letter clutched in her hands. 'Thank you for telling me this.'

He held out his hand for hers. 'You OK?'

'I'm fine. Just sad that I never knew what anguish she had suffered. She was a wonderful, loving mother.' She ignored his hand.

Anna walked into her bedroom. She put the folded letter in her little jewel box on her dressing-table and stared at her reflection in the mirror. Her mind was full of thoughts about Isabelle, trapped inside their home, reduced to painting pictures of the flowers in their garden. She was so sad that she had never been able to talk to her or comfort her, that she had never known the pain that had been in her own home.

Langton and Anna left her flat in the Mini at half past eight. The atmosphere was strained, the two hardly talking. Anna no longer believed that Alan Daniels was their killer. She had felt his pain last night and responded protectively. She was sure he was not the monster they sought.

Langton, believing Anna's silence was due to distress about her mother's tragedy, addressed the subject eventually.

'These things happen, Anna,' he said quietly. 'You just have to get on with your life. When my first wife died, I kept on working. I kept on pushing myself, so I wouldn't feel the emptiness.'

She threw a startled look at him as he continued speaking with an intimacy unfamiliar to her.

'A month after her funeral, I packed all her things away. They seemed to amount to so little; yet it was her life with me. That was the first time it hit me. I took six weeks off then sold the place; moved on, started again, met my second wife and, well, that was a mistake, apart from Kitty.

'I'd have liked to have children one day, but I doubt that I'll ever settle down with anyone again. You have something perfect; it's wrong to make comparisons, but I probably always will. Now I rent a place. Nothing in it means anything. If it burned down tomorrow, I wouldn't care.'

After a lengthy pause, he sighed. 'Well, that's me, Travis. Hope I managed to cheer you up.' They exchanged a mutual grin, then he glanced at his watch. 'Better get to work.'

'I'll make out my report as soon as we get there.'

'Good girl.

'Langton,' he snapped into his mobile as they drove into the station car park. He got out as she paused, looking around for a parking space, continuing his phone call as he headed towards the building, then turning to gesture at an empty space. Anna smiled, at least he still remembered she was with him. The space was next to the old dirty Volvo. She parked as far from it as possible, still unsure who owned it, and wary about any more damage to her Mini.

Langton called for a briefing at eleven o'clock, which was the time Michael Parks was expected. At her desk, Anna began to type up her report. No one asked how the evening had progressed; it was as if they were expecting failure.

Moira burst into the incident room an hour and a half late. She looked over at Lewis. Her eyes were red-rimmed from crying. 'Don't start. I've had a very bad morning. I need to speak to the gov ASAP.'

'He's busy. What do you want to talk to him about?'

'It's personal,' she said curtly.

Langton and the head of the surveillance team were holed up discussing the previous evening. The chauffeur had submitted his report. Anna had, as yet, no idea they had replaced the driver of the Mercedes with an undercover policeman; she had not even known about the usherette.

Langton thumbed through the reports. He knew he would get a strong-arm response from the commander. He had made a mistake in placing so much responsibility on a twenty-six-year-old's shoulders.

Of course, there were still Daniels's fingerprints to be examined. While the fifty-pound note would probably not be of any use, the glasses he had used at the Opera House and the Ivy would help. If they were a match with the fingerprints on the picture frame, it would be the only result from a very expensive operation.

Langton dismissed the surveillance chief. Moments later, Lewis called to say Moira wanted to see him. He added in an undertone that she was in a bit of a state. She seemed to have calmed down by the time she walked into his office. 'You wanted to see me?' he asked.

'Yes. It may be nothing, but there again – you never know.'

'Fire away.'

'My daughter Vicky's been dating this bloody so-called DJ. She's only sixteen and he's twenty-seven. He's right full of himself, he is. I have warned her, done everything possible to stop her seeing him, but she's been sneaking out. She's a right little bitch and very hard to handle.'

Langton winced, wondering what the hell this had to do with him.

'She's been going with him since she was fifteen.'

'Moira, can you get to the point, please?'

'Right. I was damned sure she was on something, so I grounded her. Well – one night she staggered in, obviously stoned but denying it, then said she'd had too many coco pops, or whatever they serve in the clubs nowadays. Anyway, to get to the point, last night she got out through the window and went off to this club he works at. She didn't get home until after three, right, but I was waiting for her.'

Langton closed his eyes. 'If you need compassionate leave—'

'No, listen! She comes creeping back in a terrible state, crying, her top all torn. So right away I went from being ready to crack her one to being really concerned. She was crying her heart out, saying they'd had this row and then I saw this terrible mark on her neck. Round. Bruise the size of a ten pence piece, maybe a bit bigger.'

Langton leaned back. His patience was just about up.

'I said to her, "What's that? Did he hit you?"'

'I've had a late night, too. Can you get to the fucking point, Moira!' Langton snapped.

She went straight back at him. 'I am fucking getting there, sir! Hang on and listen, all right? She said he pushed her head down on his lap. She's sixteen years old, for God's sake. This mark was crimson! Really nasty. I said, had he like, forced her to go down on him? And then she started howling, "No! It had nothing to do with him!"'

Now Moira leaned forwards, indicating her own neck and pushing a finger in it.

'Just here, it was. She said she got it from the gearstick of his car. It was the same size, same mark that Melissa Stephens had on her neck. This DJ, he drives a Mercedes Benz drop head, 280 SL. It's in filthy condition, but . . . it's automatic.'

Langton was staring, onto it now.

'The identical mark,' Moira said with conviction. 'Maybe the killer was trying to get her to do what my bloody daughter's boyfriend was after, to give him a blow job, but Melissa struggles and hits her neck on the gear-stick.'

Langton and Moira studied the board set up in the incident room. She pointed to the blown-up picture of the bruise on Melissa Stephens's neck.

'It's the same, I swear to you. That is what that mark is on my daughter's neck.'

Langton turned to Mike Lewis. 'Was the suspect's Mercedes automatic?'

'I dunno.'

'Get onto his insurance company. Check it out.'

'Will do.'

Seeing Michael Parks walk into the incident room, Langton called to his team to be in the briefing room in fifteen minutes. He stopped by Anna's desk. 'You typed up your report yet?'

'Yes, sir.' She passed him four copies.

'Thank you.'

Langton ushered Parks into his office and passed him Anna's report. 'You'll see she didn't get us much, but when you discuss the report this morning, can you go a bit easy on her? She's emotionally on edge. She was just too inexperienced. I blame myself for not seeing she wasn't up to the job.'

'All right.' Parks nodded and put on his glasses in preparation for reading Anna's report.

Lewis confirmed that the Mercedes driven by Daniels had been an automatic. The bruise to Melissa Stephens's neck could have occurred during a struggle in the car which resulted in her neck hitting the automatic gear lever. If the suspect was holding her down in the struggle, this would explain why a clump of hair had been dragged out by the roots from the back of her head. In front of the team, Langton acknowledged a debt to Moira for coming up with this theory. Moira gave a nod; she was very pleased with herself.

Langton went on to report that they were still awaiting the development of prints on a glass used by Daniels, which they would match against those from a picture frame removed from DS Travis's flat. If they matched, Daniels could be brought in on suspicion of burglary. It was by no means enough to hold him for any length of time, but it might unnerve him; a threat to go public on the burglary charge would really make his life hell.

At that moment Michael Parks walked in. Langton described Anna as having done a good job the previous evening and thanked the driver of the Mercedes. Anna flushed with embarrassment to learn that he was a plant. She was mortified, not least because she had not mentioned in her report that their suspect had kissed her and her omission would be obvious in the driver's report. She sat, her head bowed, making notes, almost afraid to meet Langton's eyes. She felt like an idiot: inexperienced, incompetent and now that she had learned of the cost of the operation, completely frivolous and wasteful.

Michael Parks drew up a sheet of big paper and pinned it on the noticeboard. She recognized her report in his hands and saw with horror that it was covered with red ink markings.

'I will take DS Travis's report section by section and break down each of them. It shows classic signs of the profile I had drawn for you of the sociopath. First example: Daniels sends his driver to bring DS Travis to the waiting car, then he steps out and helps her into the back seat. He is reassuring her she will not be confronted with the possibility of being alone with him, but there will be a third person present, the driver.'

Anna looked up, attentive, recognizing that was exactly how she had felt at the time.

'The suspect takes a call on his mobile phone, reminding her at the same time to turn her own off. This simple interaction had a dual purpose. One: he was assured she was not in contact with her superiors. Two: to show that Daniels at no time anticipates not being able to leave England due to a murder case pending against him. He is heard refusing to go to Paris, preferring his wig to be brought to London. If he is to go to Paris, he will want payment.

'Now to the arrival at the Opera House. He pays scant attention to the press, focusing instead on DS Travis. He gives a fifty-pound note to the usherette, showing how rich he is, how important he is. This man is a real player. After he has made sure DS Travis is at her ease with him, he rests his hand at her back, then on her shoulder. He still can't be sure that she isn't wired, so he asks to see the contents of her evening bag. Only now, when he is satisfied there is no hidden microphone, does he really get down to business.'

Parks wrote on the board: *I will get in trouble for talking to you about the case.*

He turned to the room. 'Travis repeats this numerous times. He assures her that he does not want to get her in trouble, that he has asked her to spend the evening with him because he has felt a connection between them. This is where he gets ready to tease information from her. When he appears distressed regarding his dental X-rays, he is putting on a brilliant act of the innocent man being hounded.'

CAN YOU HELP ME? Parks wrote in block letters.

'It is because he's alone with no one to help him that he needs Travis. He was constantly drawing on her sympathy. Twice he explains to her how his career would be shattered if news that he was under suspicion for murder was ever leaked to the press. As emotionally charged as he seems to be, nevertheless he is able to gain the information that the police have two witnesses, but it is interesting to note that he didn't ask more detailed questions about them.

'Finally, let's focus on the journey home. Daniels suggests he should be dropped off first. Considering he had behaved like the most charming courteous escort all evening, this could seem out of character. He does it to make her feel sexually unpressured by him. Then he produces his biggest draw-card. He provides a small glimpse into a wretched past: the starving little boy in the brothel. He cries. He conjures up for Travis a tragic picture. And she, wisely, allows him to think she has been suckered in. She allows him to draw her in his arms, where he will ask for her protection, that she will help him. Then, he adds that he will try and help her, that he will think how he could possibly be a help to the enquiry. Consider the audacity he displays here!'

Parks leaned forward. 'I can guarantee you that at some point, relatively soon, DS Travis will hear from him again and that this time he will suggest a suspect. I believe we have him worried. The danger is that he might take off, but I doubt he will now. By having what he believes to be contact with an insider, Daniels's ego will cloud over his anxiety. Do you see now, how the entire evening was a ploy by Daniels to gain DS Travis's trust?'

Parks extended his congratulations to Anna for consistently maintaining, throughout the evening, a façade of such endearing openness and innocence that Daniels at no time seemed to perceive her as a threat.

Anna flushed as they gave her a smattering of applause. She felt a bit better after Parks's breakdown of the evening. The meeting broke up and Langton called Anna into his office.

'I'm going to have a tap put on your phone. Is that OK with you?' he asked.

'Yes.'

'Last night, you said you didn't believe Alan Daniels was the killer. Do you remember?'

'Of course I do.'

'He got to you, didn't he, Travis?'

She didn't reply.

'You had a lot to drink.'

'I know. He just kept on ordering more and—'

'I suppose you noticed Parks didn't bring that up, or the fact you kissed him! Jesus Christ, Travis, what the fuck did you think you were doing? It was bloody unprofessional. You want to read the driver's report?'

'It would have been helpful to me if I'd known about the driver.'

'Bullshit! I said we would take care of you.'

She shrugged her shoulders.

'Look at me.'

She looked at him.

'He's going to contact you again. You know that, don't you?'

Her jaw tightened. 'I thought that was the point.'

'Well, there's not going to be a next time, Travis. I'm not putting you out there in the field. You'll probably get in bed and screw him next.'

Her instinct was to punch Langton in the chest and scream abuse at him, but somehow she managed to control her anger. She did not respond, even as he continued: 'You have got to straighten out and stop behaving like a ten year old.'

'Sir, I will do my best,' she said sarcastically.

'So far your best has not been good enough. Now get out.'

She exited wordlessly, but she was swallowing hard and trying not to break down in tears. She made it to the ladies and once inside the cubicle, covered her mouth so that no one would overhear her sobs.

In case Daniels tried to get to either witness, Barolli was sent to check on the Cuban waiter, while Mike Lewis tried unsuccessfully to contact their 'deep throat'. In the meantime, Daniels was put under round-the-clock surveillance.

Langton was called to Scotland Yard, where he detailed Parks's report on the previous evening. The commander was not impressed; they had made no significant progress. While it might be interesting to hear a profiler confirm his suspicions, it moved them no closer to making an arrest. In fact, it was her opinion they had now given their suspect too much information. She was extremely dismissive about the part played by DS Travis and hauled Langton over the coals for depending on a young, inexperienced detective for the success of the operation.

With the carpet being tugged from under his feet, his budget now way out of control and still no result, Langton was dependent on matching fingerprints to haul Daniels into police custody. There again, he had only disappointing news for the commander. The prints had still not been verified. Since the water glass had been chilled, the condensation had made the fingerprints too smudged to be any good. There were numerous prints on the fifty-pound note which had to be separated, though there was the possibility of digitally enhancing the ones on top of each other.

Even this was greeted with scepticism by the commander. She knew where Langton was going and said she did not want a feeding frenzy from the press. 'Arresting your Alan Daniels for suspected burglary does not give you enough to keep him longer than a few hours.'

Daniels was under observation all day. It was reported that he had spent an hour with his agent at the Wardour Street office. Then he caught a taxi to Harrods, where he spent time browsing in the gents' clothing department; from there he strolled along Beauchamp Place, window shopping. He disappeared into San Lorenzo's restaurant at one o'clock and lunched with a woman in a silk turban, who appeared to be conducting some kind of interview.

Daniels walked back to Harrods and got in a taxi, returning to Wardour Street, where he went to his agent's office. That's where they lost him.

Anna let herself into her flat. By now, the phone tap was on, but she didn't give it too much thought. She was depressed; after calling the Ivy, she had been told nothing had been handed in. She wondered about calling the hire-car company, but instead made herself a cup of coffee and sank into the sofa. She closed her eyes, trying to recall Daniels pulling items from her evening bag. She was certain she had seen him replace the cufflinks.

She didn't hear it at first, it was such a light tap. Then she listened and heard it again.

At the front door, Anna moved the spy hole a fraction: it was Daniels. She had a moment of panic and returned quickly to the living room to pick up the phone. But the door was rapped harder. There was no time to make a call. Should she answer the door, or stay silent? She made her mind up and called out, 'Who is it?'

'It's only me, Anna. It's Alan.'

When she opened the door, he was standing there smiling. With a mischievous look, he opened the palm of his hand.

'These are yours, aren't they?'

'I thought I'd lost them. I was frantic; I even called the restaurant. Where did you find them?'

He grinned like a naughty schoolboy. 'In my pocket.'

'You took them?'

'Yes. I needed an excuse to see you again.'

She forced herself to smile. 'You could have just called me.'

'But what if you hadn't wanted to see me again? I was too embarrassed about breaking down in front of you last night to risk the rejection. Aren't you going to ask me in?'

She hesitated.

'Anna, remember I said I was going to think back and see if I could come up with anything that might help you find the murderer?'

'Yes.'

'Well, I might have something.'

She closed the door and gestured towards the lounge. 'I've just made myself a coffee. Would you like one?'

'No, I've only got a few minutes.' He looked around the living room. 'This is very nice.'

'Not compared with your flat. Yours is much more sumptuous.'

He sat down on the sofa. 'It was a wreck when I bought it. Some of the rooms hadn't been used for twenty years. They stank of mildew and birds' droppings. When I was a child, I used to sleep in a little back room. Actually, it was more like a closet; it didn't have a window. There was a mattress on the floor: no sheets, but a couple of blankets and a pillow with no pillowcase; it was striped and stained and smelt of cats.'

He went over to look out of the window. 'I bought the flat because of the fantastic stained-glass windows. They're original William Morris. They hide the fact I have no views in a very elegant, wondrous way. In the mornings when the light shines through them, it's like a magic lantern.' He turned to her. 'I've been thinking about some of the things we discussed. In fact, I hardly slept last night.'

She perched on the arm of a chair to listen. He sat back on the sofa and frowned, looking down at his hands. 'There are things I remember, things I have tried hard not to think about. Anyway . . .' He leaned back and licked his lips.

He went on to explain that, as a child, it was always difficult to stay asleep, because of the constant noise of partying in the early hours of the morning. The police were often called to the house to break up drunken brawls. Then one day, Social Services took him away and put him in a foster home. His life changed dramatically: there were three meals a day, clean clothes. But he was always sent home. 'She would demand me back.

I never knew why; she didn't appear to want me. I'd be dragged back screaming and crying.'

Anna noticed that his voice was unemotional. He never discussed his feelings, just the facts of what happened: how he had been moved backwards and forwards until one day he ran away. Then Social Services took him to a care home and from there he was relocated to his second set of foster parents.

'Away from that hell hole, I started to do well in school. I even won a scholarship to a good public school. And in all this time I didn't hear a word from her, not a letter, or a phone call. When I was about fifteen, I looked out of a bus window and saw her. She looked hideous. Her face was bloated from booze, her tits were sagging and she was wearing a mini skirt, staggering about in high-heeled shoes with her veined legs bare. She disgusted me.'

For the first time he appeared unsettled; he took a deep breath before continuing. The boys he was with caught sight of her and not knowing she was his mother, they started laughing. Soon they were yelling abuse out of the bus window, calling out 'slag' and 'whore'. He shook his head. 'And I joined in.'

Langton was in a blazing fury. He had just been told that Daniels had 'disappeared'. The surveillance officers surmized that the suspect had used AI Management's side entrance to cross Wardour Street and had gone into the garage that way. His car was still parked. Langton swore and cursed their incompetence. The exit from the underground garage stairs would have brought him back onto the street and from there, it was just a short distance to Oxford Street where there was no shortage of buses and taxis. He could even have caught the tube at Tottenham Court Road.

Langton immediately ordered a car to take him to Anna's flat.

Anna was wondering about the reason for the visit. But she knew she had to be patient.

Daniels said he had taken the bus, alone this time and got off at the place he had last seen his mother. He found her in an alleyway, leaning against a wall, her skirt up round her waist, being slapped around by a man in a pale blue suit. She was shouting drunkenly, but he only slapped her harder until finally she started to slide down the wall. 'I charged, started to punch him, but he took out a knife. She got in between us and started to scream at me, telling me to go away and mind my own business! He warned me that if I didn't, he'd kill her. So I ran away. Later, she was picked up by the cops. She said she had been raped, as well as beaten up and she wanted to press charges.'

He explained how he had gone to the old house in the morning, to see if she was all right and the man in the pale blue suit opened the door. Running away down the street, he was arrested and thrown in a patrol car.

'She charged that I had beaten her up. I was questioned by this revolting pig of a man. He was abusive to me. The really sick thing was, I had seen this man at the house. He was a Vice Squad officer and he used to be around there all the time.'

Anna guessed he was referring to Barry Southwood. Now, Daniels spoke so quietly that his voice was hardly audible.

'They found her body about eighteen months after and arrested me on suspicion of murder. It was all unreal, terrifying. I had no money for a lawyer, nothing. I was certain it was him. I went back to that disgusting house to confront him. One of the women told me he'd done a runner, taken their money. She said he had threatened them that if they ever said anything to the cops about him, he would kill every one of them.'

Daniels was standing now, staring ahead, almost mesmerized, his hands clenched tightly at his sides.

'Did you ever find out where he went? The man in the blue suit?'

'Their pimp?' He nodded. 'I saw him on the front page of the *Manchester Daily News*. He was opening up a new nightclub. He had these TV stars around him. He looked for all the world like a successful businessman.'

'What was his name?'

'John George McDowell.'

He watched her get up and fetch her notebook. She wrote down the name.

'I'll pass it to the team first thing in the morning.'

He stood. 'I have to go now. I hope that I have helped you. It's been painful, telling you all this. I hope you will protect me, Anna.'

'I'll do everything I can.'

'Promise me?' He moved closer.

'I promise, Alan.'

He cupped her face in his hands. When the doorbell rang, they jumped apart.

At the front door, Anna moved the spy hole aside: Langton was outside. 'It's my gov,' she said, hopelessly.

Daniels shrugged his shoulders. 'We're not doing anything wrong, Anna.'

She opened the door.

'Hi, I need to talk to you,' Langton said. Before she could stop him, he brushed past her into the living room and froze. She followed helplessly.

'Nice to see you again. I was just leaving.' Daniels extended his hand. 'Anna, see you soon.'

Langton stood in mute fury as he sauntered out. Anna closed the door behind her visitor.

'What the fuck is going on?' Langton hissed.

'He came to see me.'

'Jesus Christ!' He flopped down on the sofa. 'You continue to amaze me, Travis. What the hell did you let him in for?'

She chewed her lip. 'Um – I am still here.'

'Don't you be bloody sarcastic with me. Why didn't you call in? He could have killed you.'

'Why don't you let me tell you what he came to see me about?'

'I can't wait,' he snapped.

She summarized Daniels's conversation, finally producing her notebook with the name: John George McDowell.

'It's bullshit.'

'But we should check it out.'

'Travis, don't you want to know why I'm here?' he demanded.

She blinked nervously.

'Surveillance lost him in Wardour Street.' He looked at her expectantly. 'Did you hear what I said?'

'Yes, sir. That's why you're here.'

'Partly. Your boyfriend has been in your flat. Travis, we have a match. Sweetheart, it's Alan Daniels's fingerprints on your daddy's photo frame.'

Her body started to shake. She had been alone with Alan Daniels for over three quarters of an hour.

Langton picked up her notebook. 'We will check out this "John George McDowell". From now on, Travis, you don't make a move without me and the team knowing it.'

'Yes, sir.'

'We will get someone to look after you, as you don't seem capable of acting like a professional officer.'

'Will you be staying here?'

He glowered. 'What the fuck do you think I am, Travis, your bloody babysitter? There is an officer parked outside your flat. Tomorrow, I want from you a full report of exactly what Daniels said.'

'Yes, sir.'

After Langton had slammed the front door closed behind him, Anna bolted it, top and bottom. She stood in her small hallway, feeling angry. Not at Langton this time but at Alan Daniels, who had used her so expertly, as if she were just a pawn in his game.

Chapter Sixteen

John George McDowell had a police record, a long one, with many different charges: living off immoral earnings; two years for assault; another eighteen months for dealing in stolen property. After the nightclub closed down years ago, McDowell had spent more time in prison for aggravated burglary. Then the trail went dead and Mike Lewis was having a hard time tracing his present whereabouts. He waited for the Midlands police to get back to him.

Barolli was also on the phone. He had been assigned to check out their Cuban witness which resulted in a big runaround because he had been fired from the transvestite club for stealing. Barolli eventually discovered that he was working at a restaurant in the same area. Now Barolli was at his desk, having problems tracing their second witness. Jean joked with him that to lose one witness was unfortunate; to lose two was flipping careless. He was not amused.

Yvonne Barber, the deep-voiced prostitute, had moved from her last address and no one seemed to know where she had gone. A roommate said she might have gone to Brighton, but she hadn't heard from her in over a week. Barolli cursed. It was very frustrating, especially as she had been warned to keep the police informed of her whereabouts.

Anna was finishing off her report on the previous evening when Lewis yelled over to Barolli to ask if they'd any luck with Daniels's fingerprints. Barolli shook his head.

'They're waiting for that woman to come down from Nottingham and do the digital enhancing trick again.'

Anna looked up at Barolli. 'What did you just say?'

'What about?'

'The fingerprints. I thought there had been a match.'

Barolli shook his head. 'That's news to me. Like I said, she's coming down from Nottingham.'

Anna printed out her report, clipped the pages together and headed for Langton's office. Not waiting for a reply to her knock, she walked in and slammed the door shut behind her. When Langton looked up in surprise, she dumped the report on his desk.

'You are a bastard, you know that?' She put both her hands on his desk. Her face was red with anger. 'You said the prints were a match. You bloody lied.'

'Maybe I had a reason.'

'Like what? To scare the living daylights out of me? Make me frightened to be alone in my own flat?'

'Maybe I did it because I felt you needed a kick up the arse.'

'You bastard. You had no right!'

He pushed his chair back. 'I had every right to make you see sense; you let the son of a bitch into your place.' To her rising fury, he began to mimic her. '"I don't know if he's guilty. I just really liked him."'

'I did not say that.'

'How about that tragic diatribe he gave you about his wretched background? He suckered you in, Travis. You could have been his next victim. It was lucky I came round when I did. I only came because the surveillance team had lost him!'

'So, you frighten the life out of me?'

'You needed to realize the danger you were in.'

Before she could reply, Mike Lewis knocked and entered. 'Can I see you for a minute, gov?'

Langton looked at her. 'You all done?'

She went out, this time closing the door quietly. She was shaking with anger. Every time she thought she knew the man, she found she was mistaken. She was no closer to knowing Langton, but she had learned one thing: to make damned sure not to put a foot wrong where he was concerned, because now she knew he would cut her down and perhaps even damage her career.

Inside the gov's office, Lewis pulled at his collar. 'Listen, gov – Alan Daniels might have done us a favour. This McDowell character is being held in Manchester City police station; he's been there all night. They hauled him in for beating up a prostitute and her pimp and then taking out two of their officers who were trying to arrest him.'

'He's a regular customer, I understand.'

'He's been inside off and on, lots of short stretches. He's a fucking nightmare. But he was out of the nick for our victims, I've checked.'

'Manchester?'

'Yep. Daniels told Travis that McDowell knew Lilian Duffy. He could easily have known the other women. Plus, he drives a 1987 cream four-door Mercedes-Benz.'

'Can they hold him until we get there?'

'I'd say so. They've been waiting to question him once he sobers up.'

Langton and Mike Lewis were preparing to head up north when the Sussex police called in the discovery of a bloated female body found below the old pier legs in Brighton. The pier was under orders for demolition; it had been cordoned off from the public. The woman had been strangled with a leather belt, drawn so tightly round her neck that the skin by her jugular had broken under the buckle. Could it be their other witness? She had extensive bruises and jagged cuts, which the postmortem report said could either have been from the rocks around the pier, or from the body banging against the pylons. The body had no identification; it might never have been found, except for a very high tide, which floated it closer to the shore.

Langton ordered Anna to go down to Brighton and verify whether or not it was their witness. They would also need an estimated time of death, which would allow them to check if their suspect, Alan Daniels, would have had time to make the trip there.

Anna was disappointed not to be going to Manchester to interview McDowell, but, after their last interaction, she doubted if Langton would let her accompany him as far as the station car park.

Langton had already left the station with Lewis. She waited for Moira to co-ordinate a driver and patrol car for her. From her desk, Moira glanced at Anna.

'You OK? Seem to be in a bit of a dark one today.'

'I am.'

'If you want to talk about it—'

'I don't.'

Nearby, Jean gave a raised eyebrow to Moira.

'You're getting to be quite a prima donna,' Moira said good-naturedly. 'What with surveillance at your home, the Opera House and now a private car to Brighton!'

'Just get them to allocate a car for the day please, Moira.'

A short while later, Moira informed Anna that the driver would be waiting in the car park in fifteen minutes.

'Thank you.'

'Think nothing of it.' She raised her voice slightly so that Jean could hear. 'I was a bit surprised you weren't with the gov on the train to Manchester. He usually takes you with him.'

'I won't be going anywhere with him, in the near or distant future,' Anna said grimly. 'In fact, the sooner I am off this case, the better.'

Moira pursed her lips. 'I thought you two got along?'

'Well, I've had enough; I don't know how you all stand him.'

'What's that supposed to mean?'

Anna burst out: 'He's a two-faced bastard, that's what it means. He's a selfish, egotistical control freak.'

Moira leaned closer, saying quietly: 'You watch what you say about him. Because we all rate him. And if this is about him turning up at your place and reading you the riot act, then you should think again. Because, when he knew the surveillance team had screwed up, the only thing he cared about was that you were safe. He had to check for himself. He's that way with all of us. As busy as he is, he still found time to come over to my place and talk to my daughter. Her own father couldn't find the time, but he did. And he had a word with the boyfriend. He didn't have to do that, but he did it to help me out. He'd help any one of us out, if we needed him.'

'Did he tell you what he said to me?'

Moira moved off to her desk. 'I'm not getting involved in this one; I'm just saying you should watch your mouth. We're all on his side and we've been on it a hell of a lot longer than you! I saw him going through a private hell and he never laid it on anyone.'

'I know about his wife dying, Moira.'

'Yeah, well, the second one went off with one of his closest friends. And he's still paying through the nose for her daughter.' She continued, red in the face: 'Now I've gone and said too much, so don't go and repeat it, or I'll bloody have you!'

Anna collected her briefcase and wordlessly left the station. She was driven in a patrol car by a large, over-talkative officer. He started with his hobby, which was buying car wrecks and doing them up to sell. He described how he checked out the salvage companies which often took spare parts from cars before they were crushed. He listed different prices he had paid to them, compared to buying the same thing from a main dealer.

At last, they arrived at the Brighton mortuary. Anna was glad to escape the car.

The Sussex Police had made enquiries but come up empty-handed. Their best guess as to time of death was a couple of weeks ago. She had been in the water for that length of time and she had a very high alcohol level: five times the legal limit. Though her body was in horrific shape and her face was bloated, Anna recognized her as Red Leather.

No one had reported her missing and they had no idea where she had been staying. They found no ID and lacked any knowledge of where she had been on the night of her death. Anna gave what details she could and the address in Leeds for them to contact the girl she lived with in order to find any relatives. They said they would put an appeal for information in the local press and get in touch as soon as they had any news.

Death was due to strangulation, but the MO was not the same as their victims'; her hands were not tied, nor was her underwear used to strangle or tie her. The belt was of a very cheap variety and a woman's not a man's; it could possibly have come from a raincoat.

When Anna returned to her garrulous driver, she sat in the back, explaining that she'd had a late night and planned to catch up on her beauty sleep. She phoned Barolli on the mobile to confirm that the corpse was indeed that of their second witness, then she stretched out. It was almost four o'clock. As Anna was falling asleep, she was vaguely aware of her driver talking about spraying cars: how much paint sprays cost; how some of the expensive models needed at least four coats; how he layered on the paint, then carefully rubbed it down until he got the right texture and finishing gloss. His biggest profits were always on the vintage cars, he mumbled, but it was hard to find parts, especially for the older Mercedes. But the dealers he knew kept parts for him, headlights, bumpers, even seats.

Around the same time, Langton and Mike Lewis were getting out of a taxi at the Manchester police station. Before interviewing McDowell, who was being held in the cells, the duty sergeant and the arresting officer took them into a small office, where they heard about his arrest the night before. McDowell worked for an Irish pub as a bouncer; he was doing it for the booze and a few quid at the end of the week. It was late, almost half past eleven, when the police were called. A prostitute had been sounding off in the bar. He was trying to evict her, but she and her pimp started punching McDowell. When the police arrived, the fight became a brawl. McDowell, who had been drinking heavily, charged at the police like a mad bull. It took three policemen to restrain him. He had passed out in the cells.

'How old is he?' Langton frowned, checking McDowell's records.

'Fifty-two.'

McDowell's list of crimes was part petty, but his association with prostitution was what interested Langton. He had a string of girls working for him at the club and a lot of them were on the game. He had been charged with living off immoral earnings.

'Did you ever have an address for him? Shallcotte Street?'

They had so many addresses it was like an A to Z of Manchester, but there was no record of him living in the same house as Anthony Duffy or his prostitute mother. McDowell had moved constantly from one place to another.

'He's now in the basement of an old house that's been earmarked for demolition, not far from the Granada TV studios.' The sergeant shook his head in disgust. 'It's a real stinkhole of a place. I'd say he just dosses down there, or passes out. The guy has a massive drink problem. The nightclub was a big success for a while; all the stars used to hang out there. Unfortunately the profits he didn't drink away, he put up his nose. He fancied himself as a ladies' man.'

'What about his Mercedes?'

'It's been in the pound for a week. He had fifty outstanding parking fines.'

Langton nodded. 'Right. Let's talk to him, then.'

They were shown to an interview room and supplied with coffee. It was ten minutes before they heard the thump of footsteps and a loud voice shouting: 'What was I supposed to fucking do? You got that bitch in the cells? I bet my bollocks you've fucking let her go, but I've been here all fucking day. I want to see my solicitor, because this isn't fucking right!'

When the door opened, there were two uniformed officers on either side of McDowell. Even after all they had heard about him he still took Langton and Lewis by surprise. He stood glowering before them: six foot three inches tall; bedraggled shoulder-length blond hair; a receding hairline. His tie and shoelaces had been removed, so his feet slopped out of his shoes as he walked in. His blue suit had a strange fifties look, with its draped jacket and baggy trousers. His dirty, stained shirt was open at the neck. He had enormous sloping shoulders, like Robert Mitchum.

When he saw Langton and Lewis, sitting on the opposite side of the bare table, McDowell looked confused.

'What's this about?'

Langton stood up. 'I am Detective Chief Inspector James Langton from the Metropolitan Police and this is Detective Sergeant Lewis.' When Langton shook his hand, the returning squeeze felt like iron, a big shovel. He looked down at a gnarled hand with knuckles that stood out, red-raw and callused.

'We'd like to talk to you.'

McDowell closed his eyes. 'Oh shit, I didn't fucking kill him, did I?'

'Who?'

'The cop I knocked out.'

'I'm here on a different enquiry. Please, sit down.'

'Not until I know what this is about.' McDowell stood, legs apart.

'I am leading a murder enquiry, Mr McDowell. I would like to ask you some questions.'

'No fucking way. I want a solicitor.'

Langton sighed. 'Very well, that can be arranged.'

McDowell sat down. He asked for a smoke; Langton passed over his packet and then lit McDowell's cigarette. The duty sergeant went off to find a solicitor from their lists and, until he returned, they had no option but to sit and wait. McDowell dragged on his cigarette.

'You're not charging me with anything, are you?'

'We need to ask you some questions if we're to eliminate you from our enquiry.'

'What time is it?'

Lewis looked at his watch. 'It's half past five.'

'I'm going to lose my fucking job over this.' McDowell shook his head. 'They've had me here for over sixteen hours. I know my rights!' He inhaled; the smoke drifted from his nose as his watery eyes looked from Langton to Lewis.

'Shit, this is serious, isn't it?'

Back at the station, Anna had typed up her Brighton report and handed it to Barolli. She glanced at him. 'At the time of the murder, was Daniels under surveillance?'

'No, that started later.'

'So, it's possible Daniels could have driven to Brighton.'

'But how would he know she was there?'

Anna shrugged. 'Maybe he asked your Cuban friend, back on Old Compton Street. Or perhaps when she was questioned, she found out who he was and contacted him. It could have been that way round.'

'I'll check it out,' he yawned and rubbed his eyes.

Anna returned to her desk and looked over the memos that had collected while she was away. She asked Jean: 'Am I on lates tonight?'

'Yes, with the gov and Lewis out.'

'Right.' She stood up. 'I'd better get a bite to eat in the canteen.'

'Be a love and file this for me, on the way.'

Anna collected the file Jean held up, but before filing it away she skimmed the report which detailed the information so far received on McDowell. As she stood by the cabinet, her reading started to slow down. She had reached the description of McDowell's car: a cream Mercedes-Benz. She hesitated and then placed the file in order. Now she opened another drawer and flipped through the files until she found one detailing the vehicle history for Alan Daniels. Then she found what she was looking for. The place Alan Daniels had sent his Mercedes to be crushed was called Wreckers Limited.

'I thought you were getting something to eat?'

Anna returned to her desk and picked up her notebook. 'Jean, the driver I had this afternoon, is he from downstairs?'

'Yes.'

'What was his name?'

'I can't remember, off the top of my head. PC . . .'

Moira supplied it. 'PC Gordon White.'

'Thank you. Can you do me a favour and see if he's still around?'

'He was in the canteen a minute ago,' Jean offered.

She and Moira watched Anna bang out of the incident room and exchanged bemused smiles.

PC Gordon White had just finished off a plate of steak and kidney pie when he noticed Anna advancing on him from the other end of the canteen.

'Gordon, could you do something for me?'

'Of course,' he responded.

On the table in front of him, Anna laid down the photograph of a car identical to the Mercedes formerly owned by Alan Daniels.

White nodded approvingly. 'Mercedes, drop head 280SL; lovely motor.'

'If someone had a prang,' Anna began earnestly, 'not a car smash, mind, just a prang, how costly do you think it would be to repair?'

'Depends. They're a very heavy car and they got big bumpers,' he said solemnly. 'They cost. If it was just the bodywork, you could probably be looking at a couple of grand, but they don't have spare parts for them over the counter, since it's a seventy-one model, so you'd need to go to someone dealing in those specific parts.' He grinned. 'Or you could come to me.'

'There's a company called Wreckers Limited. A breakers' or crusher yard.'

'Yes, it's up in Watford.'

'Could you take me there?'

'Now? I'm off duty.'

'No, I didn't mean . . . This is sort of private. Could we go in the morning, first thing? I'd just like you there when I talk to them.'

'I'm on at three to nine tomorrow. I could meet you there, say at ten in the morning.'

'Thank you,' Anna said gratefully. 'I'll be there at ten.'

★

McDowell's solicitor was wearing a neat grey suit and blouse. She looked like she was in her early twenties. They had waited for over three-quarters of an hour from the time she was phoned for her to turn up. In that time, McDowell had started to sweat profusely. When he drank some water, his body was shaking so badly that he had to steady the cup in both of his massive hands. He was being co-operative and answering their questions; he just badly needed a drink. When first of all he was shown a photograph of Lilian Duffy, he volunteered her name straight away. He agreed that for a very brief time he had lived at the house in Shallcotte Street. Langton asked him if he knew Lilian's son, Anthony Duffy.

'Yeah, I knew him.' Beads of sweat dripped from his forehead. 'Right little sod he was, Lilian's son.'

'Tell me what you know about him,' Langton said quietly.

'It was a long time ago,' McDowell sighed. 'One of my girls, a really lovely kid, had upped and left me. I'd heard she'd moved into Lilian's doss house, so I went over there. They said Lilian was out on the street. I finally found her with her dress up round her waist in an alley, her and a punter, having it away. I pull him off her. He starts throwing a few punches so I give him a slap. She starts kicking and screaming. I get her by the throat, say I want to know where my girl was. The next minute, this fucking kid is on my back, punching me head in. I don't even think she knew it was her kid. Anyway, when I heard the ding-dong, I left her on the ground. I didn't want to get involved with cops; this was when I was trying to start my club, right? Next I hear, she's been taken in. She's so out of it, she says she's been assaulted. She didn't even know it was me who grabbed her, she was that far gone.'

'I need to get something straight.' Langton rubbed his head. 'You assaulted Lilian. Her son, Anthony Duffy, broke up the fight. But when she reported the incident, she said that it was her son that had beaten her up, not you.'

'That's right. They do the whole business: get a doctor in to check her out, take her statement. They pick up her kid and then she denies everything. Do you mind?' He took one of Langton's cigarettes.

286

'Were you arrested over the incident?'

'Fuck, no. By then I knew to stay well clear of that bunch of whores. It was one of her drippers told me.'

'Can you recall the next time you saw Anthony Duffy?'

His brow puckered, as he sucked the cigarette he held with his shaking hand.

'Not sure. He used to just turn up. He'd be about sixteen, I guess. The time I remember, he kicked down the back door, yelling for her. He needed a passport. He'd got some school trip he wanted to go on and he'd had to come round for his birth certificate. He's ranting and raving, really uptight about wanting his fucking birth certificate and she's screaming that she doesn't know where it is. And he hits her. Then she whacks him back. And I sort of broke them up. I remember, she started chucking stuff out of drawers and he was beside himself, crying at one point. Then she finds it. And she just throws it at him.'

McDowell started gulping at his beaker of water. 'Then her kid looks at the birth certificate and asks why it's blank for who was his father. She could be a real mean bitch.'

'Go on, Mr McDowell,' Langton said patiently.

'She just laughed. Said she had no fucking idea; told him he could put in any name he could think of. And he, Anthony, her kid, stood there with this scrap of paper, crying. Because all the boys at school would know he didn't have a father.'

He described how Lilian had snatched the birth certificate back and written on the document which she threw back at him. The boy had read the name out loud. Burt Reynolds. 'I guess he was her favourite film star. When he read what she had written, I've never seen such . . .' McDowell frowned. 'He had these big eyes and they went like chips of ice.'

Langton asked McDowell if he had murdered Lilian Duffy. He blinked a few times, surprised, and shook his head.

One by one, Langton placed onto the table the photographs of the victims. When he saw Barbara Whittle, McDowell immediately identified her as one of the women in Shallcotte Street. He also admitted knowing

287

victims three and four, Sandra Donaldson and Kathleen Keegan. Kathleen, he volunteered, had a number of kids but they had all been taken away by Social Services.

'Kathleen was a terrible woman; sold her own kids to sickos. You know, for the paedophiles. I think she even messed around with Anthony.'

'What was that?' Langton leaned closer.

'I heard she had used him, too, when he was a little kid. He was a very pretty little boy. Keegan would have used her own grandmother for money.'

When the picture of Mary Murphy was presented, McDowell easily identified her. He told them she had stayed at Shallcotte Street until it was demolished and then moved on. But when Langton showed him the photograph of Beryl Villiers there was a different reaction. He started to sob uncontrollably. He fell to a sitting position on the floor, his hands covering his head, moaning that Beryl was his little girl; the only one he had ever loved. Lewis and Langton had found another piece of the jigsaw. McDowell had been the man Beryl had run away from Leicester to be with. He had met her at the health spa where he had been the manager.

Although they tried to proceed with the questioning, McDowell lost control. Not only was he sobbing and shaking, but as he cried, spittle formed in globules at the sides of his mouth. A doctor was called in, who said he was going through the DTs and would be unable to talk coherently for some time. Now the duty sergeant brought up the fact that McDowell was due to be released. It was doubtful they would get an extension to hold him for any longer. If they took him before the magistrate court first thing in the morning asking to remand him in custody, the most they would get would be three days.

'But he had a bag of tabs on him as well,' Langton snapped.

'Which is why we reckon the magistrates won't grant him bail.'

'Do what you can. We'll be back in the morning to re-question him.'

By the time they left the station, exhausted, it was already half past seven in the evening. They still did not know if McDowell had been in London or travelled to the United States. They doubted it, but he was nevertheless in the frame and they had a search warrant for McDowell's basement and a warrant for his Mercedes to be towed from the pound and examined for evidence.

Two uniformed officers from the Greater Manchester Police accompanied them to search McDowell's flat. The steps leading down to it were littered with used food cartons, syringes and beer cans. The stink of urine was overpowering. They used wire clippers to open up the padlocks and gain entry to the dark, squalid flat. The carpet was wet under the feet, as a toilet was overflowing.

'Jesus Christ,' Lewis murmured. The old electricity box had been rewired, illegally; it was connected to the street-lights. The kitchen was full of empty vodka bottles. There was a loaf of stale bread on the counter and mice droppings everywhere.

Off the damp corridor, one room was empty, another boarded up. The last room was McDowell's bedroom. They prised the padlocks away from the door. Inside, the room seemed more habitable than the rest of the flat. There was a TV set, a coffee maker and a wardrobe. One wall was lined with black and white curling photographs, mostly of women draped over those familiar sloping shoulders and minor celebrities at his nightclub. The younger McDowell had been quite a handsome ladies' man. There were a few colour snapshots of him in a T-shirt, showing off his muscles. In a corner was a set of weights and barbells.

'How the mighty have fallen,' Langton murmured, softly.

They found more empty vodka bottles stashed in drawers and under the bed, as well as some full ones in the wardrobe. Their methodical search yielded old newspaper cuttings, books, a stack of pornographic videos and magazines, knuckledusters, a cosh, two flick knives and a pillowslip containing some women's dirty underwear.

Langton lifted up the old frayed carpets, which revealed a hoard of cocaine, Ecstasy tabs and a bag of marijuana.

'We can keep him for as long as we like,' he said, feeling drained.

Lewis showed him a handful of US travel brochures.

'You found a passport anywhere?'

Lewis and the two uniformed officers shook their heads. As the two uniforms moved out into the hall, Lewis asked his gov quietly, 'What do you think? Is it him?'

'Could be,' Langton said uncertainly.

One of the officers appeared at the door. 'Sir, you want to come and look at this.'

Near the front door beside the electricity meter was a cupboard which they had forced open. Hidden beneath a torn blanket were several women's handbags, covered in what looked like brick dust.

Langton kneeled down. He looped his pen underneath a strap and drew it towards him. With a handkerchief in his hand, he opened the bag. Inside were a wallet, cheap perfume, a powder compact and a packet of condoms. He eased out the wallet and examined it.

'Jesus.' He turned to Lewis. 'This belonged to Kathleen Keegan.'

Langton told the officers they had better not touch anything else. It was time to call in a forensic team.

By ten o'clock they were back at the police station. McDowell was shouting in the cells below that the walls were full of cockroaches. Though a doctor had administered a sedative, it had yet to kick in. They waited in the room allocated, as the evidence was brought in plastic zipped–up containers: three women's handbags, contents listed and bagged. One they already knew belonged to Kathleen Keegan; the others were identified as those of Barbara Whittle and Sandra Donaldson.

In the station car park, arc lamps had been set up and the forensic team was making an inch–by–inch search of McDowell's Mercedes. So far, all they had discovered were half bottles of vodka beneath the seats and two rocks of cocaine and a crack-pipe in the glove compartment.

Langton and Lewis adjourned to a nearby pub, where they nursed a double Scotch and a gin and tonic respectively. They touched glasses.

'A good day's work,' Langton commented.

'Does this mean Alan Daniels is off the hook?' asked Lewis.

Langton stared into his Scotch for a moment, then drained it. 'So it would seem, Mike. So it would seem.'

Chapter Seventeen

Anna stood by the corrugated-iron gates that led in to Wreckers Limited just outside Watford. She was waiting for PC Gordon White.

The yard was at the end of a small, terraced row of houses. The wall was over eight feet high and big hoops of barbed wire were nailed to the top. She could peer into the breakers' yard through a crack.

She spun around when she heard the car, a Corvette. White got out, nodding at it proudly. 'A heap of rust before I got my hands on it.'

'It's amazing.' When she rested her briefcase on its bonnet, he grimaced and she quickly lifted it off. She took out the photographs of the Mercedes 280SL.

'How much do these cars cost?'

'Depends on the condition. You could pick up one in need of a lot of renovation for five or six grand, maybe even less. It's a 1970s model, so you've got to have a massive mileage.'

'How about one in this condition?'

'Well, if it was remodelled, hood in perfect condition, with no rust and the engine in good nick, you could pay anything up to fifty thousand.'

'Fifty?'

'They're collectors' items. The hubcaps alone are worth over a couple of hundred.'

She asked about the process of crushing vehicles.

'If you've written your car off and the insurance company is in agreement, you can wheel it in here. The charge for crushing it isn't that much.'

Anna chewed her lip. 'So whoever owned this Mercedes, for example, if he wanted the insurance, would have had his insurance company look at it to say it wasn't roadworthy.'

'With a car this valuable, they'd want to look at it.'

'If he described the damage as just a prang, would they pay for it to be crushed? Or would they pay for repairs?'

'Depends on how bad the prang was. Though it wouldn't really be logical to crush this. They've got beautiful steering wheels, nice big round ones, some made of wood, that would be worth salvaging; dashboard, even; ditto the hubcaps. It would make more sense to split it up, for resale of the spare parts.'

Anna nodded. 'OK, let's do it.'

'Do what, exactly?'

'Find out about the Mercedes that was brought here.' She replaced the photograph in her briefcase. 'It's connected to a case I'm working on.'

'Insurance fiddle, is it?'

'More serious than that.'

White, intrigued, eased back the corrugated gate. Wreckers Limited was far bigger inside than she had thought. The noise was deafening. A forklift truck was lifting a wreck from a pile of about fifty cars over to a massive dumper truck. It was released with a crash. Huge wheels gobbled up the rusted heap.

Rising twenty feet in the air on the other side came something that looked like a Big Dipper. Moving down the rods were cubes of metal: crushed cars.

'You'd be amazed how many villains have departed this world inside those square remains,' White said above the din.

Some distance from the pile of wrecks, a man wearing red braces over an open-necked shirt and a cloth cap stood on the steps of a caravan, shading his eyes to watch them. They headed towards him.

'Good morning,' Anna said loudly.

'Morning.'

'Is this your yard?'

'What?'

'I said, is this your yard?'

The man yelled to the driver of the forklift truck. 'Turn it off, Jim. Turn it off!'

While they waited for the silence, Anna showed her ID. 'Could I talk to you?'

He gestured for them to follow him into the caravan. Documents littered almost every available wall space, pinned up and clipped together. There were boxes spilling out more paper onto every surface: a moth-eaten sofa, two armchairs and a desk with one broken leg propped up with tatty old telephone directories.

'This is Constable White. We're here to discuss a Mercedes-Benz convertible.' She gave the vehicle identification and registration numbers.

The man nodded. 'You know, I had another copper enquiring about the same car two weeks ago.'

'Yes, I know.'

'So how can I help you?'

'Could you tell me who brought the car to you?'

When he removed his greasy cloth cap, there was a red sweat ring around his forehead. 'Chap came. He wanted the car crushed. He paid his fifty quid and he left. That's all there is to know.'

'What was the name of the man who brought the car to you? Or was it towed in?'

'No, he drove it in.' He opened a drawer to remove a dog-eared wedge of a book, which he started thumbing through. He showed them the payment slip.

'Mr Daniels. He signed for it.' He passed over the receipt. 'I faxed your lot a copy of it.'

'So Mr Daniels was able to drive the car into your yard?'

'Yes; then he paid his money and left.'

Anna hesitated. Gordon White leaned forward. 'Hang on a second – what was the damage?'

'Look, it's not up to me to estimate what the bloody damage is. He wanted it crushed, so that is what I did.'

'All of it?'

'What?'

'I am asking you if you put the whole of the car through the crusher,' White said flatly.

The manager pursed his lips. Anna noticed that his name, Reg Hawthorn, was printed on a plaque on his scruffy desk.

White sighed and hitched up his trousers. 'Reg, I have a hobby. I do up cars; I buy spare parts. Now, are you going to tell me this Merc, with its hubcaps, its steering wheel, the bumpers, the tail-lights, not to mention the dashboard – remember, I know what price these things go for – you just let it go?'

'I did nothing that anyone else in my trade doesn't do. It's part of the perks, right?' Hawthorn lit a cigarette. 'To be honest, it did seem strange.'

'What did?' Anna interjected.

'Well, it wasn't that badly damaged. I've got to tell you, I run a legitimate business. I don't do nothing without insurance and ownership documents left with the wreck. It's more than my life's worth. But he had all the papers. So who am I to turn down business, right?'

'Before you put it in the crusher, did you strip it?' she asked.

Hawthorn yanked open the drawer again. 'Nobody asked me about this before. So there was no need for me to tell them, right?'

He brought out another dog-eared receipt book and with his gnarled thumb, flicked through the pages to his grubby lists of receipts.

'I sold a number of items; stripped them out. Bought by Vintage Vehicles – VV – over in Elephant and Castle. The seats they didn't buy, though, probably because they're an unusual colour.' He looked up helpfully – 'They got a yard where they do up Mercs specifically' – before flicking further on through his receipt book. 'Seats were bought by

Hudson's Motors in Croydon. They're real bastards to deal with, cheap buggers. Oh yeah, they also bought the hood.'

'Thank you.'

Anna returned to her car. She refused Gordon White's offer to take her to the VV company. 'I really appreciate the time you've spent coming here.' She asked if he knew the Croydon company. He trotted over to his gleaming Corvette and returned with a Greater London A to Z.

'What's the address again?'

'I'll find it, Gordon.'

'I don't mind coming with you.'

'I may be on a wild-goose chase, anyway.'

'Maybe you are. I doubt there'll be anything left for you to see. It's been a while.' He leaned further in to speak to her through her window. 'Mind me asking what it's really about?'

She smiled. 'I'm thinking of starting up a hobby.'

'You're kidding me!'

'Yes, I am. Thanks again, Gordon.'

The interview room was stuffy but the noise of the traffic was too intrusive to open a window. Langton had loosened his tie. Beside him Mike Lewis, sweat plastering his hair to his scalp, had taken his jacket off. McDowell's solicitor also looked very uncomfortable, but it was not the heat that was getting to her. The case was becoming a very serious one and she was woefully aware of her lack of experience. McDowell had been charged with possession of drugs, but it could get worse. She could find herself representing a serial killer.

The interview was being recorded on audio and videotape. Far from complaining of the heat in the room, McDowell kept repeating that he was cold. He was very subdued, lethargic. A doctor had given them clearance for the interview and given McDowell a vitamin shot. Although still suffering withdrawal symptoms, the prisoner was not shaking as much. He was wearing a police-issue tracksuit, his clothes having been taken to be checked for evidence. It was difficult to keep him on track. He chain-smoked and kept repeating the questions to himself before he answered. It was a very frustrating interview.

Langton's patience was frayed. The mixture of cigarette smoke, the heat and McDowell's body odour was suffocating and asking the same question three or four times was driving him to distraction.

McDowell admitted he was an acquaintance of the three victims whose handbags had been found in his basement flat, though he insisted he did not place them there. When he learned the women were dead, he shouted, 'I haven't seen none of them for fucking years and that's the God's honest truth. I dunno what you are trying to make me say, but I never killed any of these slags. But I would have done, if I'd got my hands on that bitch Kathleen Keegan. She should have been hung, drawn and quartered; she was a disgusting woman. Used her own kids. She used Duffy's boy.'

'Are you referring to Anthony Duffy?'

'Yeah, she used him.'

'Are you saying she was procuring children for someone?'

'For herself; for anyone. She sold her kids, one only four years old. And she was forever making that boy do stuff.'

'Anthony Duffy?'

McDowell sighed with impatience,

'Yes, yes. I just said so, didn't I?'

'And you are sure that Lilian Duffy let her use her own son?''

'Yes, YES, Lilian's kid. Don't you listen? Why don't you check on the Social Service register and stop wasting my fucking time? They was always taking him away.'

As the evidence stacked up against McDowell, he became more and more angry. His solicitor had to tell him constantly to keep seated.

'I'm being set up for something here. Now I admit to the drugs; I admit to having them, but not this fucking stuff – these handbags and gear. I never seen any of these women in ten years or more.'

'Can you explain why they were in your flat?' Langton asked, forcing himself to be controlled, his voice quieter.

'No! I bloody can't tell you anything about them. My place has been broken into Christ knows how many times.'

'Did you report it?'

'Fuck off, course I didn't. I'm only crashing down there myself. I'm hardly ever there.'

'Where do you go, if you're not at home?'

'I sleep in me car. But the fuckers towed it away.'

'Do you go to London?'

'Sometimes, yeah.'

'So, having denied you ever went to London, now you admit that you did.'

'Yeah.'

'Have you recently, or in the past few years, been to the United States?'

'Never been.'

Langton put the photograph of Melissa Stephens in front of McDowell but he claimed not to know her. Desperate for a result, Langton then displayed the pillowslip full of women's underwear taken from McDowell's room. It was only then that the big man cracked. He sobbed that the underwear belonged to Beryl Villiers. He had kept it because he loved her.

McDowell's solicitor requested they break for lunch.

While the interview progressed, a forensic team was stripping down McDowell's squalid basement flat. By eleven o'clock they had not discovered any other handbags or female belongings.

Langton met up with the head of the Manchester forensic team. They turned their attention to his Mercedes. The engine was a wreck and there was so much rust under the bonnet that the car was a hazard. It had no MOT, no insurance, no tax. Two rugs were being tested. In the boot, they found some of McDowell's clothes; these were also being examined.

The tests to determine how long the handbags might have been there had not been completed. They were so mouldy that they could have been hidden away for years. Or had they been brought in from some other place? Langton sighed; could someone have planted the evidence? It was a possibility. The handbags had been found outside McDowell's own pad-locked room. Vagrants and junkies had easy access to the common areas of the basement.

McDowell was charged with drug-dealing, possession of narcotics and, at half past four, with the murders of three of their victims. Langton decided to remove McDowell from custody of the Manchester Police and have him transported to Wandsworth Prison in London for further questioning.

Tired out, Langton and Lewis caught the six o'clock train back to the capital. In the dining car they ate dried-out hamburgers and had a couple of beers. Their result had come with so many loopholes it didn't bear thinking about. However, it did show they had made some progress. For a while at least, it would take the heat off them.

A press release was issued to confirm that they were holding a man for questioning.

The incident room had significant new information for Langton on his return. The local Brighton press release had brought a result: Yvonne Barber, their 'deep throat' witness, had been seen drinking in various bars within the Brighton Lanes, then outside a disco, close to the sea front. A woman recalled seeing their witness walk past her with a youngish man. She had been shouting and laughing drunkenly.

A description of a man in his early twenties with crew-cut hair, wearing jeans and a leather bomber jacket, was circulated. Since this fitted neither Alan Daniels's nor McDowell's description, it was surmised that the murder of Yvonne was not connected to the ongoing case; it was just a sad coincidence.

Anna did not sign in until midday. When Barolli had a go at her, saying that the gov's absence was no reason to take liberties, she replied, uptight, that she was actually working. However, she had lost his attention by then, since he was on the phone to Manchester. Anna typed up her report of the morning at the breakers' yard. She put in two calls to Croydon; there was a fault on their line.

In the meantime Barolli was on the phone to Langton about whether to pull off the night-time watchdog on Travis. To his surprise, Langton said it should stay on her until he returned. Likewise, the phone tap should remain in place.

'We're not home and dry with this one yet.'

'So Daniels is still in the frame?' Barolli asked.

'Maybe. Anything come in from the prints?'

'Not yet.'

'Talk later.'

Langton hung up.

'Travis—' When Barolli turned to speak to Anna, he found himself addressing an empty desk. 'Where's Travis?'

'She just left,' Moira said.

Barolli spread his arms. 'What the hell does she think she's doing?' He crossed to Anna's desk and picked up the folder that lay there. 'Where's she gone?'

'She didn't say.' Moira returned to her work. Barolli grunted and perused Anna's half-completed report. Then, irritated, he checked the filing cabinet and dug out the officers' report on the breakers' yard.

Hudson's Motors was behind a warehouse, in a small mews made up of garages. Cars were lined up everywhere; a few mechanics were working on various sports cars. Anna approached a boy in a stained overall. 'Is there an office for Hudson's Motors?'

'Last one along, right at the end.' His head disappeared back under the bonnet of a Bentley Continental.

The only occupant of the office was a man dressed in a blazer, grey slacks and a striped shirt, sitting at his computer. When Anna tapped on the open glass door, he turned around.

'Mr Hudson?'

He smiled. 'He died ten years ago. I'm Martin Fuller. How can I help you?'

When she showed her ID, he reacted with surprise.

'Do you know you have a fault on your phone?' she asked, as he quickly gestured for her to sit down.

'Tell me about it. My computer cut out this morning as well.'

She opened her briefcase. 'You bought some items from Wreckers Limited in Watford.' She took out her notebook.

He blinked and leaned back.

'I have a copy of the receipt, Mr Fuller.'

He flushed. 'We do buy a few things; we deal in vintage cars mostly.'

'This was a Mercedes-Benz.'

Fuller reached for the receipt, but didn't really look at it. He explained that he never bought anything illegal. None of his vehicles had come from there.

'I know, just spare parts,' she smiled.

'Right. Now, what is this receipt for?'

'A pair of seats, the front ones.'

'Oh yes, I remember.'

'You do?' Her heart started pounding.

'Yes, for a Mercedes 280SL. We bought them a while back; I sent my truck over to collect them.'

'Do you still have them?'

He nodded.

'You do?' She could hardly believe it.

'To be honest, if I'd have known they were a custom-made colour, I wouldn't have paid what I paid for them. They're sort of mid-grey-blue and I can't put them in another SL if the interior doesn't match. Basically, I've been waiting for one to come in that has the right interior colour and needs replacements.'

'So you still have them?' she repeated anxiously.

'Yes, they're in storage.'

'Here?'

'Yes.'

She swallowed. 'Have they been cleaned or altered in any way?'

'No. We wrapped them in bubble wrap when we removed them, brought them straight here.'

'Could I see them?'

'We use the first garage for storing spare parts.' He took out a set of keys from a drawer.

Anna followed him back down the mews. He unlocked the door of the garage and slid it back. It was pitch black inside. He switched on the lights: the interior was stacked, floor to ceiling, with seats, bumpers, hubcabs, steering wheels and so on.

'It'll be at the back. They've been here for quite a while.'

Jean, phone to her ear, yelled across to Barolli. 'It's Travis, line two.'

Barolli snatched up his phone. 'Where the hell are you, Travis? No, no, you listen to me. You don't just take off. We're already bursting our budget to get someone looking out for you at your place at night and you – no, just hear me out – what?'

Barolli sat back, discomfited. 'Look, I can't just organize a truck to pick them up and take them to the lab. It's six o'clock. It'll have to be first thing in the morning . . .' He listened. 'Because I am telling you, that's the best I can do. If they've been there for this long, they're not likely to walk out now!'

It was eight o'clock and Langton was just opening a beer when his mobile phone rang. He listened wordlessly, which in itself gained Lewis's attention. Then, after a few moments more: 'They haven't been touched? This is fucking mind-blowing. For Chrissakes, yes! Get them there as soon as you can.' He shut off his phone and stared into space.

'Well, what?' Lewis asked. 'Jimmy, who was it?'

'Barolli. They have, believe it or not, got hold of the two front seats from Alan Daniels's Mercedes.'

'*What?*'

'The crusher yard sold them to a garage. They've been wrapped in bubble wrap, undisturbed from the day they were removed.' He chuckled. 'Travis had this blazing row with Barolli. He wasn't going to get them shifted to the lab until tomorrow morning. So she only bloody hired a removal van and shipped them out herself.'

'Bloody hell.'

'Christ, she's like her father! Jack Travis would have carried them to the lab, if he'd had to.'

Lewis opened his own can of beer and said thoughtfully, 'You still got Alan Daniels in the frame?'

Langton nodded. 'He was never out of it, Mike.'

Lewis sipped his beer. 'Well, you could have bloody fooled me. Christ, what's the point of this guy McDowell being driven down to Wandsworth nick?'

'If someone else stashed those handbags — and they could have — wouldn't it be because they were trying to implicate McDowell?'

'I suppose . . . but forensic reckoned they'd been there a good few months, way before we started the surveillance of Daniels.'

'But who gave us his name?'

'Daniels.'

'Right, so you tell me why he suddenly recalls someone he has supposedly not seen for twenty years! I would say it's down to how his sick devious mind works.'

Langton leaned back, smiling. 'So, if Daniels is our man, what do you think he's going to feel like when it hits the press that we've got a suspect in custody?' It was the first time Langton had felt good in two days.

Lewis was pissed off. 'Shit, you keep stuff close to your chest.'

'Here's something I won't be keeping close. Which stupid bastard checked out the bloody crusher?'

'You don't have to look far,' Lewis said quietly.

Langton shook his head in disbelief. 'It was you?'

'Yeah, it was me. The documents were all legit and according to them, the Merc went through the crusher.'

'Not all of it. You cocked up.'

Lewis felt like shit. 'Travis, eh! The little red demon.'

Langton was staring out of the window, then he looked back. 'More news. The prints came back in. We have confirmation that Alan Daniels's prints match the ones lifted from Travis's photo frame.'

They remained silent for a moment, aware of the sound of the train on the tracks. Then Langton started to laugh softly.

'Getting closer, Mike. We're getting closer.'

Chapter Eighteen

The next morning, John George McDowell was taken to court and charged, not only with various drug offences and the possession of narcotics but, more seriously, with the murder of the three victims. These latter charges he denied. Bail was withheld.

The press were out in force. When he was taken from the court, McDowell withdrew the blanket from over his head and yelled that he was innocent. There was a flashing of camera bulbs. Langton refused to give any statement, except the usual platitudes.

The two leather seats, shrouded in bubble wrap, underside rails intact, were placed on a raised platform table. High-powered arc lamps focused on each seat. Two forensic scientists in protective suits were using tweezers to inch away the gaffer tape securing the bubble wrap. This was a slow process since it was stuck firmly to the plastic, overlapping it like a protective bandage. They eased the tape away fragment by fragment, looking for any evidence of minuscule fibres, hair or blood spots stuck beneath it.

Meanwhile, in the briefing room, Langton led the team in congratulating Travis on her tenacity in pursuing the evidence and her diligent police work. He updated them on the evidence from McDowell's basement flat. Using a thick black felt-tip pen, Langton drew a line from the mug shot of McDowell to each of the victims, except Melissa. He began listing their connections to McDowell on the board behind him.

'McDowell: Beryl Villiers worked for him at the health club. She left home to live with him. His nightclub takes a downward turn; so does our victim. She works part-time as a prostitute for McDowell and, according to him, becomes addicted to drugs. When he gets arrested for living off immoral earnings and buying stolen booze, the club is closed and McDowell goes to prison. Beryl meets up with Lilian Duffy and that mob through the house in Shallcotte Street. McDowell has confirmed that all our victims stayed there at some point or other.'

Now Langton used a red marker pen to link all their victims to Shallcotte Street, excluding Melissa Stephens.

'McDowell admits he was the man beating Lilian Duffy when her son, Anthony, broke up the fight. She accused her son of rape though, as we know, she withdrew the charge later. This accusation first brought Duffy to the attention of the police. You see how our prime suspect, Anthony Duffy, aka Alan Daniels, is also linked to McDowell.

'This connects us to Barry Southwood, who was on the Manchester Vice Squad when Duffy was brought in for questioning.

'McDowell informed us that both Kathleen Keegan and Lilian Duffy abused our suspect as a child, actually selling the boy to customers. Both women used to sell any children living in the house for money. This ups the ante again on Daniels, but we have to remember that McDowell can't really be trusted. For someone who maintains he was very rarely at Shallcotte Street, he seems to have a lot of information. He is also still in the frame for the three murders.'

Langton went on to discuss the possibility that McDowell had been set up. 'The three victims' handbags could have been planted to incriminate him, although McDowell makes rather a good job of doing that himself.' Everyone laughed. Langton looked around the room.

'OK – that's it. The press knows we have a suspect in custody and we'll be bringing in McDowell from Wandsworth later today to continue interrogations. So let's keep at it. You all have a lot to wade through, thankfully. At long last.'

Langton asked Anna to join him in his office.

'You've seen the results from the fingerprints on the frame?' he asked.

She nodded. 'Yes. Alan Daniels was inside my flat.'

'I'm keeping up the surveillance on your place. We're round the clock on Daniels, as well.'

'So, McDowell is . . . what?' She frowned.

'A possible suspect. But also a decoy.'

'What?'

'Until we've got more evidence, I'm not bringing Daniels in. We could arrest him on the fingerprint off your photo frame, but he was also later inside your place with your approval.'

'Hold on – that was much later. I brought in the frame days before,' Anna said stubbornly.

'I know. But he could say otherwise and then it gets down to his word against ours.'

'That's ridiculous.' Anna was steaming. 'Anyway, forensic can prove him wrong.'

'I know, but we have to cover all probable explanations from his brief. We need more evidence that'll screw him. Did he go to Manchester in the last few weeks? He certainly dropped McDowell in our laps.'

'So, what's next?'

Langton pointed to her. 'We watch out for you. I'm sure he'll try and make contact with you, just to find out about McDowell.'

'If he does, how much do I tell him?'

Langton drummed his fingers on his desk. 'Oh, I think you can tell him quite a lot. We want him staying right where we can pick him up. So the more he thinks we believe our decoy is guilty of the murders, the safer he's going to feel. You up for it?'

She nodded.

'I thought you would be. Now, I want you in on the interview with McDowell, but you play by the rules, Travis. You do not, at any cost, put yourself in jeopardy. Is that clear?'

'Yes, sir.'

There was a pause. He was still looking at her; she was unsure whether she should leave. Then he smiled softly. 'The seat discovery was good, Travis. Your dad would be proud of you.'

She swallowed the emotion that welled up. 'Thank you.'

'OK – that's it for now.'

Wearing handcuffs and prison-issue dungarees, freshly washed and shaved, McDowell was escorted from Wandsworth Prison to Queen's Park. He arrived for the interview just after three o'clock. He seemed almost a new man, thought Langton, who had first glimpsed him that morning in court.

He was remarkably coherent. The medication, the meals and a good night's sleep seemed to have worked wonders. He understood the seriousness of the charges and although he would plead guilty to the drug-related offences, denied that he had committed the murders.

When Anna and Langton entered the interview room, McDowell's handcuffs had been removed. He was sitting beside his new solicitor, a thin-faced, dome-headed man named Francis Bellows. Langton introduced him to Anna; the two men had met earlier that morning in court. Bellows had been court-appointed and briefed from Manchester and had already had a lengthy session with McDowell at the prison.

'DS Anna Travis will be conducting the interview with me,' Langton explained as he drew out her chair. Anna sat down facing McDowell. He was enormous and, contrary to her expectations, had a rather jaded handsomeness.

'Right, let's get started,' Langton said, pressing the tape machine on before swivelling round to check the video camera was also ready.

The bubble wrap had been removed from both seats and was laid out in sections. The forensic team had examined every square inch with magnifying glasses. They removed samples of a wool and synthetic carpet, oil stains, grit and a fraction of sand. After these samples were listed and numbered, they focused on the seats. The disappointing news was that the two seats had been well and truly cleaned before being taken to the crusher yard. The leather was in immaculate condition but smelled of mildew and some kind of leather-cleaning fluid.

Leather is not a material that fibres cling to. The two scientists worked on a seat each, moving inch by inch, but they were unable to discover anything except a few grains of sand. They took the seats apart and removed the back to revealed the underside. Here, the leather stitching ran in parallel lines: there were accumulated dust balls and a one-pence piece. Then they got lucky. Caught in the stitching, hardly detectable by the human eye, was a strand of hair. It took a while for it to be gently teased free. It was a single long blonde hair with the root attached and it was from the passenger seat.

The next discovery was caught in the glint of torchlight. It was embedded in the crease of the stitches on the driver's side. The tweezers gently released what looked like a small sliver of pink glass. The hair and pink glass were placed in separate containers, ready to go to the lab for testing.

It had been over two hours and McDowell was tearfully explaining his relationship with the victim, Beryl Villiers.

'Beryl liked Ecstasy. She wouldn't leave the stuff alone. She loved that euphoric feelin', know what I mean? I couldn't stop her. Then I had a bit of a problem, got busted and she started taking them like Smarties. I was only in for a six-month stretch, right? But when I come out, she's up and left me. I search all over Manchester for her, then I find out she's dossing down at Lilian Duffy's place. I went fucking apeshit; they were a real bunch of slags there, I'm telling you. I wanted her back with me. I loved her.'

'So, talk me through the time you went to find Beryl. You said she was staying at Lilian Duffy's house?' Langton asked.

McDowell hesitated a moment. 'Right hovel it was, over in Shallcotte Street. By now Beryl was doing heroin and Lilian Duffy was using her out on the streets.'

Langton began to lay out the photographs of their victims and McDowell touched them one by one.

'Yeah, yeah, they were there. Or they came and went. Almost every tart in Manchester stayed over at that place at some time or other.'

Langton glanced at Anna. 'Did you see her son at the house?'

'Yeah.'

The picture McDowell conjured up was even more wretched than Anna could believe. The child, brought up in a house filled with women, was either ignored or beaten. The only temporary escape came during foster care, which was unpredictable and intermittent because his mother constantly insisted on dragging him back.

'You were questioned about Lilian Duffy's murder before, weren't you?'

'Oh fuck, that was a joke. It's because I got in a fight with her once. She was on her feet when I left her in that alley, her kid just standing there with this crazy expression on his face. Next I hear is, she was found by the cops, beaten up and covered in blood. He done it.'

'Done the beating?'

'Yeah.'

'What about the murder?'

'I dunno. It was a while after. But he certainly had reason to.'

'What reason?'

'Well, what she done to him, locking him in this cupboard and that. Days on end he'd be in there before someone opened the door.'

'So, contrary to what you said before – that you only went to Shallcotte Street rarely – you seem to have been a frequent visitor.'

McDowell shrugged. 'Like I said, I went there looking for Beryl.'

Langton tapped the desk with a pencil. 'Well, you were there before that. First you say that Anthony Duffy was just a small child, next you say he was beating his mother up.'

'Right, yeah.' McDowell sucked at his cigarette.

'So, how many times *did* you visit that house in Shallcotte Street?'

McDowell shrugged again. 'It was like this – I lost my club, fell on hard times a bit and when I needed a place to doss down, I'd go there.'

'When was the last time you saw Lilian Duffy's son?'

'Anthony? It's got to be twenty years ago, pal – that time when he come round for his passport, or it could have been after he was arrested, I can't remember. He could be dead, for all I know. Me head's a bit muddled; it's the drink.'

'So, he never made contact with you? Say, in the last few months?'

'You're not listening to me. I never seen him since he done over his mother.' McDowell was starting to sweat. 'I don't feel well.'

'Do you need to take a break?'

'I need a bottle of fucking vodka, but I doubt you're going to give me one!'

It was just after half past six when they called it quits for the day. McDowell by now was shaking, unable to think straight, and his sweating had started to stink out the interview room. He was taken back to Wandsworth to be returned for further questioning the next morning. The legal sixteen hours with breaks was almost up.

Langton was stunned to hear what forensics had found in the car seat. It was a hell of a lot more than he had expected.

He contacted the lab. By now it was after half past seven and nearly everyone had left for the night. Lewis had already gone home to his new baby. Barolli was on the late shift, organizing the surveillance on Anna's flat. Anna was sorting out her desk and putting things in her briefcase.

'You off then, Travis?' Langton asked, squinting from his cigarette smoke.

'Yes, unless I'm needed here.'

'You're not. Goodnight.'

She looked from the impatient Langton to the edgy Barolli, then picked up her coat. 'Goodnight, then.' The swing doors closed behind her.

Barolli briefed Langton, who stood in the middle of the incident room in his raincoat ready to leave. Daniels had been at home most of the day apart from a trip to the gym in the afternoon. He came back carrying the *Evening Standard*.

'At least he knows we acted on his tip-off,' Barolli said, showing Langton a copy of the newspaper. The headlines reported that a suspect was in custody for the serial murders.

Langton inhaled deeply, the smoke drifting from his nose.

'You going off, then?' Barolli asked.

Langton sat down, hunching his shoulders in the raincoat. 'A lot depends on the lab tomorrow, doesn't it?'

'Yeah. They say with the hair's root attached, they were pretty positive they'd get a result on the DNA. You know, gov, maybe we should pull the bastard in tonight?'

'I've been thinking about that. But Travis is primed to know what to say if he calls her.'

'You think he will?'

'He must be itching to know what we're doing with McDowell.'

'Why hold off? The surveillance team is costing a lot; we are way over budget.'

Langton stubbed out his cigarette. 'Because, pal, if we don't get the results we're hoping for from forensic, he'll be in and out of here like a blue-arsed fly.'

He looked at his watch. 'Who've we got on Travis's flat?'

Barolli checked his list. 'Dick Field; takes over at eight.'

'Mmm.'

'I was just going to grab something to eat before they close the canteen.'

'Who's on Daniels?'

Barolli checked his list and passed it over. Langton glanced at it and let it drop back onto the desk. He yawned; he was exhausted.

'Why don't you go and recharge your batteries, gov?' Barolli said anxiously. Any minute the canteen would close.

Langton dug his hands in his coat pockets and stood up. 'I'm going to have a sleep. Call me at home in a couple of hours.' As he walked out, Barolli sighed with relief.

'He's knackered,' Moira remarked.

'Run up and get me a bacon sandwich, would you? I'm starving.'

Moira pushed her chair back. "I hope he has something to eat; he's not had anything all day.'

'Tell me about it.'

Anna bought some groceries at her local supermarket. As she returned to her car, her mobile rang. She tucked it between her shoulder and her chin, juggling her shopping bags.

'Travis,' she said.

'Hi there.'

'Who is this?' She dumped the bags, knowing immediately who it was.

'Don't you recognize my voice?'

'I'm sorry. Is this Alan?'

'Yes, it's Alan. Where are you?'

She hesitated, her mind racing. 'I'm at Tesco. I'm in the middle of shopping.'

'Which Tesco?'

She sat in her car. 'It's the one on Cromwell Road.'

'I know it.'

She shut the door and locked it. How on earth had he got hold of her mobile number?

'Are you still there?' he asked.

'Yes. Just getting in my car. I'm actually in the car park.'

'You're not far from Queen's Gate. Why don't you wait and I'll meet you there?'

'Unfortunately someone's coming to fix my dishwasher and I've got to be at the flat to let him in.'

'Well, another time then.'

'OK.'

She wasn't sure if he had hung up or not. As she listened—

'How's it all going?' he said softly.

She jumped. 'How's what going?'

'I read in the paper you've arrested someone. He was in court this morning.'

'Yes, he was. But you know, Alan, I can't really talk about it.'

'Why not?'

'You know why not. I'm on the case and it's just not ethical.'

'But I was the one who told you about him.' He sounded peeved.

Sweat started trickling down from her armpits. 'I know you did.'

'So, did they find any evidence?'

'My gov would go crazy if I told you.'

'He's only jealous.'

'Oh, I doubt that.' She gave a soft laugh. 'I have to go now, Alan.'

'Goodbye then.' He hung up abruptly.

Barolli was at his desk, mouth full of bacon sandwich, when Anna rang. She told him she'd had contact.

'Shit, where are you?' he swallowed.

'I'm at Sainsbury's on the Edgware Road. In the car park. He wanted to meet me but I told him I was at Tesco and I had to get home to let someone in to fix my dishwasher. So he knows I'll be home.'

'Listen, let me get back to you. You just carry on and I'll talk to the gov.'

'OK.' She cut off the call.

Barolli called Langton's flat.

'He's not bloody answering,' he said to Moira.

'But he must have got home by now.'

'Yeah I know, but maybe he was so shagged out, he's not hearing the phone. Let's hope he picks up his mobile.' Barolli tried the two numbers for another few minutes and then redialled Anna.

'Travis? I can't get hold of the gov. He doesn't live far from you. Can you call in before you head home and give him an update?'

'Wait a minute.' Anna jotted down Langton's address.

She had often wondered where he lived. She was about to find out. She continued towards Kilburn. Once she found his street, to the left off Kilburn High Road, she drove along slowly, looking for the right number.

Anna climbed the front steps of number 175 and rang one of the unmarked bells. A female voice answered.

'Who's there?'

'My name is Anna Travis. Is this James Langton's flat?' She did not mention his rank for security reasons. She also knew many police officers didn't like neighbours knowing their line of work.

She was in luck. The heavy front door buzzed open. She entered a rather rundown hallway and looked up the stairs.

'Come on up. It's the second floor; door to the right,' said the voice. Anna walked through the open door to the flat and into the sitting room.

'It's Anna Travis. Hello?'

The room was fairly dark, though a lamp on a side table was turned on. Anna took in the rather shabby furniture, the heaps of newspapers and files, and noticed a racing bicycle propped up against a bookcase.

A blonde wearing a bathrobe and slippers was drying her hair with a towel. She was curvaceous and tall, at least five nine. Even without a scrap of make-up on, Anna could see she was stunning.

'Hi. Sorry I couldn't get to the door, but I was stark naked. He's on the phone. He knows you're here.'

'It's quite urgent,' Anna said.

'I'm Nina Davis. I'm your commander's DI.' She reached out to shake Anna's hand. She had a strong grip; neat, clear-varnished nails. Anna avoided looking into the woman's wide blue eyes.

'I've heard a lot about you. You want to sit down? He should just be a moment.'

'No, thank you.'

Anna was able to hear Langton on the telephone, from what she presumed was the bedroom.

'What time did he call her? Is there a surveillance report? Is he still at Queen's Gate? And the phone tap is in place? Good, yes. So, he's not moved out? What? She said what? Give me Mike Lewis's home number, will you?'

Nina was rubbing her damp hair. 'He hasn't been home long. Do you want a coffee or something to drink? I've just made a fresh pot and—'

314

'No, thanks,' Anna answered abruptly. 'From what I can hear, he already knows what I was going to tell him. So I'll go.'

There was a bellow from the bedroom: 'Travis!'

Nina leaned against the bedroom door frame. 'She says she's going.'

'Just stay put a second, Travis,' Langton shouted. Nina gave a shrug of her shoulders and disappeared into the bathroom.

Anna was pretty shaken. It wasn't nerves at the unexpected call from Daniels: she found the presence of the blonde upsetting. She had not considered that Langton could be living with anyone, let alone another officer.

Langton was wearing a tatty old dressing-gown.

'So, the bastard called you. Tell me exactly what he said. I've only had it second-hand from Barolli.'

'He started to ask me about McDowell. Said he'd read it in the papers. I was getting a bit jumpy because he said he wasn't far away and could meet me at the car park. I'm not sure where he is now.'

Langton rubbed his eyes.

'I've just checked. He's at home. Listen, stay cool. We'll know if he makes a move and you've got a watchdog at your place.'

'What do I do if he calls me again and wants to come over?'

'Keep him talking. Give him what we discussed, no more, but don't let him come and see you. Make any excuse.'

'But if you've got people on him and I've got a guy outside, then why not?'

'Because I say so, Travis.'

'Yes, sir. But if he called on my mobile once, he can call me on it again.'

'If your mobile rings, don't answer. We want him to use the land line – that way we can monitor him. You do not agree to let him come and see you, is that clear?'

'Yes, sir.'

He cocked his head to one side. 'You all right?'

'I'm fine, thank you.' She looked down, trying to avoid looking at him.

He suddenly reached out and cupped her chin in his hand.

'Just be straight with me. Do you want me with you?'

'No, no, I don't.' She jerked her face away from his hand. 'Besides, you seem to be . . .'

'I seem to be what?'

'Nothing. Say goodbye to Nina for me. It was nice to meet her. G'night.'

He turned away, checking his watch. She closed his door and left. She sat in her car for a while to calm herself down.

'It's none of your business who he lives with,' she muttered. It was not as if he even tried to hide the fact from her. He'd said he liked blondes and he'd certainly got himself one; plus a direct line to the commander. Anna put the car in gear with some irritation, wondering if anyone else knew about how close he was to Nina, including the commander.

Barolli put the phone down. 'Travis went round to the gov's place,' he said to Moira. 'Now he's double-checking everyone's up to speed! I don't like this. We should just arrest the bastard.'

'Is he worried about Anna? Thinks maybe Daniels'll try and get to her, is that it?' Moira asked, sitting on the edge of his desk.

'It's what he's bloody hoping for, Moira.'

She looked at her fingernails. 'He's playing head games. Langton should watch it. According to the profiler, that Daniels bastard is a master at it! What did he want Mike Lewis's home number for?'

Anna forced herself to stow away the groceries. Then she took out a bowl and mixed three eggs with some grated cheese. As she was adding a little butter to the frying pan, her mobile rang. She knew her voicemail would kick in, so she let it ring: five times. When it stopped, she turned on the hob and put the pan over the burner. Her mobile started ringing. She ignored it, scrambling the eggs and melting the cheese in. The mobile rang again; then twice more. She continued to ignore it. She opened a drawer, took out a fork and picked up her plate.

She ate only a couple of mouthfuls but was unable to face any more.

Wearily, she dialled her voicemail: seven missed calls, no messages, caller ID withheld.

Two more calls came in while she was watching television; her mobile phone was in the kitchen. She recalled what Michael Parks had said. Her response would drive Daniels to distraction as he was unable to take control of the situation. Nothing on the TV could take her mind off it.

She picked up her plate again then almost dropped it when the land line rang. After a moment, she answered it.

It was Langton. 'Has he called again?'

'Nine times, on the mobile. Caller ID withheld.'

There was a pause.

'It shows he's worried about calling you on the land line. You told him you would be at home, right?'

'Yes.'

'OK. He must be getting really pissed off. Well, we just sit it out. Goodnight.'

'Goodnight.'

Anna went to check every window and the front door twice, to satisfy herself she was properly locked in. Then she returned to the lounge and waited nervously. They were using McDowell as a decoy and now they were using her as the bait.

'He's using me, the bastard,' she muttered, rubbing her head. Actually, they were both using her, Langton *and* Daniels; just for different reasons.

Langton asked the officers outside Daniels's flat to verify the target was still at home. They ascertained that no one had seen him leave; all the lights were on. Langton insisted they go further: one of them should question the tenants in the basement flat to make sure there was no possible way he could have left unseen.

The officers crossed the road from their patrol car and rang the basement doorbell. It was opened on a link chain and a young girl peered out. After a couple of minutes' conversation, one of the officers followed her inside. When he returned to the car, he told the other: 'Daniels might have climbed out the back way; you get to the mews over a flat roof. She said she'd done it once when she left her keys at work. She said his flat is an easier climb.'

Langton went ballistic. He instructed the officer to make damned sure Daniels was home by going up to his flat to find out.

Lewis came on the line after a few minutes. 'You were right. Climbed over the roof. He's in a taxi; we're at Marble Arch. I'm right on his tail.'

'Stay in touch,' said Langton. 'I'll be waiting.'

'Will do.' Lewis cut off the call.

Moira raised her eyebrows as Barolli slammed down the phone, fuming. 'This is bloody ridiculous! The bloody surveillance officers had to knock on his frigging door to find out if he was still at home! And guess what? Nobody answered!'

'Wasn't there anyone out the back?'

'There was supposed to be.'

At that moment, Langton, wearing a tracksuit with the hood pulled up, jogged round the corner into Anna's street. He went to sit in the unmarked car waiting opposite Anna's block of flats.

When Anna's mobile phone rang, she counted it as the tenth time. After five rings, it went to voicemail. This time, however, no sooner had it stopped ringing than her land line rang. Feeling a kind of dread, she slowly reached for the phone.

'Hello?'

'Anna.'

'Alan.'

'Don't you answer your mobile phone?'

'I must have let the batteries run too low. Why? Have you been trying to contact me?'

'Doesn't matter. Did the washing-machine repair man come?'

'It was the dishwasher and yes he did, thanks.'

'What are you doing?'

'I'm just about to have a bath. I need an early night.'

'Have you eaten?'

'Yes, I made some scrambled eggs.'

'So, you wouldn't like to have dinner with me?'

'I'd really like to, Alan, but it can't be tonight. It's very late.'

'You're breaking my heart, you know that?' His voice had become seductive. 'I keep on remembering that kiss . . . the moment when it was happening and you were in my arms. Was it as special for you?'

She hesitated. 'Yes.'

'Thank God for that,' he laughed lightly. 'I hoped I wasn't making a fool of myself. When do you next have time off?'

'I don't have my schedule with me. It's all quite hyper at the moment.'

'Oh, right, the arrest of McDowell. Has he been charged?'

'Yes, he was in court this morning.'

'Charged with the murders?'

'Yes, not all of them. We don't have the evidence for all of them. You're doing it again, Alan. You know I'm not supposed to talk about this.'

'Now you're being silly.'

'Sorry?'

'You don't have to be that way with me. I knew one of the victims rather intimately. Of course I would be interested.'

'I'm sorry, Alan. I understand. More than ever after what McDowell told us.'

'What did he tell you?'

'How badly you were treated.'

'Is she one of the victims he's charged with murdering?'

She noticed he still could not use the word 'mother'. He hadn't mentioned Lilian Duffy's name once.

'Well, is she?'

'All I can tell you is that they found some very incriminating evidence in the basement where McDowell lives.'

'Like what?'

Anna sighed. She'd been instructed to appear uneasy about giving him this information.

319

'It was a handbag,' she said. 'Which belonged to one of the victims.'

'That's pretty conclusive, isn't it? Did they find anything else? Serial killers take tokens from their victims, don't they?'

'Yes, and McDowell was quite a ladies' man. But he's proving very tricky to question. He's very, very intelligent.'

'Are we talking about the same man? He's a drunk.'

'He didn't appear to be. He's got a top lawyer, too.'

At that moment, Anna's front door buzzer rang. She looked down: there would not be enough telephone lead to carry the phone to the door.

'Alan, can you wait a second? I left my coffee in the kitchen.'

She put the phone down. In the hall, she looked through the spy hole, but could see nothing. Then she clicked on the door intercom.

'Who is it?'

'Langton,' the intercom crackled.

Anna buzzed him in.

A few seconds later Daniels had pushed the door to her flat open. He stood in front of her, smiling and waving his mobile. 'Surprise, surprise. Aren't you going to ask me in? Good impression, don't you think?' He repeated Langton's name in a gruff voice.

'I don't know what game you are playing, but I told you I couldn't see you.'

'I just couldn't wait. Don't be hard on me, Anna. I'll go after one cup of coffee, I promise.'

'Alan, I really can't. I've told you why.'

'How do you think that makes me feel?' he said. He placed his hand to his heart. 'When all I have done is try and help you.'

At the station, Barolli listened to the conversation with a set of headphones. Two officers were sitting alongside him.

'She's doing all right. But something's wrong. She's not on the phone. I can hear her talking to someone. Oh, Jesus Christ, it's him,' Barolli said, in a panic. 'It's Daniels: he's in her fucking flat.'

The other two officers said nothing; they had been making copious notes throughout the call. One switched over to a radio contact, listened, then turned to Barolli. 'DCI Langton is already there.'

'You saying he knows Daniels is in her place?'

The officer moved his headset aside a fraction. 'I'm still picking up voices, so her phone's still off the hook.'

'Thank Christ for that,' Barolli said.

Daniels was heading towards the living room.

'I want you to leave!'

'I promise I'll only stay a few minutes. I'll be a gentleman.'

Anna could see her phone was still on 'conference' and knew it could pick up.

'You can put your phone down now,' Daniels said, nodding at it.

Her heart was racing. Picking up the phone, she pressed 'speaker on' as she replaced it.

'You said you wanted a cup of coffee?'

'Not really. I just wanted to talk.'

Langton headed up the stairs two at a time. He had seen Daniels enter Anna's flat. He also saw the front door left ajar. Silently, he edged closer and closer until he could hear them talking.

Anna had just gestured for Daniels to sit down. He put his mobile in his pocket and sat next to her on the sofa. Anna sat close to her phone, praying they were still picking up. She had not stipulated how many handbags had been found. He had already slipped up by referring to McDowell as a drunk, which suggested he might have seen him recently.

Trying hard to remain calm, she smiled at him. 'Did the Paris job work out?'

'Oh, yeah. I was able to do the wig fitting in London.'

'So, when do you do the film test?'

'Soon. You must come over. Have you ever been to Paris?'

'I doubt if they would let me off, Alan. With all that's going on, we're sometimes doing double shifts.'

Langton edged further along Anna's hallway. Then he made a fast move into Anna's bedroom, through a door exactly opposite the lounge. He could hear Daniels's voice clearly.

'But surely, now that he's been charged, all that must be over?'

'Not quite. Because he's not been charged with them all and even the ones he has been charged with . . . Well, the clever way he's handling the interrogation is making the evidence look a bit dodgy.'

'Clever? It wasn't too clever to leave some of the victims' handbags at his flat.'

'True. But there might have been someone else living there.'

Anna's nerves were jangling. The tension of keeping control of the conversation to draw him out and get him to implicate himself was tiring her out.

'Someone else living there?' Daniels leaned forward intently. 'What did you mean by that?'

'Apparently, the evidence was found in a part of the flat used by other people. Well, he's maintaining that. As I said, McDowell is very intelligent.'

His voice became angry. 'Stop saying that. Intelligent? He's a bum, a drunk.'

'Really? When did you last see him?'

Daniels stood up. 'I have had no contact with him. Why did you ask me that? I don't know him. I haven't seen him in years.'

'I'm sorry. It's just from what you said, I thought you must have met up with him.'

'What are you implying, Anna?'

'Nothing.'

'He was just a name I drew out of the past. All I was trying to do was to help you. Do you understand that?'

'Yes, of course I do.'

'I mean, if you get the case solved, you get the credit, right? That's why I am interested, Anna, that's the reason.'

'Yes, but you never seem to understand when I tell you that I could get into trouble for talking to you, because you were a suspect.'

'Not any more. I can't be suspected now. Unless . . . there is something you haven't told me?'

'No, there's nothing.'

'You sure?'

'Yes.'

'This is very important, Anna. If we are to see each other again, I have to trust you.'

'Of course.'

'You see, I care about you, Anna. I want to take you to Paris, take you shopping. Would you like that?'

'Yes.'

He was moving closer and her heart was beating so rapidly, she was certain he would be able to detect it.

'You know that dress you wore to the ballet? It was sweet, but it didn't really do much for you. You've got a lovely figure. I kept thinking all night how you'd look in really beautiful, stylish clothes. We could have such a wonderful time together. What's the matter, Anna?'

'Nothing. I'm just tired, Alan.'

'You're not upset about the dress? It just really wasn't very flattering.' He laughed softly. 'Would you like to be made beautiful, Anna?'

'Yes.'

'We could go shopping in Bond Street tomorrow.'

He was now standing very close to her. 'Give me your hand.' He took her hand and drew her up towards him.

'Alan, it's getting late. I really think you should go.'

'Are you trembling? You are. Don't be afraid, Anna. I won't do anything you don't want me to do.' He put his arms around her. 'But I think you like me.' She stood pressed against his chest. His arms were tight around her, like iron clamps. 'Don't you, Anna? I like you.' His hands touched her bra and then slid down her body. She was terrified by the strength of his grip; she literally could not move. At that moment the front door slammed shut, making them both jump.

When Langton strolled in the room, Anna was hugely relieved. Daniels sprang away from her like a startled animal.

'Oh, I'm sorry.' Langton seemed puzzled. 'I didn't know you had company! It's Mr Daniels, isn't it?'

'Yes,' Daniels said pleasantly. 'I was just passing and thought I'd drop in.'

Langton turned to Anna: 'What the hell do you think you're doing?'

Daniels seemed very much in control. 'You're working late, Inspector Langton.' He kissed Anna's cheek. 'I'll call you tomorrow. G'night.'

'I'll show you out.' Anna followed him to the front door.

'G'night Anna,' he repeated pleasantly. But he never looked back, shutting the door behind him as he left.

Anna returned to the living room, legs shaking.

'Are you all right?' Langton asked.

She took a deep breath. 'He didn't like my frock, as you called it.'

'What?'

She sat down on the sofa, her legs buckling under her. 'He wants to take me to Paris and buy me couture!'

He sat down next to her. 'Come here.'

'What?' She was stunned.

'I said, come here. Come on.'

He held out his arms and, unthinkingly, she rested her head against his chest while he wrapped his arms around her.

'Tell me everything,' he said.

She closed her eyes. 'I just don't think I can go through it all right now. I'm exhausted. I'm sorry.' She wanted to ease away from him. 'I'm just tired out.'

His arms tightened. She was reminded of Alan Daniels's arms tightening like iron bands and how she had felt like helpless prey. She pushed away from him and stood up. 'I want to know how in God's name he was able to turn up here!'

'Listen, he was monitored. Nothing would have happened to you.'

'He was here in my flat! He could have killed me!'

'Don't be stupid.'

'I am not stupid!' she said, flushed with anger.

She had a horrible feeling she was going to cry and the last thing she wanted was for him to see her in tears. She took a deep breath to calm herself down and gave Langton a brief summary of the conversation with Daniels.

'I managed to leave the phone on speaker, so anything we did say will hopefully have been recorded.' She headed for the door. 'I'm going to bed.'

'Do you want me with you?'

'What?' She froze.

He stood up. 'I said, would you like me to come with you?'

'Why don't you just go home to that blonde?'

Langton threw his arms out wide. '"That blonde" is my ex-wife. Are you jealous? Is that why you're on the attack?'

'No! What's really making me angry is that all your so-called surveillance screwed up and I was left alone with a serial killer, all right? But I played my part and only let him know what I was meant to tell him. So I did my job, didn't I?'

When she slammed her bedroom door, her mind was in a jumble of thoughts. Had she heard right? Did he mean what she thought he had meant? Did he offer to come to bed with her? She felt dizzy. Maybe she had taken it all the wrong way; maybe he didn't mean it in a sexual way; maybe he just meant that he'd look out for her. So, Nina was his ex-wife. She changed into a pair of pyjamas and buttoned them to the neck. She then cleansed her face, splashed cold water over it, cleaned her teeth. She thought for a moment, then took a pillow from the bed and fetched a blanket from the cupboard. She went back to the living room.

He was on her sofa: his tall, lanky frame curled up, his eyes closed. She dropped the pillow onto the floor and shook out the blanket, then gently laid it over him. She stood looking down at him. She turned off the lights and closed the door.

Chapter Nineteen

Anna thought that with Langton in the next room, she would at least get a good night's sleep. But after dozing fitfully, she kept waking up, the conversation with Daniels looping round in her mind. Finally, she threw the duvet aside and turned on her bedside light.

She thought about what Langton had said, confused about his intention. Or had she misinterpreted? Surely, he hadn't meant he would sleep with her? It must have been more along the lines of protecting her. But what if he had meant it sexually? She had turned him down flat and he might never make another approach. Did she want him to? She did: a realization which sent her into turmoil. She was being ridiculous; he had an ex-wife who was probably not as much of an 'ex' as he made out.

Anna opened her briefcase. She took out her notebook and sat at her dressing-table. She thumbed through most of the book to find a clean page. While she hoped the entire interaction with Daniels had been recorded rather than just the early part, she decided she would make comprehensive notes just in case. As she worked, she realized that the encounter with Daniels had actually been productive. He had made two major slips. In her eagerness to write more, she pushed aside her jewellery box, some make-up and perfume. The jewellery box fell onto the floor. She winced at the sound; the last thing she wanted to do was to wake Langton.

There was silence from the living room. She bent down to pick up the brooches, earrings and strand of pearls and replaced them in the jewellery box, which had once belonged to her mother. She held up a diamanté clip, remembering the sight of it in her mother's hair one Christmas. It was inexpensive costume jewellery. A few of the coloured stones were missing and the empty claws, where the stones had been, were sharp. She ran her finger over them.

Langton was sitting up, unsure what had woken him. He listened for a moment, then crossed to check the front door. Underneath Anna's bedroom door, he could see light. Suddenly there was a strange yelp and a loud bang. He burst into the bedroom.

'Anna!'

She whipped round. She had been standing in front of the dressing-table, the stool fallen to one side. Seeing it was Langton, she almost ran towards him.

'The pink sliver of glass, in the Mercedes' seats!'

'What?'

'I know what it might be!'

'Slow down. You almost gave me heart failure.'

She often reminded him of a kid and never more so than now, in her baggy pyjamas with the bottoms almost falling down. She dived back to the dressing-table, jerking the cord to tighten her pyjamas on the way.

'Melissa Stephens's T-shirt. The pink diamanté logo,' she was back, waving her notebook in front of him, 'had one stone missing.'

'What?'

'Forensic found a shard of pink glass. It was caught in the stitches, right down in the driver's seat. What if, when Melissa struggled, it fell out, got crushed? Forensic didn't know what it was. What if it was off her T-shirt?'

Langton sat on the edge of the bed, rubbing his eyes. 'Christ, what time is it? But weren't those things sequins?'

'No. Don't you remember? I told you. It was expensive. They use these clipper things to stick the stones onto the fabric.'

He blinked, trying to take it in. He had been in a deep sleep, one he really needed. He fell back on the bed, sighing. 'Shit. Why couldn't you let me sleep, Travis?'

Anna knelt on the bed beside him. 'I'm sorry. I couldn't sleep. I was making notes and I knocked my jewellery box onto the floor and—'

'Come here,' he said softly.

She hesitated.

'Your pyjama bottoms are falling down.'

She hitched them up again, moving away a fraction. He looked up at her and opened his arms. 'Come here.'

Slowly she put one knee on the bed.

'I could be right, don't you think?'

'I think it was an inspiration. Just lie beside me. Come on.'

She couldn't help it. She found herself inching further towards him. He was on his side, facing her and when she was almost there, he caught hold of the pyjama cord and pulled her in close beside him. He slid one arm beneath her to turn her so that she nestled against his body while his other hand gently stroked her.

'Travis,' he said, under his breath.

She loved being enveloped by him, the feel of him around her. It felt like the safest place in the world. Her head was buried against his neck, which she found herself kissing, again and again. She could feel his heart beating against hers, and the next minute he had turned her onto her back and she was beneath him.

'Can I take this off you?' he murmured, as he began to ease one button after another from her pyjama top. He moved it aside and looked at her small firm breasts, then bent his head and started kissing one, then the other. She gave a soft moan, and then used both her hands to draw his face down to hers. They kissed. It was a long, passionate kiss, and when they broke apart she had to gasp for breath.

He began to loosen his shirt from his trousers, pulling at it. There was just a beat before she began to loosen his belt buckle, then he rolled away and ripped off his clothes, tearing off his shirt as she eased down his trousers, feeling the elastic of his jockey shorts waistband. He was very aroused, and he moaned as she slipped her hand around his erect penis. She bent down and started to kiss him and he closed his eyes, moaning softly.

★

The alarm, set for seven, woke them both. She was cradled in his arms as he jolted upright, jerking her aside as if he didn't even know where he was, or who was beside him.

'Jesus Christ, what have you got there, Travis? It sounds like a fire alarm.'

She turned off the alarm clock and rested back against the pillows. She could see in the cold light of day her pyjamas and his clothes strewn around the bedroom. He lay back beside her and yawned, rubbing his head.

'What time is it?'

'Seven,' she murmured, hardly able to look at him.

He hooked one arm around her and drew her close. 'You know what I feel like? Eggs and bacon. I am starving hungry.'

'Me too,' she said, feeling shy about getting up naked from the bed, relieved when he tossed the duvet aside and jumped out.

'Right, I'll have a shower, you start the fry-up, then I'll take over and you can get dressed. Is it a deal?'

'Yes.'

He grabbed his clothes and headed into her bathroom. After a moment she got up, fetched her dressing-gown, glad he was not watching her, and went into the kitchen. She could hear him singing away as she busied herself getting out eggs and bacon, the frying pan and putting on fresh coffee.

He appeared dressed, hair washed, and shaved; he slipped his arms around her waist. 'Right, go and get yourself ready, and I'll have this all done when you are through.'

'OK. Coffee's on, but watch out for the toaster; it's got a mind of its own.'

She was glad there was no embarrassment between them; to the contrary, he was totally relaxed and made her feel at ease. He was also as good as his word, apart from the smell of burning toast: he had found the cutlery, set the small bar area she used to have her meals, and was pouring coffee when she walked in.

'That toaster is crazy. I'm going to buy you a new one.'

'It's OK, just idiosyncratic: when you put it on five, it means three, but two means five.'

Anna fetched the plates, keeping herself busy as he watched over the bacon in the frying pan.

'How do you like your eggs?'

'Runny.'

'Me too.'

They sat side by side on the bar stools, and he ate like a starving man, dipping his toast into his eggs.

'You eat too fast,' she said.

'I know; it's because I'm always hungry.'

He pushed his plate aside and then cocked his head to watch her. After a moment he leaned over and kissed her neck. 'You OK with what happened last night?'

'Yes.'

'Good.'

He got up, carrying his dirty plates. He almost put them in her washing machine before he located the dishwasher. Then he checked his watch.

'I'm just going to make some calls, and get them to check this diamanté stone, then we should leave.'

'OK, I'm ready,' she said, looking at her plate. She'd hardly touched her eggs and bacon.

Langton went into the lounge and started making his calls. She ate a couple of mouthfuls, then put the rest in the bin. She put her plate into the dishwasher and went to clean her teeth.

Her bathroom was a sea of wet towels, toothpaste left uncapped; the razor he'd used was left on the side of the sink. She looked at herself, and then bowed her head. She was hardly able to believe what had happened last night.

'Travis, let's go!' he bellowed.

She looked at her reflection a moment, ran a comb through her still-wet hair, and put on some lipstick.

'Travis!' came another bellow.

'I heard you!' she shouted back.

As Langton slammed her front door closed behind him, she winced.

She drove the Mini to his house and double-parked outside. He hurried out in a suit and clean shirt. He was still knotting his tie as he got in beside her.

'Right, let's go. Good news is, we've still got the bastard on tape. After you put the phone down.'

She gave him a sidelong glance. 'Your ex-wife do the laundry for you?'

He laughed and shook his head. 'Nope. I have a good cleaning lady. She's a dab hand with the spray starch.'

He then made one call after another until they arrived at the station. It seemed to be business as usual as he strode ahead of her into the station; she was clipped by a set of swing doors when she wasn't close enough on his heels.

'Watch it, I'm behind you,' she said, but he didn't seem to hear. He headed straight for his office and slammed the door behind him. It was as if the night before had never happened.

At a quarter past nine, Michael Parks arrived. He sat with the team to listen to the taped call between Daniels and Anna. She was flushed with embarrassment at having to listen to herself. However, no one even alluded to the fact that there seemed to be a sexual interaction. Parks replayed the tape a couple of times, making copious notes, then gave them his take on what they'd heard.

'One: he trips up not once, but twice. He refers to your suspect McDowell as a drunk, which implies that he has seen him recently. It was twenty years ago that he saw him in the alley with his mother.'

Langton glanced at his watch.

'Two: there's another leak, when he says handbag in the plural, even though DS Travis made a point of saying there was only one handbag discovered at McDowell's.'

This had also been noted by Langton, who was becoming impatient.

'Three: we can almost feel his anger and frustration as DS Travis constantly focuses on how intelligent and clever McDowell is. If he did, indeed, plant the incriminating evidence, imagine his confusion. Again, he repeats that McDowell is virtually a waste of space.'

Parks flipped through his notes, chewing at the end of his pencil. 'What does show very clearly in how he tries to manipulate DS Travis is the pattern of the classic sociopath. For instance, he is only making these calls "to help" her, see him planting the idea that she should be grateful to him, as it could mean promotion. Note again, he cannot refer to his mother by name, or cannot say the word "mother". It is always "she", despite the fact he uses his mother as an emotional reason for his curiosity about the progress of the enquiry.'

He tapped his notebook and then chuckled. 'The sequence when referring to DS Travis's clothes and saying that she didn't look attractive is classic manipulation. He's tempting her: trip to Paris, buying expensive clothes in Bond Street; he can make her attractive. He is, in other words, undermining her confidence and placing himself in a controlling role.'

He turned to Travis to tell her how well she had teased out the information; he was certain Daniels felt she was trustworthy. If he had found out they were still being taped, it could have been the exact opposite. Anna had a sinking feeling in the pit of her stomach. She raised her hand slightly.

'Do you think that my life was in danger last night? He was very close and towards the end, he was drawing me into his arms as if he wanted to embrace me. In fact, if DI Langton hadn't been in the flat, what do you think he would've done?'

'His audacity in turning up at the flat yet again shows us the cracks. He is getting very desperate. But I don't think he is earmarking you as a victim: not yet. Right now, he is really covering his tracks. But I think he is unnerved, especially by the fact McDowell is not the patsy he thought he would be. So this visit could have pushed him into making a really big mistake. It could also fuel his need to prove how brilliant he is, and that would mean another victim.'

He took a deep breath. 'So, in answer to your question, I don't think he intended any harm to come to you last night – you are, at present, too useful – but I believe he will. Your trust value went down a notch when DI Langton appeared. I hope I've impressed on you how dangerous this man is. He isn't thinking like a hunted man. He thinks like a hunter. Right now you should be regarding him as a walking time bomb.'

At no time had Langton glanced towards Anna, though he remained attentive. Everyone in the room could feel his impatience whenever Parks covered territory that he already knew.

They were, however, still dependent on the results from the forensic laboratory to come in. Without them, they still only had circumstantial evidence and not enough to either charge Daniels or keep him in custody. He had not broken into Anna's flat, but 'paid a late-night visit'.

Parks concluded 'I would say he is aware that he is under constant surveillance, which means he's already taking risks while, at the same time, proving how clever he is by outwitting the surveillance team.'

After Parks had left, Langton gave a briefing to the team. It was imperative they retain the surveillance on Daniels. Glancing at Lewis, he said that both sides of the Queen's Gate residence must be watched as from now. McDowell would be called in for further questioning and it was crucial they get from him any possible connection to Daniels. If Daniels had planted the handbags, then he must have known where McDowell lived.

Lewis lifted his hand. 'Unless McDowell really *did* kill three of the victims. It is still a possibility.'

Langton nodded, though he seemed doubtful. However, he explained, they would be stepping up McDowell's interrogation and pushing for a result. With no word yet from forensic, he instructed Anna and Barolli to go over there and breathe down their necks. He discussed the possibility of the pink shard of glass coming from Melissa's T-shirt.

'We're clutching at straws at the moment but one of them could be enough to pick him up. So get cracking and let's get a result today and get this animal off the street.'

★

In the car park, Anna and Barolli passed McDowell, handcuffed to an officer, being led away from the prison security van. He looked less fit than the day before and seemed disorientated, his feet shuffling beside the officer. His withdrawal symptoms had really kicked in and he was visibly shaking, his hair lank from sweat.

'I wouldn't like to interview him. Going to be like pulling teeth,' Barolli said, watching McDowell being led into the station. They got into the patrol car. 'Apparently, he got roughed up in the nick.'

'Can I ask you something?' she said quietly.

'Of course.'

'I've read the surveillance reports. Even though there wasn't a rear exit from Daniels's apartment, there was someone on surveillance there in case he did a roof job.'

'Yeah, that's right.'

'So they must have known when he'd skipped out?'

'Yes – well, the gov knew.'

'Was I set up?'

Barolli knew he was in trouble. After a moment's hesitation, he shrugged. 'This is off the record, OK? The gov asked Lewis to do extra time. He was the one on the rear of the Queen's Gate flat.'

'I knew it. Langton set it up, didn't he?'

'Look, Anna – even I wasn't in the loop, all right?' Barolli flushed. The truth was, he did not approve of the risk Langton had taken.

'Did he pull the surveillance from the mews behind Daniels's place?'

'Listen, it's hard to keep up with him,' Barolli sighed. 'I don't want to say anything that would put me in the shit, all right?'

She gave him a penetrating look. 'He did though, didn't he?'

'I can't say.'

From the rear of the patrol car, Anna looked out of the window, amazed at her own stupidity. Every time she felt she could trust Langton, he slapped her down.

'I met his ex-wife, Nina,' she said carefully, watching for a reaction.

'Great looker, so I've heard.'

'Did you know she's the commander's DI?'

Barolli laughed.

'No!' He shook his head, amused. 'Now I know how he knows what the commander is having for lunch! He plays women like they were violins.'

Anna pursed her lips. Plays women like violins, does he? She decided to change the subject.

'Do we know when Melissa's body will be released for burial?'

'Not yet. They already had samples, so they didn't need her hair for a match. I suppose they might have already let her family take her home. Though I doubt it, really. The gov would want us to go to the funeral, out of respect. Guess she's still at the mortuary.'

'Home,' Anna murmured, struck by the fact that Melissa Stephens was never ever going home. Whatever she herself had been put through lately by Langton meant nothing in comparison.

Langton placed a full packet of cigarettes in front of the huge man and watched him shake as he lit one. His solicitor, Francis Bellows, warned them that his client was not in good shape as his rights were read to him again.

After a quick glance at Lewis, Langton flipped open his file. 'Right, let's get started. Did anyone approach you during the past few weeks, say? Asking questions about you, where you lived? Anything that you can think of that was unusual?'

McDowell leaned back in his chair, his eyes closed. 'Yeah, the fucker from the traffic cops towed away me car. Said it wasn't taxed or insured; outstanding parking fines, an' I missed a court appearance or something, I don't know.'

'This was recently?'

'I can't remember.'

Langton slapped the table with the flat of his hand. 'You are up for three counts of murder. If you had a hard time in prison last night, think about twenty years of it, maybe more. You'd better start thinking.'

'Thinking about what?' He blinked, unnerved.

'If anyone approached you, or someone you know, asking questions about you.'

McDowell frowned. There was a long pause. He bent his head. He was 'thinking'.

Using tweezers, the forensic scientist worked intently on Melissa's T-shirt. First he matched the colour of the diamantés, then he prised the jeweller's claws open with his tweezers, unclipped a stone and laid it under the microscope.

'Colour matches,' he said softly. He signalled for Anna to come closer. As she examined it through the microscope, he continued: 'It's such a small fragment: they're probably sold in their millions. Trouble is, it'll take time to build up the surrounds.'

Anna surrendered the microscope to Barolli, saying she would see if the T-shirt manufacturers could be of any help.

Anna went into the anteroom to use her mobile. It was disheartening to hear that it was a very big company and that millions of T-shirts with diamanté designs had been manufactured. She described the specific design. She waited on hold for five minutes before a new voice came onto the phone. This woman said that this particular T-shirt was not a bulk order, but one specially commissioned by a jeweller as a deluxe promotional item. He had ordered two dozen as gifts for special occasions, to be presented to clients in a tote bag.

'Did you supply the diamanté stones?' Anna asked.

'Yes. The colour the client wanted was very vibrant, consequently more expensive than usual and therefore more costly to make up. But the jeweller was Theo Fennel, a top of the range designer, with a shop on the Fulham Road.'

Anna listened, trying to be patient. 'Yes, I recognized the logo. So you're saying the stones were not mass-produced?'

'No. In fact, the ones you are talking about were the last of a batch. They went out of business soon after so we couldn't order any more.'

Anna closed her eyes. 'Thank you.'

When Anna returned to sit with Barolli, she relayed the information. The scientist appeared and gestured for them to join him. Two massive blow-up pictures were in the light box. One contained a single stone removed from the T-shirt; the other had the shard of pink glass.

'You can see from picture one that on the entire stone there are small grooves, resulting from the claws that held the stone in place. On the second picture, we have a section of that stone. In the right-hand corner there is a very tiny indentation and at first we didn't even see it. Then it was magnified to this size.'

They stepped across to a computer and watched the broken section slide into place on the empty claw. It was a match to the right-hand corner.

'My God,' Barolli said in a hushed tone.

'Could any stone fit that claw?' Anna asked the scientist.

'Absolutely not. It's just like a ballistic test on a bullet. Although mass-produced, each stone will have some slight flaw. These are not a particularly hard stone, so when they were clipped onto the material, it left an identifying mark.'

Barolli and Anna exchanged glances.

'Would you be prepared to testify in court that, without doubt, this section of stone came from Melissa Stephens's T-shirt?'

'Yes.'

Anna spontaneously threw her arms around the surprised scientist's neck, while Barolli watched, grinning.

It was a major breakthrough.

Lewis left the interview room to take a phone call. Langton continued interrogating McDowell. When Lewis returned, he passed a memo to Langton who glanced at the information, then momentarily closed his eyes. Then he looked at the prisoner as if there had been no interruption.

'Excuse me. Can you repeat what you just said, Mr McDowell?'

'I said he was foreign.'

'Foreign?'

McDowell leaned across to whisper to his solicitor. After a few moments, Francis Bellows faced Langton. 'As you know, my client maintains that the drugs found in his possession and at his home were for his own use. He is very concerned that if he answers your question regarding this person, it could implicate him in the charges of drug dealing.'

Langton sighed, impatient. To get McDowell even to admit that someone had approached him in Manchester had taken half an hour.

'If Mr McDowell has information that helps my enquiry and assists in proving he was not involved in the murders, then it will obviously be beneficial to both parties.'

McDowell looked to his solicitor. Langton leaned forward.

'Mr McDowell, I am attempting to find out if someone set you up. Not for drugs, but for three murders. Now, about this man who approached you . . .'

McDowell spoke hesitantly: 'It was a while ago, good few months. Maybe three or four, but Barry, he was on the door, right?'

Langton interrupted. 'Sorry, who is Barry?'

'The other guy what does the doors with me, alternative nights. We work them between us; there's just the two of us.'

'Right, carry on.'

'Well, I'm in the back having a bevy before I go out front and Barry comes and tells me there's this bloke asking for me. Said he was foreign, well-dressed and he'd walked up to Barry and asked if I was around.'

He said he'd asked Barry what the bloke wanted and Barry had told him that he wanted to score. 'He's a good bloke is Barry, so he'd told the bloke that he didn't know where I was. Then he asked for me address. Said could he come around there? That's when Barry got a bit suspicious and come to find me.'

Langton nodded encouragingly.

'I said to keep him talking; ask him who put him in touch with me.'

'And?'

'When he went back out, the bloke had gone.'

Langton shifted his weight. 'So you didn't actually see him?'

'No. When I heard he'd gone and pissed off, I got really edgy, you know? Because why come to the pub, ask for me, say he wanted some gear, then piss off?'

'Did he ever come back?'

'No.'

Langton rubbed his head and looked at a note Lewis had just passed to him suggesting Daniels had followed McDowell home. Langton scrunched the note in his hand. 'You stated that your basement has been broken into many times. Do you recall if there was a break-in after this foreign man was seen at your pub?'

While this could have been a convenient lead for McDowell to follow, he responded in the negative, shaking his head and stubbing out his cigarette.

'I really don't remember. 'Cos I work most nights until three or four in the morning, there was always some bastard jemmying the padlock off the doors: kids, dossers.'

'We will need your mate's surname and address.'

'Barry Pickering.'

'And his address?'

'Well, he was living at his mother's, over in Bolton, but he won't be there. He's in Walsall Cemetery. Died of a brain tumour, six months ago.'

At that point, Langton snapped, 'Six months ago? Then how could he have seen this foreigner outside your pub?' He stood up quickly, pushing out the table and started gathering his papers together.

'All right,' McDowell said loudly. 'I met him.'

'What?'

'I talked to him.'

'Go on.'

'I didn't want to get meself into any more shit than I'm already in.

339

That's why I lied. Since Barry's not been around, it's been me doing the doors on my own.'

Langton did his best to keep his temper under control. As he asked McDowell to describe the man, his jaw muscles were working overtime.

'He was tall, good-looking. Wore a baseball cap, pulled down low. I told him I didn't have any gear on me and he'd have to wait around, so he went into the pub and stayed for a few drinks. Then he just upped and left.'

'Would you recognize him again?'

McDowell gave a half shrug. 'I don't know. To be honest, I was a bit worse for wear.'

'You must have a few punters coming up and trying to score from you. So how come you remember that specific one?'

McDowell pouted, sulking. 'Well, he was foreign for a start and for another thing, he give me a few quid.'

'And this foreigner never made contact with you again?'

'No.'

'I'll ask you again: would you recognize him again, if you saw him?'

McDowell puffed out his cheeks. 'It would depend.'

'Depend on what?'

'Well, you've got to find him first. After that, I don't know.'

Barolli signalled to Anna in the waiting area. 'They got a result; they're up on the next floor.'

Anna grabbed her briefcase and followed Barolli. Eagerly she caught up with him and then overtook him, heading up the stairs through the swinging door into the laboratory.

Towards the end of the lab, amidst rows of high-powered magnifying equipment, two scientists stood side by side, looking at their light boxes, on which sections of a single strand of hair were displayed.

'You have a result?' Barolli asked nervously.

The younger of the white-coated men pointed a thin marker at the first light box. 'This is the hair from the Mercedes. We sliced it into four sections. Though one sample was lost, fortunately we retained three sections.'

He moved to the second light box. 'This is the single hair taken from the victim, Melissa Stephens; here we have a seventy-five per cent match.'

'Seventy-five,' murmured Barolli.

'The hair follicle was weak. But the DNA match proves without doubt that the hair taken from the car seat of the Mercedes came from Melissa Stephens.'

Anna could feel her legs shaking. She looked at Barolli, moved.

'Brilliant,' he said.

Langton was so fed up with McDowell that he called it quits for the day. As Lewis and he were discussing whether to put Daniels in a line-up, Moira picked up the phone. She stood up from her desk and looked to Langton with some emotion. 'The labs have finished their tests of the hair.'

Langton stiffened, expecting the worst.

'It's a match. It belonged to Melissa Stephens.' Their eyes met. As soon as she had spoken the words, she put her hand over her mouth. He gave a brief, meaningful smile, then turned to Lewis. 'Get the warrant ready.' Then the roller coaster started.

Tension built throughout the afternoon. Everyone was waiting to hear when they would pick up Daniels, but Langton tried to remain calm, one eye on the clock. It was late. If he arrested Daniels now, an all-night session would not even get started, as he was certain his solicitor would demand sight of statements. With a case of such magnitude, Langton would refuse, but he would have to indicate what areas of questioning would be forthcoming.

When Barolli banged into the toilets, Langton was standing at the basin splashing cold water on his face.

'Put it there,' said Barolli, with his hand outstretched.

Langton slapped his hand.

'How did you go with McDowell?' Barolli perched on the counter.

Langton straightened his tie, explaining about McDowell's so-called foreigner possibly being Daniels. 'We might think about getting Daniels into an ID parade.'

While Barolli used the urinal, Langton washed his hands.

'I want Travis to be on the arrest.' He was avoiding Barolli's sour look, not wanting to be drawn into an argument.

Barolli, not liking it, muttered, 'OK.'

'If anyone deserves to see the bastard cornered, she does.'

'Right.'

'Give her a break. She's given us a hell of a lot.'

'Good.'

Barolli almost collided with Lewis as he walked out. Langton followed him out and held eye contact with Lewis until the door had shut behind him.

'Well?' asked Langton.

'Last night, I went round to talk to the kids that rent out Daniels's basement and—'

'You got a result?'

Lewis took a deep breath, slowly releasing it. 'Yes. We've got him, Mike. We've bloody got him.'

When Anna walked into the office to present Langton with her latest report, he startled her by asking, 'You want to be on the arrest?'

She chewed her lips and nodded.

'Good. We'll pick him up at dawn.'

'Dawn?' she repeated.

'Yes. Go home and get some sleep. It'll be one hell of a long day tomorrow.'

She was packing up when Barolli passed her desk.

'I hear you're on the arrest?'

'Yes. He just told me,' she said, embarrassed. 'I didn't, uh . . .'

She was aware that the pecking order decreed it should be Barolli and not her, but he winked.

'You deserve it. You won't ever forget your first murder. A word of advice? Watch his eyes. They're always the giveaway for fear.' He indicated the noticeboard, their victims' faces lined up in rows. Anna thought their dark, dead eyes looked different now, somehow.

'They're smiling,' Barolli whispered, before he walked away.

Chapter Twenty

Anna was unlocking the front door when her neighbour appeared, carrying a bouquet of two dozen red roses. Taking them, Anna thanked her and once inside the flat, tore open the note. Happily she read the words: 'Thank you for breakfast. Love, James'.

After she had undressed for bed, she huddled beneath the duvet, holding tightly to a pillow that still smelled of him. Though she doubted she would be able to sleep, sleep she did and so soundly that when the alarm went at four o'clock, she woke to find her bedside light still on.

It was the day they had all been working toward and she found it hard to keep calm. She showered and washed her hair, then dressed carefully in her new suit and blouse, with smart black shoes. As she scrutinized her appearance in the dressing-table mirror, the adrenalin started pumping again and she couldn't wait to get to the incident room.

At the station, the same feeling was prevalent. She saw that everyone had made more of an effort than usual with their appearance.

While Langton, Anna and Lewis and a uniformed driver took one car, a second car followed with two uniformed officers inside. They headed down Kensington High Street, then turned right into Queen's Gate. Langton used the radio mike to contact the patrol car behind.

'OK, let him know we're coming.'

Then he sat back and, with a quick look at the others, switched on the flashing blue light. Sirens started wailing from their back-up vehicle and the two patrol cars now sped down Queen's Gate. As they double-parked beside the residents' parking bays outside Daniels's house with the blue lights still flashing and the sirens still wailing, passers-by gathered to watch.

'Still inside?' he checked with the surveillance car.

'Affirmative,' came the response.

Langton gave the surveillance officers across the street the all clear and they moved out to return to base. Anna noticed a plain patrol car entering the road from the mews behind Daniels's house.

The two back-up officers stood on the pavement by their cars.

Flanked by Anna and Lewis, Langton moved up the steps to the front door.

'Here we go,' he said.

Langton pressed the intercom bell and they waited.

'Yes?' It was a sleepy-voiced Daniels.

'Police.'

The buzzer clicked to open the front door and the three of them proceeded through it.

After a moment, Daniels opened the door to his flat.

'Good morning, Mr Daniels,' said Langton. 'I have here a warrant for your arrest.'

Daniels took a halfstep back. Lewis moved forward and held the door wide open. Langton held up the warrant.

'I am arresting you on suspicion of the murder of Melissa Stephens. You do not have to say anything, but it may harm your defence if you do not mention when questioned something which you later rely on in court. Anything you do say may be given in evidence.'

Daniels looked in astonishment at each of them. Anna remembered Barolli's advice, 'Look at his eyes,' but the suspect's eyes seemed like dark, unfathomable pools.

Daniels walked into his dining room. They followed him.

Anna's gaze didn't waver; she was keeping her entire focus on his face.

'Is this a joke?' he said.

For a moment, she saw the glimmer of fear in the eyes, as his tongue flicked out to wet his lips. By the time he caught her glance, the fear had gone.

'Anna,' he said softly. 'What is all this?'

'Please read the warrant, Mr Daniels. We are taking you to Queen's Park police station.'

Daniels gestured helplessly at Anna. He addressed Langton evenly. 'I want to call my lawyer.'

'You may do so at the station, sir.'

As Daniels held his hand out for the warrant, he took another step back, almost tripping over a Persian rug. He read the document with an audacious calmness, then slowly glanced over it once more before handing it back. 'Well, it seems in order, but you're making a terrible mistake.' He shrugged. 'I'd better get dressed.' Lewis accompanied him.

When they had gone, Langton murmured to Anna, 'Cool bastard, isn't he?'

After a short time, they returned. Daniels was checking his coat sleeve, flicking a small piece of lint from the cuff. Then, flanked by the two men, he headed out of the house, Anna following behind. As the rear passenger door was opened, he gave Anna a slow, appraising look. Langton gestured peremptorily for him to get inside, while Lewis walked round to the opposite door.

'You'll be going in the patrol car,' Langton instructed Anna quietly, before taking his place in the front seat. He gave the nod to the driver.

Anna watched the car move off quickly, then seated herself in the back of the patrol car next to the uniformed officer. They, too, pulled out quickly to follow in convoy behind Langton.

'They're bringing him in,' said Moira, hurrying into the incident room.

Jean stood up nervously. 'Which interview room?'

'Number two's been made ready.'

Jean rushed to the window to see them entering the station below.

Barolli, desperate to have a look as well, restrained himself, busying himself at his desk.

Anna entered the incident room. They crowded around as she took off her coat.

'Any trouble?' asked Barolli.

'Nope. Apparently he didn't say a word on the way here. Now he's calling his brief.'

'What happened when you arrested him?'

'He asked if it was a joke.'

They turned quickly as Lewis entered the incident room. He cautioned: 'It's going to be half an hour or more until his brief gets here, so he's been taken down to the cells to wait.'

Langton stood outside the cell door while the duty sergeant asked Daniels to remove all items from his pockets. When he was asked to take off his shoes, he sat on the bunk bed, still silent and carefully unthreaded his shoelaces. Then came the request for his tie, which he rolled round his fist and placed beside the shoelaces.

'Trouser belt,' Langton said softly.

Daniels unbuckled his belt, snaked it through its loops and tossed it onto the bed.

'Once your brief arrives, you'll be taken up to the interview room. Until then, you will remain in the cell.'

Daniels watched as the duty sergeant noted everything down on his clipboard. Then he folded his coat neatly and passed it over.

'Can you sign for them please, Mr Daniels?'

'By all means.' Daniels did a fast, flourishing signature.

'And his cufflinks,' Langton ordered.

Daniels sighed and returned to the bed. He stretched out his arm and tugged at his wrists to unclip a pair of gold twists which he then held out to the sergeant in the palm of his hand. After they had been added to the list, a uniformed officer outside the cell took the belongings away. Now the sergeant put on a pair of rubber gloves.

'Could you open your mouth, please?'

Langton joined them at this point. Daniels tilted his head back and the sergeant looked into his mouth.

'Lift your tongue.'

The sergeant ran his hands through Daniels's hair, felt behind his ears and told him to drop his trousers. Langton walked out, discreetly closing the door slightly, as the last section of the body search was completed.

'All clear,' the sergeant said, pulling off his rubber gloves.

Langton glanced over at Daniels, who still stared at the wall ahead of him. While he had not reacted to the indignity of the body search, Langton saw that the muscle at the side of his jaw was working over-time.

When Langton entered the incident room, all eyes turned to him. He quickly summarized the situation in the cell.

'He's not a happy man, but he's not giving an inch.' He looked at his watch. 'Right, let's have a summary in my office.'

It was already coming up to eight. Anna doubted that they would go for the interrogation before noon.

Radcliff did not get to the station until a quarter to nine. He apologized, explaining it was due to heavy traffic. In Langton's office he was made familiar with the charges. At first, he showed no reaction to the development.

He looked over the warrant, then, apparently satisfied, placed it back on Langton's desk. 'On my previous visit, you had nothing but circumstantial evidence against my client. Am I to presume you now have incriminating evidence?'

'Yes.'

'And you are charging him with the murder of – erm . . .' He couldn't remember her name.

'Melissa Stephens.'

'Right.'

'We will also be questioning him with regard to a further ten victims.'

'Ten?' Radcliff spluttered.

He unzipped his briefcase and took out his fountain pen from his breast pocket. He noted the time on a small Gucci notepad. 'You are holding him here at Queen's Park?'

'Yes.'

'In discussing these allegations with my client, I will require some indication of the reason why you feel it is necessary to detain him.'

Langton flipped open one of the row of files he had on his desk.

It was a very different Radcliff who followed the custody officer down the stone steps into the holding cells.

Daniels was lying, eyes closed, on the bed.

'Sorry not to have got here sooner,' said Radcliff, somewhat subdued. 'Held up in traffic and I've been with DCI Langton.'

Daniels eased his legs down from the bed and yawned.

'Alan, we can talk here or, if you prefer, I can ask to be allocated an interview room.'

Daniels stood up and stretched. 'Just get me out of here. Full stop,' he said softly.

'I might not be able to do that, Alan. These are very serious allegations.'

Daniels shook his head with impatience, as if he was there for nothing more serious than a parking offence.

'I'll ask for an interview room.' Radcliff sniffed with distaste. The cell smelled of urine and disinfectant. 'I can't stand these places. They're claustrophobic.'

Meanwhile, the team waited in the incident room. There was yet more delay as Daniels and his brief were taken to an interview room, where the two conferred in hushed voices. At half past ten, Radcliff asked the uniformed officer outside the room if he could speak to Langton. He seemed controlled, considering the seriousness of the allegations, but was also very pale.

Anna had not yet had an opportunity to speak in private with Langton. When coffee and sandwiches were brought to his office in lieu of breakfast,

Anna took the tray from Moira, offering to take it to him. When she opened the door, Langton looked up, irritated by the interruption.

'Anything you need?' she asked.

'Nope, just some peace and quiet.'

When Langton appeared ten minutes later, looking clean cut and smart in a grey suit and white shirt, the room fell silent.

'OK, everyone, we'll be starting our interrogation of Daniels at eleven o'clock sharp. I've earmarked the files I will require at this time.' You could feel his energy. His eyes were sparkling. 'You'll have to stand by as the press is screaming. I've issued a press release to say we are holding Daniels. The phones are going to be hopping.'

When he had finished, Anna watched him conferring with other members of the team. He could hardly keep still; he was pacing around and wisecracking.

According to Anna's watch, it was ten minutes to eleven when she bumped into him in the corridor. 'The brief has said he's ready,' she volunteered. 'They took Daniels back to the cells.'

'Good. Give them the signal to bring him up. It's interview room two.'

'Yes, sir.'

As she walked past him, he caught her hand. 'Did you get something from me?'

'Yes. Thank you.' She smiled at him.

'You want in on the interrogation?'

'Well, er, yes, if it's possible.'

He touched the sun patch on her shoulder. 'OK. It'll be Lewis and you. Switch at half time with Barolli, so his nose isn't too out of joint.'

'Thank you.'

He checked his watch, then looked at her with a soft smile. 'Let's get on with it, then.'

At the newsstands, the first issue of the *Evening Standard* had on its display board: 'Film Star Held For Murder'. The front page carried a picture of

Alan Daniels. Next to his photograph was one of Melissa Stephens. Barolli had contacted her parents the night before to give them advance warning.

Flanked by two uniformed officers, Alan Daniels was led along the corridor towards interview room two. Jean had been hovering on the staircase for ten minutes in order to get a good look at him. When he passed her, he looked up momentarily to see her startled, flushed face before she quickly looked away. She hurried back to the incident room.

'I've just seen him,' she whispered to Moira.

'You were out there long enough,' Moira said dryly. 'What did he look like?'

'He is much better-looking in real life than on the big screen. He's got these amazing eyes, Moira. And he's got on this blue shirt that makes them look a really vivid blue.' She blushed. 'He looked straight at me.' She bent close to Moira. 'Where's Travis?'

Moira murmured, 'She's in there with them. Barolli's pissed off.'

Jean sneaked a glance at him. Then she whispered something to Moira, who gasped.

'Two dozen?'

Jean whispered. 'Girl in the radio control told me. Red ones.'

'You are kidding me?'

'He sent them to her yesterday afternoon.'

Barolli looked over at them. 'What you two gassing about?'

'Nothing,' Moira said, going back to her work.

Jean went to her desk and sat down. The two women exchanged conspiratorial nods.

From a seat by the door, Anna watched Langton and Lewis who sat together opposite Daniels and his brief. Daniels's hands were clasped in front of him, resting on the table. The tape was running and the video camera had been turned on. Langton selected the first file. He took out a photograph and placed it face down on the table.

'Do you, Mr Daniels, admit that you owned a pale blue 1971 Mercedes 280SL.'

'Yes.'

'Did you arrange for this vehicle to be crushed at Wreckers Limited on the eighth of February of this year?'

'Yes.'

'Could you look at the photograph, please, and tell me if you recognize these seats?'

Anna leaned to her right a fraction to watch Daniels's reaction. He cocked his head to one side and shrugged.

'Could you please answer the question?'

'They're car seats.'

'This is a receipt from Wreckers Limited, showing payment for the car seats in the photograph in front of you. They were bought after being removed from your Mercedes and they were subsequently taken to Hudson's Motors in Croydon.'

'If you say so.' Daniels showed not a flicker of interest, but remained relaxed, his hands still resting on the table.

'So, you agree that these seats are from your Mercedes?'

'I can't be sure.'

Langton related how the Mercedes dealer who had sold Daniels the car eight months prior to its accident had verified that the seats were from Mr Daniels's car, being custom made in a very unusual blue leather. They retained a complete logbook copy of previous owners and were able to verify that the seats were from his Mercedes.

'If you say so,' Daniels repeated coolly.

'There is also a serial number on the metal rods of the front right seat, 006731.'

Daniels snapped, impatiently, 'Well, yes.'

Radcliff touched Daniels's arm. 'Mr Daniels paid for his vehicle to be crushed. So it is most confusing to find the seats had subsequently been sold without his permission.'

'Can we just get on with it? What in God's name does the fact that those are the seats from my Mercedes have to do with my being held here? If I wanted to crush a brand-new Rolls-Royce, I could afford to do so. What may appear to be wasteful to you was done simply to avoid any inconvenience to myself. I do have considerable wealth.'

Langton took out the photograph of Melissa Stephens. 'Do you recognize this girl?'

'No. You asked me this before.'

Langton showed pictures of Melissa's T-shirt, indicating the missing diamanté stone. A fragment of that missing stone had been found trapped in the stitching on the seat of the Mercedes and had been determined by forensic scientists to have come from Melissa's T-shirt.

'Can you explain why that fragment was discovered in your Mercedes, Mr Daniels?'

'Perhaps whoever removed the seats from the wreckers' yard dropped it.'

'No. Both seats were wrapped and protected for the entire period they were kept at Hudson's.'

Daniels leaned back and gave Langton a confident smile. 'That would just be the word of whoever removed the seats.' However, the anger in his eyes betrayed him. He was getting rattled.

'Did Melissa Stephens ever get into your Mercedes?'

'No! She certainly did not.'

'Could you please state where you were on the night of seventh February of this year?'

Daniels gave an impatient sigh. 'I have told you before: I was filming in Cornwall for that entire week.'

'Although you were on call for that entire week, there were four days you were not required on the set.'

'I nevertheless remained in Cornwall.'

'The basement of your property in Queen's Gate is rented to a John and Carina Hood. Is that correct?'

'Yes.'

'I have here a statement they made, in which they say that you were at home on two of those nights. There is another statement from two members of the film production staff, in which they say that you were not, as you just stated, in Cornwall for the entire period.'

As Langton read the statements, Daniels leaned back in his chair, looking up to the ceiling. When Langton had finished, all he said was, 'I apologize. I must have been mistaken.'

'So you *were* in London on seventh February?'

'If you say so. However, without my diary in front of me, I really can't tell you exactly where I was. But my agent might be able to provide details.'

'His secretary recalls there was a delay in filming due to bad weather and she was granted permission for you to leave Cornwall. You were therefore not required for the four days, from fifth to eighth February.'

Daniels leaned over to whisper to his lawyer, who was jotting down the dates.

'We will need to check on this,' Radcliff said.

Langton ignored him and repeated his question to Daniels. 'Did you, whilst you were in London, meet Melissa Stephens?'

'No.'

'So, you are saying that you never saw her?'

'That is correct; I have already said it three times.'

'During those dates, did you drive your Mercedes in London?'

'I may have.'

'You may have?'

'I may have driven it, but I also had a car and unit driver at my disposal, so it is quite likely I may not have driven myself.'

'You now admit to being in London for that period?'

'Yes, I suppose I do.'

'Did you drive your Mercedes?'

'I doubt it. As I have just said.'

Langton flicked over the page. 'Would that unit driver be Roger Thornton?'

'Erm, yes, I believe so.'

'Mr Thornton has given us a statement. He says he drove you from Cornwall to your house in Queen's Gate on fifth February and then collected you for the drive back to Devon on eighth February, at four o'clock in the afternoon. He states you did not use him for the two days in between. That would be the sixth and eighth of February.'

Daniels sighed, as if bored with the line of questioning.

'So, during those two days, did you drive your Mercedes?'

'It is possible.'

'On the last day, eighth February, before you returned to filming, you contacted your insurance company in the morning.'

Langton passed over a memo from the insurance brokers, which described a phone message from Alan Daniels that he had been involved in an accident. While there were no injured parties, according to his message, he felt the car was not roadworthy and had subsequently cancelled his insurance. He did not claim for any damage or the subsequent loss of the vehicle.

'That was quite an expensive loss. Why did you not claim for the damage?'

'I couldn't be bothered,' Daniels said. 'I had to get back to filming.'

'But that same morning, before returning to Cornwall, you took the Mercedes to the crushers' yard?'

'Yes.'

'Making no claim for the damage?'

'As I acknowledged previously, that might appear unusual for someone like yourself. I simply decided to get rid of the car. In fact, I bought a new car, a few days later.'

Langton persisted calmly. 'No claim was made, although your Mercedes is valued at forty thousand pounds.'

'It was probably worth more. The vehicle was very badly damaged down one side and I did not want to lose my no claims bonus. Have you any idea how high insurance premiums are for members of my profession? These vintage cars cost a fortune for spare parts. I simply cut my losses.'

'So you drove the Mercedes to the crushers' yard?'

'Yes.'

'It was still roadworthy then?'

'Obviously.'

'Did you at any time drive Melissa Stephens in your Mercedes?'

'No, I did not.'

'Where you were on the night before you took the Mercedes to the yard?'

'I was at home.'

'All night?'

'Yes.'

Langton flipped through the file and withdrew the basement tenants' statement again. They recalled speaking to him on the pavement outside his Queen's Gate property at half past nine that evening. They could be so particular about the time and date because the conversation concerned Daniels's decision to give them three months' notice to leave as he wanted to refurbish the basement flat. The Mercedes was parked in the residents' bay directly opposite. They stated that they saw Daniels driving away from Queen's Gate, towards Hyde Park.

'So, it seems you were not at home all that evening?'

'I probably went out for a drive. I don't remember.'

Langton placed Melissa's photograph in front of him. 'Did you meet Melissa Stephens?'

'No.'

'Do you deny that she was ever in your Mercedes?'

'Yes, of course I do.'

'Would you look closely at this picture of a gear stick? It is from a vehicle the same age and make as yours. Do you agree that this car I am showing you is an automatic and identical to yours?'

'Yes, it is.'

'Now, I am showing you a photograph of the wound to the right side of Melissa Stephens's neck; an injury, the forensic pathologist informs us, caused by her head either being held or forcibly pressed down against the gear lever, leaving a clear round impression but not breaking the surface of her skin.'

Daniels glanced at it. 'So? There's more than one Mercedes being driven around London. Maybe she was giving someone a blow job; I don't know.' He got a warning tap on his arm from Radcliff.

Langton slowly closed the file. 'The hair that was caught in the seat of your Mercedes has been identified as Melissa Stephens's, so that would mean you have lied.'

Radcliff swiftly interrupted. 'Wait a moment. These seats had been out of the car for some considerable time. It is quite possible that someone other than my client transferred not only the diamanté stone but also the girl's hair.'

Anna, watching Daniels, saw the slight flicker of a smile again.

'Do you have any conclusive proof that this girl was in Mr Daniels's car? Because I do not think any of this evidence would stand up in court.'

Langton shut the file and reached for another which Lewis had ready and open. Anna was impressed by their smooth teamwork, Lewis always anticipating what Langton would need next.

Radcliff continued, 'We are all aware of transferral of fibres and as the seats were held for—'

Langton interrupted him: 'You will remember that these seats were immediately covered with bubble wrap upon being removed, gaffer-taped, to exclude any dust or possible damage to the leather and subsequently taken to Hudson's garage.'

'Yes, yes; you've told us this. What I am saying is that any one of those people who moved the seats or carried them out of the car or lifted them up into the removal vehicle could have contaminated your evidence.'

'That is a possibility,' Langton admitted.

Radcliff seemed momentarily satisfied. Daniels tried to catch his eye as if to congratulate him.

Langton did not miss a beat. Anna thought he played his hand like a professional gambler. 'However, both of those men have verified alibis for the night Melissa disappeared and we also have sworn statements that the protective wrap around the seats was not removed during their entire time at the garage.'

'You are treading water, Detective Chief Inspector. With or without alibis, either of these men could have known where her body was left. They could have returned to her corpse to remove samples of hair or whatever. I'm afraid this does not hold up to scrutiny. How many weeks was it before her body was found?' Radcliff persisted.

Daniels gave his solicitor a sly smile.

'Melissa Stephens died the night she disappeared,' Langton said, drumming his fingers on the desk. 'The seats were wrapped the following morning; they were never unwrapped.'

'It is just their word, though, isn't it?'

'Not only the word of two mechanics, but also one paint sprayer and the salesman. Also, bear in mind that if the gaffer tape had been removed at any time after being attached, it would have damaged the bubble wrap. Instead, it all remained intact. Therefore, the evidence we retrieved from the car seats was not contaminated.'

Radcliff raised an eyebrow, seemingly confident this would be easily dismissed in court. Anna glanced back at Daniels, who was now appearing more confident, even rocking slightly in his seat.

Langton held out his hand. Lewis passed him a folder. Langton took out the photographs.

'Photograph one, from file two: a close-up of the bite mark to Melissa Stephens's tongue.'

This was coming out of left field. Radcliff blinked. He knew nothing about this.

'Bite mark?' he said cautiously.

'Photograph two is from your client's dental records. It's a photograph of the impression made by a dentist in Los Angeles. As you can see, Mr Daniels's teeth have been recently capped. This dental work took place during the month of March this year.

'These were removed from Mr Daniels's study.' Langton withdrew another series of X-rays and photographs. 'Mr Daniels offered them to us as his original X-rays. As it turns out, they are not Mr Daniels's X-rays and therefore not his teeth.'

Langton slowly took out of the file an enlarged photograph of Daniels's mouth, caught in a wide grin. A ruler had been placed alongside it to measure the exact size.

'Taken as a publicity still from the mini-series *Falcon Bay*, this photograph is dated two years ago. As you can see, Mr Daniels has a very wide smile and is not yet showing the new capped teeth.'

Daniels leaned forwards, smiling.

'They made a good job of my dental work, didn't they?' he said to Radcliff. But Radcliff had smelled the sting coming and, if anything, looked more inclined to distance himself from his client than to respond to his camaraderie.

'Another picture of the bite marks to Melissa Stephens's tongue.'

Langton placed it beside the photograph of Daniel's grinning mouth. He took out two colour transparencies, placing one on top of the other. 'As you can see, it was a perfect match before Mr Daniels had his dental work. This proves, without doubt, that it was your client who bit Melissa Stephens's tongue, just as there is no doubt that Melissa Stephens was a passenger in Mr Daniels's Mercedes-Benz.'

Radcliff was sweating. He spent a considerable time playing with the sets of photographs. Anna noticed small beads of perspiration appearing on his top lip. Daniels, however, remained impenetrable. Anna thought he had lost awareness of her presence in the room, until he moved a fraction sideways and looked across at her with a barely detectable snarl before straightening up to face Langton. She found herself recoiling in horror. No one else in the room was aware of the intimacy of what had just happened. She could barely make out Langton's voice above the ringing in her ears.

'We did not find the tip of her tongue when we tested the contents of the victim's stomach, nor was it recovered at the murder site. So I'm proposing that your client either spat it out or ate it. Either way, we can prove that it was Mr Daniels who bit Melissa Stephens's tongue.'

There was a momentary pause in the room while Lewis put the photographs back into the file.

'I am asking you again, Mr Daniels,' Langton said abruptly, 'did you, on the night of seventh February, meet Melissa Stephens?'

Radcliff leaned close to his client, covering his mouth as he whispered.

'Please answer the question,' said Langton.

'No comment,' Daniels said.

Langton sucked in his breath, disappointed. The last thing he wanted was for Daniels to resort to using the 'no comment' routine for any further questions. He decided to switch tactics, informing Lewis with a quick note. Lewis nodded and brought out the case file on McDowell.

'Do you know John McDowell?'

'Yes.'

'When was the last time you saw him?'

Daniels shrugged and said he thought it had to be at least twenty years ago.

'Twenty years ago, McDowell ran a successful nightclub, didn't he?'

'Yes, he did.'

Langton planned to talk about McDowell, knowing Daniels would not be able to resist. With the pressure off from asking about Melissa Stephens, Langton continued the tactic of feeding the suspect questions that were easily answered; once more, trying to push him into a corner.

'Could you describe McDowell to me? We are trying to get an angle on the type of man he is.'

'Well, he was flashy, loud-mouthed. Ran a string of tarts out of his club. He was a fitness freak too, at the time he was visiting her house.'

'Whose house was that?'

'Lilian Duffy's house,' he snapped.

'Could you tell me what your relationship with Lilian Duffy was?'

'She was a prostitute. She ran the Shallcotte Street house as a brothel.'

'But what relation is Lilian Duffy to you?'

Daniels chewed at his lip. He hated using the word.

'Lilian Duffy is what?' Langton persisted.

'My mother,' he said, recoiling back in his seat.

'You were born Anthony Duffy?'

'Yes.'

'And you maintain you have not seen McDowell for twenty years?'

'Yes!'

Langton pressed 'play' on a tape recorder.

'I am going to play a tape to you; this is of a telephone call you made to Detective Sergeant Travis.'

Radcliff held up a hand. 'What is this?'

'It is a tape of a phone call made from your client to DS Travis.' Langton turned to indicate Anna.

'You taped the call?'

'Yes, that is correct.'

Radcliff turned to Daniels. 'Were you aware of the call being taped?'

'Of course I wasn't. We had been out together to see the ballet.' Daniels smirked at Anna. 'We had a pleasant evening, didn't we?' He sat back upright again. 'There was no reason I should not call her. Especially after she had come on to me that first evening.'

As Langton played the tape, he watched Daniels's reactions: his smirking glances at Anna and the manner in which he leaned close to Radcliff to whisper. After the conversation finished playing, Langton stopped the tape.

'You admit that this is your voice speaking to DS Travis?'

'Yes. Why on earth should I deny calling her?'

Radcliff leaned forwards across the table and wagged his finger at Langton. 'What possible justification can you make for taping my client's private phone call?'

'We were concerned for DS Travis's safety.'

'Concerned?' Daniels's mouth gaped.

'We had reason to be concerned. Your so-called "date" was under our supervision. Part of this tape recording was made whilst your client was inside DS Travis's flat.'

'What?' Daniels was losing his temper.

'She left her phone recording whilst you were in her flat. DS Travis was working undercover for our investigation.'

'For what reason?'

'I would say that is fairly obvious: you were a suspect in our murder enquiry. And I would say she did a very good job. You remained unaware of her intentions and we got the result we wanted.'

Daniels leaned forward, almost occupying the entire width of the table. 'Which was what?'

'We were able to confirm that you had gained access to DS Travis's flat. And from that you were placed under surveillance.'

'I was in her flat that night at her request. So what?'

'You had previously gained illegal entry to DS Travis's flat.'

'No.'

'We have a set of your fingerprints, Mr Daniels, taken from DS Travis's flat.'

'And I have just told you that I was her guest. It would be strange if you didn't find my prints there.'

'These prints, Mr Daniels, were removed from the premises prior to the first evening you spent there.'

Lewis produced the picture frame in an evidence bag. 'This frame was brought in by DS Travis before you spent time together in her flat. The fingerprints were subsequently matched to a bank note you handled at the Opera House.'

Daniels twisted his neck as if it was stiff.

Langton continued, 'Previously, you described McDowell as a fitness freak, running a successful nightclub?'

'Yes, that was twenty years ago, yes.'

Langton replayed the moment of the taped phone call, when Daniels described McDowell as a pitiful drunkard. 'How did you know Mr McDowell was now, twenty years later, a drunkard, if you had not seen him recently?'

'It's a foregone conclusion; he was a heavy drinker then.'

'But then he was also a successful businessman. You said so yourself. How did you know about his present circumstances?'

'It was a wild guess.'

'I put it to you it's a bit more than that, isn't it? You mentioned his present state of inebriation twice, so I put it to you that you had seen Mr McDowell recently.'

'No, that is not true.'

'You also seem to be privy to information about certain items that were recovered from McDowell's home.'

Daniels nudged Radcliff with a sly smile. 'This is obviously entrapment. The woman, Travis, told me about McDowell's condition. She also told me about the handbags they found at his house.'

'Handbags?'

'Yes, you found three of the victims' handbags. I know that. She told me.'

Langton rewound the tape. 'Please listen to the call again.'

Daniels was becoming really tetchy. 'This is entrapment.' He turned again to Radcliff. 'This tape is rubbish. They probably doctored it.'

'Just listen to the tape recording please, Mr Daniels.'

It was played again. Radcliff listened intently; he then leaned to one side to stare at Anna, before returning to an upright position, listening and tapping his notebook with his pen. When the tape recording ended, Langton moved the recorder aside and ejected the tape.

'Mr Daniels, are you prepared to take part in an identity parade?'

Daniels pinched the bridge of his nose. 'I am a well-known actor. It is farcical for you to expect to be able to assemble twelve men who resemble me. If you could, my career would certainly be in jeopardy,' he laughed.

Langton couldn't hold his tongue: 'I would say that is a foregone conclusion.'

Anna shifted in her seat. She couldn't quite fathom why Langton had taken the pressure off the Melissa questioning. She could feel the interview losing momentum and Daniels seemed to feel it, too. He was becoming more expansive and constantly swung his body away from his chair. Sometimes he seemed more interested in what was happening outside as they heard people passing back and forth.

'So you decline to agree to participate in an identity parade?'

Radcliff tapped the table with his pen. 'I agree with Mr Daniels. Owing to my client's celebrity, the notion of an identification parade is ludicrous.'

Radcliff looked at Langton. 'I am confused as to why you wish my client to take part in an identification parade anyway, especially if Mr McDowell has no connection to the charges relating to Melissa Stephens.'

'But he was connected to the other ten victims. Mr Radcliff, I believe your client was involved in their deaths. And the very fact that your client knew that three of the victims' handbags had been recovered from McDowell's premises makes me suspicious that he, in actual fact, planted the incriminating evidence.'

'Just how do you come to that conclusion?'

Langton drew the tape recorder closer to him again. 'Listen to a section of the tape again. DS Travis never makes any mention of "handbags", plural; she actually says "handbag". It is Mr Daniels who uses the plural on the tape. It is Mr Daniels who, in front of you and as recorded on video, has said that three bags were recovered.'

'It was just an assumption.' Radcliff waved his hand airily. 'He knew there were a number of victims you were investigating.'

Langton slapped the table with the flat of his hand. 'An assumption? It's the exact number: not one, or two, but three! He describes McDowell as a drunkard, yet this is a man he supposedly has not seen for twenty years.'

Radcliff was becoming agitated. 'Are you telling me that you intend charging my client with another murder, apart from Melissa Stephens? Or perhaps more than one?"

'That is a possibility, yes.'

'How tedious,' said Daniels. 'All right, I'll take part in your parade, but it's all a terrible waste of time.'

There was a knock at the door and DC Barolli stepped in. Langton duly noted his arrival on the tape. Langton glanced at a note Barolli handed him and the plastic bag that he carried. 'I suggest we take a five-minute lavatory break,' Langton told everyone. When Daniels snapped that he didn't require one, Langton good-humouredly replied that he did. He took the bag from Barolli and produced a baseball cap, which he placed on the table.

He noted the introduction of the cap for the tape and held it up for the camera to see. When Radcliff stood up, Langton offered to show him the bathroom facilities.

Lewis passed Anna the note Barolli had brought in. While Daniels watched her, she read the message that McDowell was en route to the identification viewing room where Barolli had selected a line-up of officers and other station employees of Daniels's height and build to participate in the ID parade.

Daniels leaned across the table, towards Anna.

'You two-faced little—'

Lewis said sharply: 'Mr Daniels, sit back in your seat, please.'

It was as if the suspect had sensed that something was wrong. He slowly pushed back his chair.

'Please remain seated,' Lewis said coldly.

Daniels eased himself back into his chair as Langton entered the room. 'We are ready to take Mr Daniels to the identification unit.'

'Where's my brief?' he snarled.

'He will be accompanying you to the suite, Mr Daniels.'

Radcliff had just splashed cold water over his face in the washroom and was contemplating the murky roller towel with distaste when Langton walked in. 'A witness has been brought to the viewing room. I would like you to accompany me there to oversee the possible identification.'

'This is pretty sneaky,' Radcliff said. 'I don't see what you hope to achieve, under the circumstances.' The solicitor ran a small comb through his hair, pocketed it and indicated he was ready to go with Langton.

As the two men headed down the corridor, McDowell, handcuffed to Barolli, walked towards them dressed in prison-issue overalls and a denim shirt. There was a marked improvement in his demeanour. He seemed much more alert.

'Morning.' He grinned at Langton.

'Good morning, Mr McDowell. Can you come this way, please?' Langton gestured to the viewing room.

The room was small and empty except for two hard-backed chairs.

'Mr McDowell, you must answer truthfully the questions I am about to put to you. Do you understand?'

'Yeah.'

'I want you to look into the room beyond the window and tell me if you recognize any of the men standing in front of you. Take your time. If you do recognize anyone, tell me if this is the same man who approached you outside your place of work in Manchester.'

McDowell nodded.

'Do you understand what I have asked you to do?'

'Yep. Look at the blokes and tell you if one of them was the foreigner what I spoke to. Yes, that right?'

'That is correct.'

Langton pressed the button to indicate they were about to draw the blinds from their side of the wall. The red light blinked.

In the adjoining room, Daniels entered with Lewis. Eight men wearing identical baseball caps stood silent and expressionless.

Lewis handed him a baseball cap.

'Mr Daniels, you may stand wherever in the line you wish,' Lewis said quietly.

Daniels pulled his cap down over his face and considered the line-up. He chose to stand in the centre: four men to his right, four to his left. They were given numbered cards; Daniels had number five.

'Mr Daniels, can you pull up the collar of your jacket?'

Daniels hitched up his collar to chin level.

Langton saw the red light steady their side, indicating they were set. He gestured for McDowell to draw closer to the one-way glass.

McDowell's sloping shoulders almost blocked the entire window. He stood, chin jutting out, staring for what seemed like a long time. Langton was disappointed that McDowell was unable to recognize Daniels immediately and was just about to draw the viewing to a close when McDowell turned round.

'Yes, it's him. Number five. It's a different baseball cap. That was me problem. But, yeah, I'd say it's him.'

'Thank you, Mr McDowell.'

Langton at once turned off the light and drew back the blinds.

While Langton ushered Radcliff out of the room, Barolli waited a moment before leading McDowell back to the cells.

Daniels kept hold of his baseball cap. As he was led back to the interview room, he turned the baseball hat sideways, grinning at his joke. Radcliff snatched it off his head. Langton spoke into the tape recorder to say that they had returned and that the interview would continue.

Langton waited for a moment before addressing their suspect: 'Mr Daniels, I am charging you with the murder of Melissa Stephens.'

'I gathered that,' Daniels said, sounding almost bored.

Lewis passed the folder of the victims' photographs to Langton, who continued: 'I would now like to begin to question you with regard to the murders of Lilian Duffy and of Teresa Booth . . .'

Two photographs were put on the table.

'Kathleen Keegan . . .'

A third photograph joined them.

'Barbara Whittle . . .'

A fourth.

'Sandra Donaldson . . .'

As Langton was about to present the next victim's photograph, Daniels prompted, mockingly, 'Beryl Villiers and Mary Murphy.'

Daniels raised his body up and pressed his back against the chair. He looked like a coiled snake, thought Anna. As everyone stared, he smiled enigmatically back at them. 'Thelma Delray, Sadie Zadine and Marla Courtney.'

Langton laid out all the photographs. They filled the entire table.

Anna was rigid. She could not believe what was happening. None of them could. Lewis glanced at Langton. No one spoke. Radcliff stared at his client, mesmerized by his quiet, expressionless voice.

Daniels reached out his hand to lightly touch each picture. He sighed and began counting. 'One, two, three, four.' He cocked his head to one side. 'There's one missing. Melissa; where's my beautiful

Melissa?' He picked up Melissa's picture and lay it beneath the others.

He started arranging the faces in the order that they had been killed. When he had finished his handiwork, he looked up. 'They're all mine.' He swept the pictures up into his arms and clutched them.

'Mr Daniels, are you admitting that you killed all these women?'

'Yes.'

Radcliff was shaking, his face drained of colour. 'Jesus, God,' he whispered.

Daniels stacked the photographs back into a neat pile in front of him. 'Ready when you are,' he said softly. He picked up the photograph of his mother, Lilian Duffy.

He pointed at Langton. 'No. I don't want him sitting opposite.' He turned slowly to Anna. 'She takes his place. You won't get another word out of me otherwise. I want her at the table, facing me. That's the deal.'

Langton and Anna looked at each other, their eyes locked for a moment. She gave a barely detectable nod of her head. Langton returned his attention to Daniels.

'We will take a lunch break. After that, DS Travis will sit opposite you, Mr Daniels.'

Daniels smiled. 'Thank you.' Idly, his fingers stroked the photograph of Melissa Stephens's face.

Anna's blood ran cold.

Chapter Twenty-one

Langton asked Anna to meet him in his office. He could tell that she was shaken by Daniels's request.

'Can you bear it? Facing him?'

She nodded numbly, and gave a slight shrug of her shoulders. 'I couldn't believe it when he admitted the murders. I thought it would take days.'

Langton shook his head. 'We've too much on him and he knows it. This is just prolonging the agony. I think you and I need to spend lunchtime running through how I want you to approach the interview, and it just might take days, Anna; it's not over yet.'

'Why do you think he wants me opposite him?'

'I don't know how his warped mind works. Maybe he thinks you made a fool of him. Whatever the reason, he's going to relish every minute; he's that sick and it's not going to be pleasant. He'll want to see how you react.'

'And if I don't?'

'Then you will have beaten him because this is all about wanting to break you, hurt you.'

She closed her eyes, then opened them to look up into Langton's concerned face. 'Devious bastard,' she said. 'Let's get started, I want to be ready for him.'

Barolli joined Lewis at lunch and was confused to hear that Anna would be in the hot seat from now on. Then Lewis dropped the real bombshell. 'Daniels has admitted to all the murders.'

'Christ, all of them?'

'Yeah, including the American ones.'

Word of the confession spread quickly round the incident room. Moira shuddered at Anna's situation: 'It's like putting a lamb in front of a hungry wolf.'

Jean unnerved them both when she recalled that in the Fred West case one witness experienced a nervous breakdown after listening to the horrific details of his murders and had been unable to continue working.

'She sued the constabulary involved, didn't she?' Moira remembered.

Barolli and Lewis looked at each other; then all four involuntarily glanced over at the blinds drawn down in Langton's office, against which Anna's shadow was just visible.

'God help her!' Jean said. There were brief nods of agreement and they all returned to their separate desks.

The press office had been inundated with calls. A new press release was now in preparation. It confirmed that Alan Daniels was being held for questioning in connection with the murder of Melissa Stephens and was also helping the police with their enquiries in a number of other cases. The *Evening Standard* was planning blanket coverage of the actor's arrest for its late edition. Television news programmes began assimilating as much footage of Daniels as quickly as they could in preparation for the bulletins which would go out later that evening. Like vultures, the press corps began to gather outside the station.

Langton returned from his lunch break. Anna had eaten lunch at the desk in his office while familiarizing herself with the case files and Langton's preliminary notes.

'He's been taken back in. You ready?'

She looked up, nodding. There had been no time for nerves to take hold.

'Do you need to go to the loo?'

'Yes, I'd better.'

'OK, I'll wait outside the room. Have you got everything you need?'

'Yes.'

'Good girl. Just take it at an easy pace. Don't let him ruffle you and remember: I'm right behind you if you need me.'

'Yes.'

Langton was stacking the files when she hurried out towards the ladies. She clattered into the cubicle and sat on the toilet, willing herself to pee. She was too tense; nothing happened. She gritted her teeth. 'Come on! Do it.'

At last she went. Anna washed her hands and stared at herself in the mirror. 'Watch over me, Dad,' she whispered. Shoulders back, she walked through the door.

Anna was heading up the stairs to the interview room when Lewis appeared: 'Good luck!'

'Thank you.'

'That's from all of us.'

Langton was waiting for her when she turned into the corridor at the top of the staircase. He gave her a smile. 'Files are in order on the table. You have to read him his rights again.'

'I know.'

He seemed even more nervous than she was, which in some way calmed her. They walked into the interview room together. Daniels had washed his face and swept his hair back; it looked wet. She avoided looking at him as she sat down.

Langton took his place directly behind her and Radcliff sat down beside Daniels. Anna followed the protocol of checking there was a tape in the tape machine and that the video camera was running. She looked at her watch and stated the exact time, the location and the names of those present in the interview room.

When she had finished reading Daniels his rights, he leaned close and said suavely, 'You're doing very well. I'm proud of you.'

She flushed with embarrassment. She spent a few moments looking at the first case file and composing herself, then raised her head to look directly at Daniels. He stared back, unblinking. Though she recalled Barolli saying, 'watch his eyes; wait for the fear', there was certainly no sign of fear now. If anything, the former Anthony Duffy seemed to be enjoying the unease emanating from everyone else. She began.

'Mr Daniels, this morning you admitted killing Lilian Duffy. Could you please tell me what your relationship was to the victim?'

'You know what it was, Anna,' he said smoothly.

'I require you to tell me.'

'She was my parent.' His lip curled in contempt.

Anna leaned back in her chair. Face up on the table between them was the picture of Lilian Duffy. 'This photograph: could you tell me who it is?'

'It's her, obviously.'

'Could you please identify the photograph, Mr Daniels?'

Then she saw the flash of anger. 'It's Lilian Duffy,' he snarled. 'The bitch that gave birth to me.'

Anna supplied the word he was avoiding. 'How did you kill your mother?'

'Don't you mean "why"?' He slapped the photograph with the flat of his hand. 'Don't you want to know the motive first?'

She paused. In the silence, Langton pressed against her chair, as if willing her to get on with it.

Daniels continued, seemingly oblivious to Langton: 'When I was five, she put me in a bath of scalding water. I screamed. She yelled back how she hadn't meant to hurt me, how she didn't know how hot the water was, but the truth is she was stoned out of her mind. She would have noticed the steam rising otherwise. When she lifted me out, there were scalds all over my legs, my back, my buttocks. When they festered, she got someone to take me to the emergency clinic. They called the social workers who came round to see if I was an abused child. She told them I'd run the bath myself and they believed her. After they left, she slapped me for causing trouble and told me that if I ever said anything to anyone, the next time she would hold me under and drown me. As a child, I was terrified of being bathed.'

Anna interrupted. 'Could you please tell me about—'

He slapped the table again. 'Don't fucking interrupt me again! I am giving you your motive, you stupid bitch. If you want it, you have to listen. Listen to what she subjected me to. Then you'll understand, then someone will understand, why I killed her.'

'We have a report here from the social workers that visited—'

'Bullshit! I'm not interested. Bunch of wankers. I went to school with bruises on my legs, but they were just the sort you get when you're a kid and you "fall down the stairs". Broken ribs, broken arms – you get those when you're a kid and you "play in the street with rowdy children". They did nothing! Except make my life worse. After they came round, she'd beat the living daylights out of me. I slept in an airing cupboard on a piss-stained mattress and she would lock me there for days and nights to teach me a lesson.'

He closed his eyes.

'There was a crack in the wooden slats I'd pick at to get some light. It was in the bathroom facing the toilet. For want of nothing else to do, I'd watch those whores washing their cunts, shaving their armpits. They'd use this rubber douche to wash out their stinking fannies, their sticky semen-filled arses. They'd wash their filthy underwear and hang their dripping tights and their sweat-stained bras on a clothes line above the bath. I'd watch them shoot up, burn their drugs, snort stuff up their noses. I'd see their so-called boyfriends fucking them against the wall, their pimps, big black bastards with shiny gleaming arses, pumping away at them and not one – not one – ever thought to unlock the cupboard and let me out.'

'These other women—'

Again he slapped the table with the flat of his hand. 'How many times do I have to say it, Anna? She wouldn't let me go because when I got to seven, she was able to make money out of me. Do you have any idea how she made money out of a little boy, her own son?'

Anna had to listen to such stories of depravity and horrific sexual abuse that her mind was reeling. He described being forced to have anal sex with men, being photographed sucking men off and the confusion he experienced as a young child being sexually aroused by women sucking his penis. He was expected to perform for any sick pervert that his mother could hook into paying big money for the privilege of screwing her own son, and if he refused to co-operate he was beaten, then locked up in the dark cupboard. He was saved by a schoolteacher who was supervising the boys' showers after a football match. His bruises and the marks to his wrists were obvious; he'd had to be tied up for anal penetration. The school-teacher reported the abuse.

Daniels closed his eyes, describing what it had felt like to be taken away and how, for a while, he had had respite from the abuse. But Lilian Duffy proved able to persuade Social Services that her son should be returned to her care. He joked that perhaps he had inherited his talent from his mother. 'Knowing how much money she was able to make out of me, she was inspired to give an Oscar-winning performance of motherly love. They took me back to a life of hell.'

Though he described being taken screaming from 'the only real family I had ever known', Daniels showed only cold anger towards the foster carers. He finally found sanctuary on reaching an age when his testimony could incriminate his mother. Then came the proposed school trip, which required a passport. How his mother had rubbed his nose in the fact that his father could have been any one of a hundred men. He recalled desperately searching for his mother and how he was enraged to find her up against a punter in an alley.

'She didn't even recognize me. The whore was pissed out of her mind.' He started to laugh. 'Anyway, he left and I grabbed her by the throat and pushed her against the wall. I raped her; I tore into her; I wanted to rip her apart.'

In the file in front of her, Anna had all the statements referring to the incident. Statements taken from ex-detective Southwood, McDowell and the officer they had interviewed in Manchester. All had different versions, different perspectives of the same attack on Lilian Duffy. Lost in the fire at the police station would have been the original statement from Lilian Duffy herself, but only now did they get the actual wretched, blow-by-blow account from her son.

Daniels looked at his hands, rubbed at a fingernail. 'The dripping bitch reported me. So, I went round to that shithole they all lived in and I shoved *her* in the airing cupboard. See how she liked it! Kept her there all night, too, until she promised to withdraw the charges. Soon as I let her out, the old bitch went in and identified me. So I had to beat her up again.'

Daniels described how she withdrew charges the next day. He gave a wide, expansive gesture. 'She was frightened of me by then. The tables had turned. Payback time. I started to plan exactly how I would kill her.'

His expression became gleeful as he continued quietly: 'You see, I borrowed a mate's car – an old Rover, it was. I waited. I watched her patrolling her patch. Stopping the punters. Ducking and diving.' He mimed rolling down a car window. 'Out of her head, she was. Couldn't even walk straight.' He put on a foreign accent: 'Hello, darling. You a working girl? You wanna ride with me?'

He rocked back in his chair. 'She only got in, didn't she? Anyways, she says "Anthony, what you playing at?" And I said, "I liked fucking you. I want to do it again. I've got moves." "Oh, you naughty boy," she says. She starts to undo her shirt. I says no, I want her to lay down, I want to do it properly; not up against some wall or in a back-street alley, but like I was a real man, wanting to make love. I showed her a wad of cash. Anyway, she was creaming herself.

'I drove to this wasteground. We climb out of the car and she starts undressing fast, like she's really wanting it. And then I say, "Take off your bra, Mama." And she undoes her bra. "I'm going to do it like I've seen you like it." Then I tie her hands tight, she was into that. We keep on walking, me pushing her in front. Then she lies down, legs apart. And she is all eager, saying she will do anything I want, she loves me and I tell her she's beautiful and I take her stinking tights off.'

Daniels put his head to one side and looked at Anna with a winsome smile. 'So, here's my mum: lying there as I ease off these tights, smiling as

I wind them round her neck – once, twice – and I'm saying, "I know you like it this way," and she giggles.' Daniels held his hands apart and then he drew them together. 'Well, it got tighter and tighter, didn't it, and more and more uncomfortable. So she starts struggling. I leaned in close, closer, wanting to watch her die, and I tied them in a knot. And then I leaned up and sat astride her, watching her gasping and choking. She couldn't stop me: her hands were tied behind her back.'

'Did you have sexual intercourse with her?' Anna knew they had no DNA, as the victim's body was so decomposed.

'Oh, yeah, I fucked her. I made sure she was watching as I strangled her. But my timing was off. I hadn't perfected it by then, you see. She died before I came.' Daniels burst out laughing. 'My dick went flat as a pancake. But when I was lying on top of her, watching the light go out of her eyes, I thought how it was the perfect justice. She was my first.'

Anna asked him to pinpoint on a map exactly where the killing had taken place. He frowned as he peered at the map, then turned it round. 'Oh, right. Here we are. There's the bus shelter just there and then a housing estate about a mile up that road.'

He picked up one of Anna's pencils and carefully marked the area with a cross. He passed the map and the pencil back to her. 'In the nick, this slob interviewed me for hours.'

'Was his name Southwood?' Anna interjected.

'Yeah, that's him. I recognized him. Well, it was family night. He'd shafted my mother, like most of Manchester. But they had nothing on me, so's they had to let me go.'

Anna was intrigued by the way his voice changed from his well-modulated upper-class tone to a northern accent and back again. In the accent of his early childhood, the timbre of his voice was rough with a strong nasal twang. She remembered an important question she had planned to ask him. 'Did you retain any keepsake from the murder of your mother?'

'What?'

'On the night she was murdered, did you take anything from her?'

Daniels nodded. 'I see where you're going. Yeah, she'd left her handbag in the car: twenty-two quid, a few skins and her make-up. I used to make myself up with her stuff. It was a turn on, you know?'

'Why's that?'

'It reminded me of watching her die.'

'Do you still have this handbag?'

He wagged his finger at her. 'Yes, yes. I still got it.'

'Where is it?'

'Maybe tell you later.'

'It is important that you tell me now.'

'Why?'

'It provides evidence that what you have been telling me is the truth.'

'Don't you believe me, Anna?' he asked, innocently batting his eyelashes.

'You could have been acting throughout this entire interview. After all, you are a very famous actor, Mr Daniels,' she said smoothly, though her insides were churning.

'Oh, right, I see. In my bathroom there's a big cupboard: fitted, glass panels, made especially to my specifications. Take everything out. There's a panel at the back which comes off. That's where the rest of them are. You lot would never have found them without me. You already searched my place, didn't you, and came up empty-handed? Oh, and write this down, Anna. I took out three of them and hid them at McDowell's place.'

Langton got up and left the room. Anna mentioned for the benefit of the tape that Detective Chief Inspector Langton had left the interview room. Daniels watched the door close.

Anna had selected the Kathleen Keegan file and took out her photograph. 'Could you please identify this woman, Mr Daniels?'

He gave it a cursory glance. 'Kathleen Keegan. A disgusting old bitch and that is a flattering photograph. She weighed eighteen stone, the bloated old cow. An even worse piece of shit than my mother.'

'Did you murder Kathleen Keegan?'

He grinned back, placing arms outstretched on the table. 'You bet your sweet pussy I did, Anna.'

Outside, Langton was having a quiet confab with Lewis. He instructed Lewis to arrange for a car to stand by. He checked his watch and said they would take a break at four o'clock. Then they would take Daniels to his flat and search it with his solicitor present.

'How is she doing?' Lewis asked.

'She's doing OK,' Langton said quietly. 'But she'll need a break soon.'

When Langton returned to his seat in the interview room, Daniels winked at him and then he nodded at Anna.

'She's been asking how I got Kathleen to come with me. You've not missed much. I told Kathleen there was this rich bloke I knew, an Arab, and he wanted a woman with a belly. The bitch really believed me. And she got herself all done up. This time I had borrowed a mate's van. He was a painter and decorator. So I took out his ladders and stuff and put a blanket in the back. She kept on patting my leg with her fat hands, saying she'd give me a good cut of what she made. Her fingers were like bananas, gripping onto me.' He gave a hard, low laugh.

Daniels went on to describe the disgusting murder of Kathleen Keegan; he had told her to get into the rear of the van and wait for the Arab. He said she had virtually stripped off in readiness by the time he got into the back and told her to lie face down; the Arab was on his way. 'She was so strong, even with her hands tied behind her back.' Laughingly, he painted a picture of himself hauling 'this beached whale' from the back of the van and how she'd bounced over the rough grass. 'It was no easy trip, let me tell you; she was like a fucking lead balloon. By then, I was exhausted and I didn't want to do me back in, like, so I just left her there.'

'Did you have sexual intercourse with Kathleen Keegan?'

'Once, for old times' sake. I wanted her to watch me as I wound her tights round her fat neck. She took a long time to die, so I was knackered by the time I brought the van back to my mate's. I gave him a tenner out of her handbag. He said to me, "What you been doing? You're sweating like a pig." And I said to him, "That's just what I've been doing, mate: a pig."'

Radcliff's face had gone grey. He was unable to deal with his client's monologues and the obvious relish with which he told them; the images they evoked would haunt him for ever. Daniels was seldom interrupted by Anna but when it happened, he angrily warned her he would not continue his confession if she didn't shut up and listen.

Staying attentive without showing any sign of emotion was beginning to take its toll. Anna was finding Daniels's need for her undivided attention stressful. Sometimes when he leaned towards her he came so close she could feel his breath on her face.

Yet again, when shown the map of the area where Kathleen Keegan was found, he was able to pinpoint the exact location he had dumped her body. When Anna asked for details of where he was residing at the time of the murder, he was less co-operative, simply saying he had moved around and taken various jobs, but did not come to London permanently for another four years. He then told how he had started going to the theatre as a teenager.

'Do you know the Manchester Library Theatre?'

'No, I don't,' she said.

'I got a job there as a cleaner. I could watch rehearsals and see the show for free every night if I wanted. That's when I knew I'd found what I wanted to do with my life.' Daniels described taking drama lessons and landing bit parts.

'The director took me aside. "Anthony," he said to me, "you've got real talent. You should take this up as a profession."'

He leaned back expansively. 'I done better than most of the actors that were there. I changed my name for starters. There was another actor called Duffy and I hated the name anyway. So I became Alan Daniels and I went to London. Got an Equity card by then, from all the work I'd done at the theatre, so I started looking for an agent and stuff like that.'

Anna sneaked a glance at the clock, before taking out the picture of the next victim Teresa Booth. She laid the photo down. 'Do you know this woman, Mr Daniels?'

'Oh, am I boring you? Don't you want to hear about my television roles? How I got to be famous?'

'Could you please answer the question, Mr Daniels.'

He sighed with irritation. 'That's Teresa Booth and you're all mixed up: I killed her before.'

He leaned over and jabbed a photograph. 'After Teresa, I done Sandra Donaldson. And she had it coming to her!'

'Did you murder Sandra Donaldson?'

'Yes, I did. She was a pain in the arse, always drugged up. She had the nerve to come to the stage door one night and she says to me, "Tony, I need some dough. Can you help me out?"' Daniels yawned, rubbing his head, then rested his chin in his hands, his elbows propped up on the table. 'She had this PVC mac on, white high-heeled shoes and her face looked like a clown's.'

'This was in London?'

'Yes. She was constantly being picked up in Manchester for prostitution so she'd started to travel to London at weekends. I was working at the Player's Theatre, doing stagehand stuff to earn a living, some bits of TV, nothing very exciting yet. She must have seen me going into the theatre. I don't know how else she'd have found me.'

Daniels described how he had cajoled Sandra to come with him, saying he knew a client who would pay her top money. He shook his head. 'These tarts are so stupid. This one in particular didn't have much between the ears.'

He marked a cross on the map to show the area of the park where he had met her and described in detail where he had taken her from there. 'I done her with the tights and the bra, just like the others.' He told them how he had dumped the body.

'The silly bitch had almost thirty quid on her. So I had that and I got a taxi back to my digs. Next day, I got a call from my agent and he's got this big audition, for a television series.'

Langton stood up. 'I believe we should break now.'

'Oh, the man speaks,' Daniels said sarcastically.

'We can continue this interview in the morning.'

As Anna was washing her face, Moira came into the ladies and said that she was wanted in the incident room. Daniels had refused to return to the Queen's Gate house unless accompanied by Anna.

'Now?' She felt totally drained.

'They want to search his place before they reconvene.'

'Oh, OK. Moira, can you tell them I'll be right out. I just need a moment.'

Moira touched her shoulder. 'This must be pretty awful. Anna, if you ever need to talk things through, I'm always available.'

'Thank you,' Anna said gratefully.

'Keep going, darlin'.' Moira gave her a quick hug. 'We're all behind you. One hundred per cent.'

Once Moira had left, Anna had an overwhelming feeling of wanting to scream.

Daniels, handcuffed, sat beside Anna in the back of the patrol car. There had been a gathering of press outside the police station when they left and Anna could see more of them waiting in the street outside his house.

'Shit,' Langton said. Daniels's head was lolling forwards. 'Do you want a blanket to cover your face, Mr Daniels?'

'What?' He woke up, abruptly.

'The press are out in force. We can cover your head.'

Daniels followed Langton's gaze through the window. 'No thanks.' He did an impression of Gloria Swanson, throwing his hair back. 'I'm ready for my close-up, Mr de Mille.'

As Daniels was led up the front steps of his house, the uniformed officers kept the press back. Even with his hands cuffed in front of him, he was smiling and probably would have posed for photographs had Langton not ushered him inside. The flash of cameras was blinding and Anna was reminded by the yells and shouts of their night at the ballet.

Inside the house, they waited for the two forensic officers to join them, then headed directly to the bathroom. The linen closet was large, with mirrored sides. They took out a stack of soft towels and several neatly packed rows of sheets and linen. Daniels was standing next to Langton. He announced, to no one in particular: 'All from Harrods.'

Radcliff had hardly said a word; he watched the search while making copious notes. Anna could tell he was finding the whole situation disgusting.

The linen closet was very much larger than it appeared. Once they had cleared it, Daniels drew their attention towards a fitted board on the right-hand side. 'Press that. It should slide open.' The white-suited forensic scientist pressed the board with a rubber-gloved finger. The entire rear wall of the cupboard slid back to reveal a cubbyhole with a mattress and a pillow.

'Old habits die hard,' Daniels whispered. He looked over at Anna, who was standing just outside the room.

The forensic scientist took out a large cardboard box and put it on the bathroom floor to open it up. It was full of women's handbags, each one wrapped in a plastic zip-up bag. He took out Daniels's hidden treasures, revealing the sick trophies one by one.

Anna had a shower and made herself a hot chocolate. She was relieved to be back home. When Langton asked if she would be all right on her own, she had insisted that she would, preferring to spend the time preparing for the following morning's interrogation. She felt sick. She curled up under her duvet, hot chocolate untouched and files stacked by her bed. She had a low, dull headache and the pain persisted even after she'd taken some aspirin. She fell asleep with the bedside light turned on.

Three hours later she woke up, terrified of monsters looming in the shadows and the dead women's faces alternately leering and screaming out in agony. Though her head was throbbing hard, the images remained. She got up to fetch two aspirin and a glass of water. She checked all the locks. The broom cupboard where she kept her Hoover and household cleaning things was partly open. She clenched her fists, walked briskly towards the cupboard and yanked open the door. A broom and a mop fell out, hitting her in the face; she swore, pushing them back inside. As she shut the door, she had an image of a terrified little boy locked up and left for days and nights on end.

Returning to bed, Anna hugged the duvet tightly round herself. As an adult, Daniels was still trapped in the terror of the dark cupboard. She knew how fortunate she had been to have had such loving parents; to have never known rejection or been abused. Her father had never brought the darkness home. Just once, she could remember when she had sat on his knee and the pain still clung to him. She understood that pain now, because it was clinging to her: Daniels had invaded her life with his all-pervading sickness. The tears that had been close to the surface during the day were now released; she cried aloud, like a child.

Eventually, she fell into a deep sleep, which was broken by her alarm. She made herself a cooked breakfast and sat at the kitchen bar, studying the files. By eight o'clock she was dressed and ready to leave. The doubts of the previous night had been dispelled.

The night had altered Daniels's demeanour, too. He was not as pompous or gloating when the day's session began at half past nine. Anna started by questioning Daniels about the sixth victim: Mary Murphy. Then the fourth: Barbara Whittle.

By the time they were ready to break for lunch, they had reached Beryl Villiers. Daniels characterized Beryl as 'different' from the others. He blamed McDowell for Beryl's decline from a beautiful, vibrant young girl into an addict. He said his mother would use Beryl when she was so drugged she didn't know what day it was.

'Beryl was going downhill. I felt sorry for her so I put her out of her misery. I couldn't bear to watch her changing into an old dripper: cheap and nasty.'

Anna noted that three times he had said how much he liked Beryl. Finally she corrected him. 'Beryl was not an addict when she was murdered.'

'What?'

'Beryl Villiers was not addicted to drugs when her body was found. In actual fact, she'd been clean of drugs for some considerable time. She was also a lot younger than your previous victims.'

'What are you after, Anna?' he asked, frowning.

'Were you able to maintain relationships with other women?'

'What?'

'Did you have sexual relationships with other women?'

'I have known a lot of very beautiful, sexy women.'

'That is not what I asked. I asked if you had full sexual relationships.'

'Well surely, Anna, you were in a position to hazard a guess.' He cocked his head to one side, smiling provocatively at her. She looked down intently at her notes.

Having succeeded in embarrassing her, he shrugged his shoulders.

'What the hell? The answer is pretty obvious if you have a modicum of intelligence. No.'

'You did not have normal sexual relationships?'

'No. I only have sex with prostitutes.'

'In many cases, were they women who resembled your mother and her lifestyle?'

'I never hurt any woman who wasn't the dross of humanity. That's why their cases remained unsolved for so long.'

He leaned sideways to look at Langton in his position behind Anna's chair. 'They were the dregs of society. Nobody missed them. Nobody even noticed they were missing. Nobody cared. I was helping society, in fact: clearing them off the streets with their drugs and their booze.'

'Yet you found them sexually attractive?'

'I found you attractive, Anna, but I didn't fuck you.' He yawned aggressively. 'This is going nowhere. I am tired now, I don't want to talk about it any more.'

'Melissa Stephens was a seventeen-year-old virgin. How does her murder fit in with your rationale of cleaning up the streets?'

He looked daggers at her. 'She was in Soho, walking the streets. She was a whore. She came onto me. That's the reason I picked her up.'

'No. She was not a whore.'

Daniels's lip curled, angrily. 'Yes, she was. She recognized me. She said, "I know who you are! You're Alan Daniels."'

'So you asked her to get into your car? The Mercedes?'

'She ran round to the passenger seat. She couldn't wait. I'm telling you, she was on the game.'

'No. You took an innocent girl and you killed her for your own satisfaction.'

His face became tense with fury. He pushed his chair back forcefully as the words burst out of him: 'OK. She started to scream. I said to her, "Stop screaming!" but she wouldn't. She was trying to get out of the car. My God, anyone could have seen us. I take hold of her by the hair and drag her head down. Next minute, she flops back onto the seat moaning. Out cold. Well, I couldn't chuck her out, could I? She'd recognized me. Don't you understand? She knew who I was. I had to get rid of her. She gave me no choice.' He was rubbing his head with frustration.

'She wasn't a whore. She was sweet and innocent, like the child in the photo you showed me.'

'Christ, how many more times do you have to be told? She knew me. She fucking knew who I was. She was unconscious. I bloody drove around with her half the night. I had to do it. I had to kill her. She knew me and . . .' He closed his eyes. 'Her body was perfect, firm and soft. She was so beautiful. And I took off her white sports bra, turned her over and tied her clean, pretty hands together. Then I rolled her back. She was perfect; she was so clean and pretty . . .'

He stopped for a moment, his eyes squeezed tight and his hands clasped over his knees. He described slipping off her tights, then leaning down to wrap them around her neck. Melissa Stephens was the first young girl he had ever had sex with and when she woke up, he was still inside her. 'She was moaning. I wanted to keep her quiet. But she wouldn't stop. Then she started screaming, begging me not to hurt her and I – that's when . . .'

He took a deep breath, then he described how he had kissed her and how he had never kissed any of the other women. Anna listened with disgust as he spun his fantasy where an act of murder became romance and his victim's suffering only produced self-pity. She was not going to let him get away with it.

'You didn't just kiss her, though, did you? Did you?' she said harshly.

When he opened his eyes, she saw the fear for the first time. It was because she knew him now. He was frightened of her because of it. She had seen into the dark recesses of his soul.

Maintaining tight control of her emotions, she continued: 'You bit her tongue off, then you ate it.'

'I didn't mean to. I just didn't want her crying out.'

'She never had a chance. She trusted you; she admired you.'

Now the madness erupted. Daniels sprang to his feet, screaming: 'Don't give me a fucking lecture, bitch! You were next!'

Langton strong-armed him back into his seat, grunting and struggling. Anna now charged Alan Daniels with eleven counts of murder, including the victims from the United States; to each name Daniels mumbled, 'Yes,' to confirm that he was responsible for their murder. By the eighth 'yes', with his bowed head and his half closed eyes, he resembled a sleeping reptile. When Anna reached the last count of murder, he looked up on hearing the name Melissa Stephens. The fear seemed to have gone. He leaned back in his chair. 'You'll see. I will never spend a day in prison.'

Anna raised an eyebrow then gathered up the files. Langton was holding the door open for her and she left the room without a backwards glance. It was over.

Later that afternoon, Daniels was taken to Wandsworth Prison to await trial. No hope of bail; his lawyer, Radcliff, never even applied.

McDowell was released from prison once the murder charges were dropped. He was given his train fare and expenses back to Manchester, where he would stand trial for drug-related offences. He would, at a later date, be called to act as a witness for the prosecution. His abstinence from alcohol had made him feel fit and confident, but even as he boarded the train at Euston station, he was making his way to the buffet car.

The tabloids ran headline stories and the newsreels showed old footage of Daniels at every opportunity. They interviewed actors and actresses who had worked alongside him. His celebrity status rose daily. He was a household name. The fame he had hungered for was his, but from his cell in solitary confinement, he was hardly aware of it. Many of the other inmates were eager to get their hands on him and the catcalls and screams of abuse went on day and night.

Langton and the team resigned themselves to remaining in the incident room for as long as it took to pack up their boxes of evidence. After days of preparation, a hundred and twenty boxes of files and statements would be made available to the defence team and the prosecution.

Melissa Stephens had been buried in a small private ceremony. Two weeks later, there was a memorial service and the entire team was present. Her family had arranged a beautiful service and thanked the officers from the pulpit for allowing their daughter to rest in peace at last. The team stood shoulder to shoulder as they sang Melissa's favourite hymn: 'All Things Bright and Beautiful'. The family did not allow the brutality of her death to intrude into her memorial service. She had been all those things in the words of the hymn: bright, and very beautiful, and she was remembered with great love and pride. The memorial would stay in everyone's mind as a moving celebration of her short life.

Langton and Anna worked together all day packing up the boxes. When he asked her if she wanted to go out for dinner that evening, she agreed and they decided on Italian. She had arranged to collect him at eight o'clock. She took a long time deciding what to wear. As she searched through her wardrobe, Anna caught sight of the dress she had worn to the ballet with Daniels; she bundled it into a plastic bag and chucked it into the bin.

The Mini had been put into a garage to knock out the dents and receive a thorough valet service. When she learned that her car would not be ready for another couple of days, she booked a minicab to collect her and pick Langton up on the way.

Traffic was light and the cab arrived at Langton's house a few minutes early: just in time for her to see Nina leaving and Langton kissing her goodbye. Anna instructed the cab to take her straight to the restaurant. On the way, she called Langton and said she would meet him there instead.

Langton was over half an hour late, but he had obviously taken considerable time with his appearance. They sat at a small candlelit table chatting like old friends, although they had not been alone since they had spent the night together. Langton was charming and Anna was not at all uncomfortable; unlike Langton, she knew what the outcome of the evening would be.

'You seem different,' he said, once the waiter had gone. They had been making small talk, avoiding the obvious.

'Do I?'

'Yes. More confident, perhaps? I don't want to talk shop all night, but you were very impressive. Your old man would have been proud of you.'

'Thank you. I had more than my share of self-doubt.'

'About what?'

'If I could do it. Or more importantly, ever do it all over again. You know: another case, another victim?'

'And?'

'Melissa Stephens turned me round. To see the satisfaction for her parents of him being brought to justice made it worthwhile. That's how I knew I wanted to stay on the Murder Squad.'

'I understand.'

'I did go through one night of feeling sorry for myself, for the web of squalor and abuse and violence we were being drawn into. I even thought that I'd begun to understand how Daniels became what he is. But then I realized that he didn't kill Melissa because of his wretched mother – that's what he was killing in the others: her image, over and over – but not with

Melissa. She was innocent and he knew it soon after he had picked her up by mistake. He killed her to protect himself. Protecting his image and denying his sickness was more important than sparing her life.'

Langton nodded. 'In fact, if he hadn't been stopped, she would have been the start of a whole new cycle where he killed for the sexual excitement. Finally with Melissa he could enjoy sex. It wasn't just revenge any more.'

The topic they had been determined not to discuss engaged them passionately for the rest of their meal. Langton became quite tetchy when she suggested splitting the bill, but as they left the restaurant he put his arm round her shoulders and offered to take her home.

'Erm, no thanks. I'll get a taxi.'

'What?' Surprise and disappointment flitted across his face.

'I meant to tell you in the restaurant. About what happened between us: I want to leave it at that. I'm sorry. It was just that we got to talking about the case—'

'Why?'

'Because maybe we'll work together again and I think we should keep our relationship on a professional level.'

He couldn't hide the fact that he was totally stunned. 'If that's what you want,' he said, stepping away from her.

'It is.'

'At least let me take you home,' he said, recovering fast. 'I've got my car.'

'No, really. I want to get a taxi. I'll see you at work tomorrow.'

'What was it? I mean, was it something I said tonight? Or did I do something? Come on, Anna, tell me what the matter is.'

Anna took a deep breath. 'Well, I think you have some personal issues and—'

'Personal issues like what?'

'For one thing, your ex-wife still seems to be very much part of your life.'

'Well, it's complicated, I told you, because of Kitty and – sometimes, yes: she just shows up, stays at my place when she's nothing better to do. I don't see that this has anything to do with us.'

Suddenly Anna felt so much older than him. She shook her head. 'It doesn't have anything to do with me, but it has a lot to do with you. Your life is like a tangled ball of string.'

'A what?'

Anna sighed. 'A ball of string. Sometimes it's worth untangling.'

'What?'

'You get a ball of string and if you want to use it again, you make the effort to untangle it—'

'Fucking ball of string? What are you talking about?'

'I'm talking about you. Your private life is all tangled up.'

'And you'd know about my life, would you?'

'Don't get angry at me because I'm being honest. I'm just saying, I don't think you've really come to terms with losing your first wife and on top of that you've got your daughter and Nina—'

'She just comes by sometimes, when Kitty—'

'I'm very serious about my career. I'd like to work with you again and I think any personal relationship we might have would get in the way. I just don't want to become part of the tangle.'

She had to stand on tiptoe to kiss his cheek. She had forgotten how she loved the feel of his skin and his smell. She felt a sweep of emotion through her body, strong enough to test her resolve, but he broke away first, his face flushed. 'Well, I'll no doubt see you in the morning. At the station.'

'Yes. Thank you for dinner.'

'My pleasure,' he said, walking away, throwing a 'goodnight' over his shoulder. She watched him for a moment. She could tell he was angry by the familiar way his hands clenched at his sides. Then she turned away. She decided not to hail a taxi immediately, but to walk for a while. She was deep in thought when his car caught her up, so she didn't see the look on his face as he passed her striding down the street. He was driving the old brown Volvo that had been parked beside her Mini that first day in the station car the same car that, no doubt, had scrunched the side of her own.

Observing his 'little carrot top', arms swinging, striding along the street, Langton yearned to leap out of the car and take her in his arms. But he didn't, knowing she was probably right that they might be working together again. It had never worked in the past when he'd had a fling with one of his team. But she was right at a deeper level, too. He had never got over the death of his first wife and Kitty kept him trapped in the relationship with Nina. He looked in the rearview mirror. Anna was staring in a dress shop window at a smart Amanda Wakeley suit. Without so much as a sun shadow across the shoulder.

Alan Daniels had asked for writing paper and been given a lined prison-issue notepad. His note began, TO ANNA, in capital letters, and then beneath he wrote in his fancy scrawl: 'People think that acting takes a giant ego, but it's more about knowing where to put it, where to store it. You keep on shifting consciousness to different parts of you. Acting is really all about energy. Only when I was acting was I at peace, because I was no longer Anthony Duffy, the boy trapped in the cupboard. Goodbye, Anna.'

He had spent two days and two nights in a prison cell, longer than he had boasted he would. Always resourceful, he had hidden the plastic bag from the clean clothes he had been allowed to take to the police station. He tied it tightly round his neck, almost as tight as when he used to strangle his victims. The bag was pressed so close to his face that when the officers looked in on him every fifteen minutes, he seemed to be sleeping. It was on the two o'clock check when the spy-hole was moved aside that suspicion was aroused. His hands were clasped behind him; a final show of his determination to die.

Anna received the news the following morning. She refused to read or listen to the contents of the note he had addressed to her. She felt an enormous relief at the realization that she would not have to face him over and over again in a lengthy trial. This way was really the best outcome for her, though as usual, Alan Daniels had only been thinking of himself. To celebrate what she felt was her 'release', she splashed out on a new suit. As she watched it being folded up with sheets of tissue paper and put in the box, she realized she was ready for the next case. She had cut her teeth on a serial killer, first time out. Nothing could faze her now. As she handed over her credit card, she smiled into the intense blue eyes of the helpful young saleswoman and remembered the tip Barolli had given her for the future: 'Watch the eyes. Wait for the fear.'